**John Innes Mackintosh Stewart** was born in ⌐⌐⌐ ¬ attended Edinburgh Academy b⌐⌐ Oxford where he was awarded a short interlude travelling with studying Freudian psychoanalysis edition of Florio's translation of M⌐ helped him secure a post teaching ⌐  ⌐⌐⌐⌐⌐ University.

By 1935, he had been awarded the Jury Chair at the University of Adelaide in Australia as Professor of English and had also completed his first detective novel, 'Death at the President's Lodging', published under the pseudonym 'Michael Innes'. This was an immediate success and part of a long running series centred on 'Inspector Appleby', his primary character when writing as 'Innes'. There were almost fifty titles completed under the 'Innes' banner during his career.

In 1946, he returned to the UK and spent two years at Queen's University in Belfast, before being appointed Student (Fellow and Tutor) at Christ Church, Oxford. He was later to hold the post of Reader in English Literature of Oxford University and upon his retirement was made an Emeritus Professor. Whilst never wanting to leave his beloved Oxford permanently, he did manage to fit into his busy schedule a visiting Professorship at the University of Washington and was also honoured by other Universities in the UK.

Stewart wrote many works under his own name, including twenty-one works of fiction (which contained the highly acclaimed quintet entitled 'A Staircase in Surrey', centred primarily in Oxford, but with considerable forays elsewhere, especially Italy), several short story collections, and over nine learned works on the likes of Shakespeare, Kipling and Hardy. He was also a contributor to many academic publications, including a major section on modern writers for the Oxford History of English Literature. He died in 1994, the last published work being an autobiography: 'Myself and Michael Innes'.

J.I.M. Stewart's fiction is greatly admired for its wit, plots and literary quality, whilst the non-fiction is acknowledged as being definitive.

J.I.M. Stewart

# A Memorial Service

HOUSE OF
STRATUS

First published in 1976

© John Stewart Literary Management Ltd

This edition published in 2012 by House of Stratus, an imprint of
Stratus Books Ltd., Lisandra House, Fore Street, Looe,
Cornwall, PL13 1AD, U.K.

www.houseofstratus.com

Typeset, printed and bound by House of Stratus.

A catalogue record for this book is available from the British Library
and the Library of Congress.

ISBN 0-7551-3041-3
EAN 978-0-7551-3041-2

# I

*NOS MISERI HOMINES ET EGENI* . . .

For the first time since becoming a fellow of the college, I was listening to grace in hall. It hadn't changed in twenty-five years; probably it hadn't changed in four centuries. Or had the pronunciation changed? That first consonant in *egeni* had come out as in *genius,* whereas I seemed to remember it as in *gamp* or *golliwog* or *Ghent.* But this might be a false memory, arising from the way I had been taught to enunciate Latin at school. What I was hearing now at least struck me as being close to Italian, which was no doubt proper enough. Possibly the bible clerk summoned thus to prelude the common meal was allowed to consult his own fancy. In such matters it was a liberal place.

*Per Jesum Christum dominum nostrum.* As the bible clerk, a bearded youth in a tattered scholar's gown, came briskly to the end of his task there was a murmured laughter, a ripple of applause, from his companions in the body of the hall. The unexpected sound echoed faintly among the dark rafters of the hammer-beam roof, as if a stripling wave had tumbled audaciously into an enormous cavern and broken there. Some sort of wager may have been involved. The bible clerk had been challenged, say, to get through the grace on one breath, or even to introduce a variant reading, facetious in character, which I hadn't tumbled to. Nobody at high table took notice of this small happening– – unless, indeed, in the Provost there was to be detected a controlled and temperate disapprobation. But then the Provost was a clergyman, so that was proper enough.

I had last heard grace here only a few months previously, when, still no more than as a former member, I had attended the annual Gaudy. There had been no undergraduates then, except for half-a-dozen known as academical clerks. They and the choir-boys and the Provost and the chaplain had between them sung and intoned a grace of splendid elaboration judged to be in consonance with the magnificence of the feast. As I sat down now, I was remembering how, when my uncle the minister came to stay with us in Edinburgh in order to attend the General Assembly of the Church of Scotland, my father, although not religiously inclined, would insist that we remain standing until his brother had uttered – mournfully and on a far from optimistic note – the simple presbyterian hope that for what we were about to receive the Lord would make us truly thankful. One of my earliest problems of a doctrinal nature had arisen from the thought that the thankfulness, if it were to be any good, ought to be spontaneous, and that it was futile to urge the Lord to go out of his way to make us grateful to him. I wondered what the Provost would rejoin if the new fellow put this theological difficulty to him over the soup.

Not that at the moment I could have put the question to Edward Pococke without bellowing. He sat at the middle of the high table, with a portrait of the college founder behind him and the long vista of the hall in front. I was four or five places away from him on his left hand, and looking down the hall too. He had greeted me in common room, expressing pleasure that I had come into residence so promptly. Over the Provost's sense of pleasure, or displeasure, there always hovered a hint of divine sanction – again something very proper in a clergyman, but apt to disconcert when encountered again after an interval. And the phrase 'come into residence', although I knew it to be a normal piece of academic vocabulary, struck my unpracticed ear as odd. I made an awkward reply, saying that I didn't know about residence, but that at least I was here and glad of it. At this the Provost left me, with what I think was designed as a comforting smile. Meanwhile the common-room butler had been hovering, an elderly Ganymede, anxious to explain to me where I must sign on for my sherry. He also mentioned that I got my dinner free but paid for anything I chose to drink at it. This might have been regarded as officious, but I took it to be occasioned by former experience of embarrassing misconception. Fledgling dons, if they unwarily got this small matter wrong, might be confronted with an unexpected bill later.

Several men had then come up to me, offered casual welcoming remarks, and drifted away. A couple of them shook hands, which was something they would never do again unless they invited me to an extremely formal private dinner. The others, sticking to the custom of the country from the start, refrained from this demonstration. And presently I had moved into hall under my own steam. Nobody was going to do anything so obtrusive as to take me under his wing. Had I been a stranger to the college hitherto it might have been otherwise. But they all knew that I had been an undergraduate here a quarter of a century before. This constituted me – it is another piece of academic jargon – a gremial member. It would be an immediate convention that there was nothing about the place I didn't know. My return was a matter of coming in and hanging up my hat.

I had heard that there were still colleges in which the fellows formed up in a solemn order of seniority to enter hall. With us the Provost was allowed to go first and then everybody did as he chose, short of using his elbows. I was to learn that this note of the casual was a central tenet of the society; it overlay, perhaps masked, a formidable subterranean rigidity and conservatism in matters well beyond the sphere of deportment. Such being the order of things, I expected to sit down between total strangers. But, at least on my right hand, it wasn't so. Cyril Bedworth, my contemporary and a man who had never left these sheltering walls, had been keeping an eye on me, and had all but used an elbow in the interest of establishing himself as my neighbour. (He was a physically awkward man, with no deftness in manoeuvre.) Now he had been standing beside me as we waited for the grace to be uttered. We sat down together.

'Oh, Duncan,' Bedworth said, 'how splendid to have you here!'

It was when I became conscious of Bedworth's warmth as cheering me up that I realised how much I was misdoubting my new situation.

'Thank you very much, Cyril – and I hope I can bring it off. I'm glad to arrive, and have just told the Provost as much. I've a kind of itch to teach that I'd be shy to confess to the generality. But chiefly I've come to want stable things around me – not having managed much connectedness in my life so far.'

If this confessional speech surprised me as I uttered it, I knew I hadn't gone wrong in addressing it to Bedworth. He received it gravely, although without the solemnity which I recalled as often attending his responses as an undergraduate.

'I think I understand that,' he said. 'But Duncan—do you know?—I rather wish you'd married again.' He paused to pass me a silver salt-cellar almost as big as a soup-tureen. 'Married and had children.'

'It might have been an idea, yes. But you remember Dr Johnson on second marriages. The triumph of hope over experience.'

'A college is an odd sort of place. And I sometimes think – just looking around me, I sometimes think – that it's not a terribly good place to grow really old in.'

'I suppose not.' If Bedworth's warning note struck me as a shade premature in being addressed to a man in his forties, it was far from deserving to be laughed at. 'But nobody's let do that now, surely? Some birthday comes along, and out you go.'

'That's true, or almost always true. Goodness knows what the final condition of the old-style bachelor life-fellows must have been. And senescence comes to people at varying chronological ages, don't you think?' Bedworth glanced down the table and lowered his voice. 'Look at Arnold, for instance. An ailing and lonely man.'

I followed the glance and was a good deal startled. Arnold Lempriere had changed perceptibly since I had encountered him only a few months before. Then he hadn't quite filled out clothes tailored for him a good many years back; he was even more shrunken tonight. His hair and complexion made a single indistinguishable grey, as if he were an image carved out of *pietra serena* in some shadowy renaissance church.

'Yes,' I said. 'He doesn't look too well.'

'And I think we don't always allow enough to a man's years. Our instinct's good, but perhaps we overdo it. A man's your equal – you posit in him all his old stamina and flexibility and resilience – right down to the day you attend his memorial service in the college chapel.'

'Most men wouldn't want it otherwise. The ultimate humiliation, surely, is to be allowed for in a kindly way.'

'Yes. Patronised.'

'Who is Lempriere ages with? Albert Talbert?' Talbert, once my tutor, was Bedworth's immediate and senior colleague now.

'No – Arnold is the older by several years. He's still on the strength, as a matter of fact, only as the result of our bending a rule or two. But there's another thing. Albert (he's not dining tonight) is a different type. He's an absorbed and dedicated scholar, as Arnold is not. And scholarship mummifies, I suppose. It embalms you painlessly as you go along. And Albert has his wife – not to speak of two children who stay put at home. Albert's not looking for anything he's less and less likely to get. Perhaps Arnold is.'

'When you say he's lonely, do you mean he's alone in the world? When we met last summer he seemed rather keen on family relationships. He said he was related to an aunt of mine – my mother's brother's wife – and came down heavily on me for not knowing, or remembering, her maiden name. It was Lempriere.'

'That's like Arnold – coming down on a chap heavily, I mean.' Bedworth laughed softly as he said this. It struck me that I couldn't be certain of ever having heard him laugh before – or, for that matter, call a chap a chap. He had been an anxiously formal, socially uncertain youth. It looked as if the years (and perhaps his position of authority in the college, since he had lately become its Senior Tutor) had loosened him up. 'As for being alone in the world, I believe Arnold runs to an elderly sister, who looks after his house in the country.'

'So the college isn't his only home?'

'He owns a small landed property in Northumberland.' It was the old Bedworth, at least, who said 'small landed property'. 'But in effect I'd say the college *is* his only home. Regarded in emotional terms, that is.' Bedworth was frowning as he said this; he might have been glimpsing some problem looming ahead. 'He adores the place. It's been his whole life. That's why he snaps your head off if you venture to say a good word for it.'

Bedworth, although professionally the celebrant of novelists of abundant wit and nuance, was not himself a man from whom one often expected a *mot*. I marked this one as an arrow going straight to the gold.

'I noticed that,' I said, 'on the night of the Gaudy. And he took a monstrously unjustified smack at me when he marched me round Long Field next morning.'

'You're right about his setting store on distant relationships. There's somebody's wife here that he judges it's important he's related to. I forget who.'

'A Mrs Gender.'

'That's right, Anthea Gender.' Bedworth was surprised at my knowing this. 'A formidable woman, but extremely nice. Mabel and she get on rather well together.' Bedworth plainly took pleasure in the fact. 'Knowing all about your cousins ever so many times removed is an amusing characteristic—wouldn't you say?—of the aristocracy.' This time, Bedworth didn't himself sound amused. Like many men of unassuming origins, he retained a stout if naive sense of hierarchy.

We were half-way through our dinner, or so a card in front of me seemed to indicate. I glanced down the hall, and saw with surprise that it was nearly empty. It was as if, at the clap of Ariel's wings, the banqueters and not the banquet had vanished. The undergraduates must have bolted their food in a manner I didn't recall from my own time. I commented on this to Bedworth, since the subject of Arnold Lempriere had exhausted itself.

'Oh, yes. They maintain they're hustled through dinner by impatient servants, and that the food's not fit to sit in front of for more than fifteen minutes, anyway. I'm afraid there's something in it.' This was Bedworth's note of scrupulous fairness. 'We used sometimes to sit on and on, didn't we, Duncan? Particularly at the scholars' table. There's no scholars' table now. The undergraduates prefer to be all mixed up, and I suppose it's better really. I remember how you and I once had a tremendous go at Dostoyevsky. In the end they turned the lights out.'

'Yes, Cyril. I remember that too.' I made this reply quickly, since the reminiscence had been an invoking of ancient friendship. There came back to me all the times I had made fun of Bedworth to frivolous companions of my own. I had the odd thought that it might be to that talk about Dostoyevsky – or to something it represented – that I owed the fact that I was sitting at high table now. I was about to offer some remark about Russian novels at large – picking up, as it were, where we had left off when the lights went out – but Bedworth interrupted me. The man on my other side had for the first time stopped talking to somebody across the table, and Bedworth took the opportunity to effect an introduction.

'I'm so sorry,' he said. 'Adrian, have you met Duncan Pattullo yet?'

'Good God! Nobody need introduce me to young Pattullo.' The man addressed as Adrian had uttered his profane exclamation so loudly that the Provost glanced down the table with an air of courteously dissimulated discomfort. 'I tried to teach him how to translate Tacitus, but had more success in topping him up with madeira.'

I realised that this middle-aged man, red-faced and full- fleshed, was known to me as Buntingford, who had been one of the minor annoyances of my first two terms in college.

'Absolutely correct,' I said. 'And chunks of unseen as well. "Marcellus Offers Reasons for Rejecting the Proposals of Prudendus Clemens."'

'What on earth's that?' Bedworth asked.

'Buntingford explained that there would be an English heading like that to the unseen in the exam. Just to give one a clue. He said that if I simply wrote a short essay in decent English with somebody called Marcellus chatting up somebody called Prudentius, I'd infallibly pass. He judged it unnecessary to instruct me further, and we talked about other things. It was alarming. But he proved to be right.'

'I see.' Bedworth appeared disconcerted by this harmless anecdote, presumably as suggesting irresponsible tutorial behaviour. Then he managed to be amused again. 'Adrian's gay confidence was justified. Although I seem to remember giving you a hand myself on more orthodox principles.'

'So you did, Cyril. And I taught you Greek. I hope you keep it up.'

'Oh, indeed yes. As well as I can.' Bedworth took my question entirely seriously. 'I try to read some Homer and a couple of plays every long vacation. I enjoy it very much.'

'And now Pattullo and I can again start talking about other things,' Buntingford said. 'And do you, Cyril, show some countenance to that harmless youth on your right.'

Bedworth took this injunction seriously too, reproaching himself for having so far neglected a very junior colleague. And Adrian Buntingford looked at me wickedly. 'The heartening thing I have to tell you,' he said, 'is that the first ten years are the worst.'

The majority of dons dining went into common room for dessert. Lempriere proved to be in charge here – perhaps in virtue of being the oldest fellow, or perhaps because he had been elected into some stewardship or the like. Undergraduates never grasp anything about their seniors' manner of conducting such matters, which put me in the position of now having to learn a lot. I was quite sure that nobody was going to tell me anything, just as nobody had presumed to walk me into hall. If I cared to find out this or that, I'd be free to do so. I might even ask questions. But in this event (I was soon to discover) men who had been members of common room for twenty years would produce answers framed in terms of detached conjecture, as if the whole place were as mysterious to them as on the day they had themselves arrived there.

'Come and sit down, Dunkie,' Lempriere barked at me commandingly. He had already disposed of a couple of guests by rapidly reassorting them each with the other's host, and was pointing at a minute table at one side of a large fireplace. I saw that an effect of modified tete-a-tete was in prospect. There was a shallow arc of tables of varying size facing the fire, and at these the other men were disposing themselves in twos and threes. The gap was closed by a wine-railway down which decanters could be trundled in a more or less controlled way; the effect of this archaic toy was rather that of the primitive sort of contrivance for whizzing chits to a counting-house still to be found in some old-fashioned shops. 'Did your college friends call you Dunkie?' Lempriere demanded. And he sat down with a faint creaking of the joints.

'Tony Mumford did at times. But I didn't encourage it. As you know, it's a family thing – my father's name for me.'

'Quite right. You'll be Duncan except to myself.' Thus allowing for our obscure relationship pleased Lempriere. 'How is your aunt?' he asked.

My aunt was dead, and I said so. This reply wasn't a success. Lempriere, although not upset by the information, was upset that it hadn't come to him earlier. Perhaps this was reasonable, although Aunt Charlotte's death had taken place only a couple of months before. I started telling him what little I had myself heard of the unremarkable circumstances of the old lady's end, but the subject had abruptly ceased to interest him. Instead, he was lecturing me on the two decanters in front of us, which it appeared I ought to have transferred to the next little table, necessarily getting to my feet for the purpose. It hadn't been a perfectly self-evident social duty, and I might have been irritated had I not realised that this crusty performance had two faces. I was being rebuked in a manner which would have been ill-bred if directed at a near-stranger – and I was to find that Arnold Lempriere, although he could be arrogant and rude, was never that. He was badgering me over this local custom for the same reason that he was going to address me by a family name; I held a position of privilege in his regard, and must expect to receive rough treatment as a consequence. And now he effected another abrupt transition, raising a hand to the side of his mouth as if to indicate to anybody who cared to look that I was being made the recipient of a confidential aside. It was a small but theatrically vulgar gesture which only an entirely self-confident man could have made.

'Something to say to you,' he said. 'Don't spread it around.'

Although I saw little likelihood of my doing anything of the sort, I responded suitably to this conspiratorial note by leaning towards Lempriere in an answeringly histrionic manner.

'That old fuss-pot Penwarden,' he said, 'has he got at you yet about the Cressy affair?'

This question was mysterious to me. I couldn't recall even having heard either of these names before. It seemed wise to say so. To be forthright with Lempriere was clearly the appropriate thing.

'Arnold,' I said, 'I simply don't know what you're talking about. Who are Penwarden and Cressy? They ring no bell.'

'You never were too good at remembering names.' Lempriere said this with a throaty chuckle which I knew indicated a return to good humour. 'Pull yourself together, Dunkie,' he went on. 'You were present on the crucial occasion. I wasn't here myself in those immediate post-war years – which is why you and I never met until a few months ago. I was still in Washington, God help me, lying away like mad in an effort to shore up the British Empire. But I've heard all about it. It has been debated often enough, heaven knows.'

'Well, then, I do remember.' I said this in some astonishment, for the phrase 'immediate post-war years' had given me the clue. Lempriere was calling up an incident – and now it all came back to me, Penwarden and Cressy included – which had taken place in my first undergraduate summer term. 'Something about some papers.'

'The Blunderville Papers. Poor old Blobs Blunderville – he inherited his brother's title of Mountclandon after he'd been P.M. – of course died donkeys' years ago.'

'It would be surprising if he hadn't. He must have been about eighty then.'

'Certainly he was. Well, Cressy walked off with the cream of the stuff – the key volume or file or portfolio or whatever it was – bang under everybody's nose.'

'So he did. It was the most marvellously impudent thing.'

'Aha! The target area at last.' Lempriere was delighted. 'Penwarden was our librarian – he's our librarian still, being that sort of man – and the larceny was the supreme shock of his life. Remains so, positively down to this day. And there you were, Dunkie, there you were! A shy but observant youth – and now the sole witness still in the land of the living.' Lempriere, who during this colloquy had been drinking port with unconventional speed, was in high delight. 'It's why he voted for you, if you ask me.'

'Voted for me?' I repeated blankly.

'For your university readership and college fellowship and so on. He now has his witness under his hand. So beware.'

These fantastic remarks dumbfounded me – the more so because their basis lay in fact. My father, already eminent in his profession, had been staying with the Provost; there was a dinner-party which I had been summoned to attend; after it a group of guests, Lord Mountclandon himself included, had been conducted round various college treasures, and had inspected a mass of papers (whether state papers, or family papers, I hadn't clearly understood) which Mountclandon had lately deposited with the college for learned purposes. And Cressy, then a young don who I gathered had recently moved to another college, had deftly extracted from the aged nobleman a few vaguely courteous words which he then instantly represented as permission to walk off, there and then, with some particularly prized exhibit. That an outraged Penwarden and my uncomprehending self had been the only people within earshot of the crucial exchange I now recalled as true. I could conjure up the scene precisely as it must have been – except that now, by a common yet strange vagary of memory, I was seeing my own figure as part of the composition.

'Does Cressy have the thing still?' I asked.

'Of course he has. That's the whole point of the matter.'

'But, Arnold, this is something that happened more than twenty-five years ago! Isn't it all water under the bridge?'

To this surely pertinent question I had to wait some moments for a reply. A decanter had come swaying gently down the railway to Lempriere; he seized it with no time wasted and replenished both our glasses; on this occasion I remembered to do my butler-like duty.

'There's no such thing.' Lempriere, having imbibed, produced his throatiest chuckle.

'No such thing?'

'As water under the bridge. Not here, Dunkie. Not in a place like this.'

I found it impossible to tell whether or not Lempriere believed himself to have been talking about a matter of any real substance. Perhaps he had only been putting on a turn. On the occasion of the Gaudy I had judged him given to something of the sort, heightening the actual facts of a situation so as to make them vulnerable to his own sardonic commentary. That an act of petty academic larceny perpetrated a quarter of a century before was still a live issue among a body of intelligent men appeared to be a proposition that took some swallowing. But it might be so; I just didn't know. In such matters I hadn't yet got the measure of my new environment.

About Lempriere himself, however, there were some observations not difficult to make. This was his hour of the day, and this his place. There were probably few colleges in the university at which the full formalities of dessert were observed, as here, every night of the week. That it was all very much taken for granted; that the inflexible rituals transacted themselves with the most casual ease; that nobody betrayed the slightest sense of being involved in group behaviour that was decidedly odd: these were circumstances which, on a pause to think, only revealed as the more archaic the entire presented scene. It was a survival, and over it Lempriere presided as a survival himself. He had an *ultimus Romanorum* air – but as the evening wore on suggested less a Cassius (to whom Tacitus attached that celebrated tag) than some tyrant of a later time. He flourished a more-than-imperial toga under our noses, or exhibited (in a plainer figure) the most aggressive territorial behaviour. He commanded people, as if they were his orderlies, about the room; insisted here on silence and there on speech; was charming to obscure guests and startlingly rude to persons of consequence. The decanters circulating the little tables had vanished when empty, but their place had been taken, on a buffet at the end of the room, by others holding brandy, whisky, and the alarming fluids known in their respective countries as *grappa* and *marc*. Lempriere's preference among these was impossible to determine; he grabbed whichever came to hand. Here, I told myself, was what my father had used disapprovingly to call a pale-faced drinker.

I also told myself how unreliable was the old tag about holding one's liquor like a gentleman. It did seem valid for Lempriere vis-a-vis the young and unassuming; and I was sure that, without ever putting a foot wrong, he could have conducted a tipsy confabulation with a cow-wife until her herd came home. On the other hand he could have become quarrelsome in a moment, insulting on the spot anybody whom he pleased to consider as having some courtesy title to be judged his equal.

I didn't of course spend the whole evening in dialogue with Lempriere. The little tables had been set close enough together to make general conversation possible. Indeed, the effect was rather cramped and jostling; we might almost have been the *habitues* of a kerbside continental cafe, manoeuvring newspapers wired to sticks with scant regard to the safety of one another's noses. The system had been designed for a common room less populous than it had now grown to be; I was to find that on 'big' nights (and the present was apparently 'small') the minuscule tables vanished, and everybody sat round a very large one which came and went mysteriously as occasion required.

For coffee we went into another room, and mostly wandered around. It was here that I noticed a change in Lempriere. Dining in hall, he had appeared brooding and withdrawn, so that I wondered whether his hearing was now more imperfect than he cared to admit, making conversation difficult for him against a background of considerable hubbub. Seated at dessert, he had been aggressive and touchy. But now, moving confidently if with a physical stiffness from group to group, he was an easier man. It became obvious that as an institution he was liked and his tyranny accepted; people turned to him at once and rallied him or were themselves rallied; if there wasn't any more colour in his cheeks there was a new sparkle in his eyes. Wine had its part in this. At this hour, he was a happy man.

We hadn't been on our feet for long before James Gender, the senior of the college's tutors in law, came up to me. We had met at the Gaudy – in circumstances wholly inappropriate to that festive occasion. I wondered whether he would refer to them now.

'I'm sorry that this is rather a small night,' Gender said. He spoke softly and in a tone of apology, as if it would have been more fitting if my wholly unremarkable arrival had been signalised by the entire senior body's coming on parade. Being unaffectedly no more than a polite fiction, the sentiment passed as not in the least absurd.

'I find it quite big enough to be going on with,' I said laughing. 'What an enormous place this has become.'

'Yes, indeed,' Gender had received my words consideringly for a moment, much as if I had offered him a pregnant and instructive remark. 'But wait for your first meeting of the Governing Body! We burst at the seams. And more and more of us develop a flair for sustained eloquence. It must be put down to the spread of education, I suppose. But the Provost copes with it all quite admirably. He's miles better than any High Court judge I know.'

'I'd have guessed as much,' I said – thus offering a polite fiction of my own. 'I hope it's the drill that a new member keeps mum for at least a year.'

'For a term, perhaps. Isn't it delightful to see Arnold so recovering his form?' Gender must have remarked my eye on Lempriere. 'He terrified me for years, but has a heart of gold.'

'I'm glad to hear it. It seems I have some claim to be a distant relation of his.'

'So has my wife. Anthea has never quite worked it out, but accepts it as gospel, all the same. Arnold has his quirks, and they can keep us on the *qui vive* now and then. But he's a man of deep feeling. I think you had a glimpse of that after the Gaudy.'

'Yes.'

'I was so sorry that on your first return to the college you ran into that sombre affair.'

This time, I didn't venture even on a monosyllable, for I was uncertain to what extent serious subjects were held appropriate at an advanced post-prandial hour. But Gender had drawn me up a chair in the corner where we were standing, and reached for a second chair for himself. We sat down, therefore, in a confidential manner, and for a moment he was thoughtfully silent.

'You remember,' he said, 'that Arnold spoke to us on a severe note – even an acrid note – on the way we had been arranging things: shunting around the college those boys who had to remain up for examinations.'

'To accommodate old members at the Gaudy, and because of the Commem Ball as well.'

'Just that – the wretched Ball. Arnold went to town on it, didn't he? We must remember that when he was being sharp with us it was before the dimensions of the disaster were known. It was before the news came that Paul Lusby was dead.'

'Has the disaster left any sort of legacy?'

'Well, yes. The young men have got hold of the story – the whole story, if in a distorted way – and some of them don't like it at all.'

'I can't blame them.'

'I agree. But I don't want to see a beardless boy made into a scapegoat. It would be far from fair.'

This was my own view of the matter we seemed to be approaching. I had an instinct, however, to hold my hand for the moment. As Gender's colleague, and the colleague of the crowd of strangers now thinning out in common room, I was a tiro. It wasn't for me to express any attitude to a perplexed affair. This was the clearer to me because the 'beardless boy', Ivo Mumford, was the son of my oldest Oxford friend. Gender knew it to be so, and he appeared to sense my caution and approve of it. He got to his feet without haste.

'I have to pick up Anthea,' he said. 'She's been to the Playhouse to see *The Good Person of Szechwan*. Would you call that an impressive play?'

We exchanged some casual remarks about Bertolt Brecht, and then Gender took his leave. I glanced round the room. There weren't many men remaining – just enough to form what seemed now a slightly uneasy circle round Lempriere.

I had a notion that Lempriere stayed on to the death every night. I had a notion, too, that on these occasions his behaviour might follow a curve controlled by all that wine. At the start what he drank livened him up, lifted the creeping depression of old age, and made him a companion of considerable charm. Later, perhaps, it dumped him and left him boring and cantankerous. My disinclination to verify this conjecture at a tail-end of the evening was strong. I went up to him and murmured a good-night; remembered to retrieve my gown; and walked out into the Great Quadrangle.

A large pale moon hung low in the western sky behind the college tower. For a moment I stood still, held by the spectacle as I had sometimes been at this hour on returning from a party, a not wholly sober boy – and as my father had been in broad daylight when it had been revealed to him that here must be the scene of my further education. The second memory amused me, just as I had managed to be amused (although I was also infinitely alarmed) when my father came home to Drummond Place with his astounding announcement.

Then I went on, intending to make my way back to the staircase in Surrey where I was again to live.

# II

THE WEST DOOR of the college chapel opens on the Great Quadrangle and fronts the main gate; midway between these two portals, islanded in grass, stands the fountain in a big circular basin full of fish. Both grass and fountain are frequently described in guidebooks as 'ancient' – but 'ancient' is a relative term. Within the college itself the idea of ancientry attaches rather to the great chub. More exotic fish come and go at their allotted span, but this particularly large and lazy creature is believed to live forever. I have always supposed that, in the interest of so pious a persuasion, a deceased great chub is replaced only nocturnally and under the discreet superintendence of the Governing Body's Gardens Committee. Nocturnally too, human beings are chucked into the basin every now and then, presumably as a sacrifice to Poseidon and his attendant Tritons, piled up like a disordered rugger scrum at its centre. These watery divinities, reputed Bernini's work, had been the gift of an old member of the college who, pious also, caused them to be filched from Italy at a time when any English nobleman could do that sort of thing at will. The exuberant composition stands in odd contrast to the general massive sobriety of the scene, like a tumble of music-hall contortionists erupting upon a severely classical stage. The stodgy lime-streaked effigy of Provost Harbage, occupying a similar station in Surrey Quad, is really more congruous with the spirit of the place.

I paused again by the fountain, but there wasn't a fin to be seen. There was a light high in the cavernous archway above the main gate. The Great Quadrangle, its crenellations faintly defined by moon and stars, itself lay in the complete darkness which the college porters were for some reason always resolute to achieve at night. In Surrey or Howard or Rattenbury, numerous lighted windows would attest the wakefulness of young men conducting late parties, or discussing Chomsky or Marcuse, or making a belated start on their weekly essay, due on the following morning. But the Great Quadrangle is held in the main too august for the accommodation of undergraduates. It already slumbered in a senior members' calm.

And yet there was one further gleam of light, a slender perpendicular line that seemed to define the chapel door, slightly ajar. I didn't know if there was anything unusual about this. The zeal of college chaplains sometimes conduces to minor religious manifestations at unlikely hours. As I glanced across the quad I thought I heard tenuous sounds supporting the conjecture that something of the sort might be in train. Yes – I told myself – it was a muted organ music that floated to me through the October night, faintly swelling and faintly fading, as if a small wind was wandering in distant caverns.

I forgot about going to bed, and walked across the quad – the new boy whose business it was unobtrusively to acquaint himself with what goes on. The door was certainly open and the organ was being played, although in a subdued way. I saw at once that nothing of a devotional order was in question. The chapel, so surprisingly lofty and large by Oxford standards, was dimly lit and deserted. I remembered that music at night was nothing out of the way in college; instruments of one sort or another abounded in people's rooms; nobody paid much attention to any rules there might be for restricting the hours at which they could be played. It seemed probable that somebody, perhaps one of the organ scholars – of whom there were always, I think, two or three – was treating himself to a little quiet practice while nobody was around. I walked the full length of the aisle until the altar steps were in front of me. It was into a gathering obscurity; the light, such as it was, came only from somewhere near the door by which I had entered. The organ continued to play, but now more softly still.

'It's like Milton.'

These words were uttered from behind my shoulder. They had been spoken by a young voice, not of the most cultivated sort, and conveyed an impression of involuntary utterance. I turned round.

'It's like Milton.' The young man – or boy, rather – whom I now faintly distinguished repeated his words apparently out of mere confusion at having spoken at all. 'Only I can't remember.'

I could. I wouldn't have been Albert Talbert's pupil otherwise. And it was to relieve a certain awkwardness that I now quoted *Il Penseroso*.

'The high embowed roof,
With antique pillars massy-proof,
And storied windows richly dight,
Casting a dim religious light.
There let the pealing organ blow . . .

That's it, isn't it? Even the organ laid on.'

'Yes, sir. Thank you.'

The boy's confusion had increased. I tried to disperse it with another question.

'Does someone often play it late at night?'

'I don't know. I don't belong here at all.'

I had taken it for granted that this was an undergraduate member of the college. It now seemed a little odd that a strange youth should be wandering round the chapel at so late an hour, like a disoriented passenger in a deserted railway terminus. It is improbable, nevertheless, that I was so uncivil as to hint mistrust or surprise. But the boy spoke again, as if to explain himself.

'I just came for the day. With a party from school. Kids mainly. But I've stayed on. I wanted to see a bit more. There's a train back to London at midnight.'

'It's an uncommonly uncomfortable one, I'm afraid.'

'Oh, I don't mind that.' The boy had taken my harmlessly sympathetic remark for a rebuke. 'And they let me in at the door, the gate. I . . . I gave my name. The gentleman was very nice.' The boy was suddenly alarmed. 'They won't have locked it up for the night? I shall get out?'

I'm pretty sure you will. People seem to come and go at all hours nowadays. In any case, I can let you out myself.'

'Sir – are you one of the dons?' The boy's eyes had widened on me in the gloom.

'Yes, but I'm quite a new one.' My eyes were growing accustomed to the half-light, and I could now see my companion less uncertainly. He was slight and very pale. He wore some sort of blazer and an ugly striped tie. I had a sense that his long hair, which seemed raven black, was cleaner than long hair often tends to be. And he was alert and bright-eyed. Once you'd noticed his eyes, I thought, you'd cease to notice his complexion.

The organ had stopped, and the light had dimmed further, fading out the chapel walls like the backdrop on a darkening stage. There was a sound of footsteps, and I saw that a young man was approaching us from the farther end of the nave.

'Good evening,' he said, in an accent not like that of my new acquaintance, 'I hope you didn't mind my playing that not too well.'

'Not at all. It completed an effect. I enjoyed it.'

'I'm afraid the organ isn't in too good fleece. Our organist says that playing it is like eating stale chocolate. But it's more than good enough for me, I need hardly say.' The young man – politely diffident, but very much in charge of the place – was glancing curiously at the boy standing in shadow beside me. 'I'm terribly sorry,' he went on, 'but I'm afraid I'll have to lock up. Do you mind?'

'Of course not – not if the recital is over.'

'Then we can go out together.' The young man had produced a large key. He stood aside with an air more markedly polite still; there must have come into his head the thought that we might be after the chapel plate. 'I'm almost sure that you and your son will find the gate open, sir. But I'll come across with you just in case.' His eye fell on the gown draped over my shoulder. 'Oh, I say!' he said. 'It looks as if I've got this wrong.'

'Not a bit. But we'll certainly manage under our own steam.'

We moved towards the door. The young man turned off a final light, and organ and the vague architecture backing it vanished together. Once in the quad, he said good-night in proper form and walked away.

'It was a bit of luck, that was,' the boy said. 'Meeting you, that is. Otherwise, he'd have had me in the nick, if you ask me.'

'I don't think it would have been as bad as that.' I had found the naive remark attractive. 'Look, it's not nearly time for your train. Will you come and have some coffee?'

There was a second's silence. We couldn't see each other, but I had a sense of the boy as having to brace himself before this sudden invitation into the unknown.

'Yes, please,' he said.

Between the Great Quadrangle and Surrey there is a glorified tunnel: an elaborately vaulted affair the numerous bosses of which are embellished with brilliantly gilded and painted armorial bearings of heaven knows whom. Their suggestion is neither ecclesiastical (bishops and their like own only a limited repertory of mitres and crooks and keys) nor academic. Many fellows of the college have doubtless been armigerous in their time, with no need to declare, like Baldock in Marlowe's play, that they fetched their gentry from Oxford, not from heraldry. Possibly some of these contribute to the display, but I imagine that what is commemorated in the main is one or another connection that the college can claim with persons of altogether more exalted station. However that may be, this tunnel is one of the prime nuisances of the place, since throughout the year herded droves of tourists treat it much as if it were the Sistine Chapel, so that it becomes impossible to move unimpeded from the one quadrangle to the other. But now all this injudicious ostentation was shrouded in night, like a casket closed. The darkness was so entire that I had to take my chance companion by the arm to guide him through. The action made me realise that there was no single area within the spreading curtilage of the college that I would have failed to traverse confidently even if blindfolded, pinioned and being led to execution. Like the ability to ride a bicycle or sit a horse, it was a skill, it seemed, that one simply didn't lose.

It was quite a walk; we couldn't very well accomplish it in silence; at the same time I felt I mustn't simply fire questions at the invisible boy. His having recalled Milton came back to me, and what I now produced was some allusion, obvious rather than apt, from that literary quarter. It may have been no more than 'dark, dark to me' or 'this dark opprobrious den' or 'through utter and through middle darkness borne' – something like that. Whatever it was, I perhaps expected the boy to cap it in some way. Bandying quotations had been rather the thing with us when I was his age. But I had a feeling that he didn't catch on to my effort; what came through his grasped elbow was a suggestion of renewed alarm. It was natural enough. He had been snatched up by a total stranger of great age (as he would consider me to be) and was being hurried off he didn't at all know to what. He might even suspect it as being with some improper intent. This grotesque thought, just slipping through my head, made me realise, as I often did, that the minds of a whole young generation were almost closed to me. It was a poor position for a professional playwright. Some notion of remedying this defect, I knew, had been among the motives prompting me to my present belated entry into the educational sphere. I wasn't in fact old; I wasn't a bit old; but I was – if prematurely – coming to feel that the elderly were less interesting than the young.

At least there was a light on the staircase – my old staircase. I had taken over the tutor's set on the ground floor formerly occupied by Dr Tindale (eminent authority on Pope Zosimus and familiarly called the White Rabbit), whom I had known slightly when I was an undergraduate, and rather more familiarly in Italy later on. Tindale, retired from his fellowship long ago, was now dead. So far as I knew, this wasn't yet the condition of anybody else who had been on the staircase in my time. I was only beginning, nevertheless, to shake off a feeling of moving among ghosts. Not that there was anything the least eerie about the present moment. On the contrary, there was a great deal of thoroughly mundane noise, and it came from my former rooms on the first floor, now in the occupancy of that Nicolas Junkin whom I had met on the night of the Gaudy. It was evident that Junkin was giving a party. Probably it was a bottle party, and I wondered whether

Junkin's guests would leave their empty bottles behind them – thereby contributing their quota to the impressive array of such exhausted receptacles which I recalled as the principal ornament of his abode.

It suddenly struck me that the boy at my side might be terrified by this uproar ahead of us. Such ebullitions of vinous jollity take a little getting used to. One has to learn, too, to draw conclusions from certain subtleties of timbre not to be distinguished by an unhabituated ear. I recalled that I had myself done this pretty quickly. As a mere matter of self- preservation, the presence or absence of menace is the first discrimination one has to achieve. (When very new, I remembered, one moved about the place nocturnally as alert for small signs as a savage threading a darkness inhabited by alien tribes.) Later on, finer distinctions can be made. There are parties which, on simple auditory evidence, one knows at once that one may join if one wants to; there are others even a distant susurration from which declares that this would be censurable and indiscreet. Nowadays, it occurred to me, the involvement or non-involvement of ladies must constitute a larger factor than heretofore in the manner in which such festivities are comported. I thought I could, in fact, hear girls' voices from Nick Junkin's room.

'These affairs tend to happen at the beginning of term, and then again at the end. It's a bit quieter in between.' I said this by way of reassuring my young companion. Perhaps, too, I wanted to vindicate the character of the college as a scene of orderly living and intent study. The boy might be thinking or dreaming of coming up to Oxford himself, and I should have disliked his concluding that this particular bear-garden was not for him. 'As a matter of fact,' I continued, 'the row's happening in what were my own rooms when I was an undergraduate. But I'm down here now. So come in.' And I opened my door and turned on the light.

'Can I give you a hand, sir?'

The boy had asked this after a single glance, and the suggestion was certainly justified by the state of the room. I'd forgotten how much it was still in disarray; it might have been tumbled about by rowdies (by hearties, the generation before my own would have said) expressing their disapproval of some unpopular man. Not much of the furniture had got itself rationally placed; all was higgledy-piggledy, like an overcrowded stage gone hopelessly out of one's control. Big pictures were stacked against the wall and little ones lay on sofas and chairs; books had emerged in intimidating numbers from crates without yet having got on shelves.

'Yes, please,' I said, since so prompt an offer couldn't be turned down. 'You get a couple of chairs into reasonably functional shape, and I'll find the coffee and things. I do at least know where they are. By the way, my name's Duncan Pattullo. What's yours?'

'Peter, sir.'

This was only a semi-communication, but I supposed it probably to follow a convention current with the young. I was about to ask Peter some further question. But he got in his own before me.

'Have you really only just arrived? Not, I mean, been in another part of the college for a bit first?'

'I'm brand-new, Peter. This will be only the second night I've slept in the college for something like twenty-five years.'

'Have you been a don somewhere else, then?'

'No – nowhere else. I've never been one before. I've made my living by writing plays.'

What this information kindled in Peter seemed to be a renewal of alarm. It certainly wasn't any spark of recognition, and he was pretending to nothing of the kind. For a moment he was at a loss for a further question. But then he found something.

'For a theatre, sir?'

'Yes, for a theatre – when they'll have one.' I had been at a loss myself before remembering that most plays are written for the phantasmal world of television. 'Are you keen on drama?' I asked.

'Yes, sir. I'm in the school dramatic society. We did *Measure for Measure* last term. By Shakespeare.'

It struck me that Peter wasn't as young as I had taken him to be in the dim light of the chapel. If university entrance was what he was after it couldn't be far ahead of him. Perhaps one might ascribe to nervousness that last piece of superfluous information. Even so, there seemed a slight presumption that he wasn't strikingly intelligent. Yet striking in some way I did obscurely feel him to be. He would go off to catch his train, I supposed, without my learning anything very much about him, and we were unlikely ever to meet again. But I'd remember him for some time to come.

I had at least now got him sat down. He perched on the edge of his chair, although it didn't happen to be one in which such a posture is at all easy. Whenever I got up to fiddle with the coffee percolator or open a tin of biscuits, Peter sprang to his feet too. It wasn't restful, but to tell him to relax might have been to suggest that he'd got his manners wrong. And if I wasn't clear that he was at all clever I had no doubt whatever of his being more than commonly sensitive; every now and then the needle quivered on the open dial of his face. We drank coffee and munched biscuits. Peter was in too much anxiety about the crumbs.

'Is it tremendously exciting?' he asked suddenly. 'Being here like this. Coming back.'

'Do you know, I believe it is?' The boy had asked something interesting, and I showed it. I hadn't acknowledged it to myself – not in the least. But, really and truly, it's exactly as when I came here first, when I wasn't much older than you are.' I paused, and saw that this time the boy was alert and on the ball. 'All easy assurance on top, and an air of modestly dissimulating the fact that I already owned the place. It looked as if I couldn't be knocked down – like those plastic toys wobbling on lead-filled bottoms – but in reality I was just staving off panic underneath. That was me then, Peter, and I'm not sure it isn't me now. However, I remember it doesn't last long. Have some more coffee.'

Peter passed his cup with a slightly shaking hand. He had listened to this small conversational liveliness with his striking eyes rounded on me.

'I do know,' he said, 'it can be rather life or death.'

I found this remark, or the manner in which it was uttered, disturbing. It was as if I was suddenly in the presence of something unknown. So I shifted ground.

'I don't think it's true that our responses to things don't change. As individuals and with the years, I mean. Life would be pretty boring if they didn't. Still, odd continuities and recurrences sometimes assert themselves. But there's another question: how much – in twenty years, or thirty, say – we all change together.'

'The generation gap?'

I wondered why a cliche, hopefully produced, should put it in my head that what Peter might turn out to be was a poet. He had mentioned Milton in his first words to me. But in the great Olympic pool of language, certainly, he had shown no sign of being more than a breast-stroke performer as yet.

'Yes,' I said, accepting the phrase. 'Whether it really much exists. And if it does, whether it's a constant, or whether it widens and narrows as succeeding generations trundle along. I'm going to be interested to see whether undergraduates today, for instance, are very different from what they were in my time.'

'There's the length of their hair.'

It would have been hard to say whether this remark of Peter's had been intended seriously or humorously. Certainly he hadn't smiled. It occurred to me that I hadn't seen him smile yet.

'Almost everything I've noticed so far,' I said, 'seems like straight recognition from the past – with just enough of surface change to keep things lively. I look at a man in the quad, and say to myself "He's just like so-and-so". I mean, you know, in everything I can glimpse of his manners and habits and assumptions. That rather than mere physical resemblance.' I paused on this, and saw that I was puzzling Peter now, rather than interesting or amusing him. Perhaps foolishly, I tried something more arresting. 'You yourself, for instance. You remind me a good deal of one of the first friends I made here. He's a fellow of the college now, as a matter of fact.'

As I said this I was thinking, needless to say, of Cyril Bedworth, who had been just such a youth as Peter, with the same hint of the *chetif* about his person, and a similar liability to social unease. Allowing for certain shifts in the English class structure, a similar family background, too, might have been posited of either. The young Bedworth had been occasionally pompous, as Peter was not. But that had tied in with the flexing, as it were, of his intellectual muscles. He was an intellectual – or at least a scholar – whereas Peter was something else. I didn't at all know what. Probably *not* a poet. Only I dimly felt that posterity might just conceivably hear of Peter, but not of Bedworth.

'Do many undergraduates stay on and become dons?'

This was once more Peter's sharp questioning note. I somehow knew that he felt he oughtn't to deploy quite so many demands. But an unexpected opportunity had come to him, and it was on his conscience that he must make the most of it; must discover the lie of a whole unknown terrain while he had the chance. I realised something else; that I'd done what I'd actually made a mental note not to do. I understood singularly little as yet about college entrance in the nineteen-seventies, but I did suspect that a boy like this, unprovided with any special talent of the sort examiners can readily recognise, and unprovided too with anything broadly to be described as 'connections' of a useful kind, probably had a long way to go. It wasn't for me to play the knowledgeable insider, and benevolently hand out facile and groundless encouragement. And I'd unfortunately let Peter pick up a false implication from what I'd carelessly said. He was the same type of person as somebody who'd brought off a successful academic career.

'No,' I said. "Not really. Undergraduates are many and dons are few. But then it's also true, Peter, that careers are many and university teaching is just one of them. It's a very specialised thing. Quite as specialised as being a poet or a painter, say.'

'You don't seem all that specialised to me.'

'Probably I'm not.' I had liked this firm retort. 'And whether I'm going to be any good here is still all to prove. But what about your own career, Peter? What do you want to do?' I had located my clock – perched crazily on top of half a dozen volumes of the *Oxford English Dictionary* – and noticed that it was almost time to see my guest out of college. And it wasn't possible, I felt, to part without asking this obvious question.

'I think I must come here, sir.'

'To this college?'

'Yes. To read law.'

'You might certainly do worse. There's a capital tutor in law here.'

'I know – Mr Gender.'

'Quite right.' For a moment I had found myself considerably startled – less by the boy's possessing this scrap of information than by something in his way of uttering it. 'And you have my best wishes for bringing it off. But have you thought about any of the other colleges as alternatives?'

'No, I haven't. Why?' Peter's entire spare frame appeared to have tautened. 'Is it particularly hard to get a place here?'

'I'm not sure, but I don't think so. It's just that it's usual to shop around a little. To send in a list of three or four colleges, I believe, in order of your preference. Your school will keep you right about that.'

'I suppose it has already. I've filled in a lot of forms. I didn't understand them very well. There's one master who says this college isn't much good at present. Academically, he means. Is that so?'

I knew very well it was so, but felt a decent reluctance to admit it baldly.

'Perhaps it doesn't perform too brilliantly at the moment in what are called the Examination Schools,' I said. 'But it's the college *I'd* choose, all the same.'

'Just as you did long ago?'

'Well, no, Peter. To be honest, no. My father did the choosing for me, as a matter of fact. It was a sudden thing of his. I believe he liked the architecture.'

'So do I.' Peter said this to a curious effect of momentary inattention. My mentioning my father had arrested him, but now his thoughts were elsewhere. 'Anyway, it's all irrelevant.' Surprisingly, the boy had got briskly to his feet. 'I think I'll have to say good-bye now.' He hesitated. 'You see, my parents have thought about it a great deal. And they want me to come. So I'll have to try.' Peter frowned. It was as if he felt he might be judged to have said rather a feeble thing, but himself knew that it was nothing of the kind. 'Yes,' he said. 'And I see they're right. There's nothing else for it. Please don't bother to come out with me.'

I almost agreed to this, feeling that for some reason Peter wanted to break off our encounter at once. Then I caught his glance, and it seemed to signal something else.

'Peter,' I said, 'that's not the drill at all. Of course I'll walk with you to the gate. Are you sure you know the way to the railway station?'

Making certain of this took us from the darkness of Surrey to the darkness of the Great Quadrangle – and that we traversed in silence. A curious conjecture which had been floating in my head had made me of a divided mind. Did the boy really want to say or disclose something more? I decided he did. The great gate was shut, but the little wicket in it stood open. I waited until we were both in the street.

'I'll look out,' I said, 'for your name in any lists that turn up. Only I don't know it, Peter. So it's Peter what?'

'Peter Lusby, sir.'

'Thank you. I thought perhaps it was.'

'Then you know about Paul – even though you've only just arrived?'

'Yes, I know about Paul. I was here – although not as a don – on the night the news came.'

'Paul was my elder brother. Thank you very much for entertaining me so kindly, sir.'

These last Words – which somehow showed the boy as giving every ounce of himself to the task of making a good impression in this place to which he wanted to come – were almost too much for me, and I was glad of the darkness. Only just in time, I realised that he was accompanying them with a proposal to shake hands.

'Good-bye, Peter,' I said, and watched his slight figure dissolve into the dark.

# III

I N THE SECOND week of term Tony Mumford — in his middle years 'disguised' (in a favourite phrase of Lempriere's) as Lord Marchpayne — came to dine with me. Tony hadn't yet been elected an honorary fellow of the college, although his elevation to Cabinet rank now lay some months back. Simply as an M.A., however, he was entitled to turn up occasionally at high table and in common room if he wanted to. If he had adopted this course on the present occasion his entertainment would have been at his own expense instead of mine. But he judged it more politic, he said, that his appearing should be in response to an invitation from myself. I had summoned him to dinner, he explained casually to several men, by way of celebrating my own election to a fellowship of the workaday order.

I thought a shade poorly of this — partly because such an action would never have suggested itself to me, and partly because I judged the subterfuge must be transparent to all who had any interest in Tony and his concerns, or rather in his sole concern with Oxford at that time. Ivo Mumford, who occupied his father's old rooms in Surrey directly above those which had now become mine, was under threat of banishment as the consequence of being obstinately unaddicted to passing examinations. Tony was here now to discover — from me, if possible — how the situation was developing. He had involved himself in the issue to an extent which I judged wildly injudicious. But I soon saw there had been nothing injudicious in the fiction of his having received that invitation from me. People approved of it in the interest of the *convenances*. And Tony was a model of good behaviour. He managed to talk to quite a number of men – without exuberance, and even without the charm which was one of his professional assets in simpler company. No breath of domestic concern exhaled from him. He might have been a comfortable bachelor in his favourite club. Nor did he linger over his wine. As soon as two or three departures had taken place he gave me a wink and we went off to my rooms. We settled down with whisky in front of the fire.

'I remember who had these rooms in our time,' Tony said. 'We called him the White Rabbit. An elderly queer.'

'He was one thing and another, no doubt. A mediaeval historian, for instance. His name was Tindale. I used to see something of him when he had retired to Amalfi and I was up at Ravello.'

'Men used to climb into college by way of the coal-yard and through these rooms. This Tindale got a kick out of watching them as he lay in bed. Sometimes he'd pretend to wake up and catch one. He'd offer him the choice of being reported to the Dean and gated for the rest of the term, or engaging in some esoteric flagellatory ritual on the spot.'

'What utter rubbish! It's the kind of dirty yarn people make up at drunken parties.'

'So it is – and rather in my poor old father's style.' For some moments we smoked and sipped in silence over this accurate but unfilial remark. 'Damn it, Duncan!' Tony then said abruptly. 'The sheer muddle-headedness of it!'

'Muddle-headedness of what?'

'Having the boy back for a term, and then turfing him out if he fails to clear their bloody sticks.'

'I can't say that I quite see that.' This confusion of mind in a legislator disturbed me. The college *is* a place of education, you know. That's a rock-bottom fact.'

'The boy's here under his own steam – or mine.'

'He's nothing of the kind. I'll bet Ivo touches the tax-payer for his little minimum grant. To say nothing of the college endowments.'

'Ivo's not a scholar; he's not on the foundation of the place at all, any more than I was.' Tony grinned at me. 'We know that you were, young Pattullo.'

'It doesn't make all that difference. Everybody gets tuppence for his penny, more or less. From generations of benefactors concerned to bring up the youth of England in virtuous and gentle discipline. That sort of thing.'

'I know you don't think there's been much that's virtuous and gentle about Ivo's ways of late. But he's my son.'

'I'm sorry.' And I really was sorry at having produced so tactless a quote as this from Spenser or Sidney or whoever it was. 'You must just take it that I'm on Ivo's side – if it comes to his having a side. That's because I feel he's had a raw deal. But it's a raw deal from blind fortune, not from the authorities of this college.'

'Dunkie, thank you very much. I know what you mean.'

I was silent for a space, for I didn't think Tony did know quite all I meant. He was very aware that Ivo, when visiting his grandfather at Otby, had been implicated in a rustic gang-bang hazardously like rape. He was probably unaware that a less censurable folly on his son's part had through sheer misfortune led indirectly to Paul Lusby's suicide. He was certainly unaware – since it had blown up only within the last ten days – that a breath of this lesser folly had got around, and that at present, Ivo wasn't too popular as a result. What to my mind it all added up to was the good sense of Ivo's clearing out and making a fresh and unacademic start elsewhere. The Mumfords would have denied they were wealthy, but they were by any rational standard unassailably prosperous. Their heir – and Ivo was that – was free to pursue any course of life he pleased. Nevertheless, and although the sum worked out like that, I knew in my heart I'd have to back Tony if I couldn't deflect him. But at deflecting him I'd have a damned good try.

'Look here!' I said. 'You bloody well surprise me, Tony. You belong to the great world of affairs and high policy. That's where your abilities have taken you. You might expect to become P.M. if you hadn't been so thick as to accept your idiotic life peerage. Can you renounce it, by the way?'

'No, I can't.' Tony, who wasn't above vanity, responded promisingly to this treatment. 'It seems a chap can't renounce what he's himself agreed to be created. That's built into the Act. Fair enough, I suppose.'

'There could be another Act.'

'So there could.' Tony now looked at me warily. 'We're getting off the point.'

'The point is that you're overestimating the importance of Oxford for your son in the most astonishingly naive way. The proud suburban papa. It's quite comical. And it's not as if Ivo were being absolutely singled out. There are several others in the same boat, or a very similar one. The fact is, the place seems to be trying to pull up a bit on the academic side.'

'Bugger the academic side. And I know there are others. You told me on the Gaudy night about one. A young lout called Junkin.'

It was with difficulty that I kept my temper. This class stuff of Tony's, I told myself, was the more insufferable in the light of his public speeches, which I had taken to reading occasionally since the renewal of our intimacy. In Tony's speeches we were all – gentle and simple, rich and poor – chums together, comrades in some great patriotic task.

'I thought it uncommonly useful,' Tony was saying – surprisingly on a note of gratitude. 'Your giving me the tip-off about that. I wrote to the good Mr Junkin, as a matter of fact.'

'You wrote to Nicolas Junkin!' It was in blank astonishment that I stared at Tony.

'No, no. I wrote to Junkin *pere,* suggesting that we put on a common front.'

'I see. Chums together.'

'I don't know what you're talking about. I saw it as rather a good move. Two fathers from widely differing walks of—'

'How on earth did you run the boy's father to earth?'

'That's just the word for it. Indeed, you might say deep into the ground. Some godforsaken place called Cokeville. And of course it's perfectly easy to get hold of a bit of information like that.'

'I'll bet you got a dusty answer.'

'A coal-dusty answer. Dad's a miner. Can't frame a sentence. Can't spell.' Tony grinned at me, perfectly aware of being insufferable. 'After all those millions spent on the blessings of national education! And he wrote on something that looked like bumf.'

'Perhaps it *was* bumf. Nick's father may have been feeling like that.'

'You're dead right. And it was a damned good letter.' Tony visibly enjoyed this volte-face. 'The complete brush-off. Nick's affairs were Nick's business. And if Oxford didn't like Nick or Nick didn't like Oxford, there were a dozen useful jobs waiting for him any day of the week.'

'Just what I keep on trying to tell you about Ivo, Tony.'

'Ivo isn't Junkin, Duncan. Ivo's been elected to the Uffington.'

I knew very well that Tony couldn't offer a remark like this seriously. He was simply using it as a piece of nonsense with which to bait me. Still, he did really believe that society would cease to make sense if it ceased to allow for very varying degrees of privilege. And he had a contempt for those in any station within it who didn't play for their own side. I saw that all this had been hardening in him with the years, obliterating – no, not really quite obliterating – his old power of mocking himself as zestfully as he mocked other people.

Recalling the duties of hospitality, I poured Tony more whisky. I remembered an early belief of mine that it simply amused him to pretend that he got drunk rather easily. There had seemed no other way of accounting for the fact that he sometimes appeared to *forget* that he was drunk. Later, I had been obliged to credit him with the odd power of turning from genuinely tipsy to completely sober at will. Perhaps this outrages toxicology: I don't know. Certainly – expense apart – tipping a good deal of liquor into him had long ago ceased to worry me.

'The boy's uncommonly quiet.'

I was at sea for a moment before this remark, and then I remembered that Ivo was presumably directly above us as we sat. It was as if Tony would have been better pleased if his son had been engaged in wholesome uproar. Conceivably his instinct was sound. And certainly here was the moment for me to advance something new.

'I'd say he's been rather unobtrusive since the start of term,' I began cautiously. 'And I ought to mention I haven't yet even made his acquaintance. I've felt a father's friend ought not to rush him.'

'Quite right.' Tony nodded approvingly. Approval was always at least his provisional reaction to anything seemingly of a cunning cast. 'Although I'm sure the boy's looking forward to meeting you.'

'I've just glimpsed him on the staircase. He's a handsome lad – a good deal better-looking than you were, my boy.'

'But I had a gorgeous figure, Duncan. In a manly upstanding way, of course. Don't you remember our glowering at each other in the *intime* of those baths? I must admit you were pretty smashing yourself in your slender pride. In fact, I couldn't trust myself to speak. My eyes failed. *Oed' und leer das Meer.*'

This was the old Tony – mocking, and showing off literary graces he affected to despise. It was a line of talk, too, with which it had particularly amused him to shock Cyril Bedworth. At the moment, I wasn't buying it.

'As a matter of fact,' I said, 'I sent Ivo a note inviting him to drop in here tomorrow for lunch. He hasn't replied. But perhaps he'll turn up.'

Tony frowned. Unlike his snarling father, he had no natural relish of bad manners.

'I'm sorry about that,' he said. 'Ivo's still upset, I expect, over that wretched affair at Otby – that, and being hustled off to New York. Not to speak of being persecuted by a pack of pedants over their rotten exam. But it will blow over, sure enough.'

'I suppose it may. But, as a matter of fact, there's something else blowing up. And I'd better tell you about it.' I watched Tony slightly tense himself in his chair; in his inner mind, I believed, he must always be lurkingly apprehensive over the fortunes of his son. It was probably one of the things his son had to contend with. 'Have you heard of somebody called Lusby?' I asked.

'I'm sure I haven't.'

'Paul Lusby. He was a contemporary of Ivo's. An open scholar.'

'What the devil do you mean – "was"? Ivo's only been here a year.

Has this Lusby been kicked out even quicker than they want to kick out him?'

'It's "was" because Lusby is dead, Tony. He mucked his Prelim at the end of last term. He had – well, a different attitude to such things from Ivo's. He hailed from somewhere in the east end of London – a godforsaken place, you'd probably call it. His people were, I imagine, as simple as they come. Young Lusby's failure seemed the end of the world to him. It *was* the end of the world. He went home and killed himself.'

'By God, there's something there!' Tony had sat up, excited and almost triumphant. 'How splendid of you, Duncan, to get hold of that! It's no end of a lever in the business of getting the place's mania for examinations well and truly ditched. What the hell are you staring at me like that for?'

'It's that you haven't heard the whole story.' No doubt I had looked at Tony with a certain horror, but I was far from wanting to suggest alienated sympathy. I took a moment to consider. 'Lusby,' I said, 'wasn't all that tough. It wasn't a point, I suppose, that would enter Ivo's head. So Ivo's first piece of bad luck was there.'

'Ivo? What has this—'

'Just listen. Ivo dared this boy Lusby to gate-crash the Commem Ball. I think he actually made a bet with him.'

'I can't believe a word of it!' It was almost as if Tony intuitively sensed the shape of what was coming. 'How could Ivo go out of his way to make a bet with some brat from Shoreditch or wherever? He just wouldn't know the chap. It doesn't make sense.'

'That's the heart of the trouble, really. I think your son does normally keep within a smallish set of his own. But you're mistaken, by the way, if you think there's still a great gulf fixed between one sort of schoolboy and another coming up to this place. It took me no more than a week to notice that. Of course it blows around still – the old way of feeling and acting in such matters. But to the majority it's not a bit the thing. The feeling's for a get-together. Perhaps it's no more than a kind of fraternising in No Man's Land on Christmas Day: I don't know. England at large is still, to my mind, the most ghastly class-ridden hole – though one wouldn't think it from your speeches, Tony. Anyway, just here and now a bit of a thaw's a fact. Only yesterday a freezing young Wykehamist came to see me about some course or other. Or that's how he seemed to me. But it turned out he'd spent the long vac wandering through Turkey with our Cokeville Junkin.'

'Will you just spare me those sociological musings, and get on with it?' Tony was suddenly savage. 'Just what is this, for Christ's sake?'

'It's just that Ivo is rather in a reargaurd in these things. An Uffington type, no doubt. So he was on record as having gone much out of his way in cultivating Paul Lusby and luring him into a senseless wager.' I paused on this. 'It was an awkward aspect of the thing – this element of a sort of wantonness was – when it went wrong to such a ghastly extent. Just how's soon told. Lusby spent a purgatorial night lurking round the Ball in a borrowed dinner-jacket; when he got to sleep it was unfortunately in the examination room; he slid from panic to panic, bolted home, and made away with himself, as I've said.'

'And that's all?'

'That's all. Except that a certain blame is attaching itself to Ivo in the popular mind. I'm sure he knows that by now. It's a miserable story. Ivo behaved thoughtlessly, and Lusby with considerable folly. But what chiefly stares at one is hideous bad luck all round.'

'Thank you for telling me about it.' Tony looked tired and pale, and I was reaching for the whisky decanter when he suddenly lifted his chin. 'It makes it clearer than ever—doesn't it?—that Ivo mustn't quit. One doesn't run away from a thing like that.'

'I don't see there's any question of his quitting or running away. It's only a matter of not fighting against some normal college rule about men who prove uninterested in academic work.'

'That's not my view of the matter, Duncan. And we mustn't overestimate the odds against us. All this will blow over too. I admit Lusby's story shook me a bit. But it won't reverberate. Today's stink blows away tomorrow. That's a rule in politics, and it's valid in private life too.'

I remained silent but unsurprised. The spectacle of Tony Mumford regaining confidence was familiar to me from long ago. What he said on such occasions was frequently dead silly. But, with himself, it commonly worked.

'After all,' he went on, 'who are these Lusbys anyway? Good little people, no doubt, when they don't bite off more than God meant them to chew. I never heard of them before; now there's been this; I don't suppose we'll ever hear their name again.' Tony struggled from his chair. 'I think I'll go up and have a word with the boy,' he said.

I nodded dumbly. Although accustomed to bursts of arrogance from Tony Mumford which would have done credit to Cedric Mumford himself, I had found these last remarks hard to take. There had been, indeed, a hint of the old self-mockery in them, but the irony had gone harsh or sour. I was glad that, for the moment, Tony was leaving my room. I watched his hand go out to the door-knob.

'Good God!' he cried. 'What's that?'

There could be no question of what it was. Over the past minute or so there had been a certain amount of noise in the quad, and now something had gone through a window – undoubtedly a window direcdy above our heads. The crash was followed – even as we glanced swiftly at each other, recalling former days – by a rough chorus of voices outside.

'Lusby!' the voices shouted. 'Lusby, Lusby, Lusby!'

There was silence. It was broken by a sound from above – this time, that of a heavy door being closed. Ivo Mumford had sported his oak. I didn't blame him.

'They're drunk,' Tony said. He turned to stare at me, and I saw that his face was drained of blood.

'Of course they're drunk.'

'I'll have the skin off them!' Tony was looking wildly round my room as if for some instrument that might effect this purpose. Then, abandoning so unpromising a quest, he flung open the door. It was as he was about to hurl himself through it that I caught his arm.

'No, Tony, in heaven's name! This is Ivo's thing. If his father broke in on it, it would never be forgotten.'

For a moment we actually struggled in the doorway. Then the

shouting began again. This time, it was unintelligible: a mere senseless yelling and howling amid which one or another obscenity would make itself momentarily heard. It was rather frightening. To anyone without memories of the more or less harmless coming and going of such savageries in an Oxford college at night it might have been very frightening indeed. But now there came yet another sound from above – that of a window-sash being thrown vigorously upward.

'Scrub it, you rotten bastards.' The voice, which was that of Ivo's nearest neighbour, Nick Junkin, was measured rather than vehement. 'Piss off, you filthy indecent skunks,' it went on, 'and take your dirty pong with you. Go home, you stinking shits, you paltry wet wicks. Do you hear? Or do yourselves a favour. Light a match and take a look at yourselves, you daft boozy prats. You'd be highly surprised.'

Junkin's vigorous advice continued with undiminished resource for some time, first into a dead or stunned silence, and then amid the unmistakable sounds of shuffling and retreating feet.

'That's right,' Junkin said – more loudly but still on a level note. 'Have a bit of common, and go to bed. Good-night, sweet buggers all, good-night, good-night.' He banged down the window on what was clearly an empty quad.

'Do you think I ought to go up?' Tony asked. The extent to which he had been shaken was evident in the fact of his consulting me. I don't even know if Ivo knows I'm here. So would it be the tactful thing?'

I suppose that fathers and sons, equally with persons in any other relationship, have to consider being tactful to each other from time to time. There was something rather forlorn about Tony's question, all the same. And it wasn't one I could answer – or at least wasn't one I ought to answer. I said I lacked any basis of experience for giving advice on the matter.

'You won't forgive yourself—will you, Duncan?—for not having kids.' Coming at me like this was a sign that Tony was rallying with characteristic speed. 'I don't suppose your bitch of a wife had much idea of them.'

'My wife certainly hadn't much idea of them. I'm not aware I ever told you she was a bitch.'

'One hears things, Duncan – one hears things.' Tony offered this cheerful impertinence absently, his mind still on his problem. 'No,' he said, 'I think I won't go up. The boy may have settled down to work. You remember how we sometimes worked into the small hours, Duncan? Rather fun, really.'

I said I did remember – although in fact my recollection attached the practice more to myself than Tony. As for the likelihood of Ivo's being at his books now, it would only be some demotic phrase of Junkin's that could do justice to the absurdity of the idea. But how curious – I told myself – that Tony, so ready to shout at the drop of a handkerchief that young men of spirit need take no thought of study, should in fact in his heart long for a regenerate Ivo singly concerned to take a First in his School. Tony, I had recently decided, was an odd man out among the Mumfords. His father owned a simple and straightforward contempt for all matters intellectual and artistic. His son, I assumed perhaps rashly, belonged to the same uncompromising camp. Much in Tony's personality was to be accounted for by a youth spent running with the hare and hunting with the hounds.

'The chap who pitched into them,' Tony said. 'Do you know who he was?'

'Of course. That was Junkin. Didn't I tell you he was in my old rooms, across the landing from Ivo's?'

'Yes, of course.' Tony laughed robustly; his tension was leaving him. 'A chip of the old block, your Junkin. It was a damned good speech, like his father's damned good letter. Well, I must be off. Nice of you to stand me a dinner.'

'Yes, wasn't it?'

'And – look, Duncan – you'll keep an eye on things?'

'Yes.'

'Tell me how the land lies, and the wind blows?'

'Yes.'

'There's something you might have a notion of already.' We had left my rooms now and were walking through the near-darkness of Surrey; Tony lowered his voice, as if the mouldering walls might have ears. 'If it came to a show-down, who are the men we could reckon on?'

'A show-down about Ivo and his exam? I don't think the thing would work that way: a grand meeting of the Governing Body, or whatever it's called, to decide the fate of Ivo Mumford. That kind of decision is left to college officers, I imagine, or to some committee of tutors.'

'Not if it became involved with an issue of policy.'

'Tony, you're hopeless. Get back to your Cabinet and run the country.'

'Not very helpful, old boy.'

'All right. Fair enough. I'll try to answer your question. James Gender.'

'And *why* James Gender?'

'He was Lusby's tutor.'

'I don't quite get that. What sort of a chap is this Gender?'

'Liberal minded in a perfectly sincere way, but thoroughly conservative and traditional at bottom – even, it might be, reactionary.'

'Sounds admirable.'

'His pupil's suicide utterly horrified him, and he's determined no further ill shall flow from it, or even seem to flow from it. If Ivo were in any sense made an example of on the score of his gross neglect of his work, Gender would see a danger of its being thought that the college was getting rid of the boy largely on quite a different score.'

'The Lusby thing?'

'Yes, the Lusby thing. Gender might feel that justice would be done simply by turfing out Ivo for being thoroughly idle. But it mightn't be *seen* to be done. The Lusby affair would float vaguely in people's minds; it would come to be thought that Ivo had been sent down partly at least on account of it; we'd be criticised for that; and, finally, Ivo himself might be suffering a kind of double penalty. That's why I think Gender would be for keeping your academically undeserving son quietly around.'

'Anybody else?'

'Arnold Lempriere.'

'Good Lord! I've been told he's a renegade old rascal. *Lempriere egalite,* so to speak, all for sending public-school boys to the scaffold.'

'He says this and that. But he was your father's tutor.'

'Absolute nonsense! He couldn't possibly have been anything of the sort.'

'Indeed he was – although they must have been almost of an age.'

'And the memory of this will constrain him to back Ivo?'

'Not exactly. He didn't, I'm afraid, form a high regard for your father.'

'I'll bet he didn't.' Tony thus concurred without discomposure. 'So what?'

'Well, he affects to have your own contempt for the excessive importance ascribed to examinations nowadays. And he's dead against the idea that there was any real malice in Ivo's manoeuvring of Lusby. I got these things out of Lempriere the morning after the Gaudy. The old chap grabbed a role really. I think he'd stick to it.'

'It's progress – solid progress.' Tony said this with a seriousness which revealed to me again, rather depressingly, how entirely he'd absorbed himself in this not very significant business of his son's immediate future. 'But here's my bus.'

Tony's bus was a large official limousine of the kind one sees rolling in and out of Downing Street. Now it was gliding from a discreetly shadowy corner of the Great Quadrangle as if in response to some remote-control mechanism inside Tony's head. A porter was hauling open the big gates. Tony gave me no more than a casual wave by way of farewell, and climbed into the car. There was somebody in it already besides the chauffeur: a secretary, it might have been, or a detective. As the car began to move forward again, two men on motorcycles also emerged from the shadows. I could see a police car, doing nothing in particular, on the other side of the street.

England had become a country in which bombs were liable to go off, and in matters of security Tony no doubt had to do as he was told. But as the cavalcade disappeared into the darkness I was struck by the odd contrast between his going now and Peter Lusby's going the week before. It occurred to me I hadn't told Tony that in addition to a Paul Lusby dead, there was a Peter Lusby alive. Peter Lusby wasn't his problem. But he was certainly due to be somebody's.

# IV

I WAS AWAKENED next morning by what might have been the crack of a pistol in the middle distance. Plot, the successor to my old scout Jefkins on Surrey Four, had let the bedroom blind up with a snap of its roller. Having achieved this disturbance, he pulled the blind down again by the three or four inches prescriptively approved by well-trained servants. I opened my eyes (in no alarm, since the ritual was familiar from a long time back) in time to observe the latter part of the operation. Plot, turning round, rewarded me with a glance of approbation. At this hour of the day, at least, I had by now shown that I was going to give no trouble.

'Just coming up half seven, sir — and a very nice morning it looks to be.' Plot gave both these pieces of information as if an equal sense of pleasure ought to be prompted by each. 'And your tea will be ready as soon as the boy brings my milk over from the buttery. Here by now, he ought to be. Would it be the honey again for breakfast this morning?'

'Yes, please.'

'Mr Mumford will be lunching with you, sir.'

'I'm delighted to hear it. But do you mean he has simply told you to tell me so?'

'Not that by no means.' Plot registered displeasure that I should have supposed him willing to be a party to such an incivility. 'Your invitation is on his mantelpiece — stuck up there with others the like. It's our way, you'll remember, to take a look at a mantelpiece. A kind of notice-board it is, in a manner of speaking. And often they like to be reminded of things.'

'I see. And have you reminded this young man on this particular occasion?'

'That I have not, sir. Not that easy to speak to at the moment, Mr Mumford.'

'Then, Plot, how do you know he proposes to turn up? He certainly hasn't replied to me.'

'And too casual that is by a long way. But I think you can take it from me he'll be here. These lads are a study of mine, as I think you know.' In conversing with me Plot had abandoned his conventional 'the gentlemen' as indicating the youths within his care – an indication, I felt, that I was making my way with him. 'Just how Mr Ivo gets on with his lordship, I couldn't be sure about. There's an inwardness to the relations of fathers and sons.'

'I suppose so.'

'But you being his father's oldest friend and all will count with Mr Ivo, if you ask me. I just hope he'll behave himself. He can be very nice, his lordship's son can, when he's feeling that way and things are going well with him.'

'But they're not exactly doing that at present?'

'That they're not. There was a bottle through his window last night – the very night his lordship was dining with yourself. That's a disgraceful thing, to my mind – not to speak of the trouble of clearing up.'

'Yes, Plot. And I'm afraid Lord Marchpayne heard it happen, as a matter of fact. There was quite a shindy, and there might have been more of it but for a spirited performance by Mr Junkin. I don't suppose the men making the row had any notion that Mr Mumford's father was around. But it wasn't particularly pleasant. Mr Mumford himself lay low. It made his father hope he was at his books.'

'That would be the day.' Plot must have picked up this expression of scepticism from one of his charges. 'Not that he isn't up to something with pen and ink to it. He's to be the editor, he tells me, of some magazine or the like that's to be out for the first time in a week or two. It's a fancy the young men have, every now and then. Them with money, of course. You can't set printers to work on chicken-feed. Not in these days, by a long chalk.'

'That's very true.' I had got out of bed and was assembling shaving-gear – behaviour which Plot seemed to mark as being, in his presence, an agreeable informality. 'Do you know what he's calling his magazine?'

It's something in the learned way, taken from the ancient languages. But I can't just put my tongue to it. Ah! There's that idle lad with the milk. I'll be back in a moment, sir, and we can fix up about the luncheon. Mr Ivo Mumford alone, would it be?'

'Yes,' I said. 'Mr Ivo Mumford alone.'

'I'm Ivo Mumford.'

Dead on one o'clock, the young man was standing in my doorway, although with no immediate appearance of proposing to enter the room. He was looking at me defiantly, challengingly, and (I somehow divined) out of some deep inward panic. He wasn't at all like his father or – as far as my recollection served – his grandfather either. His good looks were of a fine-boned order, and perhaps he had them from his mother's side. It struck me as odd that I knew nothing about Tony's wife: not even whether she was alive. That Ivo had two younger sisters was the sum of my knowledge about the family.

'I forgot to answer your invitation. Sorry.' Ivo's face twitched faintly as he made this minimal apology. It looked like the beginning of what might become a tic or habit spasm.

'I'm glad you've turned up. Come in, and let me find you some sherry.'

'Thank you.' Ivo took the sherry stiffly. 'You know my father. He's told me.'

'Yes, indeed. And you probably know he was dining with me last night. You may have seen us in hall.'

'I don't often dine in hall.' Ivo's tone was nakedly contemptuous. He might have been saying 'I don't often drink plonk' or 'I don't often eat fish and chips'. 'I'm sure he enjoyed it very much,' he added, formally and unexpectedly.

'I hope he did. It was nice of him to come. He must be a fearfully busy man.'

'Oh, all that! He's always been that.' This time, the contempt was fused with grievance. 'It doesn't prevent him from talking a lot of faithful old-boy stuff from time to time. Makes up for his not being able to sport an O.E. tie. He seems rather to like this place.'

'I hope, Ivo, you're finding you like it too?'

'Look – I don't want to be chatted up. If that's the idea, I mean.'

The saving clause didn't much mitigate the blank hostility of what had preceded it. It did, however, speak of a certain indecisiveness in Ivo's stance. There could be no doubt that he was a difficult young man. I had come back to Oxford as a university employee; I wasn't, I understood, going to be any undergraduate's tutor; but I glimpsed the challenge that the Ivo Mumfords of the place must present to conscientious men with the maieutic instinct. But how on earth with such a boy did one set about bringing anything to birth?

'Relax,' I said.

'Sir?' At least I had made Ivo furious.

'And for goodness sake don't call me Sir – or not by way of putting me in my place. I repeat, relax. You can, you know. You wouldn't be Tony Mumford's son if you couldn't.'

This was a rash throw, but what it produced was a quick smile – as transforming for its moment as a shaft of sunshine piercing cloud. It seemed certain to me that Ivo existed amid a crush of resentments that frightened him, and that his father came in for as much hostility as anybody or anything else. But there *was* something else; Ivo's condition wasn't pathological; it was simply that his adolescence was still on top of him, and that he was a tumble of ambivalences that he didn't know how to cope with. Or this, at least, was how I resolved to read him in a provisional way.

'Let's sit down,' I said, 'and see what Plot has fished up for us. What I've got hold of is a bottle of Andron-Blanquet.' I was about to add 'I'll value your opinion of it', but reflected in time that this, as well as being silly, would be decidedly a chatting-up. I'd had it from more than one source that Tony's son was very far from possessing Tony's brains. But this didn't mean that he wouldn't be alert to detect and dislike patronage.

We moved to the table. Ivo sat down with a superplus of composure suggestive of a man taking the dentist's chair. I wondered if our meal was going to be merely awkward. Perhaps it would have been better not to have invited the boy alone on a first occasion like this. I might have asked his neighbour Nick Junkin as well, and at least gathered something from how they got along together. But that would have cut out the possibility of any reference to a number of things about which something must be said if Ivo and I were in the fixture to hold any useful commerce at all.

'My father has told me something about you,' Ivo said abruptly.

'About the time when we were both on this staircase?' It seemed encouraging that the boy was prepared to take any conversational initiative.

'No, not that. About what happened at Otby in the vac. He said you know.'

'Yes, I do know.'

'And do all the rest know?'

'All the rest of who, Ivo?'

'The bloody ushers, of course.' Ivo said this with a sudden savagery that would have done credit to his atrabilious grandfather.

'The dons? Absolutely not.'

'You haven't told them yet?'

'No.' I suppose I was staring at Ivo in astonishment. It was in order to ask these questions that Ivo had come to lunch with me.

'And you never will? And not to any undergraduates you may get thick with?'

The notion that I might start gossiping to Ivo's contemporaries about his having nearly been had up for rape could form itself, I felt, only in a mind uncommonly hard to reach. But I could just conceive circumstances in which, on a considered judgement, it might be in Ivo's best interest that some older man – Gender, say, or Lempriere – should be told that wretched story. It would be impossible to make such a thought comprehensible to Ivo himself, however, and the contingency was very remote. I weighed this up, and decided to tie my hands.

'I give you my word.' I said, 'that I'll never mention the thing to anybody who doesn't already know about it. Or not without your permission.'

'That's something, I suppose. Thanks a lot, sir.' It had cost Ivo a struggle to get out these last words, and he was in fact scowling at me darkly. 'But there was that other chap,' he said suddenly. 'The one who got me away to New York. Is he a don? I'd never seen him before. I don't even know his name.'

I'm pretty sure he isn't.' It was with dismay that I heard myself thus equivocate. Ivo was the last person by whom I'd care to be detected in a fib, but the secret of Gavin Mogridge's identity was not mine to reveal. I couldn't possibly divulge to Ivo that he had been rescued – most irregularly – by a top man in something probably called MI5. 'Listen, Ivo,' I said. 'He's a man who had to stretch a point to help us out. And no names, no pack drill. But he's a man of honour, and you can be easy about him.'

'I'd rather like to thank him some time, as a matter of fact. I somehow didn't get a chance.' Ivo said this with extreme awkwardness; it went dead against some image of himself that he had set up and was determined to live with. 'Christ,' he burst out as if in reaction to this, 'I've had the foulest luck! Those days in New York – the ones before I knew it was okay at Otby after all – were sheer hell. Skulking at parties and trying to remember which lies I had to tell.'

'It must have been very trying.' I said this as little drily as I could. Tony, I recalled, had envisaged his son in those days as rejoicing in his escape and recklessly painting New York red. It seemed one could be as far at sea about the state of mind of a son as about that of a stranger casually reflected upon in a railway-carriage. 'But it was soon over,' I added.

'Then there was that next thing. I read about it in an English paper I picked up – there in America. I'd got dead drunk at one of the parties. I read it when I was like that.'

'About Lusby's death, you mean?'

'Yes, of course. And everybody knows about *that*.' Ivo was looking up from an untasted dish, plain horror in his eyes. 'Every silly fool in the quad! Every rotten sniggering sod! How could I have known he'd do that? How *could* I?' Ivo now looked as if he was about to burst into tears. 'First the one thing and then the other – with their filthy exams thrown in. It's just a bit too much!'

I sat silent for a moment. It still seemed to me that, when the matter was dispassionately considered, Ivo was right. A hysterical and quite improbable vagary on the part of a common village slut had landed him in one trouble; an unsuspected nervous vulnerability in a simple lad from Bethnal Green had landed him in another. In both cases his own conduct had been deplorable. But chance had swollen the penalties – of which the latest had been a bottle through a window. It was because I felt Ivo to have had bad luck that I was anxious to back him if I could. It would be quite wrong, however, to tell him I felt anything of the kind. He was a young man among whose frailties a tendency to facile self-pity was to be distinguished. It wasn't for me to encourage him in its exercise.

'You have to face up to things,' I said. 'And you might as well begin with that chop.' And I poured Ivo another glass of wine.

Ivo obeyed my injunction to eat. His distresses didn't seemingly deprive him of appetite for long. Plot may have been aware of this, for the chops were in abundant supply. In what was possibly a spirit of experiment, I let Ivo have most of the wine.

'They're going to turf me out,' he said abruptly.

'Who are going to turf you out, Ivo?'

'The damned ushers, of course.'

'I'm sorry – but these people have become my colleagues. If you use that sort of language about them I'll have to turf you out myself.'

'Fair enough.' This time I had guessed right. My words had evoked not an explosion but Ivo's quick smile. 'May I call them just the bastards?'

'It's a shade less offensive, Ivo. But, you know, they'll only turn you out if you fail that examination again. Isn't that so?'

'No, it isn't. Not now.' Ivo was again scowling at me. "They'll have their knife in me.'

'That isn't true.'

"What the hell do you know about it? You've only just turned up in the place.' Ivo gulped claret. 'They'll have their knife in me, I tell you. Because of that chap who died.'

'You mean who killed himself. Listen, Ivo – listen till the end of what I have to say. Paul Lusby killed himself at the conclusion of a chain of events which you set going in a thoroughly unamiable way. It was callow and heartless and malicious, as well as being class-slanted in a rather despicable fashion. The point is that you know all this, but that you couldn't remotely have known what the affair was to lead to. You'll live with it for the rest of your days. That's not a situation before which any grown man is going to have a knife in you. You're facing nothing at all except a dons' common-or-garden fair deal in the light of their own thing – which is a bit of mucking in at the sort of work this place is here for.'

'So it's not a chatting up. It's a dressing down.'

I thought of saying something heavy like 'It's because I'm your father's very old friend.' But I reflected instead that I was entirely an amateur in coping with what my own father would have called a kittle loon. I also thought of saying 'It's neither a chatting up nor a dressing down, but I'd rather like it to be a talking round'. But I rejected this too, perhaps as feeling that it would have been a little aside from Ivo's wave-length. The epigrammatic cast of his last remark had surely come to him unnoticingly and by accident. Wherever his future lay, it was along no path trodden by astute and able men like his father. I'd do best to try once more to bring the simple facts of his situation home to him.

'Dons,' I said, 'aren't all that different from any body of men who have to run something. A regiment, for example. You might go into the army, Ivo – pretty well straight away, I imagine, if you wanted to. And you might get a good deal of fun out of it. But it wouldn't quite do to refuse blankly to go on parade.'

'This place isn't like a decent regiment.' As he made this obvious reply, Ivo smiled again – but this time it wasn't a smile that was even faintly engaging. 'And it's just no good your trying to sell me those rotten dons. I tell you, I'm not taking this lying down! Before they put that toe in my arse I promise to give them the hell of a run for their money.'

It was as if suddenly I was listening to Tony – to Tony in one of those resilient moments I remembered very well. Or rather I was listening both to Tony and to Cedric: to echoes (for it was no more than that) alike of the father's power to bounce up again and the grandfather's displeasing liability to exhibit a malignant glee. The twitch had repeated itself on Ivo's face; it could clearly be an index of excitement as well as of other sorts of nervous tension.

'What do you mean,' I asked, 'by a run for their money? Getting as near passing their examination as you can?'

'Don't make me laugh.' Ivo's recourse to this expression, which would have been more native to his neighbour Junkin, marked his sense of the extreme absurdity of my question. 'I'm just going to shake them up a bit, along with a couple of men at Trinity. Haven't you heard of our magazine?'

'I believe I have. Are you really taking to literary pursuits, Ivo?'

This rather feeble irony did no harm. Ivo was now alive with antagonism anyway, but suddenly so pleased with himself that the effect was almost genial.

'I'm not doing any of the scribbling,' he said. '"That sort of rot isn't my thing.'

'Your grandfather would be relieved to hear it. He believes that all writers have long hair and dirty finger-nails.'

I don't quite know why I reported this. Perhaps it was simply because entertaining Ivo, even with the best of intentions, was a bit of a strain. But again no harm was done. Ivo uttered rather a vacant laugh, much as if I had produced a keen witticism he hadn't understood.

'I've been doing some photography,' he said. 'Particularly last summer term. Candid camera stuff.'

'I see.' Conscious of a dim sense of danger, I waited for more.

'In the Easter vac there was a Japanese gent toadying round Otby for a contract or something. You see, my grandfather has to hold a lot of my father's directorships now. Until my father's out of government.

Or, I suppose, until I come along.'

'You'll become a director of companies when you've been turfed out?'

'Joke,' Ivo said – again with a hint of Junkin. 'But well – yes, I suppose so. Such are the facts of life.'

'What are the facts of this Japanese gent?'

'I was hanging around. Just shooting rabbits, and that sort of thing. It's a rotten time of year. But I was dead broke, and there it was. Well, this little yellow man gave me this camera, just as part of his sucking-up-to-Mumfords act. It's a marvellous job. Pretty well able to work through a buttonhole. Would you care to see it?'

'One day, perhaps.' I didn't like the sound of this prized possession of Ivo's. I even felt that there would be a kind of complicity in taking a glance at it. 'What do they use such things for in Japan?'

'Oh, industrial espionage, I suppose. I can't say that would be a line of mine. A bit squalid, don't you think?'

'Yes, I suppose so. But you use it in the interest of candour.'

'Call it that.' Ivo had glanced at me warily. 'Anyway, about our mag. The first number will be out in no time.'

'Then I take it you've already hit on a title for it?'

'Yes, of course. It's to be called *Priapus.*'

'What?' I thought I had conceivably misheard.

'*Priapus.* He was some sort of god, it seems. There were a lot of statues of him. They had jokes written on their pedestals. Rather like limericks. I think there are some in the Ashmolean.'

'I've no doubt there are.' All this classical erudition emanated, I supposed, from Trinity. 'We'd better have some coffee,' I said.

I made coffee – a service I had last performed in this room for Peter Lusby. Ivo smoked cigarettes rolled in black paper and tipped (like his father's swizzle-sticks, a flash of memory told me) with gold. Presumably he wasn't dead broke now; perhaps a big tip from the squire of Otby had recently come in. He hadn't asked if he might smoke; on the other hand he hadn't shoved his cigarette-case at me. His manners, in fact, were an odd mixture of unconsciously good and more or less deliberately bad. I felt that our lunch had been a failure in the sense that I had made no impression on him, or at least none that would lead to his paying attention to anything I said. But at least I knew a little more about him than I had done an hour before, and I told myself I was still indisposed to turn down my thumb on him. I'd continue to read him as a potentially decent lad gone bloody-minded – and the bloody- mindedness was conceivably something transitory and developmental which a change of environment might clear up. I resolved to have one more go on this tack.

'Coming up to Oxford,' I said, 'seems to take different people in different ways, don't you think? I myself fell absolutely in love with it – but then I came from quite far away, and it represented a whole dimension of things I hadn't dreamed existed. Others—'

'You had the brains for it, I suppose. You must have had – to make all that money in the theatre. And to be able to talk my head off the way you do.'

This speech, the graceless manner of which was unremarkable in Ivo's present mood, rather pulled me up. At least it deserved thinking about, and this was why I answered it only obliquely.

'I certainly came here on a scholarship, or I mightn't have come up at all. But—'

'But you were quite one of the lads, all the same. I agree you can't have been entirely a gnome, or my father wouldn't have taken up with you.'

The insolence of this was something Ivo hadn't touched before. It was, so to speak, pure Cedric, and at least suggested that I was rather uselessly getting on his nerves. But the conviction was suddenly strong in me that I'd got at a truth. Ivo's idleness and much else was a desperate disguising of radical intellectual insufficiency. He ought never to have come to the college at all. In other words, the people who were now disposed to turn him out ought never to have admitted him in the first place. Either they hadn't attended to what was under their noses in entrance papers and available to their eyes and ears on interview – either this, or they'd been rather too ready to accept the next Mumford to come along. And to Cedric and Tony Mumford that 'too ready' had no valid existence. They saw the college as faithlessly intending to break a contract never explicitly formulated but valid, generation after generation, as a matter of traditional assumptions. So they were determined Ivo should stay.

'I must stick to my point,' I said. 'Some people find themselves dead keen on Oxford. They spend three or four years absolutely lapping it up – some of them working for their Schools like mad, and others, like myself, interested in all that only in a patchy way, and just comfortably getting by. But there are men who fairly quickly find it isn't them at all. They're pretty sensible simply to walk out.'

'My father wants me to stay up. He's dead set on it.' Ivo looked at me sullenly.

'I know he is. It was in my head a moment ago. But is he right?'

'My grandfather too. He's determined I mustn't give in. I believe he'd wreck me if I did. My father wouldn't do that.'

'Wreck you? *Can* he wreck you?'

'Oh, yes. There isn't much in the way of entails and trusts and settlements and things. We're fairly new people, the Mumfords, you know.' Ivo made this shameful admission with his chin up in his father's manner, but glowering at me even more darkly than before. 'I'd find myself shoved into a shipping office, or something like that.'

'If your grandfather is so determined you must stay, Ivo, why doesn't he simply bribe you in a big way into paying some attention to your textbooks?'

'Thanks a lot; there's an idea in that.' Ivo managed his rare and surprising smile. 'But you don't understand. They believe  –  my father and grandfather do – that all that's irrelevant. I've a *right* to stay. It's as simple as that.'

'Yes. And I understand it in your grandfather. He's pretty well out of the ark in such matters – just like an uncle of mine I could tell you about. But in your father it strikes me as positively eccentric – or sheer aberration.'

'Sir, I don't know that you should speak to me about my father like that.'

'Don't be silly. Do you think I'd say to you what I haven't already said straight to him? And I'm not in the least pledged to plug his line, although you may have imagined I was when you came into this room. I'd just like you to do some thinking for yourself. This right to stay up and do damn-all. Do *you* believe in it?'

'I don't know. More or less, I suppose. It's just that these are rotten times, isn't it? Plebs running everything.' Ivo laughed again – with an inanity that made my heart sink. 'All this is a bit of a bore, if you ask me.'

'Then we must break it up. But one more thing, Ivo. Do you ever think about Nicolas Junkin?'

'Junkin, the man on this staircase? Why ever should I? Not that he hasn't taken to trying to pass the time of day with me.'

'He's taken to that this term?'

'Yes. I expect it's because I'm in the Uffington. There's no limit to the weird notions proles will take into their heads. Lusby, for instance. Doing all that creating about a rotten exam.' As Ivo produced this really nauseous nonsense he was staring at me, without at all knowing it, in dim desperation. 'No point in chaps like that coming here at all.'

It would have been useless, I saw, to suggest to Ivo that Junkin's attempts to pass the time of day were prompted by the same impulse that had caused him to deliver that speech at his open window the night before. The notion of being championed or made a friendly sign to wouldn't go down well. I stuck, however, to my own line on Junkin.

'The point, Ivo, is this. In the business of failed examinations it seems that Junkin is in exactly the same boat as yourself. And it will be the idea of the college that the same rules should apply to the two of you. It mightn't be a bad idea to think over whether the college is right or wrong. In these concrete terms, I mean. You, and a very decent chap who gives you a nod in troubled times, there on the other side of this staircase. Not your staircase, or mine, or his. Ours. Surrey Four.'

'Damn Surrey Four. And I suppose the answer is that the bloody rule oughtn't to apply to either of us. They took us on, and they should lump it.'

I wondered whether, within certain limiting conditions, this last remark was true. It was the first ghost of a plausible debating point that

Ivo had risen to. But I was tired of Ivo by this time, and I was glad to see that he was on his feet. He went through the business of thanks and farewells with a switch to decent manners which was somehow depressing in itself. But at the door he paused, as if on something that had been worrying him.

'About that chap who got me away to New York,' he said. 'You wouldn't tell me his name, and I wonder if I know why. You see, he seemed able to give orders to anybody he bloody well chose. A whole jet trundled out for the occasion, as far as I could see – and all as hush-hush as you can imagine. So I think he must be a member of the royal family. Is he?'

'No, he's not.'

At that I more or less pushed Ivo out of the room and shut the door. This wasn't because I felt any prompting to laugh – although the idea of Gavin Mogridge as a prince of the blood was ludicrous enough. It was simply that Ivo had, in the most conclusive way, played a sudden searchlight on his own rating. I recalled his schoolfellow Stumpe, who had once asked me if there were any theatres in Scotland and declared that Surrey Quad had been built by Sir Christopher Wren. But Stumpe couldn't conceivably have been so at sea about the habits and pursuits of the House of Windsor. One was back with Ivo Mumford's bad luck. Even by the quite modest intellectual standards of the University of Oxford, he was just that little bit too insufficient to be usefully around the place at all. And his insufficiency was one of the things that had got under his skin.

# V

I T WAS ON the morning following this taxing if instructive
encounter between youth and age that I received a letter from my
brother Ninian. Ninian was now Lord Pattullo, just as Tony Mumford
was Lord Marchpayne. I was to be told by Lempriere (late one night)
that Ninian took precedence three steps above Tony's young nuisance
of a son. Senators of the College of Justice came above Viscounts'
younger sons, and they in turn were above the younger sons of Barons,
and it was below these that all sons of Life Peers came. Lempriere had
taken to occasionally mentioning Ivo as a mild pest about the place,
and this was probably why he unloaded on me these useless gobbets
of information. I knew very well, incidentally, that such depreciatory
remarks about Ivo were disingenuous. Without so much as having met
the boy, Lempriere had confirmed himself in the resolution to be on
his side. These casual knocking remarks about the heir of the
Mumfords were being conceived in a spirit of primitive guile. They
made me wonder about that wartime career of Lempriere's as a top
diplomatic liar in America.

As for Ninian, he had simply become a judge. His career at the bar
had been arduous, but had at least not taken him much out of
Scotland. Partly because of this, and partly because he was in such
matters a more conscientious person than myself, he had kept up with
our kinsfolk the Glencorrys, as I had not. Indeed, during the past few
years, and more particularly since the death of Aunt Charlotte, he had
been in remote control of things at Corry Hall. Uncle Rory still lived
there for part of the year, but when he left it the reason lay in the

expediency of his withdrawing for a time to a private asylum. His descent from King Gorse, and the virtual obligation thus imposed upon him to maintain a standing army, intermittently got on top of the now aged Glencorry.

It was about a Glencorry that Ninian wrote to me. Since I had taken it into my head to live in Oxford, he said, I might care to be reminded that our cousin Anna's daughter, Fiona Petrie, was up at one of the women's colleges. She couldn't be panting to meet an elderly relation who had hitherto paid no attention to her, but I might well feel that I ought at least to do something civil now.

I suppose that somewhere in my mind the existence of Fiona Petrie had dimly registered – although indeed it was the sort of peripheral family circumstance which Lempriere liked to charge me with being neglectful of. Perhaps there was something Freudian about my forgetfulness; what had been operative was the mechanism our minds employ to repress painful or humiliating memories. Yet the inconsiderable history of Anna Glencorry and myself had been as much comical as either of these things; and it was as comedy, surely, that it did occasionally flit through my head. That our phase of tumbling in the heather together was a little shaming even in remote retrospect arose simply from the fact that it had been ineffective and fumbling – or, more exactly, that I had been so, at least in the character of a lusty young male. But much more awkward memories might have been the legacy of any less indefinite achievement crowning these encounters. Again, Anna's shot-gun marriage to young Petrie of Garth had been preluded by episodes of a certain muted drama, including my own proposal that Anna should be preserved from nameless shame by marrying me (round about my eighteenth birthday, as it would have been). Even Uncle Rory had seen no future in this, and Aunt Charlotte had more or less terminated my Corry holiday on the spot. But this too, although absurd, held nothing to be ashamed of.

Suddenly I did remember something about Anna's daughter Fiona. Her having been thus named had offended my uncle. Although 'Fiona' sounds eminently Scottish it is in fact scarcely a genuine name at all, having been invented in the eighteen-nineties by a man called William

Sharp as part of a pseudonym under which to publish stories and sketches and poems of a Celtic Twilight character. Uncle Rory would have been incapable of estimating the literary quality of 'Fiona Macleod', but he did know that no woman of his acquaintance had borne that baptismal name. I doubt whether it was anybody at Garth who was responsible for the solecism, and suspect that 'Fiona' was the brain-child of Aunt Charlotte, who subsequently lacked courage to own up.

But was there a sense in which Fiona Petrie, now of Oxford, was my brain-child too? It was finding myself asking this question that really astonished me. Was she – to amplify – perhaps the child whose growing embryonic presence in the darkness of Anna's womb had worked on my imagination to produce that precocious proposal of a kind of vicarious fatherhood? It would be curious now to be asking this mysterious process to tea. I began doing sums, and concluded almost at once that the notion must be nonsense. Anna's child and mine (to put it in that hyperbolical way) would be beyond undergraduate age. This must be a younger daughter.

Lingering doubt took me to the *Oxford University Calendar,* in which I discovered to my surprise that Miss Petrie was not an undergraduate but the youngest (or at least most junior) fellow of her college. Further research was required, and from a reference-book I learnt that the marriage of Andrew Petrie and Anna Glencorry had produced a daughter and two sons. So it was the young woman now in residence, after all, who I had proposed should be born a Pattullo.

There seemed to be no chance of Fiona's ever having been told of this piece of untoward family history – unless Uncle Rory had communicated it to her in one of his less responsible moments. Even so, I felt it to constitute a situation. How was I to cope with it? But for another memory, I mightn't have tried; I might have ignored Ninian's information as something I was too preoccupied to do anything about. What came back to me was a promise I had given to my cousin Ruth, Anna's younger sister, at the time of my leaving school. I'd invite her to Oxford, I said, and introduce her to lots of eligible young men of her own age back from the war. (If I didn't say exactly this, I certainly implied it.) The proposal had been unrealistic, so far as my first year in college was concerned. I just didn't get to know that sort of senior man. I'd given the promise, all the same. This sense of having let Ruth Glencorry down must have lurked in me for years, even if seldom or never coming to conscious focus. I was now reflecting that I mustn't let another Glencorry girl down. All I knew about Fiona was that her maternal grandmother had recently died and that my uncle, her maternal grandfather, had to be periodically shut up. These mightn't be circumstances of any deep deprivation. But at least they could be called family troubles calling for some mild manifestation of family feeling.

It remained to decide what to do. I could invite Fiona to dine with me in college. But this was a very recent possibility so far as high table went, frowned on by the conservatively inclined, and so sparingly resorted to as not yet to have come under my direct observation. I dismissed it as too tricky for the present, particularly as Fiona was a complete unknown. So I decided on starting off by making an unheralded call. There was a presumption that Fiona was unmarried, and if that were so she probably lived in college.

She turned out to be the owner – or, as it proved, joint- owner – of a minute but agreeable house forming part of a terrace standing back from the Woodstock Road. Because it took time to run the address to earth, I arrived a little later than the tea-time hour I had proposed to myself. I knocked on the door, and was answered by a shouted summons to walk in. The noise of a typewriter guided me into a room on my right. A young woman was operating the machine, and she clattered out the tail-end of a sentence before glancing up at me. There could be no doubt that this was Fiona. She wasn't in the least like her mother, but she was uncommonly like mine. The resemblance was the more startling because of the points at which it left off. I couldn't imagine my mother sitting at a big table untidily piled with what were doubtless learned papers; I couldn't imagine her working a typewriter (or, for that matter, a sewing-machine or a culinary contrivance); I certainly couldn't imagine her smoking a cigar. Fiona's cigar was of the miniaturised and inexpensive sort, the aroma of which doesn't gratify the sense of anyone casually encountering it; and I had an impression that her jersey and slacks must be impregnated to the same effect. Yet my first response to this belatedly discovered kinswoman was favourable. Her features were indeed my mother's – but they were my mother's sharpened by a strong and alert intelligence.

'My name's Duncan Pattullo,' I said. 'It mayn't convey much, but we're cousins. I've come to work in Oxford, and I thought I'd like to call.'

'I know all about you,' Fiona said, 'and I've been wondering if you'd show up.' She gave me a long glance, quite as appraising as I'd have judged the circumstances required. 'Have some whisky.'

The whisky didn't have to be fetched. The bottle – and a glass witnessing to Fiona's present recourse to it – stood on the table. An austere reply would thus have been inappropriate, and whisky was accordingly poured for me. I had been in the expectation of china tea and a stand-by tin of biscuits.

'But what do *you* know about *me?*' Fiona asked, briskly rather than to any effect of challenge. Yet I somehow felt that it was a factitious briskness, and that Fiona had been intrigued by my tumbling in on her.

'Almost nothing, I'm afraid. Are you a mathematician?'

'Good heavens, no! What should put that in your head?'

For a moment I wondered myself. Then I realised that this recovered family association had revived my boyhood's habit of referring everything to the world of Bernard Shaw. Vivie Warren, heroine of *Mrs Warren's Profession,* had gone in for whisky and cigars, and it was as a mathematician that she had made her way to Cambridge and economic independence. But as Mrs Warren had managed brothels in a big way I could scarcely explain this chain of ideas to Fiona.

'It was a random sort of question,' I said. 'So what *do* you do?'

'I suppose I'm vaguely archaeological.'

'I see.' Not receiving any further reply, I glanced round Fiona's room to discover if any more light could be got that way. It had been furnished on the unnoticing method, so that it was tasteless in the neutral sense of displaying neither good taste nor bad. I was a little reminded of the rooms I now occupied in college as they had been during their tenancy long ago by Tindale, the White Rabbit. It certainly didn't look as if Fiona had brought anything from home. I had never been to Garth, but at a fair guess it would be much like Corry, which housed a jumble of hideous and beautiful objects higgledy-piggledy. Around me now there was nothing characterful at all – except that here and there a few aerial photographs had been pinned at random on the walls, and that on the centre of the mantelpiece there stood a large earthenware pot. This last object obscurely touched my memory. Almost spherical, and reconstituted from fragments of dimly painted clay, its surface suggested an attempted portrayal of the oceans and continents of some alien planet. Perhaps this did come from Corry. It looked ancient enough to have been originally the property of King Gorse himself.

'Do you think it odd,' Fiona asked, 'that here I am?'

'Perhaps.' I found myself not quite sure of the sense in which to take this question. 'I think it odd that here I am. But why should I think there's anything odd about *your* being at Oxford?' As I responded in this way I glanced at Fiona and saw it wouldn't do. She would give short shrift to polite remarks. 'But in a way, I suppose, yes. Family-wise and the like, Fiona. I may call you Fiona?'

'I don't suppose we're going to call one another cousin – or coz.' Fiona laughed at this. Her laugh and her speaking voice went together. They were dry, rather high-pitched, and with a faint suggestion of creak or croak which the cigars may have accounted for. It wasn't like an old woman's voice, but it was rather like an old man's – a cultivated and precise old man's. In a girl no more than half-way through her twenties the effect ought not to have been particularly engaging. I found myself liking it, all the same. 'As for oddity,' she said, 'there can be no doubt about it. You're thinking I'm a sport, aren't you, Duncan? Not a good sport, just a sport. Take the Petries for a start, if you like. They're scarcely intellectual.' Fiona paused, as if considering how to develop this family inquisition. 'Do you know my father? Young Petrie of Garth?'

63

'I've never met him.' Fiona's addendum had startled me as a disconcerting echo from the past.

'He's in the army.'

'Some soldiers are extremely intelligent.'

'Some – yes. Now take the Glencorrys.'

'Scarcely intellectual. But your grandfather, you know, was up at New College.'

This time, Fiona's laughter was silent. She was perfectly right, of course, in saying I'd been thinking of her as a sport, although the actual word hadn't occurred to me. Her background and heredity alike must have been about as heavily insulated from any current of intellectual energy as could be conceived.

'I was an unlikely person to come to Oxford myself,' I said. It had grown clear to me that in conversation with Fiona one could afford to be elliptical.

'Your father was a man of genius, so you just don't enter into the argument, Duncan. Or we'll say you don't. Come, now! You didn't have any sort of devil of a time getting to Oxford?'

'Well, no. I was just sent here, more or less.'

'I *did* have the devil of a time,' Fiona said. 'It took me *all* my time.'

'Just how much time was that? When, I mean, did you get the idea?'

'The general idea? When I was about five.' Fiona wasn't being funny. 'I began to see that it wouldn't do – being what they took it for granted I was, that is. Of course I hadn't a clue on how to proceed. I'd got the hang of having brains: that some do and most don't. That comes pretty early, don't you think? What I didn't stumble on for a long time was that somebody has to come along and train the stuff. However, the penny dropped in the nick of time – just when they were on the point of packing me off to my mother's and aunt's old school.'

'That would have been worse than death,' I said – and realised that I wasn't being funny either. 'Your mother and your Aunt Ruth couldn't honestly be called highly educated women.'

'They're unbelievably ignorant. Well, I used to be sent sometimes to stay with relations in Edinburgh, and it happened one year when I was coming up for thirteen. I managed to get into the city reference library. It was dodgy, because there was a special library for children which they were expected to stick to. But I managed it and got hold of a reference book – a kind of year-book, I suppose – about girls' schools. It was my first bit of research. I knew I had to stick to posh schools, since nothing else would have come within the comprehension of my parents. Most of them sounded quite awful – all sanitation and games and religious knowledge and that sort of thing – but there were a few that had something to say about getting girls into Oxford and Cambridge colleges, with hard facts about recent successes. I wrote down their names, and when I got home I took the list over to Mrs Mackintosh at Castle Troy. She's the wife of just one more grouse-slaughtering thickie like my father, but she'd been at Girton before she fell for that sort of manhood, poor soul. I explained the terms of the problem, and Mrs Mackintosh did some research of her own. She found that the headmistress of one of these schools had ancestors going back to King Orry. Duncan, do you know about King Orry?'

'Of course I do. He may have been the same chap as King Gorse.'

'That's right. I see you know your Glencorry stuff. And there were a couple of duke's daughters at the place, which plainly put it one up on Mum's old school. So the change of plan was successfully sold to the wee laird of Garth, and to his wife, the daughter of the wee laird of Glencorry.'

'And you never looked back?' Faced with her parents, I thought, Fiona was a little given to an unnecessarily satirical note. But we were cousins, after all, with a good deal of experience – as well as the presumption of some attitudes – in common, and to outsiders she would probably be more sparing of mockery.

'Why should I look back? But that's enough about me, Duncan.' Fiona reached for another of her little cigars. 'Have some more whisky.'

It seemed to me that I could reasonably decline, without thereby aspersing my cousin as a young drunk. She plainly wasn't. The tone of her invitation or injunction, moreover, had seemed to hint a sudden thought, not very hopefully entertained, that more alcohol might brighten me up. It wouldn't have been so, and civility scarcely required compliance with a proposal thus carrying a suggestion less of hospitable than of practical intent. If I struck Fiona as a bit elderly-dull, it couldn't be helped. And I had a feeling we might hit it off quite well without my trying to sparkle.

'Do you do your teaching here?' I asked.

'Oh, no. I have a room provided in college for that. This is for the private life, and getting on with something.'

It was to be presumed that 'something' referred to activities of a learned sort, the fruits of which got themselves tapped out on the machine in front of which Fiona continued to sit. I tried to recall what I could of academic women. In my undergraduate days my acquaintance with them hadn't been extensive, and it certainly didn't help with Fiona, who clearly belonged to a new age.

'One can't get much done in college,' Fiona said – speaking again because I had fallen silent. 'Too many kids about.'

'I suppose they can be tiresome.' I hadn't heard undergraduates called kids before.

'We run a creche, of course. But the infants break out and riot all over the place.'

'A creche?' I repeated stupidly.

'Most of my colleagues are married, and have enormous families. It used just to be cats. Cats are compassable. A nun may have a cat.'

'So she may.' This reference to a celebrated Middle English treatise on the ordering of female devotion revealed to me the field in which Fiona's studies lay, or at least the field in which they had begun. I might have pursued the point if, at this moment, another young woman hadn't entered the room.

'This is a relation of mine,' Fiona said. 'A cousin, that is. His name's Duncan Pattullo. He writes plays. Duncan, this is Margaret Mountain. We live together.'

Mountain is a respectable English surname, borne by any number of distinguished persons. It would have been unremarkable in the present instance, but for the fact that Margaret Mountain was diminutive. Here, so to speak, was a mountain turning out to be a molehill. So silly a joke wouldn't, I hope, have occurred to me but for the fact that Miss Mountain was really rather mole-like. Not in figure or features, which would be ridiculous, but simply in colouration. Just as Arnold Lempriere was everywhere a senescent grey so was Miss Mountain similarly monochromatic within a narrow range of tones or values darker and faintly lustrous in effect. It was as if the mole were in good fleece, and might in consequence be attractive to the touch. But this last was a remote thought. The young woman was far from proposing herself with any urgency as a sexual presence.

I suppose I said 'How do you do?' If so, I received no audible response. Miss Mountain, her lineaments remaining notably in repose, offered, instead, a slight inclination of the head. She then walked across the room, turned, leant her shoulders against the top shelf of a dwarf bookcase, and took up a stance familiar alike in ballet and in Victorian illustrations of gentlemen behaving nonchalantly in their clubs – the weight rested on one foot, the other being crossed in front of it with only the toe touching the ground. Thus poised, Miss Mountain produced and lit a cigarette, steadily and gravely regarding me the while.

What I have to record of this behaviour is its not noticeably striking me as an abnegation of the customary amenities of social intercourse. I might, I suppose, have felt that I was being treated like an accession, whether expected or unexpected, to the furnishing of the room, and so properly to be scrutinised in silence before a verdict was given. But Miss Mountain's level gaze – our heads were almost on a level, although I was again sitting down after the requisite getting to my feet – Miss Mountain's gaze was undeniably directed upon a person. Moreover I understood that, if she was offering no communication to me, I was at least being privileged to afford some communication to her. I decided she must be a philosopher; it would only be of another learned individual, after all, that Fiona could say 'We live together' – whatever that expression might be taken to imply. She was a philosopher perpending in me the mystery of individuation, reflecting (a trifle sombrely) that whit I did I'd become, and perhaps estimating what was to be learnt from me about the nature of the absurd.

'Whisky,' Miss Mountain said absently. Her voice, just like Fiona's, had a faint husky creak to it.

We all drank whisky – this because I decided that, in these fresh circumstances, I oughtn't to play odd man out. Miss Mountain showed no inclination to converse, but did appear to feel that conversation should happen; her glance, as it passed between Fiona and myself, was like a conductor's baton, weaving into dialogue the wood-winds and the fiddles. Both ladies were relaxed; Fiona to the extent of balancing her chair hazardously on its back legs, thrusting her hands into the pockets of her slacks, and talking with a crispness which yet held no hint of a disposition to get back to any other activity; her fellow householder appearing to regard her own stork-like posture as compatible with the comfortable reception of indefinite debate. Fiona inquired into my affairs; their present posture and past history, with an impartiality suggesting that she would have been equally willing to listen to a sketch of the political situation in Bolivia or a stringent critique of Stockhausen's contribution to aleatory music. I explained myself as well as I could, although Fiona's questions at times required a more analytical attitude to my writing than came to me at all naturally. But the effect was not in the least the tiresome one, variously familiar to me, of being badgered by women concerned with tagging on to the arts. On the contrary, it was challenging and enjoyable.

This Oxford occasion might have continued indefinitely. It was interrupted by a fresh arrival.

An old man had appeared in the doorway. He was very old indeed, or appeared so: an Ancient Mariner still on his feet decades after his encounter with the wedding guests. More prosaically, one might have taken him for a tramp, except that few tramps would exhibit his sort of eye. The eye was employed in glancing at each of us in turn: at Miss Mountain, who had stiffened and planted both feet on the floor; at myself, also on my feet, as the massive seniority of the visitor seemed to require; at Fiona, herself standing up for the first time, and now advancing towards him. Fiona kissed the old man, and drew him into the room. Something stirred in me, but it wasn't any clear sense of recognition. I found myself staring at the battered pot on the mantelpiece, and suddenly I did recognise that. I even felt the seccotine sticky on my inexpert fingers. I had glued together these shards, or others like them, myself. The old man was J. B. Timbermill.

'Duncan, son of Lachlan,' Timbermill said, 'welcome home!'

For a moment I could barely manage to advance and shake hands. When I did so, it was to be hugged – a demonstration which increased the disorder of my mind. Timbermill had almost turned me into a scholar for a while, and I had worked hard at what we both knew wasn't my sort of thing: the remote and demanding field of Germanic philology. Not, of course, that it was remote for him; he knew it as the soil upon which he could raise those strange imaginative proliferations which, gathered and sheaved in *The Magic Quest,* had brought him a notable fame in his later years. He had liked me for trying, and since he was a private scholar who took few pupils we had been almost master and disciple for a time. Nothing but all the bits and pieces of Anglo-Saxon kitchen- ware I had been allowed to stick together for him any longer witnessed to that. I had admired but not greatly cared for *The Magic Quest,* not as I'd cared for the strange drawings with which he used to ornament my essays. The book had owned a range and pitch far beyond any scope of mine, all the same.

But nothing of this could have had much to do with my drifting away from my intimacy with Timbermill. He had, of course, been very loosely associated in my mind with Penny – hadn't it been from his window that I'd scanned old Mr. Triplett's tennis-court for her in vain? – and might thus be seen as hitching on to a complex of painful feeling. But that hadn't been it either. It was rather that Timbermill had been a kind of love-object to me in an imaginative way, and that I'd let myself grow away from this without building upon it any succeeding and stable relationship of affectionate regard. And now here was Timbermill, crying out 'Duncan, son of Lachlanl' as if my last essay for him had been written only a week ago.

I saw that my old teacher wasn't wearing too well. His hair, having lost lustre, had turned from silver to grey. It no longer floated about his scalp like an aureole; unkempt and straggling limply down, it lent his head the appearance of some piece of neglected garden statuary on which birds have misbehaved. He didn't look mad or manic or inspired; he wouldn't suggest to a young man now, as he had suggested to me in Linton Road, a seer or thaumaturge with perhaps some marvellous thing to say. That was behind him. He had journeyed to and frequented preternatural regions, but what he had sought to bring home – the scrolls and tablets, the bales of figured stuffs and stoppered vials of elixirs and essences – had in part slipped from the labouring back of his imagination during the long return tramp. What remained lay in *The Magic Quest*. In the man himself the fires had died away. But the ashes were not yet cold, and perhaps a residual glow would remain with him to animate his decline. And I might – at difficult times, if he'd had them – a little have taken him on. If I'd been a better man, I might have done that.

It spoke to me strangely now that this office was being discharged by Fiona Petrie, the unborn child I'd proposed to father at a time when Timbermill was still unknown to me. For it had certainly been with that implication that Fiona had kissed the old man as he entered the room. Kissing within the wide area constituted by close friends and remote relations is of course much the habit of the class of society from which my cousin came. It would be perfectly in order if she kissed me when I presently took my leave. I didn't, however, think she would, since she struck me as not of the readily kissing sort. Her manner of greeting Timbermill hadn't been a merely social thing.

Timbermill's glance moved rapidly over the three of us. It was as if he was binding us together in some theoretical structure I didn't at all understand. Then he advanced to Fiona's writing-table, and planted on it an untidy sheaf of manuscript.

'The second appendix,' he said – and his voice held something of the vibrant *staccato* I remembered. 'You must make what you can of it, my dear. Duncan could help you, eh? Duncan could lend you an amateur hand here and there. He can't have forgotten everything – no, not everything. People, perhaps – but stuff of this sort sticks. Eh, Duncan?'

'I could try, sir.'

These words came to me from some distant hiding-place. I had uttered them often enough when leaving Timbermill's attic room – now in my imagination as vast and dusky as Hrothgar's gold-hall – after having been given some assignment totally beyond me.

'Whereas *she* won't be any good to you. No good to you at all.' Timbermill had turned to glare at Miss Mountain as he suddenly came out with this. 'She's a mistake, a blunder, a howler – mark my words, Fiona.' Timbermill was shaking all over, and his face for the moment was at once savage and pitiable. 'What can you do, in God's name? Nothing but rub each other up the wrong way.'

This startling and disagreeable speech explained the abrupt tautening of Miss Mountain's frame when Timbermill came into the room. I wondered what she was going to do now.

She might, I supposed, have indicated indulgence and compassionate regard. Alternatively, she might have given the suddenly phrenetic old man what my other tutor, Talbert, would have called the rough side of her tongue. She did neither of these things, for a moment or two remaining simply impassive and considering. Then, without haste, she walked over to the table and rolled Fiona's page out of the typewriter.

'Time's up, wouldn't you say?' she asked. 'Whisky' apart, these were the first words I had heard her utter.

'Yes, it is. Off you go.'

The two girls faintly smiled at one another, but it was in a kind of understanding that didn't, to my mind, at all definitively support what appeared to be Timbermill's sense of their relationship. Then Miss Mountain picked up the machine and carried it from the room – an operation to which her inches lent the appearance of a child grappling with an unsuitably proportioned toy.

'We share it, you see,' Fiona said to me with a hint of amusement. 'We've been planning to buy another. But unfortunately the mortgage rate has gone up.'

So had the price of whisky. Probably Fiona had little if any money of her own. The Petries might well be as hard-up as I knew the Glencorrys to be, and it would be her brothers who would come in for anything going.

'So at the moment we Box and Cox,' Fiona went on. 'Now my paper, and now Margaret's second novel. What did you think of her first, Duncan?'

I had to confess my ignorance of Miss Mountain's profession, thus revealed, and attribute it to a culpable disregard of modern fiction in general. This can't have interested Fiona, but the exchange seemed designed to give Timbermill time to recover from his unfortunate outburst. It succeeded, and if he continued in some agitation it was on the score of what he had picked up about the mortgage. He seemed to have concluded that the bailiffs might at any moment appear and turn Fiona out of her house, and he fell to evolving a rambling plan for circumventing them. His harangue was by turns serious and facetious, puerile and wickedly amusing. I was wondering how to assess the mental state behind it when Timbermill grabbed some papers and abruptly took his departure.

'He can still work?' I asked Fiona cautiously.

'Lord, yes. A bit shaky in detail at times. I tidy things up for him in a general way.'

'You were a pupil of his?'

'Yes, of course – just as you were. He used to talk about you.'

'You mean he knew that you and I are related?'

'I doubt it.' Fiona looked at me in frank cousinly amusement. 'I don't think the point ever turned up. You weren't debated exhaustively between us. It was just that you were mentioned from time to time as somebody who'd stuck in his head. I remember finding it quite odd.'

'I see.' I found this information chastening. 'You stick in his head too, don't you? He's rather jealous about you?'

'Yes.' Fiona said this as one closing a topic, and I thought it was time to take my leave. She came with me into the strip of garden before the diminutive house. I didn't feel that we had made much of establishing our family connection, and concluded it would probably lapse from any acquaintanceship we might develop. Even that mightn't come to much. I must be said to be at an awkward age for Fiona – too old for her, or not old enough.

'Fiona,' I said, 'will you dine with me one evening? Not in college, with all those people. We could drive into the country somewhere.'

'That would be very nice. I'd be delighted.' Fiona's reply was conventional, but I thought I detected her glancing at me with a kind of dry fascination. And at the garden gate she kissed me, after all – thus according me, it was to be supposed, a kind of uncle's status.

As I walked back to college I wondered whether I ought to have included Miss Mountain in my invitation. Fiona hadn't seemed to mind my neglecting to do so. And her friend, after all, was on the record as not having uttered a word to me throughout our encounter. I also found myself speculating as to which of these young women ran the other. But perhaps they were straight partners, comfortably pulling together.

# VI

CURIOSITY RATHER THAN family feeling may have prompted this episode; if so, it was in the key of a good deal of my behaviour during these first weeks of return to Oxford. My colleagues seemed to regard intellectual curiosity as the first of human virtues, and the older among them would lament its virtual desuetude among latterday undergraduates. Over against intellectual curiosity, I imagine, they would have placed a vulgar variety, oriented towards, and flourishing upon, personal inquisitiveness and gossip. I don't think that the intellectual sort is the prerogative of persons learnedly or scientifically inclined. No artist can get far without it. Yet here novelists and playwrights are in an equivocal position. The whimsies and vagaries of human conduct being an essential part of their stock in trade, they are obliged to go in for vulgar curiosity too, and there are instances in which major works of fiction are spun exclusively out of the prattle of drawing-rooms and the confidences of saloon bars. I myself hover between these two modes of mental operation – the first so much more exalted in its nature than the second. And Oxford touched me up on both flanks. I don't think I'd otherwise have been prompted to the trip with Dr Pococke I must presently describe.

It would be difficult to say whether it is intellectual curiosity that prompts to the inspection of a copy of the first collected edition of Shakespeare's plays which happens to bear on its fly-leaf the signature of John Dryden. Indeed, the interest of such a volume appears to be of a personal character, so here is a border-line case. I had never viewed – which would be the word – this notable college treasure, and the afternoon came on which I took it into my head to do so. The library was almost deserted, since the period between luncheon and tea is one at which the display of any inclination to study remains taboo in Oxford. For a little while I wandered around. The library had changed since the time when I used occasionally to work in it. The pictures had been bundled away elsewhere, and the ground floor was occupied by two reading-rooms. The effect, while lacking the magnificence of the single chamber overhead, was sufficiently impressive to suggest that the pursuit of polite letters is a dignified and gentlemanlike occupation, not to be entered upon by the inferior orders of society. The books, although constituting what was known as the 'working' part of the library, rested for the most part so undisturbed on their shelves as to hint an assumption of their owning a magical efficacy: perhaps raining down or radiating learning upon anybody who cared to drop in for a nap. There was, indeed, an old lady fast asleep in one snug and dusky corner. But as she had an expanse of manuscript music spread on a table before her and a pencil gripped firmly in her teeth it was to be conjectured that she had been overtaken when engaged upon some quite active pursuit of knowledge. For a moment I wondered whether she was dead – the pencil suggesting what one reads of in detective stories as the bizarre possibilities of *rigor mortis.* It seemed not possible to find out. If I were to bellow in her ear, and she *was* only asleep, my behaviour would be censurable as eccentric and unmannerly.

I now made my way to the librarian's room, since it was clear that Shakespeare as given to the world in 1623 would be kept securely locked up in the nineteen-seventies. Penwarden received me without much enthusiasm. He had been librarian since I first entered the college, and had remained unchanged in the interval – except for its being averred that there had not unnaturally built up in him a librarian's constitutional aversion to books. He had also put on weight, without – so far as I could see – having provided himself with a corresponding change of clothes; indeed, he appeared less clothed than corseted, and thus suggested one of those elaborated toy balloons, often hawked round fairs, which when inflated take on a manikin-form, with a trunk and limbs variously bulbous and randomly proportioned according to the strength of the puff that has gone into them.

It was only our second encounter. At the first, which had been over dinner, he had told me – if not censoriously yet as with a wise resignation to human frailty – that few of our colleagues entered the library from term's end to term's end. If this were so I thought my own quite prompt arrival ought to have cheered him up. In fact he exhibited a melancholy reserve. This deepened as we inspected the First Folio – the pages of which he turned over for me himself, as if suspecting my fingers of having been imperfectly cleansed of shoe polish or raspberry jam. He thawed a little when I happened to remark that Shakespeare seemed to have been uncommonly careless in his shaving before submitting himself to sitting for Martin Droeshout's portrait. There exists, he explained to me, an earlier and very rare state of the portrait in which this negligence is much less prominent.

I had thus been lucky enough to afford Penwarden an opportunity for the casual and unobtrusive deployment of a fragment of erudition. He closed the volume with a proper regard to its hinges, and then held up his hand to a surprising effect of muted drama.

'I don't know whether you've heard,' he said. 'There has been a development in the affair.'

'The affair?' The remark had left me at sea.

'Christopher Cressy's theft from us.' Penwarden produced this amplification in a tone of surprise, as if nobody in the college ought to be ignorant that the phrase could refer to nothing else. I recalled Lempriere's extravagant-seeming assertion that so cobwebby a depredation as Cressy's ancient rape of the Blunderville Papers was still a live issue around the place. Penwarden was now glancing at me with a wariness it would have been easy to mistake for hostility. He might have been a barrister embarking upon a tricky but necessary interview with a hardened criminal whom it was going to be his business to defend. 'Incidentally,' he said, 'it may be useful if you should prove to retain an exact recollection of the incident.'

I judged it doubtful whether it would prove useful to me. I wanted nothing less than any involvement in such a moth- eaten and surely nugatory vendetta. The truth, however, had to be told.

'As a matter of fact,' I said, 'I have. I was a freshman, as you know, snatched up and exposed for the first time to the *mores* of his seniors. The occasion has revived itself quite remarkably in my head.'

'Capital! Then you probably remember the precise sequence of events. Cressy had picked up the letter-book, realised its significance, and carried it over to Mountclandon. That's right?'

'Exactly right.'

'Cressy said something to the effect that it ought to prove interesting.'

'He said it would probably be amusing to turn over.'

'Precisely. And Lord Mountclandon – a most courteous man – said, "Then do by all means glance over it".'

Penwarden paused on this – which might have been fairly described, I felt, as a disguised leading question. But it would have been impossible to swear that he was being disingenuous. The thing had happened half a lifetime back. He might be innocently confusing fact with helpful fiction.

'I don't recall it as just like that,' I said. 'It was Cressy who suggested something like a simple glancing at the book there and then. Mountclandon said, "Entirely at your leisure, pray". I remember noting that "pray", used in that sense, couldn't, as I'd have imagined, have wholly passed out of colloquial use.'

'You must have been an uncommonly literary young man.' Penwarden made this comment with a certain grimness.

'Yes, I was. And Mountclandon then said, "It's entirely yours". I agree about the courtesy. He definitely wasn't making Cressy a gift of the thing. It was only a kind of hyperbolical graciousness. But that, you know, isn't evidence. It's just an impression.'

'You've never talked to Cressy about this?'

'I've never talked to him about anything. I don't know the man.' Penwarden's question had astonished me.

'It's simply that your report chimes with his.' Penwarden got out this necessary avowal with difficulty. 'But you agree that the man is impudently perverting the true facts of the case?'

'It would seem so.' I didn't feel I need go further than this. And Penwarden, although sunk in gloom, evidently regarded me as behaving tolerably well. 'But what's the development?' I asked. Is Cressy proposing to publish the stuff?'

'That depends on the trustees. The copyright in all the unpublished material is naturally under their control. '

'The trustees of what?'

'Oh, the whole Blunderville concern. The settled estates and everything else.' Penwarden here spoke vaguely, like a man on unfamiliar ground. 'And, of course, they tend to be the sort of people that Cressy knows how to get in with. He has the art of making himself agreeable to the right people in the right clubs.'

'I remember something of that too. And he certainly had Lord Mountclandon where he wanted him.'

'It's astonishing that the man's a competent scholar as well. But what's happened is this. The trustees have appointed a new boy. Co-opted him, perhaps – –I don't know what the jargon would be. An old member of the college, as it happens. Marchpayne's father, Cedric Mumford. Do you know him?'

If this information was surprising to me the question with which it concluded was positively awkward. I was aware, not for the first time, of the tangled web deception weaves. My sole meeting with Tony's father had been in college on the night of the Gaudy, and its circumstances had been such (or young Ivo's circumstances had been such) that it had seemed injudicious to divulge that the perturbed Cedric had been in the place at all. As a consequence I had blankly denied to somebody on the following morning that the most senior of the Mumfords had ever been known to me, and an hour later had admitted to somebody else having met him on an unspecified occasion. This uncandid behaviour couldn't now be of the slightest moment. But for a perceptible instant the memory of it held me up.

'I did once meet him,' I said. 'He wouldn't strike one as a particularly appropriate person for such a job.'

'Oh, he was a useful party man in his time, I suppose, and I believe he worked for old Blobs Blunderville in a small way. Money too, of course. Anyway, the point is we think a discreet approach should be made to him. There's no doubt, you see, that the trustees could insist on the letter-book's being restored to us if they had a mind to. We've taken counsel's opinion as to that.'

'I see.' I wondered about the 'we' thus being referred to. It might mean the college's Governing Body solemnly assembled, or it might mean some faction or cabal. At least here was evidence that the affair of the purloined papers did agitate other minds than that of the patently obsessed Penwarden. 'How are you going to set about it?'

'One thinks naturally of Marchpayne, with whom we have more recent associations than with his father himself. Marchpayne has been highly successful; he would be absolutely the coming man, they say, if he hadn't so rashly got himself into the Lords. He regrets that, if you ask me.'

'I know he does. He's told me so.'

'Of course, of course! I was forgetting, Duncan, that you were so close a friend.' (This was the first occasion upon which Penwarden had addressed me by my Christian name, and I made a note that I must call him 'Tommy' before this conversation came to an end. It was the convention that one switched to this mode of utterance spontaneously and without palaver.) 'So one might expect Marchpayne to carry weight with his father. Unfortunately our relations with him at the moment are a little delicate. I expect you know about that too.'

'Ivo.'

'Just so – if that's his son's name. The boy refuses to pass examinations—'

'I doubt whether he's up to them, Tommy. Ivo's terribly stupid. I'd say he was a bad and hasty boy.'

'You know the lad?'

'He came to lunch with me earlier in the term.'

'Well, what you say may be true.' Penwarden appeared impressed by my modest exercise of hospitality. 'And errors of that sort can raise perplexing questions. But the fact is that the boy's father – Tony Mumford, as we naturally think of him – is very much exercised over the possibility of his son's being sent down.'

'So, I ought to tell you at once, is the grandfather. In fact Cedric Mumford is quite savage about it. He's as unreasonably angry as Tony, and insolent into the bargain. Cedric's a shocking old chap, Tommy.'

'Oh dear!' It was apparent that Penwarden was dismayed by this appraisal. It was also apparent that he was impressed by the degree of intimacy with the Mumfords which I had, perhaps rashly, revealed.

'It certainly doesn't make too good a climate,' I said, 'for getting at your blessed trustees. But aren't there any other former members of the college among them? I'd suppose it almost certain there are. I'd drop the Mumfords, if I were you, and find another route in.'

'You may be right, Duncan. It's a point I've discussed, as a matter of fact, with the Provost. He's reluctant to forgo what you might call the Mumford Passage – or at least to do so quite yet. I believe he has an instinct it can be navigated. And he's a very astute man.'

'I'm sure he is.'

'There's another point about the grandson. I don't know whether you are aware of this, but it appears he bore a somewhat discreditable part in a sad affair at the end of last term.

A young man—'

'Yes, Tommy – I do know about Lusby.'

'Ah, yes. Well, I don't suppose Marchpayne has heard of it.'

'Yes, he has. I told him myself.'

'You told him about that wretched wager?' Penwarden didn't sound pleased.

'Yes – and about Ivo's being rather out of favour as a result. With his contemporaries, that is.'

'You were quite right, Duncan. In following your own judgement about telling him, I mean. You are his closest friend in the college. Nobody could criticise you.'

'I should damned well think not.' I didn't react favourably to the notion of people debating whether I had spoken out of turn to Tony Mumford. 'But what's this about Ivo, anyway?'

'The Provost thought of giving the Mumfords an account of the Lusby disaster himself. Most sympathetically, and making it absolutely clear that the college wouldn't countenance the slightest suggestion that Ivo had been other than merely thoughtless and silly in the matter, or do other than support him against any injurious misconceptions. It's the Provost's idea, of course, that this might be thrown into the balance against the examinations issue, and show that we are a fair-minded lot, perfectly well disposed to the boy.'

'I see.' For a moment the notion of the Provost's thus exploiting the death of Paul Lusby in the interest of Tommy Penwarden and the idiotic Blunderville Papers absolutely revolted me. Yet he would be saying nothing about Ivo that wasn't the proper thing to say, and would be putting himself on record as behind the boy to any academically admissible extent. I doubted whether there was much future for this, or if the Provost would suppose there was were he made aware of Ivo's present intention of producing an indecent magazine. But this was not an issue to raise with Penwarden – from whom it was, in any case, time that I should disengage myself.

'Does Cressy'—I asked by way of diversion, and as I got to my feet—'ever venture into this college nowadays?'

'Oh, yes – from time to time. He has rights, you know, as a former junior fellow or the like, and he dines every now and then.' Penwarden gave me this information without disapproval and as if it held nothing to surprise. 'Christopher is very good company. He talks very well.' These further remarks came in a tone of amiable indifference. 'Have you read his last book? It's very able – very able indeed. I recommend it to my pupils as a model of good historical writing. I'm afraid the library copy will be out. But you ought to get hold of it one day.'

'Perhaps I might even buy it,' I said.

'Yes indeed.' Penwarden spoke as one whose mind kindles to an unusual but not unattractive idea – that of conceivably accreting books around oneself other than willy-nilly. 'And he's concise,' he said – this time with almost overt approval. 'Doesn't take up much shelf-room. I'll say that for him.'

Retailing small concerns at leisure as I am, I may well be giving the impression that life in the university of Oxford is a slow-motion and even *dolce far niente* affair. In fact, things tend rather to hurry along. This may be due to the curious fact that a 'full' term (as statutes describe it) lasts eight weeks, and that there are only three such terms in a year. The tempo of undergraduate life is controlled by the ephemeral calendar thus created. Every activity is announced at short notice and achieved at the double, and the most exacting demands may be made in the confident expectation of their being fulfilled the day after tomorrow. The spectacle can at times resemble that presented by an old Keystone comedy in which the camera has been speeded up to achieve effects of ludicrous expedition. In the years about which I am now writing this was particularly evident in the field of juvenile politics. A term would begin in calm, while the young men and women rapidly hatched their plots in privacy. Then there would be eruptions. 'Demos' would be held, buildings sat in by sitters-in, strikes and boycotts decreed, walls scrawled over with cheerfully inflammatory graffiti – all in the interest of programmes beyond the power of man to achieve. It is very hard to render a correct impression of this. It could be peculiarly bewildering to wandering scholars from across the Atlantic, who were inclined to swing from the apprehension that their lives and property were in danger to the view, almost equally delusive, that it was all very much a matter of paper tigers. One strove to meet and acknowledge what it is nice to think of as the burning sincerity of youth, and what one was grappling with in no time was tiresome if innocent frivolity and a natural delight in rough-and-tumble games. Then suddenly it would all be over, since the proponents of various forms of revolution had switched to fixing up their charter flights for vacations in Isfahan or Cathay.

A little of this eight-week brio rubs off on senior members. They may pay not all that attention to the young – who in the regard of many of them, indeed, constitute a minor and even inessential part of the academic scene. The bright speed of their juniors influences them, all the same, and with results that may catch a newcomer off balance. Something of this sort was the effect of a letter from the Provost delivered to me on the morning after my visit to the library.

Dear Duncan,

Tommy Penwarden has told me of a most valuable discussion which you were good enough to hold with him about the small yet perplexed matter of the missing Blunderville letter-book. I confess that I have become tired of hearing of it over the past twenty-five years – as you may already have done over a much shorter period! An affair of the sort has indeed an odd power of rumbling on, and also a mischievous capacity for getting itself damagingly tied up with other issues. It is high time that it should be composed. We have now arrived – at least in my fallible judgement – at a propitious moment for something of the kind. The point is one upon which I shall greatly value your opinion.

But more – and let me be frank with you! I view you as a linchpin in whatever may be set rolling. Cedric Mumford's accession to the trusteeship of which you have heard, and your own long-standing friendship with his son, may be much to our advantage. With the senior Mumford himself I have now had some correspondence, and I gather he would not be entirely averse to holding a further discussion of the matter in the course of a visit to him at Otby. You are, I know, busier than any of us at the moment, and it is therefore with the greatest diffidence that I suggest our running down there together. If by any chance you feel this to be possible, I shall be most deeply grateful. Mumford's convenience once considered, I should be entirely at your disposal as to a date.

Yours ever, EDWARD

My first reaction on reading this letter was naturally to ask myself just what the Provost was after – a problem, I imagine, with which his correspondents frequently found themselves confronted. If Penwarden was to be believed, that most unsatisfactory junior member of the college, Ivo Mumford, was somewhere to be lurking in the picture. His grandfather was to be told about the unfortunate end of Paul Lusby, and to be assured that the college took the most temperate view of any blame that Ivo must bear – this with the notion of emphasising how even-handed the justice dished out by the place. It was in itself a harmless proposal, although I didn't myself see Cedric Mumford making much of it. If, on the other hand, the Provost were to offer a deal – saying, in effect, 'You get us back that letter-book and we'll refrain from turning out your grandson' – this would be something which Cedric Mumford would at once regard as talking sense. That the Provost would be capable of squaring anything of the sort with his conscience appeared to me, however, highly improbable. Again, he was a man very well able to distinguish between small issues and large ones, and it was hard to understand how he could regard the matter of the letter-book as meriting any great deployment of his diplomatic powers. There was certainly enough of a puzzle in this to set curiosity stirring. And it was stirred too, I found, at the thought of encounter between two characters so little likely to delight each other as Cedric Mumford and Edward Pococke. Otby, moreover, was quite unknown to me, so that the scene of Ivo's grave and nearly disastrous misconduct in the course of the past summer existed only as a vaguely conjured up terrain in my head. All this prompted me to agree with a good grace to the Provost's proposal, although I found it impossible to envisage any useful part I could play. But even if I had totally disrelished the plan I could scarcely have got out of it. It was the first request I'd received from the impeccably courteous Dr Pococke since returning to the college.

# VII

THE DAY APPOINTED for our expedition was grey and chilly. When I turned up at the Lodging it was to find Mrs Pococke in the role of Andromache arming Hector for the field. Although it was a matter only of a warm overcoat and muffler the customary nobility of the Provost's bearing makes the comparison not inapposite. He was now an elderly man, but to look at him was to think of heroes – if not at windy Troy at least at Wimbledon, where his triumphs had been notable in their time. (He was probably the only Oxford scholar to be known by name to my Aunt Charlotte, whose historical sense had been confined to the chronicles of lawn tennis.)

This task had interrupted Mrs Pococke in another activity, in which she was being helped by Mabel Bedworth. A table in the hall of the Lodging was piled with chrysanthemums and late dahlias, and these the ladies were sorting through preparatory to decorating the college chapel. It was the custom, I imagine, to accord the Senior Tutor's wife the privilege of this assistantship, and Cyril Bedworth would not have cared to have Mabel decline it. What Mrs Bedworth thought I don't know, but it is possible that her satirical inclination conditioned her attitude to such performances. She might have been looking at me mischievously now had she been looking at me at all. But of course she wasn't; her gaze was modestly on the floor. The habit was ascribed by some to the forthcomingness of her husband's pupils, but I am inclined to think it constitutional, so that she would have continued to exhibit it even after withdrawal to a nunnery. The effect could be embarrassing. When we met in company I had to wonder whether she might not be suspected of ineffectively dissimulating some guilty association with me. The further thought that she was probably aware of the possibility of such a misconception and paradoxically extracting her own brand of amusement from it didn't render these occasions any easier.

The Provost was being fussy about his gloves; it seemed important to him that he should be appropriately accoutred in this regard for arrival at Otby. As he seldom misjudged the relative status and consequence of one man or institution and another I found myself wondering whether I had got Otby and the Mumfords wrong. Otby might turn out to be a young Hatfield or Knole. Yet this wouldn't make its present proprietor a Cecil or a Sackville. Cedric Mumford could evoke no aristocratic glamour in a mind so well informed as Edward Pococke's; and this being so, I found puzzling a certain deference to the general Mumford idea which he seemed to be developing.

Mrs Pococke seemed puzzled too, and even disapproving. I supposed that she was judging incompatible with the dignity of her husband's office this wild-goose chase in pursuit of a letter-book of the Fourth Marquis of Mountclandon. She owned a firm character and clear head, and one wondered to what extent her husband had the good sense to take her into his confidence about the problems of his job. Perhaps he was not by temperament likely thus to go all the way with anybody; he had an instinct to comport himself *en prince* and to act as his own Privy Council.

'I hope the old man at least gives you both a decent meal,' Mrs Pococke said briskly now. 'But I very much doubt it. His son would be altogether more reliable in that department, I imagine. And even the grandson is said to have excellent champagne.'

'Gossip merely, Camilla.' The Provost – who was now deliberating before a row of hats – said this with good humour.

'If the young man had the gumption to invite us to a party, Edward, I'd certainly take you to it. Mabel, you and Cyril are invited to undergraduate parties?'

'Yes, we are – sometimes.' Mabel Bedworth's soft and motile

features hinted alarm, as if some dangerous topic had been abruptly obtruded on her. 'Yes, young men do ask us – Cyril and myself – to parties quite a lot. And Cyril thinks we should always make an effort to go.'

'I'm sure he does. And, of course, men do ask their tutors and their wives to such things fairly regularly. But they stop short of Edward and myself.'

'They regard you as beyond their star.'

'Perhaps so. But it would be agreeable to be treated as a human being, all the same. I do manage to extort that from them when I get them into my drawing-room.'

'You came to my going-down party,' I said. 'Mine and Tony's.'

'So we did. I remember it perfectly well. But that was because Tony Mumford borrowed the Lodging garden for it, and so you *had* to ask us.'

'Mumford?' It was Mabel Bedworth who had repeated the name – and with an odd sharpness. 'There's an undergraduate called Mumford.'

'Yes, my dear. Ivo Mumford. His father is now called Lord Marchpayne – a name he must have chosen as a joke, one imagines – and it is his grandfather, a Mr Cedric Mumford, that Edward and Duncan are going chasing after now.'

'I know quite a lot about the Mumfords.' Mrs Bedworth perhaps resented Mrs Pococke's instructive note. But this didn't quite account for her having suddenly coloured – and much less for her looking, as she now did, positively dangerous. 'Provost,' she said, 'has Cyril told you that this Cedric Mumford wrote him an exceedingly rude letter?'

'Dear me, no. I am deeply sorry to hear it.' The Provost looked less sorry than annoyed. 'He is said to be occasionally a man of somewhat intemperate speech. And, of course, one must allow for age. Yes, Mabel – one must remember one always has to allow for that.'

'Cyril knows very well what to allow for, Provost.' Mrs Bedworth was not disposed to accept rebuke. 'And it was Cyril who simply called the letter rude. I called it insolent. It was about his grandson – the boy who is up now.'

'Parents must be bad enough,' I said, 'without grandparents piling in as well.'

"Yes, indeed.' The Provost was quick to avail himself of my effort at an emollient word. 'I sometimes think that it will come to our having to hold an annual parents' day, in the manner of preparatory schools. But before a grandparents' day I shall draw a line. Duncan, I think we had better be off.'

We all moved to the front door of the Lodging. Mrs Bedworth, I thought, had done rather well, and I actually managed to catch her eye for the purpose of indicating this sense of the matter. She responded with a smile so cautious and momentary, and therefore so suggestive of the darkest complicity, that a less well informed woman than Mrs Pococke might readily have inferred the worst. The Provost was now amply wrapped up, and not looking particularly martial after all. On the contrary, he might almost have been rehearsing the mildest, the most benign, of moods. Had his wife finally advanced upon him, not with shield and javelin, but with one of the pastoral staves from her own choice collection, she would have been making no more than an appropriate addition to the general eirenic effect. Nothing of all this abated my sense of a certain perplexingness as attending our expedition.

There had been some thought of my driving the Provost, but it had ended up with his driving me. He was, as one would have expected, the most considerate of road-users. It would have been impossible to imagine him impatiently touching the button of his horn or – a yet more fantastic thought – winding down a window, brandishing a fist, and uttering raucous yells. There was a steady purposiveness about our progress, all the same, and we were not often taken advantage of.

'I ought to tell you, Duncan, that Cedric Mumford mentioned you in a recent letter – one of the two or three I have had from him of late about one thing or another. A flattering reference, I am happy to say. He had heard of your casting in your lot with us.'

We were approaching one of the big roundabouts on the outskirts of Oxford as the Provost made this disclosure, and as he now had to concentrate on negotiating the hazard I was dispensed from any immediate response to what had a good deal startled me. With a straight road before us again, the Provost continued his remarks.

'He said he had found your head to be screwed on the right way – his manner of expressing himself is often more graphic than polished – and that I might do worse than take your advice. So, you see, he must be a wife man after all.'

The Provost made this comment with a lightness of air that didn't come altogether easily to him; it was doubtful whether he would relish being told to take advice from anybody. As for myself, I was much more disturbed than gratified. Here on my neck was the hot breath of that nocturnal deception once more. Should the Provost proceed to question me on the extent and occasions of my acquaintance with Cedric Mumford it was hard to see how I could avoid embarking on outright lies. I knew perfectly well why Cedric Mumford had a good word to say of me. It was I who, at our sole and clandestine meeting, had produced in Gavin Mogridge as it were the celestial machinery which had wafted Ivo Mumford to his alibi in New York. Ivo's father now made light of all this, his resilient temperament enabling him to regard it as having been a ludicrous over-reaching to a mare's nest. Ivo's grandfather, harder-headed if less intelligent than Tony, would retain a better sense of the grim crisis we had faced. But nothing of all this could be recounted to the Provost without putting him in possession of the facts regarding Ivo's most disreputable exploit. He wouldn't take kindly to the thought of a member of the college having been at risk of appearing in court on a charge of violating a village virgin. In any case I couldn't tell him that story now. I had promised Ivo not to tell it to anyone.

So for a time I was silent, and my doubts about our expedition grew. Cedric Mumford's personality hadn't commended itself to me; he had offered me, at the start of that nocturnal encounter, some singularly disobliging remarks; and he had struck me as an ageing man fast losing any realistic sense of what he could, and could not, get away with. A burst of arrogance from him might sink Ivo for good, and that was something I still hadn't a mind to see. But all this, though tiresome, didn't add up to calamity. Moreover it was aside from the actual purpose of our trip. It occurred to me to seek more light on that.

'Was the particular letter-book of the fourth marquis that Cressy walked away with,' I asked, 'quite peculiarly important?'

'It covers, we are given to understand, a period of major crisis in the then Cabinet.'

'So it's entirely concerned with affairs of State?'

'I believe we are unable to say that.' The Provost steered round a bend with care. 'It is, of course, with matters of public consequence that Penwarden and the others are concerned.'

'There are plenty of other letter-books of more or less the same period still with us?'

'Dear me, yes. There must be dozens of them.'

'So one must be able to infer from them the general character of the one still in Cressy's hands?'

'One would suppose so.'

I judged these brief replies unsatisfactory. I was, after all, being dragged into the country in quest of this vagrant volume – or so it seemed – and too much of the secrets-of-governance stuff just wouldn't stand up.

'What happened right at the start?' I asked. 'I mean immediately after Cressy borrowed the thing.'

'At Tommy Penwarden's instance, I wrote to Cressy – Penwarden himself being still rather a junior man. I said, if I remembered aright, that we judged it would be awkward to broach the matter with Lord Mountclandon, but that we were quite clear he had not intended that the volume should be lent away to Cressy. I received no written reply. But a few nights later Cressy came in to dine. He has always been a great accession to our table. He told me that his reading of the letter-book was almost concluded; that it would be back in our hands within the following few days; and that he had, of course, not the slightest intention of making any public use of it. This being so, he felt he had been acting quite within the spirit of the permission Mountclandon had so generously accorded him. In the circumstances, I judged it prudent to agree.'

'I suppose you were quite right, Provost. But what about since then?'

'There the matter has rested. Cressy, like Kipling's soldier, would appear to have a faculty for misremembering things.'

'I don't understand the matter in the least.' I said this perhaps too vigorously, since the Provost had contrived to annoy me. 'A donkey's age ago, Cressy undertook to return the letter-book at once. It sounds like a gentleman's agreement to me. Then nothing further happens. Yet you don't all forget about it as unfortunate but not all that important. It becomes a kind of folk memory around the place, and I'm not sure it hasn't bred considerable animosities. But Cressy comes and goes, and everybody is delighted with him. I find it odd.'

'It *is* odd.' The Provost with the largest open-mindedness nodded over his wheel. 'But we have our conventions, my dear Duncan. We have – as you will come to find – our ways.'

Like Mabel Bedworth, I had been rebuked.

Otby was rather smaller and a good deal more elegant than I had imagined it. Built of white chalk with bold stone rustications, it was very square and very tall, with a steep roof pierced with dormer windows rising to a balustrade, and above that again a lantern tipped with a big golden ball. The effect of a Brobdingnagian doll's house baldly perched on a yet more Brobdingnagian nursery table was a little mitigated by the building's being withdrawn behind a forecourt constituted by two blocks of domestic offices. I wondered when Mumfords had acquired the property. So dutchified an affair couldn't date from long after the Restoration, and that must have been anything up to a couple of centuries before the Mumford family was much around.

Its senior living representative received us with a considerable effort at civility. I couldn't think why. On my previous meeting with him his attitude to the learned had been even more disparaging than his son's. Perhaps he had decided that Ivo's academic insufficiencies might be coped with better by guile than by a more spontaneous recourse to outrageous bluster;

'Very glad you could spare a day from your scribbling,' he said to me, plainly with this ideal of courteous behaviour in mind. 'Afford it, I expect, since you've hitched on to that idle college crowd. Sitting on their backsides all day reading Julius Caesar.' Mr Mumford barked out a laugh at this, as if the picture evoked were a very funny one – as indeed, perhaps, it was.

'I assure you,' I said, 'that my new colleagues are a most conscientious body of men.' This colloquy was taking place while the Provost had withdrawn to the loo. I wondered how matters were going to proceed when he emerged from it.

'Conscientious?' Mr Mumford said. 'My arse! Conscientious in lining up for their pay packets, if you ask me. This is my old chum, Jiffy Todd.'

Mr Todd, thus informally introduced, might have been judged to be, almost in the literal sense, out of Mr Mumford's own stable. He was a small man, brown and wizened; and if I'd proposed to bring on stage an actor in the character of a groom I'd have expected him to be dressed in such garments as were now on view.

'Jiffy,' Mr Mumford went on, 'here's the author-fellow. Devilish smart at it, he's said to be. Name escapes me. Potato, or some such.' Mr Mumford laughed loudly.

This was so far over the odds that I had to wonder whether my host was going to prove to be embarrassingly drunk. Albert Talbert, it was true, had long ago been prone to address me from time to time as Monboddo. But that error had arisen respectably from a familiarity with Boswell's *Life of Johnson,* whereas Cedric Mumford appeared to be unseasonably reviving the wit of his private school.

'Pattullo,' I said placidly. The distinguishable fact was that, since our meeting less than five months before, the eldest of the Mumfords had taken a further dip into senescence. It seemed astonishing that anybody evincing such mental unreliability could be appointed a trustee of anything at all. His encroaching social disabilities, I supposed, must have been unknown to, or discounted by, those responsible.

'How do you do? Mumford ought to add that I'm his nearest neighbour. That's my sole title to having the great pleasure of meeting you.'

These words from Jiffy Todd, which might have been excessive in other circumstances, were just right in the context of the Potato joke. It could be conjectured that his having been summoned to the forthcoming feast represented a further fond and doomed intention on our host's part that a graceful amenity should obtain.

Dr Pococke emerged from seclusion, and appeared not disconcerted by Jiffy's presence, although our luncheon was presumably in furtherance of business matters of a confidential sort. On the contrary, he could be seen to take to the old chum at once. He almost certainly regarded Cedric Mumford with an inner horror, and I felt he was still far from sure about me. But he had an instinct for any quarter in which social decorum could be relied on. And here Jiffy Todd smelt, not (as might have been supposed) of saddle-soap, but of those who get a clear alpha mark.

We drank whisky in a room which (to stick to one's nose) smelt of the stuff already, as also of the aroma of long-since extinct cigars. It was the carpet and the curtains, I conjectured, which preserved these testimonies, redolent of the Edwardian age. They had probably been undisturbed for some time by any spring-cleaning campaign. I had no knowledge of when Tony Mumford had lost his mother. Otby pervasively suggested, although in indefinable ways, that it must have been a long time ago.

Topics appropriate to our rustic situation were discussed. The Provost introduced them; he seemed equally well up in field sports and the problems of rural economy, and spoke with quiet confidence on the diet alike of turkeys and dairy herds. Mr Todd followed with attention, speaking in amplification and appreciation, rather than correction, of anything that was said. Mr Mumford on the whole behaved well. He may have been prompted occasionally to tell the Provost that he was talking damned nonsense, but when this threatened, Mr Todd chipped in with some more accommodating remark. Gratitude could then be deciphered on Mr Mumford's features; there could be no doubt whatever that some dim notion of good behaviour struggled in him. But something like this was also observable in Dr Pococke. Had he been less courtly a man, or the word without inappropriately demeaning connotation, 'ingratiating' might have come to one's lips as adequately descriptive of his manner. I have no doubt that one consequence of this was Cedric Mumford's being more convinced than ever that the fellow was a damned parsonical sycophant, and being much prompted to say so aloud. This really would have set Jiffy a stiff problem in the preservation of *bienseance,* but I have little doubt that he would have acquitted himself well.

We went into a dining-room and sat down. Or rather we were about to do so when Jiffy Todd addressed himself to me in the most charmingly casual manner.

'Do you know,' he said, 'I find myself becoming most pitifully absent-minded? If I were in Cedric's position now I'd probably clean forget to ask Dr Pococke to say grace.'

This deft prompting (in addition to drawing from Mr Mumford the robust assertion that he was damned if he himself hadn't been going to forget the drill) seemed to tell me that the old chum hadn't been a member of our college – since otherwise 'the Provost' and not 'Dr Pococke' would have been natural. It occurred to me to check up on this.

'Were you at Oxford with Mumford?' I asked.

'Yes, indeed. We were exact contemporaries, but not at your distinguished college. I went up to New College.'

'Then I wonder whether, by any chance, you knew an uncle of mine called Roderick Glencorry?'

'Rory – how very interesting!' Jiffy temperately signalled the gratification proper to be felt on establishing this sort of *rapport* with a stranger. 'I knew him quite well; in fact I helped him to shoot his father's grouse on one occasion at Corry. A delightful place. I've no doubt you know it intimately.'

'Yes, I do.'

'But it's a long time, I'm afraid, since I had any news of him.' This was Jiffy's way of asking 'Is he dead?', and I took it in that sense.

'He's quite robust,' I said, 'at least as to the physical man. But he lives rather a secluded life from time to time.'

Mr Todd received this information as fully explaining itself, and went on to talk about Glencorrys not within my recollection. The Provost listened with complacency. He would have heard from Arnold Lempriere, I imagine, of my possessing these respectable connections in a middle distance, and approved the circumstance as augmenting, in its microscopic way, the consequence of the college. Cedric Mumford, on the other hand, grew suddenly impatient, and manifested the fact by bidding us stop talking about 'a pack of tin-pot bonnet- lairds'. This, being extremely rude, caused momentary embarrassment. I noticed it, however, as seeming to relieve the mind of the elderly woman waiting on us. One or two other servants had been in evidence, but this one was in charge, and I took her to be the devoted housekeeper who had providentially been unsupported at Otby on the night of Ivo's escapade. She had been beginning to fear that her employer must be ill. His return to his proper form reassured her.

Even so, this recrudescence of the natural man was momentary. We got through the predictable pheasant (which was predictably dry, and predictably accompanied by little deserts of dry breadcrumbs) in tolerably good order. Cedric Mumford even managed to inquire about Mrs Pococke's health. I found myself rather admiring both the Provost and his host. The Provost had the easier role. He spent a certain amount of time every day exercising himself amid the pleasures of society, and the thing came to him as effortlessly as his round of golf. Yet it wasn't quite without strain that he was making himself agreeable to Cedric Mumford – and all (so far as I could see) in aid of nothing more than restoring to the control of some of his colleagues a letter-book of a politically minded nobleman flourishing in the earlier part of the nineteenth century. Viewed in this way, Dr Pococke's pertinacity was a meritorious instance of devotion to duty. Cedric Mumford had a more personal motive for the effort he was making. He had concluded, it must be believed, that if Ivo was to be served those damned Oxford ushers had to be spoken fair. This family piety, too, was wholly meritorious in its fashion.

'And now,' I heard the Provost say, 'I propose to be a little indiscreet.' He paused on this interesting announcement, and drank as much claret as was decent at one go – no doubt in the interest of converting into a swallowable bolus the last of his pheasant. 'I know I can rely on your discretion, I need hardly say.' Having thus built up expectation – or fancied himself so to have done – the Provost paused again, perhaps with the thought that his host would wave the elderly female attending upon us out of the room. But this didn't take place, and the Provost had to proceed. 'I am happy to say, my dear Mumford, that at its next meeting our Governing Body will unquestionably accept the advice of one of its committees, and elect your son into an Honorary Fellowship.'

'And what the devil is—?'

'How very nice!' Mr Todd said firmly. 'A most pleasant thing to happen.'

This came from the old chum much as if designed to forestall in Mr Mumford a transport of enthusiasm excessive even in face of the announcement just made. It couldn't quite obscure the fact that what Mr Mumford had been proposing to say was 'And what the devil is an Honorary Fellowship?' Since ignorance here was not possible in one of his standing, this was even more uncivil than had been the remark about bonnet-lairds. It produced pallor behind the Provost's beard. He had, perhaps, been canvassing a little more gratification than was reasonable. The college couldn't well do other than accord this titular distinction to a former member now forging ahead in the Cabinet; if anything, it had been a little belated on the job. Tony's father could properly have received the news with polite reserve – instead of which he had let nature take another airing. But once more he manfully checked himself. I felt almost sorry for a man who, so accustomed to wound, was yet in the present instance so afraid to strike.

And the Provost, aided by a receptive Jiffy, again played his part. The roll of the college's Honorary Fellows, he explained, was unhappily not dilatable instantly and at will; there was a statutory ceiling on the number of persons who could hold the high distinction at any one time; so sometimes, before acting agreeably to its own wishes, the Governing Body had to wait for an Honorary Fellow to die. Fortunately – the Provost continued with a momentary roguishness

– this happened fairly frequently, since not many elections were made of men so vigorously in their early prime as was Lord Marchpayne.

By the time that Dr Pococke had given the matter this graceful turn I believe his rhetoric had caused him to forget what his intellect must have told him clearly enough: that to Cedric Mumford the laurels of a college could mean nothing at all. Oxford was a place at which you did, or did not, belong to the Uffington – and at which, if you did so do, you periodically smashed an appropriate number of windows as a result. The very simplicity of this archaic view of the student life made it hard for the Provost to grasp. Had it not been so, he would scarcely have proceeded as he now did.

Over blancmange (which had been served to Mr Mumford's guests before it became apparent that a handsome Stilton was to be regarded as an alternative rather than a sequel to this dish) we were treated to a short historical account of the institution of honorary fellowships. It didn't seem a rewarding subject, objectively regarded, but the Provost talked about it (as he could talk about most things) very well. At first I thought he was simply carrying off any awkwardness that the first introduction of the topic had occasioned. But this proved not to be so. The Provost was discoursing by design, and the chase had a beast in view. The beast (almost literally that, one might be tempted to say) was old Mr Mumford.

Was there any recorded instance, the Provost was asking, of a father and son holding honorary fellowships at their old college at the same time? He confessed to being unable to name one, and the thing must have happened rarely, if it had happened at all. The more the pity, so agreeable (even edifying, the Provost's tone hinted) would such a coincidence of distinctions be. And it was certainly possible to think of circumstances in which the phenomenon might occur.

What Cedric Mumford made of all this it would have been impossible to say. Conceivably it was very little. He was heavy alike with his years and his whisky and wine, and he may simply have switched off under the persuasion that the fellow was doing no more than produce his customary idle usher's babble. Jiffy Todd on the other hand, was certainly not at sea, and I thought I detected as glimmering in his eye mild surprise, even gratification, before this comedy of misconceptions. It was certainly that. Mr Mumford saw as a self-important bore a man who was in fact capable of considerable subtlety of address. Dr Pococke believed himself to be dangling a kind of spectral carrot before somebody who would assuredly prove to be without the slightest impulse to snap at it. I don't know whether I found all this amusing. I am sure I remained puzzled. If Cedric Mumford were known to have the missing letter-book locked up in the next room (rather than as being merely one whose voice might be listened to on the making of some demand for its recovery) there would still be something disproportionate about all these blandishments and manoeuvrings.

But there was more to come, for the Provost proved to have worked out a two-pronged attack. When Mr Mumford had finished his Stilton (and the rest of us our wobbling nursery pudding) we returned to the chamber of our first resort for what our host declared to be coffee. Coffee, however, whether or not it had been prepared, did not appear. Whisky did – or rather it was on permanent view. Its consumption was obligatory, since our entertainer's sense of hospitality was of that aggressive sort which treats a protesting hand or an unacquiescent murmur as a personal affront. It was impossible to imagine the Provost as ever flown either with insolence or wine; even in his greenest youth, one felt, he must have held himself proudly aloof from the sons of Belial. Yet something of the vigour with which he now developed a new theme may have been in part attributable to a hint of vinous warmth. Of Cedric Mumford's temperature there was no doubt. He wouldn't spontaneously combust, but I questioned whether we'd get away from Otby before some vexatious if minor explosion had occurred. Jiffy Todd was hovering over him like a fire-tender warily circling a smouldering tanker.

'We must not fail to congratulate you, my dear Mumford,' the Provost said, 'on the new responsibility you have been invited to take up.' He paused on this to give me a steady look, so that I was constrained to interpolate 'Yes, indeed' in a tone of earnest conviction. 'It would appear,' he went on, 'that various crucial decisions have shortly to be arrived at by the men who administer the Blunderville Trusts. So much is common knowledge among those who read the more responsible journals reporting on such matters. Not everybody knows how fortunate the trustees are in having been able to persuade you to afford them the benefit of your unrivalled financial skill and experience – and your proven wisdom, let me add.'

This was pitching it pretty steep – indeed, laying it on thick. From Mr Mumford it produced, disconcertingly, a cackle of harsh laughter.

'Wisdom my arse!' he said. 'Cunning's what you need to survive in the City, Pococke. Low cunning. You might be not too bad at it. Why not have a try, eh? Never too late to learn. Make your pile, my boy.'

These coarse pleasantries were naturally painful to the Provost. I didn't much care for them myself. Uncle Rory, I thought, would detect something decidedly bogus in the most senior of the Mumfords; it was as if Cedric had treated himself to a persona based on the backwoods squires of English fiction from Fielding and Smollett onwards. This last was, of course, an implausible supposition – Cedric Mumford having so clearly never opened, or at any rate finished, a book.

'Cedric, old chap,' Mr Todd murmured, 'ware wheat!'

This admonition (of a provenance chiming with what had been passing through my head) had considerable effect. Mr Mumford mumbled something in an abashed fashion, and the Provost took heart to proceed.

'We know full well, Mumford, that you will have numerous onerous matters to perpend. We hope, nevertheless – and Pattullo and I have really come over to express this hope – that the interests of your old college will not be wholly absent from your mind.'

'Are you talking about that confounded copybook you keep harping on in those damned pompous letters? I know nothing about it.'

The Provost was silent, as he well might be before Cedric Mumford thus at his hideous best. For a moment, even, he appeared to me uncertain that it *was* the confounded copybook he was talking about – and uncertain, too, whether there was any point in talking at all. For the first time in my experience, Dr Pococke was a little at a loss. I didn't blame him. Our host's latest return to civilised courses had lasted for not much more than a minute. But the Provost recovered himself, not being a man to give in. He expounded the matter of the letter-book. He represented the impropriety – almost the occasion of scandal – constituted by its remaining so irregularly in the possession of Christopher Cressy. To a man of affairs like Mr Mumford, he said, to a man habituated to taking broad views of momentous issues, it must all appear very trivial, almost absurd. He, the Provost, although living so secluded a life in the harmless pursuit of learning, was not without a glimmer of that. But the susceptibilities of scholars were not unworthy of some slight consideration, since they were a class of people who in their own unassuming fashion contributed something to the general seemliness of things. So if, happily, Mr Mumford could see his way to setting this small matter to rights he would decidedly deserve well of the ancient foundation within which he had for a time reposed so much to the satisfaction of all.

If the Provost didn't employ exactly these words he did manage to convey their effect. I realised with dismay how much there was yet to come – notably the theme of kindness to Ivo as a topic much engaging the college's corporate mind. This – to put it mildly – would be a distorted picture. I was sure that, at this moment, the majority of my colleagues would not so much as recognise the name of Ivo Mumford, and that it would take some quite striking activity on that young man's part to elevate his affairs above the obscure sphere of purely administrative determination. If the Provost were really to pursue this line with the object of securing Mr Mumford's admiring regard he would be permitting himself to draw a very long bow indeed. He would also be misjudging – I came back to this – the thickness of Cedric Mumford's skull. Cedric might be no genius, but he was at least more astute than his grandson.

But I doubt whether the Provost would now have introduced Ivo – let alone the Lusby aspect of his affairs – into the conversation at all. The atmosphere created by our host's ill-concealed animosity not only to ourselves but also to the universe at large would have overtaxed even the Provost's power to go about anything of the sort with the slightest appearance of a maintained propriety. Softening up Mr Mumford (in whatever obscure interest it was being proposed) would have to await a less unpropitious occasion. To my relief, and also to Mr Todd's, the Provost was showing signs of calling it a day. In the issue, however, Ivo did after all rear his handsome young head – through the agency, not of the Provost, but of Mr Mumford himself.

There could be no doubt that the squire of Otby was finding his Oxford visitors increasingly trying. He poured me more whisky – which this time I didn't propose to touch – much as if he had been a Borgia turning unwontedly candid about the potion. Then he moved brusquely away, lurched across the room, and came back to us brandishing a piece of writing-paper. I saw Jiffy Todd stiffen. He knew his man, and was probably realising that he might murmur not merely *Ware wheat!* but even *Ware wire!* in vain. Indeed, our host was now yelling at us as some enraged MFH might yell at a couple of fools riding down the hounds.

'What's all this old wives' fiddle-faddle?' he shouted. 'What about my grandson? Here's a damned impertinent letter from God knows who – calls himself Piddlebed, or some such.'

'Bedworth,' I said, I hope stonily. 'Our Senior Tutor.'

'Bedworth, Bedpan – I don't give a fart for the fellow's name. A rigmarole about examinations in this and examinations in that. To hell with your messing the lad around with such pig-shit! A tiresome little brute I don't doubt he can be. But if you have it in for him, why don't you turn him over the buttery hatch for six on the backside and forget about it? That's how such things were settled when ushers were still more or less men and not schoolmarms.'

This atavistic vision, which appeared to envisage the Provost in the flagellant character of a Busby or a Keate, struck me as not wholly without attractiveness. But it was devoid of utility, and merely witnessed to a certain obsession with posterior matters which Mr Mumford's vocabulary betrayed from time to time. It brought Dr Pococke to his feet, and I could hardly suppose he had any thought except for his overcoat and muffler. He did, however, make one more effort.

'My dear sir,' he said, 'I beg you to compose yourself. So far as my knowledge goes, your grandson has done nothing to merit castigation even in a metaphorical sense. He is at present sadly deficient in application, but we are not without hope of bringing him to a better mind.'

'Bugger your better mind!' This time, Mr Mumford bellowed. The Provost had made one measured speech too many. At least for the moment, our host was the helpless mouthpiece of a senile frenzy. 'And bugger your Honorary What's-it-called,' he added for good measure, 'and be damned to you both for a couple of arse-licking toadies.'

It was at this moment – or after a further moment which elapsed in not unnatural silence – that a fresh voice spoke in the room.

'Hullo, Grandad,' it said, 'may Bobby Braine and I drift in?'

We all turned and stared at the doorway. Ivo and another young man were standing in it. It would have been impossible to say for how long they had been edifying themselves with the scene.

For a moment the Mumfords eyed each other silently. It seemed to me that Cedric's glance wasn't at all that of a man likely to approve of a stick being taken to his grandson. Those had been but wild and whirling words, or more probably a consciously mocking affront to the decorum which the Provost so constantly exhibited. The sort of family attachment that misses out a generation existed between these two. One evidence of this was that Ivo's arrival had with bewildering abruptness put Cedric on his shaky tolerable behaviour once more. He had welcomed Bobby Braine civilly, and sat down again. So the Provost and I were in difficulty. Minutes before, we had been so grossly insulted by the owner of Otby as to be left with no resource other than that of quitting the house forthwith. Now here was the authentic snarling Cedric withdrawn into the depths of his den, leaving at its mouth an uneasily tail-wagging old creature momentarily deprived of either bark or bite.

The Provost, who had almost certainly never before been addressed by a host as an arse-licking toady, was admirably calm. Whether or not he regarded the extreme instability of Mr Mumford's moods as wholly pathological he had clearly resolved that, for the moment, that was how to take them. His attitude became that of a practised visitor to the more taxing wards of a geriatric hospital. 'Oh hullo, sir!' Ivo said to him breezily. Ivo's manner wasn't too good. It was the habit of undergraduates who went in for nice behaviour to accord the Provost a formal deference which they would have judged it inappropriate to direct upon their tutors or anybody else. Ivo addressed the Provost precisely as, if in good humour, he would have addressed me. And he *was* in good humour – a condition in which I hadn't seen him very securely established before.

'Good afternoon, Mumford.' The Provost may have been writhing inwardly at the thought that these young men had come upon him involved in a scene so grotesquely ludicrous that they could, if minded, dine out on it for the remainder of the term. But he was not likely to betray a discomfort of this sort. 'How pleasant,' he went on, 'that your grandfather's house is within jaunting range of Oxford.'

'Yes, isn't it? It means that when I have a good idea I can come straight out and put it to him. That's what Bobby and I have tumbled in about now. Bobby's at Trinity, poor chap, but he and I are going partners just at the moment. I'm letting him be the great Braine in the affair.' Ivo, who was seldom at his best when reaching for a stroke of wit, paid this one the tribute of his vacuous laugh. 'But the point is that I've had a brainwave myself. My grandfather can become a partner too. A sleeping one, that is. Grandad'—Ivo had turned gaily to Mr Mumford—'we see that what's needed is a spot of the lolly.'

'An infusion of capital,' the young man from Trinity said. He was flaxen-haired, clear-complexioned, and without much chin. The correction he had offered may have been humorous in intention or merely designed to put the matter in a dignified light. 'The fact is, sir, that printing turns out to be most damnably expensive. And illustrations and line-blocks and things. They do frightfully mount up.'

'So it's a fresh capital issue, is it?' Mr Mumford asked. He spoke with a grimness which was to be detected as assumed.

'There will, of course, be a return on it,' Bobby Braine said. He clearly regarded himself as the business man of the venture, well-prepared to put a convincing proposition before a judicious investor. 'Only there may be difficulties over the cash flow for a time.'

'Ivo will have no difficulty making the cash flow.' Mr Mumford, although producing this with a return of his familiar snarl, aimed at jocularity, and was rewarded with a quick laugh from his grandson. 'And just what are you up to, eh?'

'We're starting a magazine. Don't you think it a good idea we should start a magazine, sir?' Ivo had turned to the Provost with this question, and its tone was so impudent that the wholesomeness of the buttery-hatch idea again came home to me.

'It must depend, Mumford, on the quality of the venture. Are your interests in the main of a literary sort?'

'Yes, of course. And artistic.' Ivo felt there was a very good joke here. 'It's going to be no end artistic as well.'

'Have you yet decided on a name for it?'

'A name? Oh, I see.' The Provost's question, which struck me as acute, disconcerted Ivo for a moment. He had conceivably been finding out more about the associations of fertility gods. 'As a matter of fact, that's a tremendous secret.'

'Ah, yes.' The Provost now felt that the duties of civility had been discharged. 'Pattullo and I', he said to Cedric Mumford, 'must not get in the way of these deliberations. A most delightful luncheon.'

Mr Todd took charge at this point, perceptibly in the conviction that the sooner we were out of the house the better. For a moment, however, he contrived to draw me aside.

'A little sticky at times,' he murmured. 'A forbearing chap your Provost. Nice to the lad. How's he getting on in college?'

'Ivo has his difficulties,' I said cautiously. 'You've heard about some of them.'

'No good at his books, eh? A pity, that. And there was a spot of trouble down here at the beginning of the long vac. Cedric rather close about it, even to me. But not too good a show, if village tattle is to be believed. I hope he'll be able to stay at Oxford, and steady up. Make some clean-bred friends. Desirable thing.'

'I entirely agree.' It had scarcely occurred to me that Ivo's escapade, although scotched at the level of police investigation and newspaper publicity, must continue for a time to have its reverberations in village legend. But Dr Pococke, fortunately, was not likely to go gossiping with smock-frocked boors in Berkshire pot-houses. 'I suppose,' I went on, 'there's no chance of dissuading Mumford from putting up money for that magazine?'

'I don't imagine so. What sort of an affair is it going to be – not too decent?'

'Not too decent by any means, if my guess about it is right.'

'Then that settles it.' Jiffy Todd spoke decisively and in a spirit of sober realism. 'Cedric will shell out.'

Our further farewells were predictably formal, and within five minutes Otby was behind us. The Provost drove with even more than his usual care. His lips were compressed and his brow was stern. He might have been a bearded Abdiel, retorting scorn upon the Satanic fastness behind him. I wondered what he would first find to say.

'My dear Duncan, I do most profoundly apologise.'

'I don't see, Provost, that there can be any occasion for that.'

'I apologise most profoundly.' The Provost was not to be balked of his contrition, which was that of a monarch who has inadvertently trodden on the toes of some attendant courtier. 'Had I known how little our poor friend is in control of himself I would not have dreamt of involving you in this luckless expedition.'

'It certainly wasn't comfortable, but at least it was instructive. It hardly looks as if Cedric Mumford will be a great deal of help in the matter of Lord Mountclandon's letter-book.'

'No indeed.'

'It's lucky it's not a very momentous matter.'

'The fate of the wretched letter-book certainly isn't that. But one might still have occasion to value the foul-mouthed old ruffian's good will – and I have had the thought that his ability to conjure the thing back for us, if proved in the event, might flatter his vanity.'

Having offered me this oblique and obscure view of the matter, the

Provost hesitated, and I had a momentary impression that some less insubstantial confidence was to be offered me. But if this was so the Provost thought better of it. The mystique of the councils of princes was uppermost again.

'Perhaps,' I said, 'the good-will may be recoverable. This could just have been one of Mumford's bad days.'

'It may be so.' The Provost paused for reflection. 'What did you make of that business about his grandson's magazine?'

'I'd heard about it before. Including their name for it, as a matter of fact. It's to be called *Priapus*.'

'That scarcely sounds propitious, Duncan – the less so if, as now seems probable, it is to be financed by our late host.'

'Quite so, Provost. Don't the Proctors have a say about the launching of such things?'

Indeed they have. But they are obliged to tread warily nowadays in anything suggesting censorship. At the lowest, the venture won't make the young man any more attentive to his books.'

'A lost cause that, perhaps.'

'So his tutors are inclined to suggest. A pity. The lad didn't show to advantage this afternoon – and this project of his holds a hint of the bloody-minded, if you ask me.'

'I'm afraid I agree.' I was rather impressed by the Provost's making use of this expression. 'But he has had bad luck.'

'Quite so. And he is not, at other times, without something of his father's charm. My wife has entertained him, and tells me she finds him not unattractive.'

'Which is decidedly one up to Ivo.'

The Provost's response to this was no more than a grave inclination of the head, and we drove back to Oxford almost in silence. I meditated on old age – on old age and the dotage to which it is the grim portal. Lempriere, Timbermill, Cedric Mumford: they had been bringing rather a stiff dose of it my way.

# VIII

Nick Junkin, on the other hand, was twenty, and thus of an age agreeable to contemplate, although not perhaps invariably to live through. Junkin, indeed, was often harassed and occasionally glum: moods which he attributed to a general mysteriousness and unaccountability in the world around him. I could remember something of the kind in my own near-nonage. And as he now occupied the rooms which had been mine during that phase of my career, I was disposed to see in him myself when young. I can't imagine I told him this; on the contrary, I probably took care to give no hint of it. He wouldn't have resented any communication of the sort, but it might have added to the burden of his perplexities. Any attractiveness I held for him must have been akin to that felt by an explorer when coming upon a primitive type of society unexpectedly preserved in tolerable working order. This didn't in the least mean that Junkin condescended to me, or even bent upon me the objective regard of the cultural anthropologist. He took me flatteringly for granted alike as an equal and a repository of wisdom – although he perhaps saw the wisdom as standing in need of a certain measure of interpretation in terms of his own epoch, much as one might do if faced with sacred books dredged up from the drowned civilisation of Atlantis.

When Junkin felt harassed it was often for the same reason that his immediate neighbour Ivo ought to have felt harassed but seemingly didn't. He could be charged, in the august terminology of the Provost, with being sadly deficient in application. Every now and then he made good resolutions, deciding to get clear at last on which had been treaties and which battles: Ramillies, Oudenarde, Utrecht. But in no time the siren-voices of theatrical activity would have seduced him again. Sticking his head through my door, he would demand to know whether I judged it feasible to produce *Fear and Misery in the Third Reich*, or would consent to furnish the college dramatic society, in three weeks time, with a stage adaptation of the latest novel by John Updike or Alexander Solzhenitsyn. As I was around the place at all only as being the university's speciously accredited authority on this sort of thing, I was scarcely in a position to tell Junkin to go away and mind his book.

This field of common concern, however, had resulted in Junkin and myself meeting – briefly and casually, for the most part – two or three times a week. I didn't look in on Junkin except by invitation, it being my memory that senior members refrained from violating the privacy of their juniors by unheralded calls. Junkin looked in on me when the fancy took him – or rather tumbled in, since I was frequently not aware of him until he was half across the room. Something of the sort happened on the morning after my visit to Otby. Junkin burst in and flung himself on the sofa.

'I say,' he said, 'are you fearfully busy? Do you mind if I come in?'

'Not a bit, Nick. Please do.'

'May I sit down?' By this time Junkin had put his feet up on the sofa cushions and let one arm drop limply to the floor. The posture, and his marked inability to synchronise words and deeds, suggested a more than common perturbation on the young man's part.

'Yes, of course. Take a pew. How are you?'

'Confused. Don't know whether to be chuffed to the bollocks or not. *Quid loquor aut ubi sum?* It's like that.'

'I see.' What I had been treated to represented, I believe, Junkin's only preserved fragment of Latinity, and I had heard it before. 'But why?'

'It's Lempriere. You know he's my tutor? Yes, I've told you that. He doesn't take many pupils, being so frightfully old, but for some reason he does take me. And I've just read him the week's essay, you see. It seemed to me as big a balls-up as I'd managed yet. Do you know what he said at the end of it?'

'I'm not likely to, am I? What did he say?'

'He said, "Well, I'm blessed!" Just like that.'

'Encouragingly, you mean?'

'I hadn't a clue. And then there was what he said next. "Here I've been taking you," he said, "for a true and amiable son of Goodman Dull. And now it dawns on me that you're simply a dead-idle little brute." Would you call that encouraging?'

'Yes, Nick, I would.'

'Well I didn't think so – or not at first. As a matter of fact, I thought it rather rude. And who is Goodman Dull, anyway?'

'You ought to know that one. He's a constable in *Love's Labour's Lost.*'

'With sons?'

'I don't recall their being mentioned. But it's scarcely a relevant point.'

'I suppose not. Then the old chap suddenly said, "I'd call that one a beta-query-plus". What do you make of *that?*'

'What you do, probably. That he was uncommonly pleased.'

'Well yes – exactly. And he went on with something about the denser fogs thinning out a bit inside my skull. Quite casually, you know. No drama. And then he turned me out of the room. Only, you see, I wasn't back in the quad again before I remembered something I was told by a man who's reading Greats. His tutor's another old party – not *quite* so old – called Buntingford. Do you know Buntingford?'

'Yes, I do. He taught me for a time, as a matter of fact, when he was a very young don.'

'Good Lord!' Junkin was impressed. 'When you were both back from the Kaiser's War or something?'

'Not exactly that.' Junkin's chronological haziness exceeded even that of my Uncle Rory. Neither, one could feel, had acted judiciously in devoting himself to historical studies. 'But what was it Buntingford said?'

'He told this man that that sort of thing is called the medicinal buttered bun. I think it means something like buttering you up. Don't you?'

'It sounds like that, Nick. I've heard it called the psychotherapy of warm praise.'

'So Lempriere was just kidding me?' Although himself plainly inclining to this view, Junkin was dashed at my appearing to support it.

'No – not exactly that, I'd say. He's seen reason to feel you might have a juster confidence in yourself.'

'It might be that.' Junkin brightened. 'He has that sarky manner, you know. But he's very kind, really.'

I was struck by this. 'Kind' is the undergraduate's ultimate in commendatory words about a tutor – a fact which witnesses, perhaps, to the chronic desperation attending upon the happiest days of one's life.

'Of course,' Junkin went on, 'it depends on whether there was an objective basis for it.' He had sat up and was glancing cheerfully around the room. Judging that his eye tended to linger on the table where I kept some drinks, I got up and poured sherry. 'I mean,' Junkin continued, 'it depends on whether the wretched essay did have some small gleam to it. If I believed that, I think I'd work like mad. And I'll know by the end of the week. Because of the Mumford test.'

'What on earth is that, Nick?' This had left me quite at a loss.

'You know Mumford, the man opposite me on the staircase?'

'Indeed I do.'

'Well, we're rather in the same boat, you see. Only, he's not going to anybody here – not this term. They've farmed him out to a chap in some obscure college across the High – a kind of crash-course crammer disguised as a don.'

'They've done that, have they?' The information, although obviously containing a dash of undergraduate mythology, interested me. 'So what?'

'It seems that part of this chap's technique is to tell you to write your next essay on whatever most interests you in the rotten course. So now Mumford just borrows my last essay and takes it along.'

'I see.' The morality of this procedure didn't seem to fall within my province. 'Have you two become friends?'

'Mumford and me? Oh, no. I don't think I frightfully care for him really.' This remark of Junkin's had to be received as an understatement; thus firmly to employ a contemporary's surname was a stiffly distancing gesture. 'But it's reasonable to do the friendly turn. Mumford's been rather up against things lately. He did something damned silly at the end of last term.'

'Yes, I know.'

'Pitiful character, in a way. You won't have seen it, but he has an enormous great wank picture in his room. Makes the place like a porn shop.'

'I know that picture too, as a matter of fact. It's wanky, all right.' I wasn't sure that Junkin quite approved of my taking over this modish word. 'But what's all this in aid of?'

'I was explaining. If this last essay of mine really has beefed itself up a bit this crammer is sure to notice and tell Mumford so.'

'And you'll see that as a green light for doing a bit of work?'

'For doing an awful lot of work. That's sensible, isn't it?'

'Nick, I don't think I ever heard anything sillier. This crammer, as you call him, will have a pretty clear view of Ivo Mumford by now, and he mayn't just be alert for that gleam of dawn. The chap for you to trust is Arnold Lempriere himself.'

'I suppose you're dead right. Only, you know, your tutor's the last man you can rely upon for a straight word about your chances. Everybody says that. I suppose it's the buttered bun again. They're always softening the harsh truth, and so on.'

Junkin paused broodingly for a moment. I said nothing, having reason to believe there was a modicum of fact in the proposition he had just advanced. Long ago – I asked myself – hadn't Timbermill got a vast amount of work out of me by pretending I was a born scholar? The analogy was imperfect, but it did exist. 'Look here,' Junkin said suddenly, 'you know Lempriere quite well, don't you?'

'Tolerably well. We're distant relations, as a matter of fact.'

'You mean he's your uncle or something?'

'Of course not. An uncle isn't a distant relation. We're simply cousins in some obscure fashion. But what of it?'

'Couldn't you chat him up, and ask him casually what he thinks of my chances? We might get at something objective that way.'

'I suppose I could. In fact, I will – if you think it useful. But I just wish I was *your* uncle, Nick. A Dutch one.'

'You'd advise eight hours a day in the History Library?'

'Six.'

'From now till the end of term? You must be joking. I'd be in the funny-farm.' Junkin paused, and seemed to read scepticism in my silence. 'Right off my squiff,' he elaborated. 'And you'd be responsible.'

'Go away, Nick. You're wasting my time.'

'And we *might* manage *Fear and Misery*. It could be absolutely marvellous.' Nick got to his feet and scowled at me. 'Oh, all right,' he said. 'I'll think about it.'

'You'll be wasting your own time in that case. Just try getting cracking straight away for a change.'

'You're getting more and more like a don every day.'

'I'm paid to get like a don. But I shan't go in for the psychotherapy of warm praise.'

'That's something.' Junkin, having reached the door, turned and grinned at me cheerfully. 'Seeing you,' he said. A moment later his feet were pounding up the staircase.

It was the staircase, I decided, that would make it possible for me to inquire of Arnold Lempriere about Junkin's examination chances. In Lempriere's Oxford (which was becoming a dream-Oxford, no doubt) there was what politicians would call a special relationship between a senior member and the half-dozen or so youths who happened to run up and down the same flight of steps as himself. Lempriere would approve of my taking a fatherly interest in Junkin, whereas if I asked about the academic progress of one of his pupils living elsewhere in college I might receive a strong hint that the matter was no business of mine. The same consideration, of course, licensed my interest in Ivo.

I decided to come at Junkin by way of Ivo. Indeed, I was under some obligation to give Lempriere an account of the late Otby episode. He was perfectly capable of enjoying any comedy it contained.

Things didn't, however, work out quite this way. I had intended to drop in on Lempriere that evening, but was forestalled by an initiative of his own. When I went into common room to lunch he spotted me at once and gestured me brusquely over to him. But there was no vacant place beside him, and our exchange was necessarily brief. It was also of that obtrusively confidential order of which he was fond – his hand going up to the side of his mouth and his voice coming in a hoarse but penetrating whisper.

'A delicate matter blowing up,' he said. 'Come for a walk. Howard Gate two o'clock. Say absolutely nothing to anyone.'

I was obliged to give a conspiratorial nod, while being aware of the cautious amusement of two young lecturers on the other side of the table. Lempriere's particular version of the councils-of-princes idea must have been well known. He had been Senior Tutor in his time, and believed that the college's affairs, ostensibly so democratically controlled by the entire Governing Body, were in fact most properly in the hands of an inner ring of persons holding, or having held, such offices. Whether this was really so nobody seemed to know, and men who had been fellows for a dozen years would dispute the issue warmly. There may, for that matter, have been such a caucus without Lempriere's any longer belonging to it. Having become prone in old age to form eccentric judgements, he might no longer be thought of as 'sound' or 'reliable' as these qualities are interpreted in close cabals. But it would be my guess that he had no sense of any exclusion or relegation, and he evidently derived genuine enjoyment from occasionally divulging to some favoured outsider one or another supposed secret of this hypothetical oligarchy. Albert Talbert sometimes evinced a similar disposition. Only whereas Lempriere's arcane confidences were invariably on what might be termed the inner mind or higher thought of the college, Talbert had the air of cautiously admitting one to some aspect of universal knowledge normally available only to the deepest and most capacious scholarship.

Our afternoon walk began in a silence that Lempriere indefinably indicated as properly to be maintained for some time. This was perhaps by way of emphasising the portentousness of whatever disclosure was to be afforded me. It seemed improbable that he proposed an expedition of major scope. He was wearing stout walking-shoes, and carried a stick which terminated in a once-formidable but long-since blunted steel spike. The shoes, however, appeared a little too heavy for his feet, and with the stick he was inclined to feel forward on the pavement as if it were uncertain moorland terrain. Much more then when commandingly prowling common room, he revealed himself as quite as old as his years.

We went up the Turl – the colleges fronting upon which own in a singular degree that effect of mild conventual presence which Oxford at large once hinted to Henry James. The *grisatre* effect is very soothing, and as Lempriere was so *grisatre* too I was drawn to reflect upon how well he composed with the scene. Apart from those Washington days, he had presumably spent his whole adult life in Oxford, and had thus become one with its stones and with its grey misty uneventful vistas. It was not, I told myself, a place by which he could ever be betrayed – or even, in his old age, bewildered or surprised.

The narrow street was quiet. Much traffic had lately been filtered out of the centre of Oxford by civic authorities of a pedestrian turn of mind; and around us, at least for the moment, was an almost Venetian tranquillity. There wasn't a vehicle in sight, and the only sound was the click of a typewriter from some upper chamber in Jesus. As if judging this calm propitious for his revelation, Lempriere raised a hand to command my full attention. No words came from him, however, and for a moment I wondered why. The empty Oxford afternoon was still around us; an elderly don, a gown slung over his shoulder, was approaching at a moderate pace on a bicycle; on the other pavement a young woman had stopped to switch from one hand to the other a recalcitrant child and a heavy shopping-bag; in the doorway of a travel agency a fair-haired youth in rowing kit had paused to study some brochure or hand-out which he had just obtained in the interior. Thus sparsely peopled, the Turl was still entirely silent. Only from somewhere away on our left, perhaps in the Cornmarket, a low-toned indeterminate sound was making itself heard – a sound the chief suggestion of which was multitudinousness, as if a long way off great waves were churning up the pebbles on a stormy beach, or as if, equally far in distance, contending rugger teams were being cheered on by armies of dwarfs. Then, with surprising abruptness, this mysterious phenomenon explained itself. We were listening to a great deal of shouting of that semi-organised sort favoured by marchers and demonstrators of a political cast. It was, in fact, a 'demo' that was going forward.

'We seem to be running into a certain amount of liveliness,' I said. Lempriere made no reply. He simply walked on.

It was a large demo, as Oxford demos went. By the time we reached Ship Street the gates of Trinity, straight ahead of us across the Broad, had vanished behind a mass of young people. The Broad is a thoroughfare most appropriately named, since it is very broad indeed. Even so, the procession – or whatever it was to be called – jammed it, bringing all traffic to a stop. Any space the marchers didn't take up was occupied by bystanders, male and female, of their own age. The marchers carried banners and placards of a somewhat unimpressive showing, but there was no mistaking the sheer physical exuberance at their command. The bystanders, on the other hand, seemed concerned to exhibit an air of nonchalant ease, as if they found the whole spectacle absurd rather than alarming. Yet alarming it undeniably was. Even a mob of clergymen yelling its head off would be not without a perturbing effect. And university students in the mass (I suddenly saw) are capable of being a good deal less pleasing than they commonly are as individuals or in small groups.

What Lempriere was thinking I don't know. His silence was now so resolute that I decided not to be chatty myself. It was impossible to cross the street, but we edged our way eastwards in the direction of the Sheldonian Theatre. This, one of the two masterpieces achieved in Oxford by Christopher Wren, is guarded (as all readers of *Zuleika Dobson* know) by a semicircle of gigantic carved heads set upon pillars. The busts (believed by the uninstructed to represent Roman emperors but known to the learned to be learned persons like themselves) had lately emerged from near-obliteration in new and staring stone. These colossi were now surveying some four or five hundred pygmy undergraduates who had sat down on the road in front of them; they were also surveying perhaps a score of pygmy policemen lined up on the steps of the Clarendon Building and before the portals of the Indian Institute. Their mute spectatorship added a bizarre touch to what was already a surprising scene. I had myself, indeed, seen something like it only a few months before. That had been in Florence. There, the students had appeared younger, and their concern had been with matters far away: in Chile, I think it was. Here, such manifestations were understood to be in the interest of establishing a kind of super-cafeteria – declared by the insurgent forces to be essential to their well-being, and believed by many of their seniors to be in fact a demand for the building of a miniature Kremlin on the Isis. Here, the policemen were 'stolid' – as if they must abide by the journalists' description of them; in Florence, they had been demonstratively bored. In Florence, there had been water-cannon lurking in the side-streets; here, the police had solemnly brought out a kind of Black Maria or prison van. It didn't look as if it could do anybody any harm. I felt it to be a somewhat tactless object, all the same.

One aspect of the spectacle was without continental parallel. It is among the facts of Oxford life that the civil power (meaning the Thames Valley Constabulary) treats as territorially inviolate all university and collegiate property. The buildings of the university, and those of its constituent colleges, are a kind of Vatican City in the midst of England's green and pleasant land. The police are never 'called in' – or if they are (as they must of necessity be in the event of murders, major larcenies and the like) it is in an unobtrusive fashion. The university provides its own police, even its own fortifications; and these were in evidence now. The Clarendon Building, its administrative nerve-centre, is traversed at ground level by a tunnel which, within daylight hours, serves as a public thoroughfare. At the Broad Street end of the tunnel are massive wrought-iron gates; at the other end there had lately been erected (in preparation for such field-days as the present) a whimsically insubstantial wooden door, topped by ornamental metal spikes so diminutive that they would scarcely have served to impale a sparrow. It was the iron gates that were under siege now – or at least it was the iron gates that the squatting mob seemed to be shouting at. Without, it was guarded by helmeted policemen; within – but peering through the bars not without a certain comic effect of the menagerie sort – were the university's own forces of law and order: half a dozen bowler-hatted men with a Proctor in their midst. The Proctor – whether Senior or Junior I couldn't tell – was in full battle-dress, which in his case consisted of an elaborate gown fabricated largely from black velvet, together with a kind of bifurcated white linen bib which my Uncle Norman, as a minister of the Kirk, would have described as his Geneva bands.

Lempriere continued to push ahead. His edging through the crush was something he contrived to an effect of its not being there at all. It was true that the young savages now sprawling or dancing around us, and bellowing with the full force of their lungs that somebody or other should be 'out', parted before him the moment they had taken a glance at his years. Even so, I found myself wondering whether for Lempriere they *really* weren't there; whether he owned some power simply to exclude from consciousness a situation in its essentials totally incomprehensible to him.

This extravagant speculation was interrupted by a sudden change in the scene. The police may have decided they must clear a lane for traffic, or they may have succumbed to their innate persuasion that it is the prime duty of a citizenry to 'move on'. For one reason or another, a number of them had advanced upon the sitters down, and this move had been interpreted by a few as a declaration of war. Above the general confusion a single voice made itself heard shouting 'Scrag the fuzz!' The response to this was a certain thin scattering of objects in air. They weren't stones but they were undoubtedly missiles – eggs and tomatoes, for the most part, brought along by persons with Dickensian views on what is requisite on political occasions. The police didn't like being pelted; the whole lot of them charged in what looked like a well- rehearsed snatch raid. Within seconds – in the newspaper phrase – scuffles broke out.

Lempriere and I, having seen some delusive chance of quickly gaining Parks Road, spent a couple of minutes in the middle of this melee. Under our noses a couple of policemen grabbed a girl and attempted to march her off to their van – an essay in incarceration which may or may not have been deserved but which was injudicious in either case. Angry young men piled in; the girl was rescued and vanished; an ugly fight was still continuing when we gained the pavement outside the New Bodleian. Free of the fracas, I turned round to take a look at it. The police were on top, and quite a number of young men were being dragged ungently into captivity. It was no doubt a historic occasion – any number of demos having taken place in Oxford without even this mild approximation to 'mass arrests' succeeding upon them.

Lempriere had walked on, and I hastened to catch up. He was a little breathless, but he still said nothing. I might have been conducting someone blind and deaf through the whole commotion. It was a commotion that faded behind us with surprising speed. On our right Wadham slumbered; on our left the great gardens first of Trinity and then of St John's reposed in their autumnal dignity. As we rounded Rhodes House and moved down South Parks Road the last hint of tumult faded on our ears.

'Something disconcerting has happened,' Lempriere said. 'That poor lad who made away with himself – Lusby, you remember? – proves to have a brother. A brother who is seeking entry to the college next year. It's as tricky as anything on the horizon.'

'Peter Lusby,' I said.

'No, not Peter, Paul. The poor boy's name was Paul.'

'I mean the brother – the one who wants to come up. He's Peter.'

'You've had the papers?' Lempriere was surprised and perhaps offended. 'They're not supposed to have gone round yet.'

'I haven't had any papers, Arnold. I doubt whether that lot come to a professorial fellow. But I've met the boy.'

'You've met Lusby's brother?' Lempriere paused in his cautious progress to stare at me. 'Where on earth did you do that?'

'In the college chapel, quite late one night.'

'At prayer?'

'I don't at all know. He may have been praying, but I didn't see him at it.' I found myself surprised that this possibility hadn't occurred to me. 'He'd come to sight-see in Oxford with a party from his school, and had stayed on to look around.'

'He'd probably been praying. It seems he's a religious boy. His headmaster says so. A serious family, and so on. Did you gather anything more about him, Dunkie? It may be most important.'

'I don't quite see that. But we had a certain amount of talk. He came and had coffee with me before catching his train.'

'Humph.'

When Lempriere produced the ungracious noise commonly thus written it meant that he was inwardly approving of you. I had gained a good mark by my unspectacular hospitality to Paul Lusby's brother.

'He told me about wanting to come to the college,' I said. 'I wished him luck.'

'I suppose we all do.' Lempriere's voice had abruptly taken on the acrid tone I remembered from my first acquaintance with him. 'You'd have done better to wish him a larger dash of brains, it seems. Did he strike you as at all clever?'

'I'm not prepared to give any guess at that.'

'I don't ask you for a guess. I asked you for an impression.'

'You're not going to get it, Arnold.' I had decided by this time that there were occasions when a certain arrogance in Lempriere had to be firmly dealt with. 'The boy was my guest for half an hour. I'm not going to offer any judgement on him. Examiners can do that.'

'Humph.' Lempriere resumed his silence. We were passing through what had come to be known as the 'Science Area' of the university – a development of which he probably took a dark view.

'The boy wants to read law,' I said.

'Of course he wants to read law. His brother was reading law. You can see what he has in his head, can't you?'

"Indeed I can.'

It seems his brother gave promise of being very clever indeed.

Although not clever enough to keep clear of that damnably silly wager with young Mumford. The fact is, Dunkie, that Charles Atlas—you know that Charles is Tutor for Admissions?—is uncommonly worried about the situation. This present Lusby doesn't look promising at all.'

'On paper?'

'Yes. His O Levels or A Levels, or whatever the confounded things are called.'

'Does it matter all that?'

'It didn't use to. We'd take on boys we liked and begin with the alphabet if they needed it. But times are said to have changed.'

'Can Peter Lusby come up so far as the university is concerned?'

'Lord, yes. That hurdle wouldn't stop the village idiot. But Charles will maintain it's what comes afterwards that matters. And he has a case, as you can plainly see. This Peter Lusby isn't an Ivo Mumford – not caring a damn about his work so long as he has the run of the place for a time. He wants to come to us to redeem his brother's disaster, to honour his memory – Lord knows what. So one has to honour *him*.' Lempriere had quickened his pace, as if his feet were coming with less difficulty off the ground. Sideways, he threw me a challenging glance. 'But the boy mustn't come up and then crash. That's imperative, eh? So it requires an uncommonly hard look.'

'Yes,' I said, 'I agree.'

'There's not a stiffer problem, I'd say, blowing around the whole university at the moment.' With this extravagant remark Lempriere had nailed a flag to his mast. It appeared to have done him good. For a score or so of paces he strode ahead like a young man.

'Have you any idea, Arnold, how Jimmy Gender, who was Paul Lusby's tutor and would be Peter's too, is likely to view the problem?'

'It will worry him even more than it worries Charles. If we do find the boy a place Jimmy will feel an enormous burden of responsibility towards him. He'd work like a beaver to get him through his blasted Mods or Prelim or whatever it is, and then his Schools. That goes without saying. It would be a kind of memorial service.'

We had entered the University Parks – which are quite obviously one park only, although of considerable extent. We proceeded now on firm asphalt and now on a slippery carpeting of russet leaves. Lempriere trod with a similar care on each. Here and there vigorous youths were pursuing hockey or lacrosse: spectacles before which we paused one by one. Lempriere, I believe, possessed or retained no informed interest in athletic activities, but was attracted to them in a general way. Much the same sort of panting and pounding was going on as we had been witnessing in front of the Clarendon Building, but here it was of a sanctioned sort: the playing fields of Eton stuff. Gleams of sunshine filtered down through the October sky, and these encouraged us to seat ourselves on a park bench for a time. On the path before us elderly academics exercised dogs, young academics pushed prams, and academics yet to be – the juvenile population of North Oxford – darted to and fro on prohibited bicycles and tricycles.

I became aware that a very senior academic citizen had paused before us. He was an emaciated and even cadaverous man, and what trembled above his neck was much less like a head than a skull.

'Ah, Lempriere!' this person exclaimed. His tone suggested displeased surprise. 'Good afternoon, good afternoon.'

'The President of Magdalen,' Lempriere said grimly. 'Dr Duncan Pattullo.'

I was becoming accustomed to 'Dr Pattullo' or even to 'Professor Pattullo', although the one was as inaccurate as the other. Lempriere, of course, was merely being silly.

'And are you here for long, Lempriere?' The President had acknowledged our introduction with no more than a curt if wobbling nod. 'Are you here for long?'

'My tenure is as indefinite as yours, President.' Lempriere's reply had an incisiveness in which I found myself taking a loyal collegiate satisfaction. 'The common lot, I suppose, since they did away with the death penalty.'

'Good, Lempriere, good!' The President of Magdalen was delighted. He swayed uncertainly forward, and punched Lempriere on the shoulder with surprising vigour. 'Good day to you, good day to you!' He tottered on his skeletal way.

'Malicious old devil!' Lempriere said – again with the chuckle that might have been a clearing of his throat.

'Just what did he mean?' I asked. The senatorial exchange had surprised me.

'It's what you say—isn't it?—to a man who has retired and taken himself decently out of Oxford. You suppose him to be visiting his great-grandson at St Catherine's or Pot Hall. The President and I took Schools together. No doubt it was in Victoria's golden reign.'

We appeared to have enjoyed an interlude of comic relief. In Oxford at that time I was always learning things. And the idea of comedy put me in mind of Otby. I now gave Lempriere an account of the visit upon which I had accompanied the Provost. He made an appreciative listener.

'Dear old Edward,' he said. 'I've nothing against the man. He gives an honest attention, God bless him, to the duties of his station. But this Ivo Mumford, now – he's another matter.' Lempriere was suddenly grave again. 'Part of the problem, eh?'

'He's certainly a problem. But I don't know what problem he's a part of.'

'Lusby's, of course – the second Lusby. Suppose young Mumford rescues himself, or suppose we do the job for him. And suppose this Peter Lusby comes up to the college. They're not going to be exactly comfortable bedfellows, are they?'

'I don't see, Arnold, they need be bedfellows at all.'

'Be serious, please.' Lempriere, disconcertingly, had supposed me to be extracting a salacious joke from his figure of speech, and had come down on me hard. 'Peter Lusby would be in residence with the man who – indirectly, of course – was responsible for his brother's death.'

'But he's not going to know that! The business of the wager didn't emerge at the inquest, did it?'

'Thank God, no. But everybody in college has heard about it.'

'I know a lot of people have. But they wouldn't hand the story on to the dead boy's brother. It's inconceivable.'

'It certainly ought to be.'

'There's an unpleasant outside chance, certainly.' I paused for a moment, aware that for Arnold Lempriere matters of this sort were very important indeed, and anxious to say anything that might be useful. 'Jimmy Gender might think it wise to tell Peter Lusby about that aspect of the thing himself. It would at least be better than the boy's hearing about it in a confused way from some young drunk. But it's not an urgent matter now. The chance of Mumford's surviving and staying up isn't going to be made a reason for not taking on Lusby – or Lusby's coming up a reason for turfing Mumford out.'

'Of course not – or not in anybody's conscious mind. But there's an awkwardness in the situation that might imperceptibly strengthen a sense that Ivo Mumford is a general nuisance about the college.'

'So he is, for that matter.' I said this incautiously, being preoccupied by the sudden perception that Lempriere's concern over the affair might conceivably become obsessional.

'Damn it, Dunkie! You're for the boy, aren't you?'

'For Ivo?'

'Yes, for Ivo, confound you. Why, at almost our first meeting you put him to me as a hard-luck story! And he's the son of your oldest friend in the place.'

'Arnold, I'm very anxious that Tony's boy should have the best possible chance of a good start in life. Only I'm not confident – I think I have ceased to believe – that his remaining in college for nearly another two years is his likeliest way to that.'

Lempriere got to his feet, painfully but at the same time abruptly. I realised – without his speaking a further word – that I had said something which appeared to him outrageous and nonsensical. We all have somewhere in our minds a patch of madness. Lempriere's was a large overestimating of the particular privilege which, over all other inhabitants of earth, Ivo Mumford and some four hundred of his contemporaries at present enjoyed. Everybody alive might go to heaven on Judgement Day. But these young men were members of the college now.

We rounded the Parks in a resumed silence, and I supposed that we should head back for the centre of Oxford. But Lempriere turned east, in the direction of those windings of bits and pieces of the Cherwell which provide Magdalen's Water Walks and the region known as Mesopotamia. I took the extending of our perambulation to indicate that I was not totally disgraced. And although the subject of Ivo Mumford was becoming tedious I resolved to have another go at it.

'Look,' I said, 'I've told you about my encounters with that boy, and more or less what I make of him. He's stupid – I'll bet a good deal stupider than Peter Lusby—'

'Aha! An impression of Lusby after all.'

'Fair enough.' I was lucky thus to have put Lempriere in good humour again. 'Ivo hasn't got his father's brains, and not even his grandfather's low cunning—'

'I hope he has better manners than that old ruffian.'

'Yes, he has – up to a point. But you must have judged for yourself.'

'I haven't met the boy.'

'Never?' I was surprised by this. 'But if he's reading history—'

'I do very little teaching now. They think me past it, you know, and so they say I'm entitled to a very senior man's very large leisure.' Lempriere was amused rather than indignant at this. 'I've stopped even arranging who's to be taught by whom.'

'I see. Still, I'd have expected you to entertain an old pupil's grandson, Arnold. It's your sort of thing.'

'Boys aren't interested in meeting their grandfather's tutors. But the fact is, you know, that I have an eye on the strategy of the affair. By which I mean edging or wangling the boy round their damned rules and regulations.' Lempriere now chortled happily; he must have seen that I had been startled by this scandalously subversive speech, almost worthy of Cedric Mumford himself. 'Trouble is, Dunkie, I've been thought to make pets of people in my time.'

'What sort of people?'

'Nice lads from my old school. Or nice lads like your neighbour Nicolas Junkin, who can scarcely be said to be from any school at all.'

'You're quite wrong there. Cokeville G.S. is one of the best schools in Yorkshire. They get about as many open awards as Ampleforth.'

'Is that so?' This statistic (which I had made up on the spur of the moment) impressed Lempriere. 'Then it's a pity they didn't teach

Junkin to spell.'

'Will that spoil his chances with his examiners?'

'Oh *he'll* be all right with them. Nick's turning teachable, more or less. And we have several weeks in hand. I'll show him a trick or two to outwit the brutes.'

'That's a good tutor's job?'

'Cokeville Junkin will think so by the time I've finished with him. But to get back to Ivo. He's said *not* to be teachable, I admit. All the more occasion for his having a friend at need, eh? And it's going to be a chap who has never so much as passed the time of day with him. No chance of somebody like Charles Atlas going round murmuring that Mumford is one of the old dotard's little chums.'

'I see.' This primitive guile on Lempriere's part was something I had glimpsed already. 'Would you so much as recognise the boy?'

'Lord, yes! I've taken a good look at the heir of the Mumfords often enough. A handsome lad in his way. Keeps his hair clean, too. Glint of bronze in it.'

'Yes, so there is.'

'But I doubt whether he could put a name to me. Astonishing how little curiosity the young men can have about the old men in their midst.'

The Cherwell was now in front of us, but behaving not entirely as I remembered it. They had been messing it about. Here and there it sluiced its dirty skin over concrete as it had always done, carrying autumn leaves and autumn litter indifferently down to Thames. But the weirs had shifted their positions and so had a couple of bridges. Or so I thought. The contraption known as the rollers, however, was exactly as it had been; it helped you – although not much – to haul your punt to a higher level of the stream. On our left, beyond a muddy swamp, was a large dismal structure that rang no bell at all: a system of wooden and corrugated-iron palisades, some eight feet high. It vaguely suggested a small abandoned concentration camp, too inefficiently designed ever to have been in a good way of business.

'What on earth's that?' I asked.

'That's Parson's Pleasure.' Lempriere was staring at me, really shocked. 'Don't tell me you never came to swim here?'

'Well, yes – I did sometimes. And took a punt through quite often. Only I just didn't recognise it.' I was struck by a recent memory. 'You suggested our coming the afternoon after the Gaudy – but I had to go to tea with the Talberts. Do you bathe here often, Arnold?'

'Not at this time of year.' Lempriere surveyed the depressing scene, chuckling softly. 'But we might just take a peep. Come on, Dunkie.' Abandoning his usual cautious gait, he plunged into the mud. It seemed not decent to decline to follow him, and I plunged forward too. Submerged under an inch or two of the stuff there was some sort of footpath. If Lempriere managed to keep to it I did not. We reached the barrier in front of us where it stopped off at the river-bank, and where there proved to be a notice reading *Ladies are not allowed beyond this point*. I stared at it much as if I had met a traveller from an antique land.

'It really happens *still?*' I asked.

'Of course it does. They had a place for mixed bathing next door for a time. But it faded out.'

'Nude mixed bathing?'

'Certainly not.' Lempriere was displeased.

'Why did it fade out? Perhaps the ladies judged the Cherwell rather too dirty for their children and themselves?'

'I don't know what anybody judged. Take a look round the corner, Dunkie. But mind the barbed wire.'

I minded the barbed wire and surveyed the empty bathing- place. It naturally didn't afford much interest.

'Truce awhile to toil and tasking,' Lempriere said.

'What's that?' I had recovered my balance without falling into the Cherwell. It really looked very uninviting indeed.

'Truce awhile to toil and tasking,
Dream away the hours with us,
With a bun and towel basking:
*Pur is naturalibus!*'

Lempriere recited these lines with affection – despite their having their origin, I believe, not at his own but at a rival school. He recited them, too, with the largest innocence, although nothing could be more certain than that an old gentleman's fondness for summer bathing and basking amid naked striplings must nowadays occasion ribald comment from time to time. I felt no doubt about the innocence. Lempriere belonged, spiritually if not chronologically, to the pre-Freudian era, when bachelors were respectable and you prompted little speculation if not 'a ladies' man'. And he was certainly not the only representative of his generation to frequent this guarded stretch of the Cherwell – now so forlorn, but doubtless joyous and Arcadian in June. In my own time it had been a recognised foible, and the ribaldry no more than amusement, muted in a civilised way.

'It could do with chlorination,' I said. 'But I'll risk it with you in the summer term. Swimming's something I can still manage.'

'That's a promise, Dunkie. It's not the Corry or the Garry, I'll admit. But it serves, it serves.'

We made a circuitous return to the city, managing to take in Addison's Walk and Magdalen Grove. Lempriere was tiring and again fairly silent, but perceptibly in a contented mood. My undertaking had pleased him. I reminded myself (as I frequently had to do) that he regarded me as a kinsman, and this suggested to me something that might engage his interest.

'Talking of the Corry,' I said, 'do you know that I'm not your only kin in Oxford from across the border? There's another Glencorry – and she's a Lempriere by descent, not just by devious alliance. She's a grand-daughter of my Aunt Charlotte, called Fiona Petrie. And she was a pupil of J. B. Timbermill, as I was long ago.'

For a moment I thought I'd put a foot wrong, having failed to reckon with the indignation Lempriere was likely to feel at having been left so long in ignorance of this tenuous family connection. Fortunately he took it well, and I told him whatever I knew about Fiona. By this time she had been out to dinner with me, and I found her straying quite frequently into my head. That she could be represented as one of the up-and-coming learned women of the university, however, didn't please Lempriere at all. He seemed to take the view that, had he been – as would have been proper – apprised of her presence at an earlier stage of her career, he might have headed her off from a walk of life so unbecoming to her sex.

'And you say,' he demanded challengingly, 'that she shares a house with a lady novelist?'

'Yes.' I hadn't actually described Miss Mountain in these archaic terms. But as she wrote novels and was undoubtedly a lady the description couldn't well be taken exception to.

'Oxford seems an odd place for lady novelists.' Lempriere reflected for a moment. 'Of course,' he said concessively, 'there was Mrs Humphry Ward.'

'I believe there are several at the moment. Perhaps it's an odd place for gentleman novelists as well.'

'So it is. I've never heard of one.'

'I don't think many dons persist in the practice.' This conversation was amusing me. 'But a surprising number of them might be found to have perpetrated a single novel in their youth, or even a single novel in their riper age. Professional novelists, on the other hand, are hurrying themselves into university chairs and fellowships all over the country. They must suppose theirs is a dying industry.'

'At least we know a dramatist who has done that.' It delighted Lempriere to plant this just if obvious barb. 'Eh, Dunkie? But did you say something about J. B. Timbermill? I suppose that rum book of his might be called a novel of sorts.'

'I said that it seems he was Fiona's tutor. It's my guess that she was his favourite pupil, a kind of child of old age. And she appears very fond of him.'

Is she very fond of this Margaret What's-her-name?'

'Mountain.' This question struck me as surprising from a pre-Freudian man. 'I really don't know.'

'You must bring her to see me. Miss Petrie, that is. You can leave What's-her-name behind you.'

'I'll do that sometime.' I thought this promised rather an odd encounter.

'Good. Up Longwall, I think.'

This was a further detour from our route back to college. It proved, surprisingly, to be because Lempriere wanted to survey the late battle-field. A single policeman stood at the door of the Indian Institute, and there was a second on the steps of the Clarendon Building. The only other sign of the afternoon's manifestation was a thin scattering of abandoned hand-outs here and there in the gutters. Lempriere impaled one of them on the spike of his walking-stick and examined it cursorily. He seemed to judge it not interesting.

'Plenty of riots in mediaeval Oxford,' he said. 'Knives as well as staves at times, and no end of broken sconces. Probably not much vice in them, all the same. Still, a mob's a mob, and there's not much to be done with it. Except ignore it, eh?' He shook his stick, and the crumpled little sheet fluttered to the ground. 'No good beginning except with the individual, you know, or with three or four reasonable people gathered in a room. I'm convinced of that, and it's why I've never been other than what they call a college man. See that the college does the right thing by its own people, and the university will look after itself. A sermon, Dunkie, a sermon. Take it to heart.'

# IX

I RECEIVED LEMPRIERE's sermon in good part, perhaps because at this time I was myself turning rapidly into a college-oriented man. My job was with graduate students and undergraduates from all over the university, but the college held for me very much the centre of the stage. And this is an accurate image. I was a playwright still, with an instinct for the compassable scene. Surrey, Howard, Harbage and Rattenbury: lurking in these four quadrangles and in the dozen half-hidden but commodious nooks disposed around them were enough goings-on to stoke a modest imagination for quite a long time.

There were plenty of people around whose temperaments might have been called non-collegiate, and whose habits largely removed them from the public eye. J. B. Timbermill was one of them. As I had discovered in my first undergraduate term before running him to earth in his hideous North Oxford villa, there was a small string of colleges in which he was entitled to lunch and dine. Even at that time, however, he was understood never to enter any of them. Indeed, among the many legends attaching to his name there was one declaring that, even as an undergraduate, he had insisted on occupying strictly inviolable apartments in the Mitre Hotel. Unlike some other reclusive eccentrics indulgently regarded around the university, Timbermill was an authority of the first eminence in his field – and virtually a 'private scholar', as it used to be called, without the need of regular employment since provided with independent means. I now knew, what had never occurred to me as an undergraduate, that I had been Timbermill's pupil simply because it was with a small amount of teaching that he cared to lighten his solitude, and not on the score of any financial consideration at all.

There were other men, in some degree akin to Timbermill in temperament, who had worked perhaps for a long span of years as college tutors before attaining to university posts which left them free to attenuate their college connections as they pleased. Here I am thinking not of those heavyweights moving out to the university in search of scope for administrative and organising talent, but of men whose interest is so exclusively in scholarship and research that appointment to a university professorship or the like virtually removes them from the public ken. They appear in their lecture-rooms with decent regularity, but are seldom otherwise on view.

It was into this last group that I had concluded there must fall somebody I hadn't yet glimpsed during the course of the term, but who was for a sufficient reason occasionally in my thoughts. It wasn't because we had been schoolfellows that Ranald McKechnie would thus bob up in my head. There were several other dons in Oxford who had been my contemporaries or near-contemporaries amid the Doric colonnades and pebbled yards of that citadel of a bleakly classical education. To these I never gave a thought. McKechnie – 'Wee Dreichie' to my irreverent father – had a different claim to my consideration.

Not having run into the elusive McKechnie, I had been unable to inquire about McKechnie's wife. Could Janet – I asked myself rather needlessly – be ill? Some weeks of term had gone by without her having made me a sign. I did obscurely feel that it was up to Janet to do this, although the book of rules might have it that I ought to go and ring her front-door bell. My coming back to Oxford made me an intruder on her settled scene; if only ever so faintly, there might be something disturbing about it that she acknowledged as calling for reflection. I was conscious of this last notion as generating in me an interest, almost an excitement, that wasn't at all sensible. At Oxford, I had ended by telling myself, everybody runs into everybody else sooner or later, and Janet had decided that a key to our future relationship would be prudently set by letting this happen now. It wasn't a course of conduct that would have recommended itself to the Janet of my first love. But Janet was now a mature woman on the threshold of a tranquil middle age.

It was in the expectation of this sort of meeting that I accepted in those weeks every invitation I received, and a few days after my walk with Lempriere I went to a party given by the Genders. They owned, in St Giles', a beautiful Georgian house which made discreetly evident the possession of means not of an academic order, and on this solid basis they entertained a good deal. Jimmy Gender, although not invariably a resourceful conversationalist, was an accomplished host of the diffident sort. There was nothing diffident about his wife. To be Anthea Gender's guest was to be conscious of being very much in her hands.

'Does one ever see anything of the McKechnies?' It was with some surprise that, quite early in my conversation with her, I heard myself ask this somewhat gauche question. I had no doubt designed that it should carry only the suggestion of a topic reached for at random in the interest of sustained chat. But it hadn't come out like that. I might have been charging my hostess with a culpable failure in not having the McKechnies on parade.

'Ah, they're both shy birds – but particularly Ranald. They may be here later this evening, but Janet couldn't be definite. She has the excuse of only just having got home.'

'She's been away?' I was overjoyed at this obvious explanation of Janet's silence – the possibility of which hadn't occurred to me.

'Visiting her father, Professor Finlay, in Scotland. I believe he has been ill.' Mrs Gender was looking at me with a quickened interest I distrusted. 'You know the family?'

'I don't remember Professor Finlay at all well. His wife died and he made a second marriage. I rather supposed he'd be dead. My own father is, you know.'

I had made an indefinably awkward little speech – but it didn't perturb Mrs Gender. She glanced round her drawing- room and apparently decided she could allow me another minute or two.

'The McKechnies did come to Camilla Pococke's luncheon party the day after the Gaudy,' she said. 'Perhaps you remember that.'

'Yes. I do. Decidedly.'

'Tell me, Duncan, was that your first meeting with Ranald for a long time? I know you were at school together.'

'Yes, it was.'

'And with Janet? You knew her when you were a boy?'

'Yes, with Janet too. And I did.'

I was disturbed by these plain intimations of knowledgeableness. Women can behave with staggering unpredictability – yet I didn't for a moment believe that Janet had communicated our history to Mrs Gender. I myself in youth had buried it all in my heart. I hadn't even told Tony Mumford about Janet.

'I was rather in love with Janet once,' I said. 'But you couldn't know that – could you?'

I was now laughing at Anthea Gender, since I had to make the best of this small situation. Moreover, the explanation of it had come to me. The Glencorrys must have known at the time something about my abortive love-affair with Janet Finlay; Arnold Lempriere, obscurely my Aunt Charlotte's kinsman, had got hold of it through circuitous family channels I knew nothing about; quite recently he must have passed it on to Anthea Gender – again as a piece of Forsyte-like family intelligence.

'It was long before your marriage, Duncan? That you were in love, I mean, with Janet McKechnie?'

'Oh, yes – long before.'

'Was your wife English or Scotch?'

'English.'

'And if you were to marry again? Would it be a Scotch girl or an English one?'

'Scotch.' I was more surprised by the unthinking decision with which I said this than I was by the *outre* character of Anthea Gender's catechism – although indeed the very crispness of her address made her assumption of intimacy inoffensive. And now she did see fit to change the subject.

'I believe,' she said, 'that Jimmy wants to talk to you about his latest crisis. He has heard you actually encountered the boy.'

'You mean the second Lusby? Yes, indeed.'

'He'd be Jimmy's pupil. It would be all on Jimmy, once the boy was here. But what Jimmy says at the moment is that the college mustn't plump too readily for playing safe.'

'Meaning?'

'Concluding there's a clear case that Lusby's not up to it, and that disappointment now is preferable to humiliation and disaster later on. By the way, do you know that Arnold has the boy on his mind?'

'Yes. He harangued me on the subject the other afternoon during a walk to Parson's Pleasure.'

'Good heavens! He's not disporting himself there at this time of year?'

'Lord, no. The place is locked up and rather gruesome. We just took a nostalgic peep. But Arnold was quite impressive on Peter Lusby. He has a talent for making that sort of thing come vividly home to one. He did it over the first Lusby's plight. I was there, as it happened, and heard him.'

'I remember you were. But here is Charles. We must ask him what he thinks.' This was a reference to Charles Atlas, who was now approaching us. 'Ah, and Dr Cressy!' Mrs Gender broke off to welcome this new arrival. 'Dr Cressy, you know Mr Pattullo?'

Dr Cressy didn't know Mr Pattullo, and received the introduction with a thin smile not suggestive of taking much satisfaction in being thus required to enlarge the circle of his acquaintance. I looked with some curiosity at the hero or anti-hero of the rape of the Blunderville letter-book. This was the easier because he had barely looked at me – or at his hostess or Atlas either. He was occupied with a preliminary survey of Mrs Gender's gathering – in the hope, one somehow instantly felt, either of larger intellectual stimulus than one was oneself likely to afford or (even more desirably) of association with persons of higher social consequence. I hadn't myself set eyes on Christopher Cressy since the moment at which he had walked composedly out of the college library with the letter-book under his arm. Now here he was, still its deeply wrongful possessor, bestowing his company with complete assurance upon people who were supposed to be furious with him.

I believed that I'd have recognised Cressy at once, although this must be unusual with somebody encountered only on a single occasion many years ago. He was of a type that doesn't perceptibly age except suddenly and belatedly at a close. His hair was dark and abundant; his complexion was fresh and clear, and congruous with features singularly unlined and an expression somewhat on the impassive side – set, as it were, in a static mould of temperate and somewhat inattentive benignity; his eyes, although they possessed that disconcerting trick of wandering from you, remained as bright as a boy's.

'We are discussing a problem of college entrance,' Mrs Gender said to him. 'And Charles is our authority on the subject. He must tell you about it.' And at this our hostess glided away. Some sticky corner of her entertainment must have hove into view, and to disengage herself for it she had adopted the first resource that came into her head. Atlas – declared an authority on the strength of being Tutor for Admissions – was displeased. He glanced at me with some severity, as if the introduction of this unsuitable topic had been my fault. I said nothing, and it was left to Cressy to speak. He did so with his glance upon our retreating hostess.

'I wonder,' he murmured, 'whether Jimmy was the first of his family to make that sort of marriage? One knows about the Genders. Gender's Original Canine Biscuit – you'll have seen the advertisement in Victorian magazines. Hence their present commanding position in the pet food industry. But now this problem of college entrance. It sounds not exactly convivial ground. But Charles'—and Cressy turned to me urbanely—'can irradiate any subject with his wit. With Charles conversing, one forgets all time, all seasons and their change. My dear Charles, proceed.' Cressy's glance was again wandering round the room. Atlas, a serious young man in whom I had never remarked either the ambition or the ability to coruscate, must have been perfectly capable of recognising insolent banter when it came to him. But he gave no indication of this, merely glancing at me as if to make sure of his bearings.

'Is it the boy whose brother died?' he asked.

'Yes.'

'It's something sad and rather difficult.' Atlas had turned to Cressy. 'One of our last year's scholars, a most promising man, mucked his Mods. He felt he'd done something silly, and it seems he was a depressive type. He went home and took his own life. And now we find that a younger brother, not nearly so clever, wants to follow him here. With a mission to succeed where the dead boy failed. That's all.'

I supposed it would be all – since Atlas clearly wanted it that way, and Cressy's mind appeared occupied elsewhere. Cressy, however, pursued the matter.

'No doubt there is a problem,' he said. 'Just how do you propose to deal with it?'

'I suppose – although I'm not happy about it – that we must judge the boy entirely on the merits of what he writes for us and on what interviewing him reveals. It's the safest thing from his own point of view. Nothing else would be fair to him in the long run.'

'If you manage to be fair to him in the short run you will have done very well. But your proposal, you know, is entirely unrealistic. What will this boy do? Write borderline papers, indistinguishable from those of half a dozen other weakish candidates. As soon as you try to discriminate his quality further you are bound to be influenced by temperamental responses – conscious or unconscious – to what you know of his situation. Detached intellectual appraisal of schoolboy scribblings is a will-o'-the-wisp. Were the brothers at the same school?'

'Yes, they were.'

'Then the same consideration must apply to any estimate of the younger boy his headmaster sends you. Your only resource, as I see the matter, is to employ some examiner whom you keep totally in ignorance of the lad's situation.'

'I don't think we'd care to abnegate responsibility in that way.'

'Precisely! My poor Charles, how readily you involve yourself in contradiction.' Cressy said this in an absent manner, as if it were a judgement so universally acknowledged as to be incapable of engaging serious attention. Suddenly he raised a hand delightedly in air, and his normally frozen features were lit up with pleasurable expectation. He had spied, it seemed, somebody with whom it would be agreeable to converse. Then his glance returned for a moment to Atlas and myself – the glance of a man whom inflexible courtesy constrains to suffer all.' The fact is', he said, 'that your problem must be declared insoluble. How fortunate, then, that it is totally insignificant.' He offered us his bleakest smile, and walked away.

'Well, I'm blessed!' I said. 'What a god-awful man.'

'Christopher?' Atlas was startled. That he was also shocked appeared in his delaying further utterance until he had indulged his habit of a momentary tautening of the lips. 'I suppose,' he then said, 'that his tone tends to be astringent at times. But he's terribly good company, you know. That about the dog biscuits, for instance. It just came into his head.'

'You mean he made it up on the spot?'

'Oh, I'd suppose so – wouldn't you? It's a kind of holiday from history, that freakish strain in him. His history's tiptop. Christopher has a marvellously objective mind.'

For a moment or two I was left on my own, with leisure to ponder what some men can get away with. Atlas had withdrawn – had backed away, indeed, so that I suffered a sense of having misconducted myself in offering so frank an estimate of a fellow-guest. There was also the consideration, perhaps of greater weight, that Cressy, although for long attached to another college, remained a member of our own common room: this no doubt made my solecism doubly heinous. Yet treating as bad form any personal censure not phrased obliquely or periphrasically struck me as tiresome – and as having little to do with the substance of charity. I resolved that, upon challenge, I would always declare my conviction that Christopher Cressy was a god-awful man.

Ruffled as this absurd resolution shows me to have been, I glanced round Anthea Gender's party and found assuagement in the spectacle of Cyril Bedworth gesturing to me across the length of the room. It was Bedworth's habit thus to call me into any circle of which he formed a part at the moment – an action the gratifying spontaneity of which was commonly pointed by something physically inept in the achieving of it. This time his beckoning hand had more or less brushed the nose of a stout elderly woman – demonstrably as academic as everybody else in the room – with whom he was conversing. Robert Damian was on his other side, and all three were standing by a window. I made my way across the crowded floor.

'Oh, Duncan!' Bedworth said – and since our second term as undergraduates I couldn't recall his ever having begun to address me other than in this vocative fashion. 'Oh, Duncan – do you know Professor Babcock?'

I failed to identify Professor Babcock. If anything faintly signalled recognition it was the sense of her suggesting some picturesque figurehead in a maritime museum: one designed to actualise the common metaphor which describes a ship as breasting the waves. Bedworth, accordingly, performed an introduction in due form. My memory still functioned uncertainly, so he went on to produce for the lady a useful word about me, and for me a useful word about the lady. Professor Babcock, however, rejected this channel for polite intercourse.

'Are you related to the painter?' she asked briskly. 'I once met him at a dinner-party at the Pocockes.'

'Yes, indeed. I'm his younger son. And you met me as well. I was there too – the only near-child in the company. You were extremely kind to me.'

'Then I ought to be recalling a double pleasure.' As if to make clear that a mild facetiousness was designed to attend this courteous expression, Professor Babcock advanced her cutwater (for the nautical image must be retained) and afforded me a surprising nudge – the more surprising for having been administered not by a shoulder (figureheads aren't strong on shoulders) but by a more protuberant part of her person. The effect of this idiosyncrasy was magical. There was instantly nothing I didn't seem to remember about Professor Babcock.

'Your father was a most impressive person, Mr Pattullo. But of course I had expected that. He was also quite delightful, which is a different thing. We admired your college pictures in the library, and then there was something about another picture. We went to look at it somewhere, but there was a hitch.'

It was by my father, and in my own rooms. *Young Picts watching the arrival of Saint Columba*. Only somebody had substituted another picture as a silly joke.' Suddenly I found that I was staring at Damian. 'Robert,' I said, 'it was you!'

This called for explanations. In the course of them I realised that Professor Babcock's memory was entirely of her meeting with my father. Of the stray undergraduate who had been present she had no recollection at all. I found this vexing – a fact illustrating the oddity of the filial relationship. Lachlan Pattullo was a memorable man, and I hadn't in the least been a memorable boy.

'But just what did you and I talk about, Mr Pattullo?' Unexpectedly – for scholars are not commonly sensitive to what Nick Junkin would have called vibes – Professor Babcock had become aware of this small stir of feeling in me.

'We made fun of somebody who's at this party now: Christopher Cressy. You rather led me on, I think, and were amused when I didn't quite know how cheeky and clever I was allowed to be. My schooldays, you must remember, weren't far behind me.'

'We vied with one another,' Professor Babcock asked me, 'in the fabricating of destructive epigrams?'

'Something like that.' I didn't offer this reply with much conviction. I had been precocious at that time only in my reading, and I could now recall my chief feeling as having been that the alarming lady who had befriended me was a little too anxious to talk like somebody in a book: Meredith's Mrs Mountstuart Jenkinson, perhaps, or a figment of that kind. Of course I'd done my best to play up. Conversationally, Professor Babcock had toned down by now. So probably had I.

'And do you still, Mr Pattullo, view Dr Cressy as a figure of fun?'

This improper question had to be thought of, I supposed, as a trick of the old rage in Professor Babcock. It was a shade on the lively side. So, equally, would have been my keeping faith with myself to the extent of announcing that I judged Cressy to be god-awful.

'Still as a figure of fun?' I repeated. 'Well, no. Perhaps he rather enjoys making other people just that.'

'I agree with you. But one has to remember—' Professor Babcock broke off. 'Good heavens I' she said. 'It must be another of those vexatious demonstrations.'

It was certainly that. For the second time within a few days I was listening to the voice of young Oxford in insurgence. The same sort of shouting in ragged unison was coming from the same sort of distance. As demos commonly assembled at one point and marched to another the sound would presently fade or swell according to the objective in view.

'They don't usually come out again after tea,' Professor Babcock said. 'And they always break up in time for it – just as with their rowing and rugger and so on.'

In this remark I recognised one resource of senior Oxford in coping with the phenomenon unleashed on it. Demos were rags and nothing more. It was becoming apparent, however, that few people were continuing to find this vision plausible. I doubted whether Professor Babcock did, although she had offered a kind of token bob at it.

'I think,' I said, 'we're going to have a closer view of this lot. They're coming our way.'

'Are they indeed?' There was a pause while Professor Babcock superintended the replenishing of her glass. 'Then their goal is probably my own college. They are interesting themselves in the sad case of Mr Elijah.'

'I haven't heard of him.'

'I'm sure that Mr Bedworth and Dr Damian have. Indeed, he has stalked abroad in the public prints. He is, or was, our boilerman. A nice fellow, but unfortunately liable to get most terribly drunk – and incipiently psychotic into the bargain. Do you know our hall, Mr Pattullo?'

'I don't think I happen ever—'

'I shall hope to persuade you to dine in it. It's not unpleasing, as Victorian structures go, and we use it for our more formal lectures.

Our annual Samuel Wilberforce Lecture – commonly delivered by a dignitary of the church – is a case in point. This year's lecture was particularly impressive. The bishop's peroration rose to the most elevated considerations. But it was just then, unfortunately, that the central heating went wrong. It is no doubt of somewhat old-fashioned design. Mr Elijah, it appears, had sunk into a vinous stupor and let the boiler out. Any drop in temperature was scarcely perceptible in the short space of time involved. Not so the acoustic effect. That, Mr Pattullo, is not describable with any approximation to delicacy. The pipes and radiators excelled themselves in digestive noises. There was general embarrassment. But the bishop, needless to say, behaved very well. Some appearance of edification was preserved.'

'And Elijah?' Damian asked.

'Ah, here is the sad part of the matter. Our domestic bursar judged it to be her duty to admonish him. She declares he took it very well. Unfortunately, having withdrawn and thought the matter over, he deemed it useful to return to her office and resume the discussion while provided with a cleaver.'

'A cleaver!' I exclaimed.

'A butcher's chopper for cutting up carcasses, Mr Pattullo. Fortunately as it happened, our bursar keeps in a drawer of her desk her father the general's pistols. She has a sentimental regard for them, I suppose. Needless to say, the weapons were unloaded – but the appearance of one of them gave Mr Elijah occasion for second thoughts. While he was perpending these the police were summoned, and our college doctor along with them. The poor man was hospitalised forthwith, and has since retired on a pension. But the victimisation of Mr Elijah has been much in the generous minds of the young, and I think they are letting off a little steam about it this evening.'

Professor Babcock having delivered herself of this narrative at proper Meredithian leisure, the demo was now in sight and its vociferations were beginning to drown even the hubbub of a large Oxford cocktail party. Few of Mrs Gender's guests appeared much to react to the disturbance. They were rather carefully neither amused nor indignant nor even attentive. Was it fondly believed that, if simply ignored, this unprecedented behaviour on the part of our juniors would go away? Or were people really taking it very seriously, so that I was witnessing something like the preserved sang-froid of an aristocratic French salon as the mob howled and the tumbrels rumbled in the next faubourg?

'They're chanting "Basket Out",' I said. 'Who's Basket?'

'Our bursar, Mr Pattullo. We have the highest regard for Cecilia Basket. She combines looking after our practical affairs with maintaining a considerable reputation as a research chemist.'

'I see.' I said this mechanically, and if I was really seeing anything it was only my own bewilderment. I could glimpse that, once one had picked up the habit of this sort of noisy parade, the Mr Elijahs of society were a pretext as good as another. I thought I could hear in the shouting (only of this I wasn't sure) quite as much generalized high-spirits as focused hostility. Still, here were a couple of hundred young men employing the full force of their lungs in objurgating Miss Basket by name in the public street. It was true that the lady was a general's daughter and the proprietor of a brace of pistols. And I found, curiously enough, that I had some memory of her. She had been the very young don in whose society I had exhibited an extreme of social ineptitude on the same occasion as my meeting with Professor Babcock herself. It was by way of rallying from that debacle, no doubt, that I had later in the evening so determinedly kept my end up with the elder lady. In all probability Miss Basket was now no more tender a flower than was her senior colleague. But bellowing 'Basket Out' seemed to me not one of the numerous forms of bad behaviour in which it is held venial for young men to indulge.

I saw Robert Damian glancing at me with amusement. He must have caught my feeling, and been tickled to recognise something of the undergraduate in the middle-aged man. As a boy I had been genuinely possessed of some old-world views; where they came from I don't know; perhaps it was from my mother's reading aloud in Scott's novels. Now here I was, inwardly aspersing as louts beyond the pale a crowd of excited young men taking unmannerly freedoms with a woman's name.

'But what's it truly all about?' I asked hastily. 'Robert, you always used to say a college doctor is essentially a child psychiatrist. So how is all this diffused disturbance generated? Just what makes the kids tick that way?'

'Social mobility, for a start. Patterns from the field of industrial conflict taking over. Fags expect to become prefects, but workers hang bosses from lamp-posts. That clear?'

'Crystalline,' I said. 'What next?'

'Earlier maturition. Enormous problems there. Then consider a related thing: the revolution in sexual *mores* in society at large, and the muck we make of coping with it in these immemorially monastic dumps we call the colleges. Take what all this demo-nonsense is most frequently about at the moment. It's the providing, at the university's or the government's expense, of a kind of Kubla Khan pleasure dome with everything laid on. A common meeting-place for all students – and the running of it probably more or less left to them. Fairly rational, I suppose. But it's prompted by the imitative instinct and a rather dreary reversed snobbery – being as like a polytechnic or whatever as possible. It's also prompted – much more it's prompted – by straight anti-college feeling. They don't want any longer to live in groups of two to four hundred chaps, presided over by fatherly dons and big-brotherly don-lets. They want to be out on their own – ten thousand of them, or thereabout.'

The demo was now passing beneath the Genders' windows. It was a slow-moving affair, partly because of the display of a number of large banners which it appeared difficult to keep poised in a condition of adequate legibility. A few of these claimed, whether veraciously or not, the status of a kind of personal standard of one individual college or another; others announced various Marxist-Leninist, Maoist, and Trotskyist affiliations; and a surprising number spoke of regions remote from Oxford's dreaming spires. These last appeared to afford Professor Babcock considerable satisfaction.

'Mr Elijah,' she said, 'is clearly gaining my beloved college, hitherto obscure, a far-flung fame. Mr Pattullo, did you remark the Dotheboys Hall Anarcho-Syndicalist Group? And here are the Boiler-makers. It is eminently proper that Mr Elijah should enjoy their support.'

'There really are people from half a dozen other universities,' Bedworth murmured to me seriously – so that I somehow felt that Professor Babcock annoyed him. 'That takes a certain amount of organising. The immediate issue's plainly nonsense, but I don't think the whole thing's just funny.'

'Neither do I.'

'One almost has to admire their being so good at being so unreasonable.' Bedworth paused to make a clumsy bow to the lady, who was now carrying her wit elsewhere. 'It's the same in college. Of course I don't think many of our men turn out to affairs like this—'

'It might be better if they did,' Damian interrupted briskly. 'As a college we've always been considered superior and standoffish – and with bloody good reason.'

'Perhaps so,' I said. 'But I want to hear how Cyril struggles with the unreasonableness of the young. Deans and Senior Tutors are obviously on the job all day, but they keep uncommonly close about it. Cyril goes round with a weight of public care on his brow, but never lets me in on its specific occasions.'

'I don't think I'd be popular if I prowled the college pouring out tales of woe.' Bedworth, although always perplexed when made fun of, usually responded with a manful attempt to achieve his own lighter note. 'There are quite enough Doom-Watch characters around, wouldn't you say? And one must guard against going about making gossip and small-talk out of people's private problems – or even out of their group conspiracies.'

I felt admonished, and accordingly held my peace. Damian glanced through the window.

'The circus has come to a halt,' he said. 'The police have a trick of holding up these affairs pretty frequently in order to clear the traffic ahead. They hope people will grow bored and go home. It's equally likely to produce bad temper, I'd suppose.'

I looked down at the marchers. Halted, they were continuing their monotonous shouting about poor Miss Basket. It seemed a singularly profitless exercise – unless, indeed, it served to keep people warm on what was turning a chilly evening. I saw no sign of bad temper, but no more did I see much sign of that eruptive jollity or gamesomeness which might lend support to the 'students' rag' reading of the occasion. The demonstrators, like Cyril Bedworth, were seriously disposed. About the precise contours of the Elijah affair the majority of them were not likely to be well-informed. Generously propelled, it might have been said, by that most hazardous of fuels, a sense of righteousness, they were marching and shouting under the simple large persuasion that their seniors had pervasively made a criminal mess of things. It struck me as a tenable view.

We continued silently to watch the halted mob. It seemed in some literal sense steamed up; a faint miasma now hung above it, as above a lowing herd. The appearance of many of the males contributed to the bovine suggestion; shaggy in their persons, many of them affected jackets streaked and patched with fur, so that the general effect was of moulting or tettered yaks. Among the females a majority favoured duffle-coats worn over what seemed to be superannuated ball-dresses gone ragged and trailing at the hem. For some years nothing had more struck me about the external appearance of the young than the ability of both sexes to extract elegance from garments as unpretending as a charity child's. On a present view it looked as if a cult of ugliness had taken over. I found myself hoping that this was a passing phase or my own subjective conclusion.

'Then I'll tell you what's bothering me today,' I heard Bedworth say suddenly. He must have been brooding over my very mild joke about his reticence. 'It's this french-letter machine.'

'This *what*, Cyril?'

'I suppose most people have heard about it. They're demanding one in the J.C.R. A coin-operated machine for dispensing male contraceptives. That's what they call it in a letter. They do exist, you know. You come across them, for instance, in the wash-places of transport cafes.'

'How very difficult,' I said.

'Difficult? Not a bit of it!' Damian spoke briskly. 'Aren't french letters, Cyril, eminently objects for which a sudden need rises up every now and then? I advise the more elaborate form of equipment. You put in five p. or ten p., and the thing comes out plain or coloured accordingly.'

'It's not a subject for ribaldry, Robert.' Bedworth's glance, despite these words, admitted amusement. Long ago Tony and I had subjected him to a pretty stiff training in the reception of *facetiae* of this sort. At the same time he was very properly looking round Mrs Gender's drawing-room to make sure that nobody else could overhear and be offended. 'And I'll tell you my feeling. Funny or not, the notion just isn't decent.'

'Rubbish, man. The machine needn't be stuck up next to the colour television, or among the beer kegs in the buttery. Shove it in one of the loos. Or shove two in two of the loos. That will obviate all embarrassment among the modest or furtive patrons. And I expect the machines are rent-free. The college might even get a rake-off on sales if you pressed for it.'

'Robert, have you any *serious* thoughts about this?'

'Yes, I think I have. Consider the main point you make – I mean that the college makes – about all this sexual activity around the place. You've abandoned an orthodox Christian view—'

'We've done nothing of the kind!'

'All right. I amend that. You've abandoned the right to impose old views on young people who subscribe to new ones. What you stand by is the fact that a college is a place of learning. Most people turn up because they want to learn, and it's your duty to provide them with a reasonably undistracting environment for just that. Is that right?'

'Perfectly right.'

'You have to take any rational steps you can to protect them from the graver anxieties incident upon the sexual development of young males?'

'All right, Robert. Go on.' Bedworth gave me a surprisingly whimsical look. He wasn't at all at sea as to the drift of Damian's argument.

146

'Do you know what it's like, Cyril, to be a decent and penniless young man who isn't sure he hasn't got his girl up the stick?'

'Yes, I do.'

This reply, being unexpected, momentarily threw Damian off his stride. I myself supposed that Bedworth was merely indicating by it a certain capacity for imaginative identification with the predicament described. Yet what did I know of the intimate life of the adolescent Bedworth? Nothing at all.

'Or to be the girl?' Damian demanded. 'I'm at the receiving end of the mess quite often, and I can tell you it's the very devil. Pregnancy tests, depressions, anxiety states, covert inquiries about abortion – all the works. And every now and then – for don't let us exaggerate – it could all have been obviated had this harmless facility been to hand.'

'But Robert – this is nonsense!' Bedworth had become distressed. 'Any reasonably intelligent young man who thinks he's going to make love, and who isn't sure his girl is on the pill or something, provides himself with these things well in advance. He'd be a moron not to.'

'Then he's sometimes a moron. Or sometimes the situation just jumps at him and he takes a chance. Whereas he could, you see, nip over to the J.C.R. while the wench is getting into bed! So think of this poor chap, Cyril. Think of him in concrete terms. One of your own pupils, perhaps. He wants to get on with his essay for you but he just can't. He can't fix his mind on the job because of this awful fear that he's put his girl in the club. The poor benefit of a bewildering minute, you know. Or a single crafty reef and all's confusion.'

Damian's first-hand familiarity with his theme struck me as authenticated by elements in his vocabulary, which presumably came to him in the conversation of agitated young men. Bedworth's perturbation had increased; it was evident that the picture of the pupil impeded in his studies by a consciousness of the possible consequences of his irregular behaviour had caught his imagination.

'But Robert,' he cried, 'just think of bringing such a proposal before a college Governing Body!'

'Administrative action is all that's required. You and Jimmy Gender just run up to town, inspect the latest models, and have your particular fancy sent down the following day.'

'Talk sense, for goodness sake! The idea simply bristles with difficulties. Imagine the attitude of our clerical members.'

'It's not the attitude of *those* members that's most relevant, surely? It's—'

'If you can do nothing but produce indecent cracks, Robert, we'd better shut up.' Bedworth wasn't really offended. His own conversation never deviated from the academic proprieties, but he was a resolutely tolerant man.

'Here's Albert Talbert advancing on us,' I said. 'Shall we put the problem to him? He might be worth hearing on it.'

This suggestion, itself frivolous, was at once rendered abortive by the circumstance that Talbert proved to be accompanied by his wife. Damian rapidly took in this situation.

'I leave the literati to it,' he said cheerfully, and plunged into the thick of Mrs Gender's party. It was now a very populous affair.

# X

MORE, PERHAPS, THAN any couple in Oxford, the Talberts maintained an air of learned concern upon social occasions. The modest entertainments upon which they themselves ventured amid the domesticities of Old Road were inaugurated and brought to a conclusion with a ritual closing and reopening of enormous folio volumes upon their sitting-room table. At parties like the present you almost expected them to appear unarming such objects in a symbolic manner, much as saints and martyrs parade with gridirons and wheels and hatchets in sacred iconography. And Mrs Talbert in particular did in fact carry round with her a certain emblematical suggestion. Tall and gaunt, with crag-like features disconcertingly crowned with an outmoded *coiffure* of small serpentine ringlets, and addicted to trailing diaphanous scarves which at a breath would rise and curl like scrolls awaiting explanatory annotations, she might have appeared with acceptance in a Jacobean masque (a literary kind upon which she was an acknowledged authority) as a figure of imposing if somewhat imprecise allegorical signification.

The Talberts were invariably much at one in the direction of their current research. If Talbert pondered the possibility that *The King of England and the Goldsmith's Wife* might be nothing other than Heywood's *King Edward IV* his wife would develop the theory that *The Proud Woman of Antwerp* was a lost piece by Day and Haughton. Rightly maintaining that their function was not merely to make knowledge but to diffuse it as expeditiously as possible, and too eminent to think of scoring scoops in learned journals, they were never slow to embark upon informative talk in general society. They did, however, exhibit here a slight difference the one from the other. Mrs Talbert, the more enthusiastic of the two, would scarcely pause to be handed a drink before plunging in with *Crafty Cromwell*, or *Far Fetched and Dear Bought is Good for Ladies,* or even *Give a Man Luck and Throw him into the Sea*, for the benefit of anybody who came to hand. She was commonly listened to with interest even by agronomists and cyberneticians, since her articulatory eccentricities were becoming more pronounced with age and there was something curiously compelling in her ability to produce entire sentences on an indrawn breath. Talbert, possessing beyond everything else a sense of the high consequence (or deep import) of all fruits of scholarly labour, was accustomed to look round such a gathering as the present for persons of the gravity which he himself – except upon rare and perplexing occasions – habitually exhibited. But if nobody measuring up to this standard was on view he would accord honorary status as a full-fledged savant to any receptive-looking individual with whom he could claim acquaintance. Bedworth, his immediate colleague, must have enjoyed a position in the first category, and I myself was at least not sunk beneath the second. These estimations were now bringing Talbert towards us at a brisk toddle. His wife had detached herself from him in the middle of the room for the purpose of addressing herself to Professor Babcock – possibly about Mr Elijah, but more probably about *Lust's Dominion* or *The Two Sins of King David.*

The demo was in movement again, and had raised a ragged cheer in consequence. Alerted by this, Talbert walked up to the window and looked out.

'A political rally,' he said huskily and informatively. He might have been a connoisseur of ceramics who, glancing into a show-case, at once identifies for uninstructed companions the dynasty or whatever of the objects on view. 'A remarkable turn-out.' Talbert added this approvingly – a circumstance which might have surprised a stranger, since his complexion was that which, in a coloured comic-strip, conventionally indicates that the baby has swallowed its rattle. This fiery hue, which would have entitled him to take his place beside his wife, pageant-wise, as representing *Furor, Ira* or some similar personification, was the more striking for being set off by his large white moustache and the mild glint of his gold-rimmed spectacles. Yet any reading of Talbert as a choleric man would have been in error. Disapprobation, even measured indignation, could be aroused in him by the fact or fancy of insufficient scholarship being somewhere abroad in the land. But I couldn't recall his ever having allowed himself anger even at times when my own juvenile silliness must have been very trying indeed.

'It may well be the university branch of the Fabian Society,' Talbert added on reflection. 'I am told that they have been very active of late. This may be an anniversary celebration – of the birthday, maybe, of Mrs Sydney Webb. I see that one of the young men is waving at me.' Talbert raised a hand in measured response to this supposed greeting – which had actually, I imagine, been the random elevating of a clenched fist in an approved revolutionary fashion. 'A pupil, no doubt. Cyril, might it be Montgomerie – or perhaps Skeffington-Jones? Yes, I think it may have been Skeffington-Jones.' Talbert paused on all this fallacious rambling, and must have found it good, since he gave a pregnant and approbatory nod not apparently directed at anything else. 'A pleasant party,' he went on. 'Gender's wife has the art of contriving such things. *Misce stultitiam consiliis brevem* – eh, Duncan? The injunction affords some of our colleagues singularly little difficulty.' Suddenly Talbert's eyes lit up: a small but arresting phenomenon, like that of dipped headlights coming on full-beam very far away. Or it was as if glints from those gold-rimmed spectacles had floated free and were now harbouring deep within the irises of this learned man. Simultaneously, moreover, there was manifested that curious auditory effect, again peculiar to Talbert, faint as visceral noises emanating from some gnome or elf, which one took to reveal the existence of a deeply internalised mirth. Was Talbert's amusement a simple tribute to his wit in quoting Horace or whoever it may have been? Or was he tickled by a just sense of his own mild absurdity? As often before, I found it impossible to say. And abruptly and with an equal familiarity, I was aware that he had switched to an extreme of the Talbertian *gravitas*. It had been one of his disconcerting habits in tutorials. Confident that merriment was being hinted, pleased with one's own acuteness in detecting it upon evidence so slender, one would still be obsequiously guffawing when made aware that nothing but the most uncompromising intellectual severity was any longer present in the small bleak room.

'It ought to have been cancelled, nevertheless,' Talbert said.

Into these mysterious words my old tutor had put a maximum of *ex cathedra* effect, so that one felt the verdict to do no more than articulate the silent judgement of concurrent centuries.

'Cancelled?' The word was echoed by Bedworth, who seemed as much at a loss as I was. 'What ought to have been cancelled, Albert?'

'The present entertainment.' Talbert (who was provided with what looked like whisky on ice) glanced darkly round Mrs Gender's now thronging and animated guests. 'So hard upon so sad an event! But, hearing nothing, it was civil to attend.' Making a deft half-turn, Talbert succeeded in getting his far from empty glass usefully in the path of some ministrant person carrying a decanter. Like many men notably abstemious at home, he enjoyed getting full value out of parties. 'On one of their treacherous motorways,' he resumed. 'Crushed between Juggernauts, in the popular phrase. One might better say Symplegades, particularly since he was so brilliant a classical scholar. Your own classical training, Duncan, will have enabled you to appreciate his last *opusculum*. To my mind, there has not been its like since Housman's Manilius.' (Talbert, although so eminent an 'English' scholar, frequently emphasised that he was originally a classical man.) 'One of Oxford's finest minds is extinguished, Cyril.'

'Albert, who are you talking about, in heaven's name?'

'Or, better still, one might say crushed by the Planctae. Duncan, the twelfth book of the Odyssey will be familiar to you. The Wandering Rocks. And so young a man! Far short of fifty, I believe. An irreparable loss to scholarship.' Talbert pronounced this last opinion with his unvarying effect of weighed and considered utterance. 'Poor McKechnie,' he concluded.

In the romances of my boyhood it was frequently stated that, as a consequence of one or another well-nigh insuperable challenge to his young manhood – from a Martian, say, or an unexpectedly surviving Brontosaurus – the hero's blood ran cold. The sensation which has generated this cliche beset me now. But I was unaware of any interpretable conflict of emotions, and the possibility of anything of the kind was to be short-circuited in a moment. I knew only that the appalling thought of Janet bereft by fate of her second husband as she had been of her first left me utterly numb. It is surprising that I heard as clearly as I did Cyril Bedworth's immediately ensuing Words.

'Good God, Albert, you've got it utterly wrong!' It was very rarely indeed that Bedworth allowed himself, as now, any hint of impudence with our old teacher. 'You must have been hearing of an obscure man called McNally, who teaches some outlandish lore at Wadham. He's had a smash-up on the motorway, sure enough. But he isn't even dead. They're busy putting him together again in the Radcliffe at this moment. As for Ranald McKechnie – can't you see that he's in this room – and his wife as well, for that matter?'

Fleetingly, I remembered that this was a line of Talbert's; that he was prone to getting his disasters a little mixed up. Dimly, I was conscious that his immediate reaction to Bedworth's correcting him was also familiar; being indicted of a factual error went against the grain of his calling; he was showing some disposition to dispute the facts of the matter, even in the face of the evidence. It was that evidence which was now before me. Scanning the crowded room, I had spotted McKechnie, undeniably alive and well, in the same moment that he spotted me. He had actually flicked up a hand – jerkily, like an old-fashioned 'trafficator' on a car – in greeting. From McKechnie, this was an oncoming and uninhibited gesture, by which I'd have been touched had I taken leisure to give it a thought. But this I didn't do. He and Janet, although they could not have been at the party long, had already separated as well-conducted couples do on such occasions, and my glance had taken another sweep to find her. As our eyes met I had the impression that she had already seen me, and even that she had been studying me seriously across the length of the room. Now she smiled. It was the smile – a dispersal of some more thoughtful regard – which she had given me from the other end of Mrs Pococke's luncheon-table a few months before, and which had re-established between us I didn't quite know what. But I did know that we were going to be perfectly easy together. I knew this so clearly, indeed, that, despite all I had been asking myself about our new relationship, what I now sent her in reply across the room was nothing more complicated than a cheerful grin. At this, and to my joy, Janet began disengaging herself from the people she was talking to. I spent no time on any such civilities with Bedworth and Talbert, and within seconds Janet and I were converging upon one another – purposively, although necessarily on a zigzag course. This joint impulse, spontaneous and innocent, evoked in me a moment of extraordinary happiness. The fact must have been apparent in my features – for suddenly a woman's voice spoke at my shoulder.

'Duncan,' Fiona Petrie said, 'you look as if you'd had a very good day.' And Fiona kissed me.

I probably comported myself reasonably well, and I suppose it must be said that Janet did too. She turned away and was presently talking with her host. But this correct behaviour on Janet's part happened only after she had taken a sideways step in the interest of a clear view, and studied the ambiguous rencontre between Fiona and myself with a brief dispassionate regard such an anthropologist might direct upon two primitive persons rubbing noses or engaging in some similarly commonplace social behaviour. This mischievous action – it wasn't in the least obtrusive – disconcerted me more than it need have done. Here I was, a middle-aged man, the next thing to a bachelor, enjoying the mild pleasures of cultivated female society. And there was Janet, remembering other times and laughing at me.

It mayn't have been like this at all – and in any case I hadn't further time to think about it, since I had to cope with Fiona.

'Perhaps,' she was saying, 'you've just finished another play?'

'No, I haven't just finished another play. How can I finish another play, Fiona, when I've turned myself into a don in this desperate fashion?'

'But it has been your own choice, hasn't it? And arrived at in what may be called full maturity?'

'Chock-full, I suppose.' It occurred to me that Fiona and Janet had more than their nationality in common. They both went in for mockery, and neither overdid it. But then had I ever known a woman who hadn't regarded it as a weapon in her armoury? Penny had mocked me – and with her the mockery had eventually grown claws. My cousins Anna and Ruth Glencorry both used to have a go; being rather stupid girls, however, they had seldom got beyond a jeer. What attracted me in Fiona was largely the oddity of her being a Glencorry who exhibited an intelligence nowhere distinguishable on her genetic horizon. It was a rum reason for fancying a girl. But there it was.

'How is Margaret?' I asked. 'Has she finished another novel?' I had not met Fiona's fellow-householder Miss Mountain since our first encounter, and mentioned her in this light-hearted manner now out of a vague sense that her existence ought to be taken account of.

'She's very well, thank you. But she works rather slowly. Even although we do now have a second typewriter. It arrived last week.'

'Congratulations. By the way, is Margaret a don too? I scarcely know about her.'

'You must be found an opportunity. No, she isn't. She got a senior scholarship, and there was almost certainly a junior fellowship coming along. But she decided she wanted to be a full-time writer. Could you get me another drink?'

I got Fiona another drink. Like Talbert, she was drinking whisky. I remembered that – unlike Talbert – she drank it at home as well. One could speculate as to whether here at least was something that had come to her in a hereditary way. Uncle Rory had drunk glass for glass with his fellow lairds, but his dottiness (related, I suppose, to my mother's) certainly wasn't the consequence of inebriety. Aunt Charlotte drank at all socially requisite times, but caused sherry to be dispensed in glasses like thimbles, and at table added water to her wine as one might do to a distasteful tonic from the apothecary. About the Petries of Garth I knew, of course, nothing at all.

All this, although interesting, scarcely seemed a feasible topic for conversation, and in the few steps I had to take to satisfy Fiona's demand I tried to find something that would be brief and lively: lively, because I found Fiona lively; brief, since I had Janet still, as it were, waiting in the wings. It was Fiona, however, who spoke first.

'Duncan, has it occurred to you that when I'm sixty you'll be eighty or thereabout?'

'Of course it hasn't. And why on earth should it have occurred to you?'

'It's as a result of looking round at all these people. Their ages range from the twenties to the eighties, but it's something very little acknowledged in any formal way. Wouldn't you say that there's a convention in Oxford to minimise the fact that the young are young and the old are old?'

'Perhaps there is – but, if so, it only reflects and possibly exaggerates a drift of behaviour in society at large. You'd have to go a good long way to find old ladies still wearing lace caps. Do you think we ought to return to a Victorian Oxford?'

'Why not? Take those people stumping around shouting in the streets. They're extremely young. Younger even than I am, Duncan.'

'So they are.'

'They've been suddenly treated as grown-up; told they have to stand on their own feet, organise their own time, and so on. In every sort of social situation their seniors treat them as contemporaries. It bewilders them a good deal. Then they discover it's all a sham; that as far as the government of the university goes we're a rigid gerontocracy. They'll be listened to with an inexhaustible courtesy that becomes irritating in itself. But damn-all happens, so far as their demands and proposals are concerned. And that's why they start this idiotic demo stuff when they ought to be at their books or playing their muddy games or making love.'

I don't see what it has to do with my approaching eightieth birthday.'

'Older and younger getting along in terms of acknowledging themselves as being so. I was thinking about our getting married.'

'But we're not getting married.' The odd challenge had been disconcerting; it seemed to come from an area of Fiona's mind I knew nothing about.

'Quite so. It's a pure hypothesis, and we can speculate about it freely.

It would be a Victorian marriage – although in a non-Victorian Oxford.'

'Why would it be particularly Victorian?'

'Victorian husbands were often a good deal older than their wives, at least in the middle classes. A girl's husband might look like her father. The disparity in years was something economically determined, I suppose. Commerce, industry, the professions were largely based on the family. Every letterhead said *Dombey and Son,* or something of that sort. So the sons came to any measure of independence late; they often couldn't afford to marry – set up an establishment, as it was called – until they were middle-aged. But they still wanted fresh young brides, with plenty of kick ahead of them. So you see how you and I would have been.'

'You make it sound quite awful.'

'Nothing of the kind. Those marriages were completely stable, more often than not. There's a paternal component in every normal male, isn't there? Well, it got off to a good start.'

'I see. I'd be protecting and counselling my child-wife, and making sure she toed the line?'

'Just that. And it works very well.'

'Fiona, what an extremely unfashionable view!1'

'So much for twenty and forty. Now pass on to sixty and eighty. The snag's supposed to lie there. If I told my parents I was marrying Duncan Pattullo they'd pipe up with this tail-end of life stuff at once. But they'd be wrong. Or, at least, they wouldn't necessarily be right.'

'Because when I'm eighty and a helpless dotard, Fiona, your maternal component will get its chance?'

'Just that. There's a reversal of roles, but it's in consonance with basic sexual differences still.'

'Fiona, I feel we'd better not get married. Our first sprightly running would be splendid, more likely than not. But sixty and eighty might be trickier than you reckon. As far as that maternal component goes, you'll do well to stick to Timbermill.'

Fiona looked at me in surprise, and for a moment I thought she was offended. But she had merely detected me as having stopped talking nonsense.

'When I'm sixty,' she said, 'J.B. will be round about a hundred-and-twenty.'

'And you'll still be keeping an eye on him?'

'I hope so. I went to see him the other day. He talked about you quite a lot. In fact, he might be said to have been recommending you to my regard. Strange, don't you think?'

'Good heavens, Fiona! Is that what has put this rum chat into your head?'

'Perhaps it is.' Fiona was suddenly smiling at me like the very young woman she was. The effect was oddly incongruous with the dry precise quality of her voice and idiom – and was the more fetching in consequence. 'Will you come and dine in college?' she asked abruptly. 'Face up to the full-dress *Princess* stuff?'

'Yes, of course.'

'I'll call you, or write. And now we'd better go and talk to other people. It wouldn't do to be judged singular, would it, Duncan?'

It wouldn't do at all.' I realised, as I turned away, that I hadn't known what, if anything, to make of this ironic archaism. Perhaps Fiona, leading some kind of way-out life of which I knew nothing, had typed me as a very conventional, as well as elderly, cousin.

# XI

D UNKIE,' JANET ASKED at once, 'who is she?'
      'The girl I've just been talking to? She's a very learned young
person called Fiona Petrie, an authority on Anglo-Saxon pots.'

'I'd say she was setting her cap at you.'

'You weren't being unobservant. But it wasn't exactly that. She
appears to have rather a peculiar sense of humour. And we have
warrant for a certain intimacy of manner and address. We're cousins.'

'You're old enough to be her uncle.'

'Yes, indeed. It's something she was making quite a point of. And
she's that sort of cousin – an uncle's grandchild.'

'Would it be one of your grand lairdly relations that she'd be,
Dunkie?'

'Yes, it would.' This hadn't been Janet's natural idiom; it was one –
supposedly catching the rhythms of cottage talk – with which she had
sometimes teased me long ago when the vexatious topic of the
Glencorry connection came up. 'She's my cousin Anna Glencorry's
eldest child. And I'll tell you another thing, Janet McKechnie. There
was a point at which I did my best to father her.'

'To what?

'To father her. After she was conceived, you see, but before she was
born. It looked for a time as if a father would be the missing factor in
the affair. So I volunteered.'

'Dunkie, when was this?' It was apparent that Janet had realised I
wasn't producing some foolish joke.

'In my last school holidays, just before I came up to Oxford. When you and I—'

'Yes, Dunkie. And what happened?'

'Anna's parents failed to entertain the suggestion seriously. And then the authentic father turned up. A thoroughly eligible youth, who'd just been a trifle backward in coming forward.'

Isn't this rather an odd story to tell me now?'

'No.'

There was a silence. Janet appeared to be considering my reply with some seriousness. Her first gay remark about my encounter with Fiona had been designed to set a tone which would at least be a useful start between us. But now we had got on different ground. She was pretty well the only person in the world to whom I could have divulged this ancient story of the circumstances of Fiona's birth with any shred of decency.

'No,' I repeated. 'I'd have told you almost at the time, I think, if matters hadn't taken to moving as they did. We'd probably have managed, even then, to see it as rather comical and touching.'

'It certainly presents itself as that now.' Janet was smiling again. 'Who would have thought that young Duncan Pattullo was capable of making a proposal of marriage?'

'It wasn't exactly what one thinks of as that.' I had myself smiled – distinctly feebly, I imagine – at this shaft. I didn't put forward the idea to Anna herself – only to her father.'

'Well, well! The worthy laird might well have suspected—'

'I think he did, for a moment.'

'But then he took another look at you, and realised you were the soul of honour. Juvenile honour, perhaps – but honour, all the same.'

'Stop making fun of me, Janet.'

'I'm not – or not just at that precise point. And now, Dunkie, we can stop being sentimental.'

'So we can.'

'In fact, I think I'll drop Dunkie and use Duncan.'

'You'll do no such thing. Not if you ever want to see me again.'

'I hope I'll always want that.' Janet had returned to gravity. 'It would be a pretty kettle of fish if I didn't. Here's Ranald.'

McKechnie and I hadn't done too well on first re-encountering one another at the Gaudy, and I wondered whether this was again going to be a constrained occasion. We were all three of an age: myself the eldest, Janet the youngest, and McKechnie in between – with a total span of a couple of years covering all our birthdays. We had been brought up within bowshot of one another in Edinburgh's new town. We probably shared, it occurred to me now, a variety of more or less unconscious assumptions alien to anybody else in this crowded room.

One would have taken McKechnie to be a good deal older than his wife. He was stringy to the point of desiccation, a state of affairs suggesting nothing if not durability; short of authentic disaster on a motorway, he would infallibly celebrate his ninetieth if not his hundredth birthday. Although an unobtrusive man he was keen-eyed and nervously alert as many very shy people are; he suggested a formidably specialised creature, and I felt that a single glance at him would leave me disinclined to question Albert Talbert's persuasion that here was another A. E. Housman in our midst. Not, I imagine, that these two classical scholars were temperamentally akin. If McKechnie wasn't a man readily to conjure up warmth around him he had at least an impulse to try. I could see that he was anxious to make some genuine contact with me now. It was possible to feel that he was seeking means to this as he talked – thinking me out, as it were, as the problem currently on hand. This might well have been off-putting, but I don't think I took it that way. It was my duty to develop a cordial regard for Janet's second husband; my consciousness of this didn't seem off-putting either. I began to suspect that between McKechnie and myself there was some positive if tenuous bond going back quite a long way and having nothing to do with the fact (still strange to me) of his marriage. Perhaps we had each of us lurkingly admired something the other possessed. There would be a sort of bond in that. Or perhaps I was imagining things and had scarcely ever been in McKechnie's head. I had been an idle boy, day-dreaming when I wasn't simply fooling around. He had been a purposive and intellectually precocious child, unexampled – I don't doubt – in his command of Greek irregular verbs.

'Whenever I think of Ranald,' I said to Janet at a venture, 'I think of Greek irregular verbs. They positively chinked in his pocket – as if it was pocket-money day every day of the week.'

'They're the small change of juvenile erudition.' McKechnie was perfectly capable of responding to this sort of thing – although his sort of thing it was definitely not. He had a jerky manner of speaking, idiosyncratic and not unpleasant, as if his vocal apparatus was powered by some intricate system of tiny springs. 'Whenever I think of Duncan, I think of the most thumping and staggering lies.'

'The Secret Service Boy,' Janet said. I could see that she was pleased with the way this encounter was going. I was also struck by something else. Long ago I had provided her with an enormous amount of information about myself, but had probably suppressed any mention of the main activity of my tenth year, which had consisted in offering to my form-mates as gospel truth the high adventures perpetually befalling the Secret Service Boy out of school. McKechnie must have told Janet about this. And now a sudden vision of the McKechnies sitting by their fireside and giving a little time to exchanging memories of me was accompanied by a moment of poignant feeling which I should have found it difficult to define as either pleasure or pain.

'And now,' Janet was saying, 'Duncan has produced a new tall story. He claims to have come upon a long-lost cousin, here in Oxford, who is an authority on Anglo-Saxon pots.'

'A girl called Fiona Petrie,' I said. 'A second cousin – or what's called more precisely a first cousin once removed.'

'How very interesting!' McKechnie said politely. 'I know her name. She gave one of the British Academy's lectures last year, and I remember somebody commenting on how young she was to receive the invitation. It was partly, I believe, by way of compliment to J. B. Timbermill. One thinks of him as belonging to a past age, and Miss Petrie must have been one of the last of his pupils.' McKechnie was now on familiar and congenial ground. 'A sad case,' he concluded unexpectedly.

'Timbermill's, you mean?'

'Yes, indeed. A notable scholar, it seems. Unchallenged in his field.

But he ran off the rails somehow, and produced a long mad book – a kind of apocalyptic romance. Did you know him, Duncan?'

'I do know him. He lives in Oxford still, and I saw him not long ago. He was one of my tutors – long before he taught Fiona Petrie. I hope *she* won't run off the rails.' Having seen that McKechnie was upset at having seemed to disparage somebody I turned out to approve of, I was casting round for a diversion. 'Fiona, you see, has formed a dangerous association, and may be corrupted. She's living with a novelist.' This sounded comically wrong. 'She shares a house with another girl, called Margaret Mountain, who has published a novel and is working on another one. Not that I think my cousin will readily be lured away from scholarship. She seems the real thing to me.'

'I'm afraid I haven't read Miss Mountain's book, or even heard of it.' McKechnie spoke apologetically, as is customary among the learned when this sort of nescience has to be avowed.

'I haven't read it either. I don't even know its title.'

'I've read it,' Janet said. 'It's called *The Orrery.* I don't remember why. Perhaps the characters are supposed to revolve round one another in an extremely complicated way, as if governed by clockwork.'

'Is it highly cerebral?' My recollection of the severity of Miss Mountain's manner must have prompted this question.

'Well, you do feel she's thought it all out. But it's full of searing and irregular passions.'

'Good heavens!' This description amused me. 'Such as?'

'The principal character is a musician or a painter – I've forgotten which – who longs to go to bed with his aunt. He's in a frenzy about it. Nowadays writers of first novels are often amazingly young. Perhaps Margaret Mountain was barely twenty when she started working on the thing. We can all manage a certain amount of absurdity at that age.'

'Yes,' I said, and wondered whether this hard saying had been offered to me advisedly. McKechnie may have wondered too, since it was he who somehow gave the impression of being responsible for a moment's silence. He then grabbed a fresh topic.

'I feel remiss,' he said to me, 'at having been so little in college lately. I do greatly enjoy coming in to dine. But our living so far out, and

Janet's having been away from home, has made it a little difficult to organise just lately.'

I managed some reply to this unconvincing speech. McKechnie's impulse towards friendliness was released only when some actual social situation had been firmly contrived for him; without that, his reclusive side – the withdrawn scholar syndrome, it might be called – remained on top. He had probably been hauled along to this party now.

But any further awkwardness the conversation might have run into was obviated by Tommy Penwarden's joining us. In honour of Mrs Gender's entertainment our librarian had donned somewhat formal attire, and as the garments evidently belonged to an even earlier period of his life than those he wore every day his appearance of being in some unnatural state of distension was more marked than usual; he might have been a small boy painfully inflated through an injudicious orgy of ginger pop. He proved, however, to be in a condition not of physical discomfort but of gloomy indignation.

'I can hear them coming back,' he said. 'The demonstrators, as they call themselves. They seem not to have spent very long in their unmannerly bellowing at the ladies. The whole disruption is becoming totally scandalous, and the university's handling of it increasingly inept.'

'One hears different views expressed,' McKechnie said mildly, 'and I fear I haven't given the situation as much thought as it plainly calls for. May I ask, Penwarden, in what you yourself consider the ineptitude to lie?'

'In this intolerable nonsense of the university's setting up now one and now another comic opera version of a court of law. You may not know'—Penwarden turned to Janet, apparently as an immigrant likely to be uninformed on the Oxford scene—'you may not know that, historically, the university has the undoubted right to conduct quasi-judicial proceedings. There are all sorts of distorted views of what that means. I once had a pupil who seriously believed that the Vice-Chancellor has the power to hang wrong-doers from Folly Bridge. His persuasion was erroneous, I am sorry to say. But a court there can be, with Queen's Counsel briefed to appear before it, if anybody has a fancy that way. And such a court is sitting at the moment, amid every circumstance of indignity and absurdity.' Penwarden paused to take breath, and appeared about to resume. McKechnie, however, raised a nervous but resolute hand, thus indicating that he had an immediate point to make.

'One moment, please,' he said, again in his mildest manner. 'All this must remain very much an open question, so far as I am concerned. I am shockingly ignorant about it, as I said. So do tell me this. Is it your opinion that these unusual disorders in the streets are not such as to be dealt with suitably by any process of law whatever?'

'Nothing of the kind!' Penwarden seemed to turn puffier still from some internal pressure as he enunciated this rebuttal; his cheeks were like a trumpeter's; I suddenly noticed that his spectacles, like his jacket and waistcoat, looked a size too small for him. 'The city police should do their proper duty, and bring the entire unruly crowd before the beaks. They'd then end up before a judge of the high court, committed for making an affray, or whatever it may be called. They'd learn something, and we'd be rid of a confounded nuisance.'

'And yet,' McKechnie said, 'it would be satisfactory to feel assured that sufficient attention is being paid to the root cause of our difficulties. Who is to blame for them? It can scarcely be in any large measure these malleable young people themselves. External influences are, of course, at play upon them; we live in a period of social instability, and so forth. But ought we not to begin by looking nearer home? I am inclined to think that the people most at fault are the college tutors.'

The majority of the men now in Mrs Gender's drawing-room were tutors, so a certain boldness attended McKechnie's speech. Penwarden didn't care for it.

'Are you among those,' he demanded, 'who lay most of our troubles at the door of what they call those damned boarding- houses?'

'Most certainly not!' McKechnie, in his turn, produced an indignant disclaimer. 'But it is surely undeniable that college tutors, unhappily, are subject nowadays to a great deal of distraction. They carry novel administrative burdens. They are many of them in demand by an enlarged and extramural public through the instrumentality of what people call the media. They often feel obliged, through a supposed professional exigency, to make constant, diffuse, and even supererogatory contributions to the scholarship of their subject.'

McKechnie paused in this civil indictment. I reflected, not for the first time, that the men among whom my lot had suddenly fallen in middle-age owned resources of vocabulary and syntax exposing them to the hazard of talking like books. Yet their command of this was so effortless that some decent effect of the human and colloquial was commonly preserved.

'And as a consequence,' Penwarden took the opportunity to interpolate, 'they neglect their pupils?'

'Far from it. They are in general a most conscientious body of men. But they have let their syllabuses – the mass of mere information which students are expected to acquire in pursuit of a first degree – proliferate at the expense of any absorbing and satisfying intellectual discipline.'

'I confess to feeling a little on common ground with you there.' Penwarden, although managing this measured response, wasn't placated. Indeed, just as when, long ago in his library, the unspeakable Christopher Cressy had tucked the fateful letter-book under his arm, he was having detectable difficulty with his breathing. 'But it is generally supposed that such matters are ordered by boards and committees which are by no means exclusively composed of college tutors.'

'That is true; we are all, of course, at fault. The fact remains that in Oxford, considered as a place of education, the tutor remains the student's key man. It's up to the tutor to generate and sustain that intense intellectual excitement which you and I know to be the finer breath of all knowledge.'

I glanced at Janet and caught a gleam of fun in her eye. But her amusement, I could see, was at the expense of our total situation rather than of her husband. When that mild and withdrawn man thus stood up to be counted she undoubtedly found the spectacle invigorating.

'And a further relevant point occurs to me,' McKechnie went on. 'Faculty by faculty, both in this university and others, there is said to be a marked difference in the incidence of obsessive political preoccupations. In the more severe sciences, where people have to keep thinking hard to hold their place at all, this kind of agitating, and marching around, and occupying the offices of busy people and so forth apparently makes comparatively little headway. It's when you come to the woolly and light-weight subjects that you gain recruits. The mere lores and superstitions and parlour studies: geography and economics and sociology and English literature. Oh! I beg your pardon.'

McKechnie's sudden dismay was very agreeable, and even Penwarden managed to laugh at it. One of my recent discoveries had been that the wisdom of Oxford University saw Modern European Drama as falling much within the field of English Literature, and this made me an 'English don'. But I had no disposition to take umbrage at McKechnie's momentary failure in fact. I did feel, however, that I ought to rally him in some way.

'But, Ranald,' I said, 'isn't it something rather primitive that you propose? It used simply to be called keeping their nose to the grindstone.'

'Only so that a few sparks may fly.'

This repartee pleased Janet; she glanced at me quickly, expecting more; it was as if she liked the idea of her husband and myself in some sort of amicable antagonism.

'Intellectual excitement,' I said, 'is undeniably quite splendid, of course. We all wish we could experience it every morning in our bath. Yet there's something almost servile, it seems to me, in the whole business of driving young people along the hard narrow road of competitive examinations. You can't really want nothing but that for them – however exciting clever tutors might make it – full time? It's not a liberal idea at all. Don't all those chaps of yours – Aristotle and Plato and that crowd – assert that free citizens have not only a right to political activity but also a positive duty to engage in it?'

Rather unexpectedly, McKechnie responded to this by throwing up both hands in a nervous and comical gesture. He was saying, more or less, that there was no serious coping with such harmless nonsense as

I was dishing out. And his gesture was familiar. I hadn't seen it since we were boys together, but it suddenly came back to me with a whole setting out of the past. The worn wooden floor was spotted with ink; initials and rude rhymes were carved on the desks and benches; there was a smell of blackboard chalk in the air; through open windows came the concerted shouts of boys smaller than ourselves marking some triumph in their bat-and-ball game. I was arguing – with McKechnie, who was what we called the Dux of the school, and in the presence of other of my betters – about I don't know what. And an idle fingering of popular books on the glories of Greece and the grandeurs of Rome had armed me with some such debating point as I had now made – one just short of the frivolous, and baffling to a serious mind.

One makes up a good deal of one's past. But this, I saw, could scarcely be a false memory, since something had flashed between McKechnie and myself that spoke of his recalling it too. We were both laughing – to the perplexity of Penwarden, who thus saw an almost acrimonious debate dissolve in mirth.

Anthea Gender's party was breaking up with an unmetropolitan abruptness, since it was the hour of the day at which all Oxford moves to an exigent clock. The colleges dine early – and did so, I believe, even before it was by servants that such matters were ordered. Within the next twenty minutes a substantial proportion of the academic guests would be seated at their high tables – the husbands among them having parted from wives who would return home and there discuss with their children what Mabel Bedworth, that stout feminist, called the family poached egg. I had as yet no means of determining what degree of domestic infelicity this slightly uncouth social custom occasioned. A surprising number of Oxford wives turn out to be recruited from Oxford – or, if not Oxford, Cambridge – daughters; they have been habituated to the arrangement; perhaps they set a tone.

I promised to lunch with the McKechnies at an early date.

The invitation came from Janet, and her husband's enthusiasm for it extended to his bringing a crumpled envelope from his pocket and attempting a sketch-map of the route to their dwelling. This discovered itself as being in some rural back-of-beyond in darkest Berkshire; the final turnings to it seemed intricate and confusing; McKechnie clarified the problem they presented by a liberal employment of the letters of the Greek alphabet, together with an explanation of these *sigla* in the margin. I took the point of this performance to be again reminiscent; he was making fun of the puerile mockery I used to direct upon boys more classically accomplished than myself.

On the walk back to college I fell in with Buntingford, who had been among our domestic contingent at Mrs Gender's party. He remarked to me with satisfaction that Tommy Penwarden had appeared to be 'in good gloomy form'.

'Well, yes,' I said. 'He was for Draconian measures against our juvenile Jacquerie.'

'Tommy would be. But they're not infuriated peasants, you know, although they dress that way. They're Jacobins, my boy, educated beyond their station or prospects. And that's much more dangerous.'

'Perhaps so, Adrian. Incidentally, I wonder whether Tommy knows how stout the Provost is being about those blessed Blunderville Papers? The other day I went on a kind of diplomatic mission with Edward to a place called Otby. I don't know if you've heard of it.'

'Otby I Isn't it a house your crony Tony Mumford, now Marchpayne, is due to inherit?'

'That's right. It's rather complicated to explain, but we were on the trail of the missing letter-book. And I can report that Edward is prepared to make enormous efforts – sustain untold indignities, indeed – to secure its return.'

'You must be joking.'

'Well, that's how it appeared.'

'How more than odd! Wheels within wheels, Duncan. And Tommy ought certainly to be grateful. He's obsessed with that cobwebby affair. Nothing would please him more than to hear that Christopher Cressy had been caught robbing a bank and clapped in the Scrubs.'

'Quite so – yet he has insisted to me that Cressy is a man of enchanting address.'

'Queer convention, isn't it? Dog-fights galore, but instant solidarity on the nice-chap front.'

'Yes, I do find it queer, Adrian. But I suppose it's the civilised thing.'

'Nothing of the kind. Politicians go in for it like mad, and there's nothing civilised about *them*. And I used to meet it, when I was more or less a kid, among Foreign Office types. They'd insist on the total charm of their opposite numbers in other countries who professionally might be industriously endeavouring to deluge the world in blood. And small things with great we may compare, don't you think?'

'No, I don't. It's the same Inner Ring ethos, I suppose. But academics – I hate to say it – strike me as a thoroughly blameless crowd.'

'*O saneta simplicitas! Just you wait.*'

# XII

M Y ROOMS WERE now becoming a good deal frequented by two distinct species of junior members of the university. The one lot consisted of those graduate students whose researches into more or less modern drama I was expected to supervise or give advice on. These were a gentle race, living for the most part on exiguous grants, desperately worried over the grim state of the market job-wise, considerately trying to dissimulate these distresses, and most impressively absorbed in their subjects. I had very little notion of how I was getting on with them or what use I was being. As most of them − whatever their degree of ability − had more of the scholar's temperament than I had, I was frequently reduced by them to a state of humility of an unwholesome and nervy sort. My other species of visitors were younger, rather more care-free, and much more aggressive: undergraduates − again from all over the university − who, like Nick Junkin, judged ceaseless theatrical activity to constitute a sufficient higher education in itself. My relations with this agreeable but exhausting tribe were informal and unofficial − which simply meant that they dispensed with their seniors' polite notes and anxious telephone calls, and blew in as they pleased. It was all quite fun and undeniably what I'd signed up for. But I did remind myself at times that eight weeks was the limit of full-scale assault. Plot, responsible for the light refreshments it was proper to offer these conferring or inquiring or demanding persons, probably had the same thought.

One body of people, however, never came near me. These were my colleagues, and here was one of those conventions of the place which

I was being left to find out for myself. It obtained, if not quite rigidly, even at after-dinner hours. Conversation (and compotation) was something that happened in common room, and when people did get together in each other's sets it was usually to listen to music or stare at television. During the day a certain amount of communication took place by telephone, but this was limited because some of the older fellows (including Talbert and Lempriere) refused to have such an instrument in their rooms, judging summons and interruption by bell or buzzer at a caller's whim to be an uncivil practice to be discountenanced in a polite society. It was my impression that even those who declared the prejudice absurd substantially agreed with it. As a result people were perpetually writing notes to one another, and I don't think there was a man in college who would not have had to be adjudged highly skilful at rapid and succinct performance in that medium.

This being so distinctly one of what the Provost would have called 'our ways', I was surprised one morning when Jimmy Gender walked in on me at breakfast. The irruption was not achieved without ceremony. Plot, who could never so much as dodge into my room to replace an egg-cup without knocking, in this instance simply flung open the door and said 'Mr Gender' in an unnaturally loud voice – a nuance of behaviour in dealing with one entitled to command the *grande entree* which he had presumably acquired through watching the comportment of butlers and majordomos in television plays of high life.

Gender was in a dark suit, wore a bowler hat, and carried a tightly furled umbrella. It was evidently his London day. A number of my colleagues maintained this weekly institution, in one manner or another combining duty and some more recreative side of life. Gender, I imagined, lunched at his club, attended private views, went to auction sales at Sotheby's or Christie's, and frequented one or another of the inns of court in the discreet furtherance of the future careers of his more promising pupils. He had called on me on his way to the railway station, and he started off on a note of anxious apology.

'That dead boy's brother.' Gender spoke at his quietest. 'Peter Lusby.

I've been seeing him, Duncan. And I'm just a little worried.'

'I'm sorry to hear it. But he can't be other than a bit of a headache, I'd have thought. And other people have been perturbed about him. Arnold Lempriere, for instance.'

'Yes, of course. It seems you mentioned something of the sort to Anthea.'

'So I did – at her very enjoyable party. Near the beginning of term Arnold marched me round Oxford, haranguing me on the college's moral duty to take young Lusby on.'

'He may well be right. But he hasn't put the point to me.' Gender was not too pleased. 'Arnold is becoming just a shade eccentric, wouldn't you say?'

'Perhaps so. He was certainly in one of those "Say nothing to anybody" moods that afternoon.'

It's the dead Lusby he's mentioned to me, not the living one. And that's because he's turned rather odd about that tiresome Mumford boy. He professes to hold a poor opinion of the Mumfords over several generations, but is obviously keen in a devious sort of way that we should keep the present brat on the strength. That's how Paul Lusby has cropped up in his talk. He says the lad's suicide must have been such a terrible shock to Ivo Mumford that it wouldn't be fair not to give him the rest of this year to recover. What do you think of that, Duncan?'

'Not a great deal, I'm afraid.'

'Quite so. But about the younger Lusby. Of course he's a headache – and now there's something extra and unexpected. I oughtn't to bother you with it – only you were so kind to him when he came exploring the college, and did have a chance to size him up. So may I tell you about this development? Not that it perhaps deserves to be called quite that. It's entirely tenuous – which is just what makes it troublesome.'

'Go ahead. And will you have some coffee, Jimmy? It's still hot.'

'That's most terribly kind of you.' Gender produced this extravagant assertion with his customary grace. 'But I've just bolted my breakfast, as a matter of fact. So do you yourself go ahead. Well, it's like this.

Charles Atlas and I decided to have Lusby up for early interview. You know the system.'

I'm afraid I don't.'

'Of course not. I'm so sorry. It's just a practice we have developed of seeing a few schoolboys ahead of the entrance examination on the strength of their school record and 'A' levels and so forth. If we judge them to be genuinely impressive we offer them a firm place at the college straight away. It began as a method of preventing Cambridge getting ahead of us – but I needn't explain all that. We call this small group of candidates the supermen.'

'You and Charles had Peter Lusby up before you as a superman?'

'Of course the boy can't be called that – which made the move a shade delicate. It always has the appearance, you know, of a short-cut in, which means we have to go carefully. We'd think twice, for instance, of having some don's son, or an old member's son, present himself as a superman. As Tutor for Admissions, Charles is careful to avoid possible misconceptions as to what's going on.'

'I'm sure he is. But Lusby is at least an old member's brother.'

'Quite so.' Gender said this after what might have been taken for a moment's deep thought, much as if I had presented him with a highly perspicacious remark. 'The fact is, we'd both made up our minds about Peter Lusby – about what course it's proper to adopt, I mean. He has gained the modest qualifications for university matriculation; he has a claim on us of a very unusual – indeed, of a quite exceptional – sort. We decided the honourable thing was to admit him through a channel more or less formally acknowledging the claim's validity, and chance his proving up to taking a degree. I don't know whether you'd approve.'

'It would be cheek in me, Jimmy, either to approve or disapprove. But I'm glad – and simply because I liked the boy. I will say he struck me as a staunch sort of lad – and a trier.'

'Good. And Charles and I were both encouraged in that view – up to a point.'

'Jimmy, just what happened at your blessed interview?' As I asked this I realised it was graceless of me to sound a note of impatience.

Dons – I must have been thinking in a juvenile fashion – are a fussy crowd, much given to hesitating before molehills as if the Andes or Himalayas were confronting them. If two experienced men had made up their minds about young Lusby they should back their hunch and not start vacillating over something that Gender had characterised as entirely tenuous. But this was a deplorable thought in a new fellow of the college, and I tried to retrieve myself. 'For instance,' I went on, 'did the boy have a clear notion about reading law, and where it was going to take him? Or was it all vague to him, except that he must do what his brother had done?'

'He was quite good on all that – quite clear-headed. At the lowest, you might say he knew the answers. He's been to the courts; he reads the *Times* law reports; all the proper things. Of course he'd have had a lot of the gen from Paul, but he did strike us as uncommonly well-informed. Would you have called him well-informed, Duncan?'

'No.'

'Well, they must be working hard on him at school. A certain amount of what he said came rather pat, of course. But that's to be expected from well-taught schoolboys. Charles must keep an eye on that school; it sounds surprisingly tiptop.'

'So what, Jimmy? What went wrong?'

'The boy wasn't candid with us. You might almost call it not quite straight.'

'That surprises me very much indeed.'

'We both felt it – and it wasn't something we wanted to feel, heavens knows! Things were going well, and then suddenly there was this cagey and evasive effect.'

'Nothing of the sort registered with me, Jimmy.' I thought I was entitled to say this firmly; I'd been credited, after all, with having had a useful opportunity to size Peter Lusby up. 'In just what context did this unfortunate impression emerge?'

'It was quite late on. We'd been pretty testing with the lad one way and another, and Charles was moving to relieve the pressure. A little concluding bit about spare time and hobbies and so on. "What have you been doing lately out of school?" That sort of thing.'

'And what had he?'

'He wouldn't say. In fact, he dropped straight into panic. It was most uncomfortable. It was as if we'd taken him unawares and he could only flounder.'

'Dash it all, Jimmy, need you call that being not quite straight? Perhaps he frequents railway stations and writes down the numbers of the diesel engines – and realised it would sound incredibly childish if he told you about it.'

'It didn't sound quite like that.' This time, Gender spoke so very quietly that I knew I was being reproached. He had practiced at the bar, and was entitled to regard himself as unlikely to get this sort of thing wildly wrong. 'And East End boys, one supposes, indulge in slightly less blameless spare-time activities now and then.'

'I don't doubt they do.' I may well have been staring at Gender in astonishment, so much had this flicker of class prejudice taken me unawares. And I found it had also irritated me quite a bit. 'Would it have been your sense of the matter,' I asked, 'that Lusby is the sort of person who might go Paki-bashing?' And I might almost have added, 'Or on a gang bang, like Tony Mumford's boy?' had I not remembered that Ivo had my word that I'd keep silent about that.

'No, of course not.' Gender in his turn was not unreasonably surprised. 'But there are all sorts of wretched possibilities. Pot smoking, for example.'

'But when I cast my own eye on the courts I seem to notice that, so far as juveniles are concerned, drugs are a middle-class thing. In a working class it's precocious drinking that makes all the running at present. Perhaps Peter Lusby's a young drunk.'

'Duncan, you're getting this all wrong.' Gender looked most unhappy. 'I'm desperately concerned to see this boy as in the clear and fit to come up to the college. If he did, we'd work hard to see him through. But we can't risk two crashes in that family. And, well, there was this small unaccountable thing. He ended up by saying something quite odd. That there was something he didn't feel at liberty to talk about.'

'In connection with how he spends his spare time? Dash it all, isn't he entitled to a bit of private life, just like you and me? He may go and look after a grandmother in a state of senile dementia. That kind of thing – if I may unload another scrap of common sociology on you – is thought of as an awful disgrace among the sort of people I'm assuming Peter Lusby comes from.'

'Yes, I know. And I suppose I'm being a fool, Duncan. It's just that I distrust a whiff of mystery in what's already a tricky situation.'

'That's perfectly proper, and I've no business being critical. But – look here – would you let me go and try to find out?'

'Let you? I'd be grateful for any help whatever. That's why I've come in and taken up your time.'

'I do feel that, if only in the most fleeting way, I did establish a kind of relation of confidence with that boy. It might just stretch to having a go at him, or at his people. It wouldn't be much fun, setting up as an amateur private eye. I'd only dream of it because I feel – if you'll forgive me – that there may be a mare's-nest element in the affair. So do you think that I could, at least with some shred of decency, manage a small job of work that neither you nor Charles could properly do? What do you think?'

'What we could do, Duncan, is to rely on you entirely.'

'Then that's it. I've a couple of men coming in this morning. But I'll take the lunch-time train.'

So I found myself eating a bumpy meal with British Rail, and trying to give my tricky embassy some preliminary thought. I was clear that I must at once declare myself – to Peter, or even to his parents, if it was his parents that I encountered first. Even so, I'd be a kind of spy. As I faced this, much misgiving assailed me. And I was still of this doubtful mind when I arrived in Bethnal Green before a block of flats, old rather than new, fronting a small public park full of swings and seesaws and climbing-frames. The building was so large that on passing through a passage-way from the street I found myself in a spacious quad. The word came to me at once before this familiar spectacle of grass, two or three small trees, staircases at regular intervals round about. In another part of London Barker Buildings – thus surprisingly academic in suggestion – would have been called Barker Mansions, and been essentially similar in architectural conception but pitched to incomes four-fold beyond those obtaining in the Lusby world.

I rang the Lusbys' bell: theirs was a ground-floor flat. The door was opened to me at once – and to an instant banishing of any sense of spaciousness that the exterior design of the building might suggest. The woman standing before me wasn't generously framed; on the contrary, she was small and spare; but the passage in which she stood was so exiguous that I couldn't see how, were I to be admitted, we could both occupy it at once. For the moment, at least, the woman gave no ground, and when I caught her glance it suggested a swift suspicion the more striking because, at a glance, she didn't seem made that way. She may have been wondering whether I had come about the rent or the rates or the gas, or possibly to sell her an encyclopaedia guaranteed to set her children on the road to wealth and fame. She looked to me the sort of woman who is likely to be a better hand at that than any reference book – at least if for 'wealth and fame' one substituted expressions more consonant with a sober and moral view of things. This was undoubtedly the mother of the boy who had munched my biscuits and been careful about the crumbs.

'Mrs Lusby?' I said. 'My name is Duncan Pattullo, and I come from Oxford. I met your son Peter when he was there some time ago. And as I know he hopes to come to the college where I work I felt I'd like to call and ask him how he's getting on.'

I suppose that with these words I was keeping to a bargain with myself. They said nothing untrue. They were disingenuous, all the same, and I wondered at once whether Mrs Lusby found them so. Her moment's silence was apprehensive rather than suspicious. But when she spoke it wasn't in any sort of agitation.

'That is very kind of you,' she said. 'But I'm afraid Peter isn't at home. He'll be working in the public library. His school sends him there in the afternoon, now that he's one of the older boys and going for his Oxford entrance. And my husband's out as well. He's disabled – one of the hundred per cent war-disabled – but has light work of an afternoon and evening at the cinema. In the foyer, it is. Only what they like is that he can go in and make the children behave. He has a way with them. But won't you please come in?'

I thanked Mrs Lusby and followed her into a sittingroom. It was very small, and being provided with all the prescriptive furniture made it appear smaller still.

'Peter won't be long,' Mrs Lusby said. 'For a boy of his age he's very regular in his ways. Can I make you a cup of tea?'

'Thank you. I'd like that very much.'

This reply had the effect of taking Mrs Lusby quickly into her kitchen. Perhaps it gave her an opportunity to collect herself. I was left standing between an over-stuffed sofa and an over-stuffed chair – and not without a fear that I was going to exhibit a kind of physical awkwardness. I looked about me and then sat down. As I did so I became aware of what was the dominant object in the room. It hung over the mantelpiece: the photograph of a boy, blown up from a snapshot, and coloured, one could feel, by a conjecturing hand. There could be no doubt who it was. And when Mrs Lusby reappeared I spoke on impulse and at once.

'Mrs Lusby, is that Paul?'

'Yes, Paul.' Mrs Lusby answered quietly, but then produced a small determined rattle of tea-cups. 'Don't you think it's like him?'

'I never knew Paul. I haven't been back at the college long enough.'

'I see.' Mrs Lusby was disappointed. People who had known Paul interested her much more than people who had not. It being chiefly Peter who was in my head, I was inclined to forget what a short space of months had elapsed since the elder boy's death. 'But you'll know,' Mrs Lusby said, 'how Provost Pococke came to the funeral. And Mr Gender, who had been Paul's teacher. Then a Mr Bedworth, rather a quiet gentleman, came home with us – just for a few minutes, because he wanted to tell us how much Paul had been liked.' Mrs Lusby paused on this, and I murmured what I could. 'And some weeks later,' she went on, 'there was a little service in the college chapel: a memorial service, they called it. Peter came with us to that. It was in the holidays, of course, but several of Paul's friends came back for it specially. Provost Pococke read the lesson. One John four, seven to the end: "Beloved let us love one another, for love is of God." Paul's life was short, Mr Pattullo. But we gave thanks for it.' Mrs Lusby paused again. 'And then,' she added, 'Mrs Pococke gave us tea.'

It wasn't exactly true that all this seemly conduct on my colleagues' part had been actively concealed from me. But at least nobody had mentioned it – not even Jimmy Gender when he knew that I was setting off for the Lusby home. And what this formidable standard of reticence had veiled from me didn't make the present situation any easier – a fact borne out by Mrs Lusby's next remarks.

'All that kindness, Mr Pattullo, from learned gentlemen with so much on their minds. And from young people too, where thoughtlessness is common enough. It makes us feel we have a connection with the college. For that service – I forgot to tell you this – there was a printed sheet with the college arms, and "Paul Lusby Scholar of the College" underneath them.'

Again making what reply I could, I thought of the Mumfords, and of their arrogant assumption that an intermittent tenancy over four generations of certain rooms in Surrey Quad constituted a 'connection' carrying very large privileges indeed. But that was an irrelevance. Everything said by Peter Lusby's mother so far simply made it the more incumbent on me to get the boy's situation sorted out.

'And it has been a great thing that Peter should have his own chance,' Mrs Lusby said. 'We're sure it's right he should try – feeling as he does that he owes it to Paul. It goes very deep with him, and I wouldn't say my husband and I have any full understanding of it. But we respect it as being something on the spiritual side of life. Or we hope it's that. It might be pride – which is something religion warns us against.'

I avoided, I trust not disrespectfully, any invitation to theological discussion this apprehensiveness may have carried. What I wanted first to get clear was the degree of the Lusby's understanding of the implications of Peter's recent interview.

'I'm sure Peter is working very hard for the entrance examination,' I said. 'Did the college interview he had the other day encourage him?'

'He hasn't said much.' Mrs Lusby's voice had suddenly sharpened in anxiety. 'But then he's often rather a silent boy.'

'How do these things happen, Mrs Lusby? I'm rather new to the system.'

'I think it's so that some boys can know early about there being a vacancy for them – I suppose the ones the college feels sure about – and then they can go on with the right work for when they start there. Peter was very excited when his headmaster told him there was a letter saying he must go to be interviewed. He said it was a great thing, and was quite keyed up about it. But he was very quiet when he came back – and very quiet he has remained.' For the first time, Mrs Lusby hesitated. 'Mr Pattullo, I'm afraid it didn't go well. And he's working so hard still! Long hours away from us, and comes home dead-beat. This morning his father told him it was early days to be hearing anything. But he said no – his headmaster had told him that if you get a place this way word of it comes to the school at once.'

'Mrs Lusby, something did go a little wrong, and I very much want to clear it up with Peter, if I can. I think you've guessed it's something like that I've come about.'

'Yes – and you're Peter's friend.'

'I'm certainly that. Only you must understand that I have no share at all in this whole matter of admissions. I can only try to get some facts sorted out, and brought to the notice of my colleagues who are charged with the work.'

Mrs Lusby responded to this with no more than a nod, and I realised that she had been listening intently for something else.

'It's Peter,' she said. 'He's putting his bicycle away in the shed.'

While talking to Peter's mother I ought to have been thinking ahead. But if I had failed to do so, and had no plan at all for coping with the boy, it was at least partly because there wasn't the slightest telling how he would cope with me. If he really felt his private life to have been violated by some innocent badgering on the part of Charles Atlas, he might turn out uncommonly touchy at the sight of me. I had a moment of panic in which I felt my whole venture to have been misconceived. And then Peter was in the room – in this tiny room in which three people could scarcely stand beyond arm's reach of one another.

'Here is Mr Pattullo from Oxford, Peter.'

Mrs Lusby spoke, I think, from a feeling that her son, immobile in the doorway, was remaining improperly silent. Her words suggested, rather wildly, that without them my presence might have escaped his observation.

'Good afternoon, sir.' Having said so much, Peter waited. He was even paler than I remembered him, and there were dark smudges under his eyes: this and the black tangle of his hair lent an incongruously theatrical suggestion to his appearance, so that I found myself wondering what part he had sustained in *Measure for Measure* by Shakespeare. But he was only a tired and strained schoolboy, his confidence shaken – and not likely to be restored by my untoward turning up in Bethnal Green. Or not initially. The ultimate issue of the encounter was up to me. But in fact I somehow didn't feel discouraged. He was up against it, and there was something about his bearing in that condition that I liked the look of. I told myself that he was tougher than his dead brother seemed to have been, even if not nearly so clever.

'Hullo, Peter,' I said. 'I haven't come just to pay a polite call, but because I think there's something on the record we must get straight. Would you say that's so?'

'Perhaps.' Peter waited again. He was looking at me with a level and stony glance. And his mother again seemed to feel there was a silence that must be filled.

'Did you get a good afternoon's work done in the public library, dear? I was telling Mr Pattullo about that.'

'I got some work done, I suppose.' Peter hesitated. 'It's quite a good library for my sort of thing.' He frowned suddenly, so that his dark eyebrows came together with a narrow furrow between them. He was dissatisfied with himself, dissatisfied with what he had just said. An odd fellow-feeling came to me. I remembered how I'd said to his mother, 'I felt I'd like to call and ask him how he's getting on'. Peter Lusby didn't relish being driven into disingenuous speech. He'd brought together two remarks each true in itself, but constituting a prevarication when juxtaposed. He'd been in no public library that afternoon.

It isn't possible that at this point I had even a glimmer of what was going on. And the situation didn't look encouraging. Even so, I had a faint sense of light at the end of the tunnel.

'Peter,' I said, 'I've walked you through the college, haven't I? We'll be quits if you'll walk me round your park now. Will you?'

'Yes, of course – if you want to. But, please, I don't want just to be chatted up.'

If these words perturbed me it was because I had last heard them – or words very like them – from Ivo Mumford. I could only hope that this encounter was going to go better than that one had done.

'Then come on,' I said, and turned to thank Mrs Lusby for my tea and bid her good-bye. I wanted to make it clear that I wasn't settling in on the family for the evening. Poor Mrs Lusby's anxiety was now at a pitch constituting an unfavourable element in the affair. And Peter himself, I felt, breathed a little more freely when we were out in the street. As we entered the park I had a shot at catching on to this slight relaxation. 'When I was a boy,' I said, 'there used to be an advertisement in the papers for correspondence courses of some sort. It always carried a photograph of a very benevolent-looking elderly man. He was smiling out at you in an encouraging way. And there was a caption saying, "Let me be your father". We used to repeat that to each other as a kind of joke. But it's a tricky role.'

Whether it was judicious or not, this entirely authentic anecdote at least acted as a trigger. Peter stopped, faced me, and threw at me words suddenly filled with passion.

'What business was it of his?' he cried. 'What business at all? I'm not a kid! Can't I have something to myself? I didn't expect it. I hadn't thought. It caught me out. I made a bloody, bloody fool of myself. And after it had all seemed to go so decently. Oh, damn, damn!'

'Peter, I know what you're talking about. And I know that somehow it isn't just a storm in a teacup, although it sounds a bit like that. Listen. I was asked about my miscellaneous doings at my own interview long ago. It's a regular thing, and supposed to show friendly interest. Perhaps dons keep it up ineptly when there's a new sort of relationship between old and young. It can have an irritating smack of "Let me be your father", I suppose.'

'What were they thinking of? What were they suspecting me of? They weren't just peering into my class, and all that. They knew all about that long ago. And they were such a decent crowd when—when we had death in the family.'

'Yes. And they weren't suspecting you of anything. But you shut up on them in a puzzling way, and it worries them. Dons are rather nervous people, I sometimes think.'

'*I'm* nervous. I went as if I'd robbed a bank. And I just refused to answer one question. I didn't have the sense even just to keep mum. I said something about not being allowed to talk about it. Could anything sound sillier? Not sinister, it seems to me – although that's what they seem to have made of it. Just silly.' Peter paused for a moment, and then walked on. 'Only, you see, it was true.'

'There doesn't seem to be much doubt about that.' I ventured to give Peter a sideways glance that wasn't all gravity and despair. 'Isn't this something we can get in perspective? Can't you tell *me?* I belong to the college. But I'm not one of those tutors and examiners. I'm kind of detached. So out with it, Peter.'

'No.'

Peter said this so quietly that I felt the issue was settled. We'd reached a point at which I seemed to be trying to force not merely his confidence but his conscience as well. So there was no further road that way. We continued our circuit of the park in silence. It wasn't a big place. We'd be back at our starting point within five minutes. And then, rather unexpectedly, Peter spoke again.

'What worries me most,' he said, 'is that perhaps it was a promise I oughtn't to have given. But somebody was being so kind and generous that I felt I had to. And he was quite, quite specific. "Say absolutely nothing to anyone," he said. Well, I haven't.'

Yeats's Happy Shepherd says that *words alone are certain good*. It's a shockingly extravagant claim. But at least working with words as one's job a little sharpens the ear. After a moment's sheer astonishment I realised that with one swift shove I'd be through.

'Peter Lusby!' I cried. 'Do you mean to say all this connects up with an old gentleman called Lempriere?'

'But I haven't said anything!' Peter's dismay was tragicomical. 'I can't think how—'

'Never mind. It doesn't matter. It doesn't matter a bit. And I could work it all out now, just sitting in a dark room. But listen. Anything you tell me about it in confidence I promise shall remain our secret and Mr Lempriere's.'

There was a moment's silence. I had leisure to reflect that this sort of undertaking appeared to be becoming rather my thing. Here was very much what I'd felt constrained to say to Ivo, in somewhat different circumstances, no time ago.

'I saw it as a secret,' Peter said slowly. 'But I didn't see it as involving lies. Of course it has. Even to my parents. All that about the public library. It's quite disgusting. But Mr Lempriere said it was entirely honourable and proper in itself.'

'Then so it was. He's that kind of man. But what has he been up to, Peter? Sending you to a crack coach?'

'A crack—oh, I see. Yes – a very, very good tutor in the West End. The best in England, Mr Lempriere said.' Peter reported this estimate with considerable solemnity. 'He's certainly being pretty marvellous. Only he laughs at Mr Lempriere – at Mr Lempriere's idea, I mean, that examiners are brutes you can be taught tricks about. I think he's probably right.'

'I think he probably is.' Peter, I was thinking, possessed an encouraging amount of good sense; rather more of it, perhaps, than his benefactor. And the barrier was pierced. Peter was eager to talk. He'd been bottling up rather a lot.

'I don't think Mr Lempriere was at the service for Paul, sir. But then, you see, he turned up at school, and saw the head, and took me out to lunch. He said he wanted me to have this coaching, quite privately, and wanted to pay for it. He said he happened to be quite well off, but I'd see that was just an agreeable irrelevance. I had to work that one out. He said he knew nothing about me, and that it was because of Paul. He said he'd liked Paul very much.'

'I see.' I was, in fact, seeing a good deal. The top liar in Washington, for one thing, had taken on a sudden reality. I judged it not improbable that Lempriere hadn't so much as known Paul Lusby's name until the day the boy died. But there was nothing spurious about his sense of what the college owed Peter, and he'd found his own distinctly wayward method of lending a hand.

'Sir – what happens now?'

'Nothing at all dramatic, Peter.' This direct question had been a matter of good sense again. 'You go on being taught by this thoroughly efficient chap, and then you sit the entrance examination. Everybody has to do that, you know, whether they've been promised a commoner's place or not. If they have, it's a matter of trying for a scholarship.'

'I couldn't remotely—'

'It doesn't matter a bit. Only do as well as you can.'

'I will. But about my parents—'

'What you tell your parents is your own affair.' There were limits to this business of digging Peter Lusby out of the difficulties Lempriere had not very judiciously created for him. 'But it's my guess you needn't now worry too much. And you'd better be off to your tea.'


I rang up the Genders from my club. Jimmy had just got home.

'Jimmy,' I said, 'this is Duncan. About young Lusby. I've seen him. He's in the clear.'

'He is?' Gender's voice was eager and reassuringly well- pleased. 'Just what—?'

'It's something I don't feel at liberty to talk about.'

'Good heavens, Duncan! Isn't that something I've heard before?'

'Yes, it is. And that's it.'

'Good.' Gender didn't hesitate for a second. 'We'll act.'

'The next post, Jimmy. If you can oblige me so far.'

'Right. It's for the Senior Tutor to send the letter. I'll ring up Cyril now. Shall you be dining?'

'No. I think I'll go to a theatre.'

'Enjoy it, Duncan. This has been most terribly good of you. We're most grateful.'

'Good-bye.' I rang off, and went into the club dining-room to get an early meal. I felt – childishly, I suppose – an enhanced regard for our Tutor in Law. He had accepted my verdict as if at the drop of his London hat.

# XIII

I N THE EVENING following this London venture I was the guest
of a man called Alexander Pentecost at a dining club of the
traditional Oxford sort that meets now in one college and now in
another according to who is host for the occasion. Pentecost was a
physicist, and as he had won a Nobel prize more or less in childhood
it was to be presumed that he was one of the most distinguished
scientists in the university. But he also owned a consuming interest in
the theatre. He was active in producing plays for the OUDS and for
college societies, and the highlight of his life appeared not to be the
occasion on which he was summoned to Sweden to be handed a
cheque or scroll or whatever by the king of that country, but one on
which he had successfully stormed the West End stage. It had been a
matter, I think, of propitious acquaintance with certain top stars
powerful in that area. But as the play had been the *Prometheus* of
Aeschylus, and as Prometheus may be regarded as the archetypal atom-
buster, a certain eclat no doubt attended its superintendence by so
highly nuclear a character. Pentecost was interesting to me because he
presented the odd spectacle of a supremely intelligent man (as he must
certainly have been) in whom there lurked a Nicolas Junkin who had
never grown up.

We had met several times without my having felt that he had any
designs on me in my professional character, but now this proved not
to be so. At least he had something to discuss, and he got going on it
over the champagne before we sat down at table. There was still
prejudice, he was maintaining, blowing around against the Junkins in

general. It was often asserted in senior common rooms that no human activity – not even playing cricket for the university – was more disastrously time-consuming than play-acting. As soon as a college began to do damned badly in the Examination Schools it started a witch-hunt in this regard. And it couldn't be said—could it?—that my own college was exactly at the head of the academic league-table. So was this sort of persecution going on there? He only wanted to know.

I said that on the general situation I didn't yet feel competent to pronounce, but that so far as the narrower issue went I was unaware of ducking-stools, let alone faggots, being prepared around me. On the contrary, the college subsidised juvenile dramatic aspirations with ready cash to a tune unimaginable in my own undergraduate days. We even allowed ourselves – and it was a much harder thing – to be bundled out of our hall for nights on end in the interest of staging in it theatrical ventures which sometimes proved extremely bizarre. Pentecost wasn't to mistake me. I was all for this more liberal and accommodating attitude. As for what militated against the success of the academic studies of the young – and again I was all for modest success being there achieved – I was perpetually being treated to all sorts of theories, the kind of distraction we were discussing being only one of them.

Pentecost said he was glad to hear it. But he didn't let up. Instead, he went into what I sensed as a routine about aristocratic education in the Elizabethan age. The great schoolmasters of that golden time had regularly encouraged skill in the actor's craft as a proper part of their curriculum; the same attitude had obtained in the great houses of England as well; there were recorded instances of former wards having instituted actions against their guardians – men puritanically inclined, perhaps – for having denied them, in this as in other particulars, the due education of a gentleman.

Not having heard of this evidence from the law courts, I asked for details. Pentecost produced them at once. He had got the whole thing up – I imagine without the slightest effort – and now gave me the benefit of that not inconsiderable aid to intellectual eminence which consists in the humble endowment of a photographic memory. This lasted us well through the dinner, and the attention Pentecost exacted from me made me slow to take stock of the company. I was the only man from my college, although one old member of it was present in the perplexing person of Lord Marchpayne. I say 'perplexing' because I was at first at a loss as to why Tony should have turned up – presumably as a guest, like myself – at such an unassuming academic jollification. Ministers of the Crown, I believed, were very busy people. And Tony's presence could scarcely be part of his campaign to have Ivo retained in residence – a matter with which none of the dons present could have any connection or concern. Then I remembered recently reading that the government was judged likely soon to undergo one of those 'shuffles' that English political mythology declares to be periodically essential for prolonging the tenure of administrations. Being in the Lords must make Tony's political life particularly tricky, and if his present job was wanted for somebody else it mightn't be easy to find him another Cabinet post which could reasonably be held by a peer. Perhaps – I didn't at all know – the Ministry of Education was one capable of being so regarded, in which case Tony might well be accepting a round of engagements designed to assert his keen interest in pedagogy at its every level. This would have been so like him that I was presently taking it for granted that I had found the key to the riddle.

So far, I'd had no more from him than a wink across the room, and had myself given more attention to something else. Entirely to my surprise, the host of the evening had turned out to be Christopher Cressy. This made me, in a formal sense, his guest at one remove, and I rather thought it also meant that he was paying for my dinner. I couldn't, indeed, be certain that this was the set-up, but the structure of the thing had that feel. Dining clubs like this one were a survival from more spacious days. With due permission asked, a man might bring along another man and there would be no thought of splitting bills. Cressy – so chilly at our first encounter – had welcomed me benignly on my arrival; had made a few remarks which, although conventionally polite, contrived an amusing turn of phrase; and had actually managed to keep his eyes on me in an interested way for twenty seconds on end. I tried to feel this as a gratifying promotion in his esteem. It seemed paltry to be speculating on whether he was paying for my entertainment or not.

'Cressy must have given thought to this meal,' the man on my other hand said when I had disengaged myself momentarily from Pentecost. 'It's what must be called serious dining, wouldn't you say?'

'Decidedly. And the company owns a certain gravity as well.'

'Indeed we do. This club is seldom gamesome. My name's Corlett. How do you do.'

'How do you do. My name's Pattullo. I'm Pentecost's guest.'

'So I see. And yes – gravity in every sense. We get up weightier than when we sat down. *Vino gravis* too, of course, although not to any point of indecorum. Do you like getting to bed early?'

'Moderately.'

'A pity. A sustained discussion ensued, and the club dispersed after midnight.'

'I beg your pardon?'

'It's what an enthusiastic secretary minuted of some meeting round about 1910. Nobody has ever ventured to drop the formula since.'

'Or to disperse until the small hours?'

'I wouldn't say that. Occasionally a bold spirit will wait for eleven o'clock, cry "Aha! The witching hour of twelve has struck", and reach for his muffler and galoshes.'

'What is sustainedly discussed?'

'A paper. Somebody reads a paper. Sometimes it's the host and sometimes not. About fish-names in mediaeval Spain, or recent developments in biblical exegesis in Holland, or the Yamato-E tradition of narrative scrolls in twelfth century Japan.'

'I see. Can one do a bit of homework? Is one told of the subject in advance?'

'Oh, no. Everybody's likely to know something, of course.'

'Of course.' I hope I looked round with respect at a company so erudite as this must be. 'What's your own subject?' I asked at a venture.

'International liquidity,' the man called Corlett said. 'I'm an economist.'

We went into another room for coffee and whatever further drinks we had a mind to. The lighting was dim, and there was a spread of sofas and chairs of the capacious leathery sort – the rich relations of Mrs Lusby's three-piece suite. The dominant suggestion was of comfortable repose. Several members of the club, happily provided with brandy and cigars, closed their eyes and sank back into obscurity with the deep sighs of men relaxing after toil. A very old man, making use of spectacles tethered to him by a broad silk ribbon, contrived some inaudible dealings with a minute book; he was presumably reminding his fellow-members that at their last meeting a sustained discussion had taken place.

At this point there was a short break, occasioned by Cressy's need to make additionally sure of the comfort of his guests. He made a circuit of the room, and it was again curious to remark how, although endowed by nature with that vagrant eye and features of a notably immobile cast, he could radiate mild charitableness at will. This ambiguous regard now fell upon me, and he appeared to become aware that I had not been introduced to the man next to whom I had sat down.

'Clark,' he said in a clear and penetrating voice, 'do you know Duncan Pattullo? He is the author of that dazzling series of purified bedroom comedies.'

I didn't think it necessary to seem amused. Tony, near-by, struck a match with a gesture sufficiently large to attract attention, and in the resulting spurt of flame was to be observed as directing raised eyebrows upon our host. I felt grateful to him. Cressy's joke had been what used to be called a start of wit: an improvisation floating free of the facts of the case. He may have guessed that I hadn't taken to him at our previous meeting, and been prompted to this mild slap in consequence. Or it was possible – I told myself – that he was one of those habitually malicious men whose victims can comfort themselves with the Freudian thought that their impulse to self-destruction must be very strong. But it seemed uncharitable to credit our host with being in the grip of Thanatos, and I gave my attention – or tried to give my attention – to the next stage in the evening's proceedings.

It was a paper, as Corlett had promised, and read by another man noticeably stricken in years. Strangely enough, I recalled his voice at once, although not his name; he must have delivered one of the half dozen or so lectures that I had thought fit to attend during my three years of undergraduate residence. His present theme was the order in which Shakespeare's sonnets must be rearranged if the poet's original intentions are to be disclosed. There are 154 sonnets, many of them enormously famous, and it was at least reasonable to rely upon most of us being more familiar with them than with the Yamato-E tradition in ancient Japan. This venerable scholar, however, owned a faith in us more robust than that, and proceeded on the assumption that he had only to give the number of an individual sonnet to recall it *in toto* to our minds. The postulate conduced to mental fatigue and, I am afraid, inattention. I found myself recalling the only fact in this field of investigation to have stuck in my head. An American inquirer of sceptical habit had computed that the number of possible rearrangements of these 154 poems considerably exceeded the number of electrons credited by Arthur Edding- ton as being in the universe. The universe, of course, had been a more primitive affair in Eddington's time than it now was in Alexander Pentecost's. But the computation probably remained sufficiently valid to be discouraging. The witching hour of twelve would certainly have struck before the possibilities of the subject were exhausted.

The club, however, didn't fidget, and those of its members who had fallen asleep had the good manners not to snore. The paper came to a close on whatever its just conclusion was. There was a long silence. It didn't appear to be the convention that somebody was required to say 'Thank you very much'. Such of the members as I could at all clearly see had opened their eyes and assumed thoughtful expressions, as if here had been much to perpend. Then somebody shrouded in darkness spoke.

'Each changing place with that which goes before,
In sequent toil all forwards do contend.'

*Like as the waves make towards the pebbled shore* . . . that was the sonnet the lines must come from, and the quotation had been notably pat. It didn't, however, sound like a beginning to discussion, and I wondered what could follow. But the man who had read the minutes, pouring himself a little more brandy, said something over his shoulder about the Dark Lady – a disreputable person who has always held a strong attraction for the academic world. Amid various long pauses for consideration, half a dozen people made remarks about her. One or two others framed questions, and to these the man who had read the paper gave judicious answers. General talk went on for some time. It wasn't exactly animated, but I found it quite impressive, all the same. Here were a dozen people representing a wide diversity of learned and scientific interests, all perfectly capable of keeping this rather specialised ball rolling.

They didn't do it, however, until midnight. By imperceptible stages the talk ceased to be general, and equally imperceptibly Shakespeare and his sonnets faded out of it. Once dropped, I don't think they were referred to again. The man who had read the paper stuffed it unobtrusively into the pocket of his dinner-jacket, and was among the first to talk contentedly to his neighbour about other things. The evening had turned into one of the common gossiping sort.

People had begun, moreover, to drift around, and I was about to cross the room to join Tony when Cressy came up to me, a decanter in either hand. Very properly, he was again making the round of his guests in this way – pausing, I think, to talk punctiliously to anybody insufficiently thus favoured earlier in the evening. He had left me to the last, and now he put the decanters on a small table beside me and sat down.

'We are so delighted,' he said, 'that you have been able to dine with us. Lintot read a most worthy paper, didn't you think? But I found myself wishing that it had been you on the job. We might have heard something as distinguished as your *Shakespeare's Use of Song.'*

I expect I was foolishly taken aback by this reference to something of mine which was at least a far cry from bedroom comedy. The remark didn't strike me as in the nature of a palinode. What Cressy's manner seemed to suggest – if he felt, indeed, that any suggesting was necessary – was the untroubled assumption between us that a man says now this and now that. I had an impulse to thank him for having referred to me so kindly earlier in the evening, but managed to refrain.

He continued to talk, and he talked uncommonly well. I had heard about this endowment of Christopher Cressy's, and here it was. There was nothing excessive about it. He didn't propose himself as out of charm. He was tentative, thoughtful, considered; he listened; when he looked away it was in quest of his theme and not of more exalted society. His manner at first had a little reminded me of the Provost's. Edward Pococke could have said just that about *Shakespeare's Use of Song.* But Cressy had a wit which the Provost either didn't command or judged inapposite to his station. Cressy in his talk could be as brilliantly wicked as he chose to be. He had perfect command, as it were, of the tap labelled 'malice', and could let just as much of this quality percolate into the stream of his talk as was appropriate or permissible in its context. I wouldn't describe myself as captivated. But I'd have been a poor wooer of the Comic Spirit if I hadn't listened with respect and kept my end up as I could.

'By the way,' Cressy said, after consulting his tumbler at leisure, 'have you ever chanced to hear about the famous letter-book?'

'To hear about it?' I experienced the feeling of coming awake with a jerk. 'I was there.'

'I beg your pardon?' There was the effect of a sudden glare in the cold eyes Cressy had turned on me.

'At the *fons et origo* of the entire affair. I happened to be standing beside Lord Mountclandon when you approached him with your interesting discovery.'

'My dear Pattullo, how excessively odd!' As Cressy said this I felt confident that he was really surprised. Our present conversation wasn't a consequence of his having got wind of the facts of the case. 'You must forgive me,' he went on. 'Your presence has left no mark on my memory.'

'I was an undergraduate, and only at that dinner-party because my father was staying in the Lodging. You may just possibly remember him. His name was Lachlan Pattullo.'

'My dear man!' As he uttered this exclamation softly, Christopher Cressy actually laid a hand – equally softly – on my arm. He was indicating that one wouldn't readily forget meeting a person of my father's eminence. I am delighted,' he said. 'Quite delighted.'

'You have reason to be. I can't say I make much of this letter-book affair. Its longevity seems incommensurate with its consequence. But I must tell you, Cressy, that my recollection of the precipitating occasion is substantially yours – in the matter of words actually spoken, that is.'

'How very interesting.' Cressy didn't in fact sound interested, but I felt he was perhaps weighing the qualified character of my statement. 'The whole thing probably strikes you as a rather tediously sustained academic joke. It may be the best way to look at it. Of course Tommy Penwarden takes a serious view. But then Tommy, although a dear man, is almost pervasively absurd.' Cressy paused as if soliciting some reaction to this sudden impropriety. Not getting it, he proceeded as smoothly as before. 'Nobody else can really be much concerned. Your Provost for example. I have a small collection of his wonderful letters on the subject. But they render, to my mind, an impression of solemn shadow-boxing. He isn't honestly exercised.'

'You're quite wrong there.' I hadn't uttered these words before acknowledging to myself that I had perhaps been deftly led into a trap. But I was a little impatient of the whole thing, and decided to go ahead. 'The Provost, as a matter of fact, has been taking almost dramatic steps in the matter quite recently. And once more – strange as it must sound – I was there.'

'Really? Dear Edward! Whatever can be in his head?' I saw that Cressy wasn't going to seek any elucidation of these gnomic utterances of mine. 'Why should he be interested in a lot of mid-Victorian kitchen accounts?'Kitchen accounts?'

'Ah! Perhaps you don't know. That's the peculiarity of that particular letter-book – it's having considerable concern with Blunderville domestic affairs. Social history, you might say. The relations of masters and servants, for example, in that curious age. One could get an interesting little paper out of it on that. I wonder, by the way, whether any of Tommy's colleagues – still around, perhaps – had glanced through it before dear old Blobs so kindly presented me with it? The whole subject is very boring, Pattullo – very boring indeed. But the more I turn the matter over in my mind, the more inclined I am to judge it may be wise and charitable in me to continue holding on to the thing. Won't you have a little more brandy?"

'No – I'm very happy, thank you.' This conventional response wasn't true. I had become uneasy, and for two reasons. It was clear to me that I was being fed through the bars with intriguingly mysterious gobbets which I was then to run around with among the other animals. And I had a feeling that the evening had treated me to what the musical comedy people call a *reprise*. Just as when he had produced his flight of fancy about my plays, Cressy had been beginning to fabricate something suddenly perceived as susceptible of exploitation in pursuit of the ludicrous. The victim now appeared to be the Provost. If I disliked this it was no doubt because I myself had a weakness that way. Hadn't I often, for instance, built up Albert Talbert as a figure of fun? And I was fond of Talbert, whereas I didn't imagine Cressy cared twopence for Edward Pococke. So it wasn't for me to be censorious. Not, therefore, having anything to say, I was relieved to observe a couple of men hovering with the evident intention of thanking their host for their dinner and taking their leave. I got to my feet, and fairly promptly ceased wondering what all this had been about. I had myself two hosts to thank and extricate myself from. I set about this at once.

Tony and I left together, emerging into the darkness of an alien quad. It was our first chance to talk.

'Damned cheek, that fellow's crack at you,' Tony said. 'Bedroom comedy, indeed! Not that your plays mightn't be more entertaining, Dunkie, if they sometimes inclined a little that way.'

'Thank you, Tony. You're a true friend.'

'That's right – plain words by thy true-telling friend. And what were you nattering to the man about, anyway?'

'Heaven knows.' I had become clear that I wasn't reporting Cressy's obscure remarks to anybody. 'But he's a notably entertaining talker.'

'Just another confounded usher a damned sight too pleased with himself, he seemed to me.'

'Still down on the dons, Tony?'

'Blast the dons.' Tony was silent for a moment, and I saw that this had prompted another train of thought in him. He came to a halt half-way to the college gate. 'I say! Have you heard that Ivo is starting a magazine?'

'Yes. He told me about it himself. He did come to lunch with me, you know.'

'I'm very glad to hear it. Ivo's grandfather is putting up some money, it seems. It might be quite a good thing, don't you think? Blameless literary activity earns him a mark or two.'

'Perhaps.' I hesitated on this dishonest reply. In relation to his son, Tony had an astonishing capacity for wishful thinking. 'The magazine,' I said, 'is to be called *Priapus.*'

'Oh, Christ! I did think the senile old rascal sounded suspiciously pleased with it.' It was entirely affectionately that Tony contrived to refer to the most senior of the Mumfords in this way. 'There's my car,' he said abruptly. 'Let me give you a lift back to college. It's confoundedly late.'

Just as on our previous nocturnal parting at the beginning of term, Tony's big ministerial limousine had nosed its way out of darkness, bodyguard and all. The men on motor-cycles weren't on view, but no doubt they were around.

'Thanks awfully,' I said. 'But I think I'll walk. It clears the head.'

'Clears the head? Stuff and nonsense! Your head's as clear as mine, and I work on papers all the way back to town. Anyway, what about the muggers? Oxford's said to teem with them.'

This was almost true. Amazingly, the sacred town had become one in which nervous people didn't altogether like to walk alone at night. Drunken undergraduates had become a rare and reassuring sight.

'I never carry more than a couple of pounds,' I said. 'That's held to be enough to get you off without having them put the boot in for luck. The bloody government should do something about it, all the same.'

'You're a rotten socialist,' Tony said. And at this we punched each other in the chest and parted with good feeling.

I wasn't myself fearful of a mugging. Late at night the streets of Oxford are quite deserted, but behind the colleges' sober facades there is always a good deal of wakefulness going on, chiefly because undergraduates have the habit of writing their weekly essay through the small hours. One is seldom out of sight of several lighted windows. I felt that, if attacked, I'd only have to give a shout to have these flung open and a shower of bottles and cricket-bats and handy bits of furniture descend in the happy faith that they would brain the villains and not their victim.

But Radcliffe Square lay in darkness. Brasenose, at least, had suspended the pursuit of learning, and in All Souls, which houses nothing but dons, nobody had turned up the lamp. The Radcliffe Camera, and beyond it the university church of St Mary the Virgin, were only uncertainly silhouetted masses against a dull starless heaven. Amid all these solemn presences I paused. *In the deserted, moon-blanched street How lonely rings the echo of my feet!* Arnold's lines didn't quite fit, but it was perhaps to still such an echo for a moment that I had come to a halt. And in the resulting silence I was prompted to abandon my direct route back to college in favour of a meditative detour among the dreaming spires.

I retraced my steps for a little and walked down New College Lane. My uncle Rory had been at New College, the only kinsman of mine whom I had ever heard of as an Oxford man. This surprising episode in his past had always pleased me, and it may have been the memory of it that led me in the direction I was now walking. The lane twists, narrows, and displays a good deal in the way of high blank walls before, on a further turn, it broadens again and calls itself something else. There was a single street lamp, set high up in the angle of a building, but otherwise the place was pretty dark. My own footfalls were the only sound still. I had placed myself, it came to me, in something like a clichéd situation from a gangster film. The hunted man is in some tunnel-like space: only a long way in front of him and behind him is there any way out. Sinister figures suddenly appear ahead; perhaps they wait, perhaps they slowly advance. He turns, and an identical menace closes the vista. He is trapped. This hackneyed fantasy was actually in my head when, some thirty yards before me, a figure – a single figure – did appear, walking towards me. The figure came to an abrupt halt, and I felt that it was the sight of me that had occasioned this. There was nothing alarming about it, but I looked swiftly over my shoulder, all the same. The lane behind me was empty. I looked ahead again. The figure had vanished. There was plenty of shadow to vanish into, but it had happened too quickly not to be disconcerting. Perhaps it had slipped through some doorway I'd forgotten about; perhaps, for some sufficient reason of its own, it was lurking unobserved until I went past. The man's movements or motives – for I thought it was a man – were no business of mine. I quickened my own pace – not particularly perturbed, I imagine, but nevertheless quite willing to gain Queen's Lane and a straight walk back to bed. There was a faint ribbon of light before me, and I walked down it without attempting to peer into the shadows on either hand. Then I heard a step behind me, and in the same moment felt myself gripped firmly by an arm. One tends to act instinctively in the dark. I flung off this grasp not at all gently, and swung round as if to defend myself.

'Duncan, son of Lachlan!' J. B. Timbermill said.

I hadn't seen the author of *The Magic Quest* since the afternoon upon which he had burst in on Fiona Petrie, Margaret Mountain and myself in the house on the Woodstock Road. I knew that he still lived in his old attic dwelling – thus remaining the Wizard of the North – and I had twice made my way there in quest of him. Faded ink on a discoloured card and a drawing-pin from which the head had rusted away constituted, as long ago, the only intimation of his tenancy. On both occasions I had knocked on his door in vain and then, as when I was his pupil, attempted simply to walk in. But the place had been locked up and that great shadowy space – Hrothgar's Heorot, as I thought of it – denied me.

The first thing I had ever learnt of Timbermill was that he never left home, and thus twice drawing blank discomposed me. His visit to Fiona was evidence that he had to some extent changed his ways, but I found it hard to suppose he had done so radically. Fiona herself, of whom I was now seeing a good deal, was noticeably reticent about our old teacher; it was almost as if she were harbouring a slightly jealous indisposition to go shares in him. I didn't press her on the subject. But I ought to have been more pertinacious in my efforts to contact a man whose personality had once so powerfully impressed me. And now here he was, casually encountered round about midnight in an Oxford street.

'J. B!' I exclaimed, and took both his hands in mine − a gesture prompted by the fact that, moments before, I had been prepared to do my best to knock him down. 'Where have *you* been dining?'

I asked this question − in the circumstances a very ordinary Oxford question − before I had really seen my old tutor clearly. His behaviour on spying my approaching figure had been nothing out of the way; he may have had the same thoughts of possible marauders in his head as I had, and it had been only prudent in an old man rapidly to conceal himself until it was apparent no such threat existed. But we weren't now in anything like complete darkness; a second lamp, again clamped high up on a building, faintly illumined the narrow street where it turned between St Edmund Hall and Queen's. I now saw that Timbermill didn't look like a man who has been dining − even as an acknowledged eccentric − in academic company. His clothes were ragged and I suspected them of being dirty as well; he had neglected to attach a collar to his shirt; his feet were in carpet slippers which had seen better days. Yet it wasn't these matters of external appearance that were striking, so much were they overshadowed, dominated by the inner being of this great scholar in his decline. Not that he looked like a scholar, great or small. It would have been hard to say what he *did* look like − except that, if one tried, contradictory literary associations would be likely to jostle in one's head. I could have viewed him instantly as a Dickensian grotesque − Oxford dissolving round us and being replaced by some bizarrely-conceived mid-Victorian London *decor*. Or alternatively − and this perhaps did more justice to the effect

– here was a wild and preternatural figure as conceived by the original Wizard of the North – bobbing up on some darkened Scottish moor to affright a lonely traveller with mysterious intimations of doom.

'Dining, Duncan?' There was the old vibrant note in Timbermill's voice as he took up my question sharply. 'I'm soon to be dining with the crows, my dear lad. Not with the feasters but with the feasted upon, as the old sermon has it.'

'Donne,' I heard myself say. '*Mundus Mare,* J. B. Both the dishes and the guests.'

'Good, Duncan, good!'

This was astonishing. Just for the moment, Heorot was around us again, and the favourite pupil was showing off. Or say he was loyally keeping his end up – I don't know. But I did in the succeeding seconds realise it wasn't an hour for histrionic effects. Timbermill had better be got home. It mightn't be much good, but that was the present job. I believe I knew at once that I was in the presence not of an aberration but of a habit. The eremitic Timbermill had become a nocturnal wanderer. There must be a medical term for this manifestation of senescence; *by per kinesis,* it might be – or something ending in *agitans.*

'It's fairly late,' I said. 'Walk back to college with me, J. B., and I'll get out the car and run you out to Linton Road.'

'That's too kind of you, Duncan.' Suddenly it might have been Jimmy Gender speaking, and I tried to take comfort from this switch to the commonplace polite Oxford man. At the same time I was thinking that Fiona, if she was fully aware of the state of affairs now revealed to me, might reasonably have been a little more confiding about it. I had no idea whether Timbermill had any living relations to be at all concerned about him. He had certainly never been married. When I was his pupil I had already been aware of him as strangely isolated, and I believe I had thought of him when, at the beginning of this present term, Bedworth had remarked to me that an Oxford college is not a terribly good place to grow old in. Timbermill hadn't even a college. Or rather he had three of them according to the book, but for years had never entered one of them. He must have had contacts with fellow-scholars; he had, I knew, gained real satisfaction from taking a handful of pupils. But that had been it. Of course there had been the creatures of his imagination and he must have done a lot of living with them. Yet that insubstantial pageant had faded, and he had been left with his vocation as a philologist. I supposed that such a man, long habituated to much solitude, was all right as long as he kept his grip on that sort of exacting intellectual work. When that slipped there was the void. I imagined Timbermill to be facing that now.

We walked on together. Even in carpet slippers one of which had a flapping sole Timbermill didn't totter or dodder; he was firmer on his feet by a long way than Arnold Lempriere, a younger man, had become; the tree would perish from the head down. This gloomy thought was in my head when he spoke again.

'The question is,' he said with sudden amazing incisiveness, 'are you going to marry her?'

Since Fiona had been in my head only a minute earlier it was to be presumed that a telepathic process had been at work. And I couldn't pretend to be in the dark.

'Dear J. B.,' I said, 'only think! She's young enough to be my daughter.'

'Have you spoken to her about it?'

'No, I haven't. But she has spoken to me.' It was impossible not to own any relevant truth to Timbermill.

'To the laggard in love? Duncan, you made a mess of things long ago through not speaking out to a girl. You didn't know that I knew it, but I did. It was written all over you. And then you went further and fared worse. Years afterwards, when you hadn't even youth as an excuse. I heard about it, although our ways had parted by then. Duncan Pattullo that way went.'

I believe I said 'Meredith' to myself dumbly. J. B. Timbermill suddenly restored to his demonic character was hard to cope with.

'Listen, J. B. It wasn't like that – Fiona's way of speaking to me.'

We walked on through a minute's silence. The High was deserted. We could have walked down the middle of it from end to end unthreatened by traffic, like gowned and capped scholars in some old print. No – I told myself – it hadn't been at all like that, Fiona's perplexing banter at Mrs Gender's party. If Timbermill, possessed by some *idee fixe,* was now badgering me about her, he had already badgered her about me. Faced with this embarrassing nonsense, Fiona had taken care to show me that she placed the whole notion in the region of the absurd.

'You could do great things together,' Timbermill said.

'Do great things? We could have children, I suppose.'

'Children?' Uttering the word vehemently, Timbermill came to a halt, and I realised I had said something which would never have entered his head. 'Between you, you could complete my *corpus.* And *finis coronat opus,* Duncan.'

I had no idea what precisely Timbermill's *corpus* was, but clearly he referred to some large labour of systematic scholarship. Perhaps it had something to do with all those broken pots and kitchen-midden shards. There was a certain relief in our being back on demonstrably obsessional and impersonal ground. It wasn't ground on which I could conceivably have a place. My talent, slender as it was, stood committed to men and women; to what I could make of the bewilderment and vehemence – or mere comedy – of human life. Ink had replaced seccotine on my fingers long ago.

'But there's a further thing.' I knew before he went on that Timbermill was up to another of his intuitive performances. 'There's a human thing. You can rescue her from that unnatural woman.'

'From Miss Mountain? I've no evidence that Miss Mountain is what can be called that, and I hope I wouldn't condemn her if I did. Emotional attachments between women can be happy and stable and rather beautiful. Think of the Ladies of Llangollen, J. B.'

'Rubbish, Duncan!' It was evident that my attempt at a whimsical note hadn't been a success. 'Women ought to bear children. If an emotional attachment, as you call it, isn't within hail of that, then it's of no use to them. You agree there, don't you?'

I supposed I did agree, although the generalisation was rather sweeping. But if I could have been angry with Timbermill I'd have been so now. It was I who had introduced the theme of children, and he had unscrupulously appropriated what would not spontaneously have occurred to him.

'It's fair to mention,' I said, 'that the girl you think I ought to have proposed to as a schoolboy now lives in Oxford.'

'Married?'

'Happily married, I think – and to an old schoolfellow of mine that I've a considerable regard for.'

'Then the fact's irrelevant. Try to think clearly, Duncan.'

I don't believe I resented this tutorial accent, but I couldn't think of more to say. We were both silent again, but not for long. This was because Timbermill began to mutter to himself, and was presently doing so vehemently and quite incoherently. He had shot his bolt. More exactly, he had made a tremendous effort in what he conceived to be Fiona's interest and mine, and now his mind was wandering. I was distressed by this, as well as upset by the general tenor of our talk. Perhaps it was true that I hadn't been thinking clearly; that I had been thinking increasingly unclearly, indeed, about Fiona Petrie since my first meeting with her not many weeks before.

Timbermill wouldn't come into my rooms for the brandy I thought might do him good. So I got out my car at once – a manoeuvre of some complexity at night – and we drove off to North Oxford. Heorot was just as I remembered it: a vast cavernous room, overflowing with books and periodicals and pots, with subsidiary caves disappearing into darkness under the various eaves of the house. It now struck me as strange that I had once felt in so close a discipleship to its owner without ever thinking to find out what his domestic dispositions were. He had ceased any continuous muttering and seemed to have forgotten our odd debate; for a minute or two he was reluctant to let me go; then suddenly he said 'Dear Duncan, how like a former time!' and waved me from the room.

# XIV

THE FOLLOWING MORNING brought me a letter from Peter Lusby. He must have sat down and written it immediately upon hearing he had gained a place at the college.

Dear Sir,

I write, please, to thank you very much for your help. It has been a most timely interposition and I am sorry for the inconvenience I have caused you. However I get on at Oxford, and I do promise to do my best to justify the confidence reposed in me, I shall be grateful always for your lending a hand in trouble. I have explained certain matters to my parents and they are a bit upset about my untoward reticence as they must feel it to be but are coming round as I knew they would do because we are all right as a family, at least nearly always. Please pray for me when you are next in the college chapel. I didn't like to tell you that night that I'd gone in to do that, pray I mean.

Yours respectfully, PETER
(P. L. Lusby)

It was, perhaps, a laboured composition, but I reflected that Peter was at least one up on Nick Junkin in being able to spell. I also wondered whether Peter would be disturbed to discover that the fellows of the college didn't file into their chapel with any great regularity. Perhaps it was a subject upon which Paul hadn't been communicative. I liked the letter, and felt that, at least for the present, the Peter Lusby problem was adequately tied up.

Yet it wasn't quite – or not so far as I myself was concerned. Nobody was going to ask me questions about the mystery I'd solved in Bethnal Green. But what was I to do about Arnold Lempriere? I hadn't set out to spy on him. But spy I had, and up he'd bobbed in the path of my investigation. I couldn't ask Peter to keep mum about me in the further contacts he was bound to have with his eccentric benefactor; to do so would be unfairly to commit the boy to prevarication precisely as Lempriere himself had done. But if I left it to Peter to come out with the story of my 'interposition' Lempriere mightn't like it at all. The ticklish communication, in fact, was up to me. I'd promised Peter not to let the secret go any further. But he'd find it quite natural that I should speak to Lempriere about it.

I went about the job as we walked round Long Field together that afternoon. Lempriere was entirely unruffled. The doubts raised in Gender and Atlas as a consequence of the state of confusion to which Peter had been reduced before them he seized upon as an occasion for sardonic comment, and he contrived to view my visit to London as part of a family conspiracy in which we were involved together. This was to carry our kinship by way of Aunt Charlotte decidedly far, and it also violated the facts of the case to an extent suggesting that Lempriere was ceasing always to be very clear in the head. I reminded myself that, so far as his years went, he was entitled to be a little dottier than his old pupil Cedric Mumford. Compared with that phrenetic old creature he was wearing fairly well.

'But the boy will continue with the coach I found for him?' he suddenly demanded. 'Right up to the entrance examination?'

'Yes, of course. I wasn't coming between him and your generosity, Arnold. I told him to carry on going to your man.'

'Good. He'll pick up a trick or two to puzzle them – even in these remaining few weeks.'

'He doesn't need any tricks. He's in. It's just a matter of his doing his best, and showing he'll make a decent commoner. We mustn't expect him to get an award, you know. Although I think that in some ways he's a remarkable boy, he's not in that intellectual bracket.'

I waited in some expectation to hear what Lempriere would make of this. One of his most fixed ideas was the duty of good and faithful tutors to treat all examiners as persons to be conspired against in every lawful way. The vision of tutor and pupil hand in glove together was precious to him. It was possible to square this attitude with another to which he was almost as firmly wedded: the conviction (and here he was on common ground with the Mumfords) that the university's entire system of competitive examination was an absurdity. But there was a further persuasion – one shared by nearly all dons of Lempriere's generation although scarcely by their juniors – which seemed incompatible with this. It could be called the mystique of the Open Scholarship. A schoolboy who, at the age of eighteen or thereabout, has persuaded two or three college examiners to nominate him for such an award, has thereby established himself in the intellectual *elite* of the nation. It was just like that. If anything went wrong with him the thing held the dimensions of tragedy. It seemed to me almost impossible that this antique superstition didn't lurk in Lempriere. At the moment, however, I failed to coax him on to this ground.

'That's enough of young Lusby,' he said. 'The place has been persuaded to do its plain duty by him. He'll come up; he'll take his chance; and that's all we can do. So what we have to think about now, Dunkie, is the brat.' Unexpectedly, Lempriere gave his throaty chuckle. 'And talk of the devil, eh?'

It was true that Ivo Mumford – whom Lempriere now commonly referred to thus – was approaching us. Like ourselves, he was on a path which had narrowed for a space between high banks, and he would be rubbing shoulders with us as he went by. He was by himself, and sauntering gloomily with his hands deep in his trouser-pockets. I had lately come across him like this more than once.

Undergraduates when not gregarious are commonly at least companionable; they seem seldom to have occasions obliging them to walk alone; observe one so doing two or three times running and you may fairly infer that, whether for the nonce or for keeps, he is some sort of odd man out. Ivo, although unpopular with many of his fellows, was unlikely not to be able to command congenial society if he wanted it, so his solitude was probably of his own choice. He had an air, too, of being withdrawn within himself, and had the path been a couple of feet wider he might have gone past us quite unregardingly. It struck me that this would be habitual with him. Like Christopher Cressy, Ivo would divide his world into the noticeable and unnoticeable, and the second batch he just wouldn't notice at all.

But he did now notice me, and what first signalled his recognition was not any acknowledging glance but that involuntary twitch or spasm which I had remarked on his face when he came to lunch. He then looked quickly at Lempriere – we were at no more than arm's length now – and his features took on a startled expression which lasted only for a fraction of a second. After that he smiled. It wasn't his attractive smile. There was something secretive about it that I didn't like at all.

'Good afternoon,' Lempriere said.

'Good afternoon, sir.' Ivo had jumped as he walked, and this involuntary nervous exhibition he endeavoured to convert into a sideways swing allowing us to pass. But he mistimed this, and his shoulder bumped heavily into mine. 'Sorry!' he muttered angrily, and hurried on – his hands deep in his pockets still.

'Graceless little brute,' Lempriere said. He spoke almost affectionately, as if graceless little brutes constituted a category of persons for whom he had a particular regard.

'Ivo has a long way to go,' I said, 'before he matches his father at making friends and influencing people. By the way, was that greeting the first word you've ever uttered to him?'

'Certainly it was. But I suppose a very senior man can pass the time of day with a junior member if he wants to?'

'Yes, of course. It struck me you startled him. Perhaps, Arnold, he was suddenly saying to himself "That must be my grandfather's tutor". It would be quite a thought suddenly to come into an undergraduate's head.'

'No doubt. But the point is that we have to have *him* in *our* heads. For as far as this damned examination goes the brat's now past saving.'

'I'm not surprised to hear it.'

'Fortunately Edward is softening up.'

'The Provost?' My surprise was for some reason so marked that I had to make sure of this identification.

'Yes, of course. Don't be a fool, Dunkie.'

'He'd let Ivo stick around even after another flop?'

'It isn't to be seen quite that way. These are matters of general policy – how to deal with various classes of undergraduates in one situation or another. They naturally vary from time to time. Various expediencies have to be weighed. Edward's good at that. But he needs support when some sensible notion strays into his head. You can lend a hand there.'

'I think what you mean is that he needs leaning on. And I'm not sure I want to lean on him about Ivo. As I've told you before, I've come round to the view that the boy's best chance is to clear out – gracefully if possible.'

'You mustn't cross the floor of the house, confound you!' Although Lempriere said this humorously, he was clearly serious. 'You're a key man, there in the Lodging. Mrs P. is fond of you. She was fond of you as a kid, it seems.'

'She was fonder of Ivo's father, as a matter of fact. And you know how she quite tolerates the boy himself. But I'm damned if I care for petticoat politics, Arnold. Particularly when they're basically unaccountable to me. And this affair is that. Edward and the Mumfords make a petty puzzle – with a piece missing bang in the middle of it.'

'Irritating things, jigsaws,' Lempriere was amused. 'My sister does them like mad, and when she gets held up there's just no reasoning with her. The dogs suffer.' He paused on what was presumably a glimpse of squirarchal life in Northumberland. 'She'd do better playing bridge.'

We were back within the walls of the college, and the Great Quadrangle was before us. Following his custom, Lempriere surveyed it briefly, before finding some formula of dismissal.

'Can't offer you tea,' he said. 'Never touch the stuff. Afternoon to you, Dunkie.' And with a light touch on the arm – his occasional way of asserting our cousinship – he walked away.

Minutes later I was offered tea by Nicolas Junkin. He had seen my approach, and was waiting for me at the doorway of Surrey Four.

'You'll do me a favour,' he said. 'For I'm chuffed to the bollocks.'

These were both familiar locutions on Junkin's lips, but each offered its quota of perplexity. The first, it seemed, could be employed at need without any implication of irony or challenge. The second stood beyond the reach of interpretation – 'chuffed' belonging to that small and interesting group of words which are employable in diametrically opposed senses. Only Junkin's tone could indicate whether he was announcing himself as pleased or as disgruntled. All that I could actually catch was that note of perplexity or bewilderment which he so frequently exhibited.

'Guess where I've been to lunch,' he said, leading the way upstairs.

I became conscious of scanning the rear view of Junkin which our relative positions alone permitted me. My first glimpse of him, which hadn't been many months before, had been in brightly coloured pants and nothing else; since then I had never seen him except in jeans below and pullover or anorak or combat-jacket above. What Junkin now wore was a pin-stripe suit. When he turned to usher me into his room I was confirmed in the impression that the outfit was tailored on modest and conservative lines. I recalled the pleasing fact (first revealed to me by Plot) that Junkin enjoyed the favour of an aunt whose Cokeville wealth ran not merely to a sweetshop but to a number of desirable urban dwellings as well. Junkin's gent's suiting, as well as Junkin's Honda, must have its origin in this resource. But what made me conscious that a small chunk of social history stood before me was something else. Had the undergraduate Cyril Bedworth – a Junkin of sorts in his time – dressed himself up like this he would have looked like a shop-boy on holiday. Junkin, because without any social self-consciousness to speak of, was indistinguishable from the first Harrovian or Rugbeian one might have run into. He might even have been, so to speak, Ivo Mumford from across the landing, appropriately habited for a London jaunt. I wasn't sure how I felt about this evidence of assimilative pressures as at play upon Junkin.

'It would be my guess,' I said, 'that you were lunching in the

Lodging.'

'You'd be dead right.' Hospitably intent, Junkin grabbed his electric kettle. 'Do you remember when I didn't even know it was the college H.Q? I thought the Provost was just the chap who preached the sermons and that kind of thing.' Junldn said this on a reminiscent and nostalgic note, although the particular nescience to which he referred was distanced from us by not much more than a long vacation. 'Do you mind chocolate biscuits?'

'I like chocolate biscuits. Were the Pocockes kind to you?'

'Vigorously kind. It was a bit disturbing, really. You might say I lacked orientation. Tell you in a minute.'

Junkin disappeared to fill the kettle, and I glanced around the room which had seen the end of my own youth. Like its present proprietor, it was in process of change. The prized collection of empty bottles which had paraded below the ceding had vanished – chucked out on the landing, no doubt, for Plot to cart away. The bug-eyed Ishii Genzo still held his place where my own *Young Picts watching the arrival of Saint Columba* had hung. But the op-art reproductions had gone, and in their place were displayed Bosch's *Garden of Earthly Delights*, Roy Lichtenstein's *Whaam!,* and Blake's tondo of *Saint Michael binding Satan.* These were all outsize affairs, and thus represented value for money as well as artistic taste. Another innovation was the presence of a framed photograph on the writing-table; it was of a very pretty girl with eyes thoughtfully downcast upon an open book. Junkin had currently opted, I knew, for a settled attachment to a Cokeville maiden. And here she was.

'Of course they get round to everybody in time,' Junkin said, returning and getting out his teapot. 'But I gather they don't usually come at you till about the end of your second year. So it was a bit of a shock – specially with me being rather a doghouse type at the moment, examination-wise.'

'Such things aren't permitted to affect social intercourse.'

'I see.' Junkin had greeted this remark with proper suspicion. 'The Provost called it a working lunch. Could I possibly spare the time, he said in a note, to drop in for a working lunch. I thought it a shade casual.'

'I'd have thought it a shade mysterious.'

'That too – you're telling me. And I'd rather have expected the invitation to come from the old trout.'

'Not necessarily.' I was a little depressed by this further evidence of Junkin's increased trafficking with convention. 'And not if Mrs Pococke wasn't going to be part of the working-party.'

'Oh, but she was. She's a decent old bag, I'd say, and was quite a comfort to both of us. The Provost has his overpowering side, don't you think? Have a biscuit while you're waiting for the brew-up.'

'Thank you, Nick.' I took a biscuit. 'Who's both of us?'

'Larry and me. Larry Andrews. He's president, you know, and I'm secretary.'

'Of the Dramatic Society?'

'Yes, of course. That's what the working lunch was about. It was a plot about you, among other things.'

'What on earth do you mean?'

'About roping you in to do the summer term production. The Provost turns out to be fearfully keen on our next effort. It's funny. Larry says the old boy has never registered all that interest in the Dramatic Society before. He always turns up to one of the performances, of course. But Larry says it's a gracious-behaviour turn rather than a thirst for dramatic experience.'

'I get Larry's point. But perhaps it might be a bit of both.' I offered this, I suppose, out of an instinct to defend the elderly from the too penetrating eye of youth. 'Did the Provost discuss the choice of a play?'

'No, not that. He said he'd be enormously interested to hear what we decided upon, but it wasn't for him to influence us in any way. He's rather a correct man.'

'So he is. There's much to be said for it in his position.'

'I suppose so. But listen – I haven't really told you. Oh, how do you like your char?'

We got this settled. I realised that Junkin's point of main perplexity was yet to come.

'The Provost paid more attention to me than to Larry. It was the wrong way round, it seemed to me – Larry being a fourth-year man and having enormous experience. *Armstrongs Last Goodnight* is what everybody says was our highlight for years. And it seems that Larry humped it pretty well on his own.'

'But Larry wasn't awkwardly left out?'

'Oh, no. The Pocockes know their stuff. You have to give them that. Mrs P. had all the gen on Larry; you felt you couldn't have stumped her on his old grandad's favourite brand of fish paste. But it was the Provost who knew all about me. And do you know what it felt like? That medicinal buttered bun again. He was quite ignoring that I might no longer be in Oxford's land of the living six months from now. We'll do this, Junkin – and we must think about that. It wasn't natural. It seemed like he was due to hand me a medal for meritorious services to the college. Stalwart contribution to an important aspect of the life of the dump, he said. I ask you! Do you think perhaps Lempriere put him up to it?'

'More psychotherapy of warm praise? No, Nick, I don't imagine so. Did you manage a decent show?'

'A decent show? I tell you, man, I felt like doing a quick cop out. But yes, I suppose so. Junkin fights back. That sort of thing.'

'Capital! The Provost will now be able to say that he happens to have become well acquainted with you, and is impressed by your firmness of character, tenacity, sagacity, modesty, and all the other unassuming virtues.'

'Stop making fun of me.'

'I'm not – nor of the Provost either. He does his homework – knows his gen, as you've remarked.'

It's rather worrying.'

'Forget it, Nick. Is there any more tea? And I'll have another biscuit'

'Any amount of tannin, mate.' This circumstance cheered up Junkin much, I imagine, as it would have cheered up his affluent aunt. 'I say I I'm doing no end of work. And Lempriere's being terribly stout. No end cunning.'

'I don't doubt it.'

'For instance, do you know what a parliamentary train is?'

'I haven't a notion.'

'It's a train carrying passengers at not more than a penny a mile, and has to be run daily each way over the company's system. It's 7 and 8 Vict. 85.'

'What on earth's that?'

'I suppose it's an act or regulation or something, and of course it's the hard part to remember. But Lempriere says it amuses examiners to have mugged-up out-of-the-way facts ingenuously unloaded on them. I think "ingenuously" was the word. Puts them in a good humour. Generates favourable vibes.'

'I see. I'd imagine it's a technique to be adopted with discretion.'

'Lempriere says that too.'

It was something, I thought, that Junkin had come so stoutly to believe that he had a paragon of a tutor. Perhaps he really had. Lempriere must possess something like fifty years' experience of shoving young men through examinations, and his methods weren't for me to assess. Junkin and I talked about Joe Orton for the rest of our tea.

As I left Junkin's room I was bumped into, for the second time that afternoon, by his neighbour Ivo Mumford. Ivo seemed to have emerged from his own room and dashed for the staircase in some excitement. He had a letter in his hand.

'Sorry,' he said perfunctorily, and then recognised me. 'Oh, Lord!' he added. 'Done it again. Sorry about Long Field. I wasn't feeling too good. However, things are looking up. The bastards are caving in. Only I'm not sure I'm going to let them.'

I was less struck by these remarks – although they were mysterious – than by something that appeared to have happened (or to be happening) to the young man uttering them. It was as if Ivo had put his hand on the tip of something he'd been looking for.

'Just who are caving in, Ivo?' To let curiosity loose in this way went a little against the grain with me. I'd tried to get on terms with Ivo and it hadn't come off; there wasn't much point in attempting to advance again on chit-chat with him. But I did want to know what he was talking about.

'The dons, of course. Or at least the Provost – and I'll bet the others follow him like sheep. I've just found a letter from my father. I was going to show it to somebody I'm fairly thick with in Harbage. But I'd like to show it to you. You're the only person who's ever given me any good advice about the damned place.' Ivo paused on this handsome acknowledgement, which somehow I found myself not quite trusting. 'Look, won't you come in for a minute, sir?' Rather amazingly, Ivo had turned and thrown open the door of his room. I went in, and he at once offered me a drink. It was still afternoon, so I was able civilly to decline. Ivo hesitated, and then refrained from pouring anything for himself. I supposed him to be on his best behaviour.

'I say,' he said abruptly, 'who was that old man?'

'That I was walking with this afternoon? Don't you know? His name is Arnold Lempriere.'

'Really?' Just as when he had first glimpsed Lempriere and myself side by side, Ivo looked distinctly startled. 'I don't think I've ever noticed him around the college before. But I've heard of him. He was my father's tutor.'

'He was nothing of the kind. He had a job in America when your father and I were up. But he was your grandfather's tutor – which is quite something, Ivo, you must agree.'

'He couldn't have been!'

'I assure you he was. I don't suppose there were four years between them.'

'And he's still a don at this college? How very odd.'

I have probably remarked before that undergraduates are capable of remaining in the most astonishing ignorance about those aspects of college life that fail to interest them. But this unawareness of Ivo's was quite out of the way. I reminded myself again that he was a very unnoticing type of young man.

'No – I don't think I've ever spotted him shambling around,' Ivo said, much as if obligingly confirming me in this conclusion. 'Comes, perhaps, of not going in and eating those awful meals in hall.'

"If you haven't been aware of him, it doesn't mean he hasn't been aware of you.'

'Just what do you mean by that?' Ivo's voice had sharpened. I wondered why he was suddenly so interested in someone whose very existence within the college he'd contrived to remain in ignorance of.

'I mean that Mr Lempriere has been doing his best to have people view your affairs and prospects, Ivo, in as favourable a way as possible. You might pretty well call him your friend at court.'

'I thought it was you who'd tried to sign on for that.'

I was now so puzzled by some unknown factor underlying Ivo's bearing that this familiar flash of insolence struck me as almost reassuring. I found it rather too offensive to reply to, all the same.

'So he's another guardian angel, ' Ivo said. 'I've had enough of guardian angels. They can all get stuffed, as far as I'm concerned.' Ivo's face twitched, and then suddenly he laughed – wildly, and to an unnerving effect of momentarily releasing panic. 'I suppose it makes it a damned sight funnier,' he managed to say. 'I can see that.'

'Ivo, I don't know what you're talking about. But you obviously need to sort yourself out. I'll leave you to it.'

'No, don't go away. I want to tell you about . . . about the capitulation.' Ivo was still holding his father's letter. He now raised it in air, but didn't offer to show it to me. He seemed to have thought better of this. 'The Provost has given my father lunch at the Athenium.'

'Do you mean the Athenaeum?'

'That's right – a club. Or not exactly a real club. Not like Boodle's or Buck's. A place for bishops and people of that sort.'

'Quite so. But what's so remarkable about this bit of news?'

'Well, for a start there's another bit. The plot's thickening, speeding up. My father's coming up to dine in their grotty Lodging. And he has a nose for such things. The way the Provost talks and writes, tells him that what's in the wind is a little quiet wheeling and dealing about the black sheep of the family.'

'Does your father express it that way?'

'No, of course not. But it's what he means. I've got a bit of a nose too.'

'Why should the Provost wheel and deal about you, as you express it?'

'I haven't a clue. And I don't think I like it much, as a matter of fact. Which is jolly decent of me, wouldn't you say?'

'I don't think I'm prompted to say anything. Except that if you feel this whole business is a bit silly, I agree.'

'Families are a bit silly, if you ask me. I'm fed up with being clucked over. When a man's my age he ought to be through with all that. Here's my father talking about a conciliatory move, and a reasonable accommodation. It's not my sort of language at all.'

'I'd suppose not. Do you mean your father is giving you advice?'

'He wants me to scrub *Priapus*. That would be conciliatory.'

I had forgotten about *Priapus*. But now I remembered it was clearly a venture the character of which made it very relevant to any politic efforts Tony was still making on Ivo's behalf.

'If I know anything about *Priapus*' I said firmly, 'any sane person would advise you to scrub it. But can you? What about your associates?'

'What do you mean – my associates?'

'That man Bobby Braine – and the other people at Trinity or wherever it is.'

'Oh, them! They've all ratted.'

'You mean you're on your own?'

'Yes – right out on a limb. Except, of course, for my grandfather. I'm still in partnership with him. I think perhaps I'll consult him – although I can pretty well guess what his advice would be.'

I judged the behaviour of Mr Braine and his colleagues ominous. Their sudden circumspection was unendearing, but it clarified the character of the forthcoming publication, supposing one felt in any doubt about it. I wanted to tell Ivo that for good advice he need look no further than the letter in his hand. I refrained out of a sense that this would be counterproductive. Ivo, whom I had always sensed as being his grandfather's man, was in some phase of confused antagonism towards his father. I even had a notion that, if something new was really stirring in his mind, it actually had to do with what he was pleased to call his partnership with Cedric Mumford. I tried a fresh tack.

'Ivo, your grandfather's quite an old man – and I've a feeling that, as he grows older, it will be your job to protect him a bit. His judgement's not too good already, if you ask me. And I rather wonder about the effect of its becoming known that he's backed your magazine and put up the money for it. Young men can do outrageous things and in a sense get away with it. Even if they're clobbered at the time, people feel it has been high spirits and inexperience and so forth. But for a much older man to be mixed up in something even mildly scandalous is quite different. It will be held to be demeaning, or embarrassingly and disablingly gaga, or something of that sort.'

'Yes.' Ivo nodded decisively, and I realised – rather to my surprise – that he had understood every word of this. 'You're quite right in a way. I've thought about it. But the point about my grandfather is that he's tough. He's a damned sight tougher than my father. And he likes guts.' Ivo paused, and suddenly his face lit up with a vivid smile. 'I say!' he exclaimed, 'do you think my grandfather liked that guardian angel of mine? One's supposed to venerate one's old tutor. His signed photograph in one's book-lined den. That sort of thing.'

'I doubt whether your grandfather cherishes Mr Lempriere's photograph, although it's you who ought to know about that. In fact I'm fairly clear they didn't care for each other very much.'

'Understatement?'

'Probably.' The drift of Ivo's thought had become obscure to me. But at least it wasn't moving in an attractive direction. Deciding that I'd again had enough of his society, I moved towards the door.

'My grandfather doesn't much like the Provost either, does he? Think of that day at Otby.'

'I'd rather not, Ivo. It was distinctly not a success. Not that your grandfather didn't try quite hard at times. But the academic classes are not congenial to him. No more are they to you. But you know what I think about that.'

'Yes, I do.' Ivo was smiling again, and seemingly even more pleased with himself than before. Observing my disposition to depart, he stepped quickly forward and opened the door politely. "Don't worry,' he said.

'Grace! Gentlemen!'

I got into hall that evening just in time to hear the butler bellow out this injunction to silence. It had always struck me as a curiously phrased prelude to common supplication – the more so as we were at once going to be described therein as miserable and needy wretches. And nowadays there was the further circumstance that dinner was no longer a one-sex affair; the young men had gained the right to bring in girls if they wanted to, and their seniors had followed them in this abnegation of an immemorial rule – only with the austere proviso that at high table female guests had to be of a certifiably learned sort. The butler was thus chargeable with ungallantly insinuating that the *deus omnipotens, pater caelestis* whom the bible clerk was about to address might be offended if it were divulged to him that there were ladies present.

I communicated these thoughts to Charles Atlas when he presently sat down beside me. Very decently, he managed to be amused. Perhaps it wasn't before reflecting that having been an undergraduate at the college I was entitled to talk nonsense about it if I wanted to. Atlas never talked nonsense. A disposition to give much time to administrative affairs was making him, at what was almost a tender age, a man of mark on our local scene. Any chore shoved at him would be faithfully carried out. His background differed from Cyril Bed- worth's, but it seemed to me he would be the Bedworth of the place a generation – or half a generation – on. It may have been this association that made me inclined to tease Atlas, much as Tony and I had gone in for teasing Bedworth long ago. Atlas and I got along very well on this basis – a circumstance much more to his credit than to mine.

'Charles,' I asked, 'does being Tutor for Admissions automatically make you Tutor for Expulsions as well?'

'I haven't tested my powers in that direction, Duncan. But I rather imagine not. When useless people go down prematurely it's commonly a matter of *saeva necessitas* on the economic front. The Secretary of State for Education and Science, rummaging round on her desk, has come on a chit telling her that such and such a young gentleman refuses to pass any examinations. So she stops his grant, and that's it.

He transfers his energies to selling detergents or motor-cars, and never looks back.'

'What if there's no grant? What if it all comes on dad?'

'The college loses patience at precisely the point the Minister would. Or at least I hope so.' Atlas paused for a moment. 'The chap departs with its blessing – although he probably feels he's had a kick on the arse.' Atlas, always rather prim in manner, employed a normal public school vocabulary. 'I don't think there's any large problem involved.'

'Look at those rows of young men,' I said, 'swallowing tepid soup. About three hundred of them, I suppose. I can't see half a dozen who look as if they ever opened a book in their lives.'

'No, indeed! It's thoroughly heartening, wouldn't you say?' Atlas wasn't going to show himself unequal to this banter. 'Actually, two hundred are working hard, and ninety-four are working like mad. Or thereabout. But it's all most splendidly disguised.'

'That's on the charitable side, isn't it?'

'Well, yes. We could do a bit better in the Examination Schools, I admit. And even a few dead idle people are potential sources of infection, whom it's wise to keep an eye on. But we needn't panic. For example, your old friend's son – Ivo, is he called? He sounds a complete young nuisance, with singularly little claim to be tolerated around the place much longer. Arnold seems to think otherwise, but I doubt whether he really knows much about the boy.'

There was a moment's silence while we both finished our own soup – which had arrived tolerably hot. I didn't think it was quite casually that Atlas had narrowed this desultory talk to a specific instance.

'You're entirely right,' I said. 'Arnold's young Mumford is pretty well an imaginary creation.'

'My point is that the boy oughtn't to be blown up into an issue of principle, or anything of that kind. It would be perfectly proper and reasonable to go quietly easy with him for a time – even on the score of some extraneous consideration unconnected with his own merits.'

'Yes, I suppose so.' I wasn't going to dispute the proposition, although for a moment it surprised me. I'd known Atlas express opinions less accommodating in this field. Here in our academic microcosm, I told myself, was the political man whose macrocosmic representative was for me Lord Marchpayne. Tony would avoid head-on collision, feel ahead into a situation in the interest of compromise, precisely as I suspected this young man of doing now. 'Only,' I said, 'the thing mustn't be ludicrous? What you call the extraneous consideration must have a bit of weight to it.'

'Exactly!' Having agreed with emphasis, Atlas compressed his lips and glanced round him warily. 'I've heard something about your mission to Otby,' he murmured. 'Would you say the Provost was prepared to go a long way in the interest of that confounded letter-book?'

'It *looked* like that. But Cedric Mumford was so impossibly outrageous that we simply got nothing off the ground.'

'You were surprised, Duncan?'

'I was surprised.'

It must be Tommy Penwarden, you know. The thing has become a perfect King Charles's Head with him. And he has simply badgered our unfortunate Provost into losing all sense of proportion about it too. Don't you think?'

'I don't know that I do. The Provost doesn't strike me as that sort of person. And there's another thing. That Otby expedition wasn't – or wasn't in the first instance conceived as being – to do a slightly shameless deal over young Mumford. We were going to show ourselves as a thoroughly fair-minded crowd Ivo-wise – not much more than that. And hint that we might make Cedric Mumford an Honorary Fellow, like his son the eminent Lord Marchpayne.'

'Good God!'

I had difficulty in not laughing. My incautious revelation of this particular wile on the Provost's part had really shocked Atlas. It had to be concluded that Honorary Fellows were Sacred Cows of no common order.

'Yes, it's deeply alarming,' I said – and at once repented a remark so patently offered in a spirit of frivolity. 'But the Provost does at least think round a situation. He knows he couldn't on his conscience go easy – as you call it – on one boy, and not easy on another boy identically circumstanced. You'll find he's got anything of that sort well in hand.'

'The whole affair could so readily become an occasion of ridicule in the university at large. We're not popular, the Lord knows. One has to face it, although it's uncommonly unfair. It's not as if we had delusions of grandeur. We *are* grand, and damned well can't help it. So why should we get the stick? But there it is.'

This time I did laugh, although not by way of denying the justness of Atlas's remarks. I said I supposed it to be the sort of penalty attached to being cock house in a public school.

'It's much worse. *That* jealousy is mitigated by the knowledge that one house pretty rapidly succeeds another house at the top of the tree. But we've been in permanent possession for centuries.' Atlas stared gloomily at a fresh dish which had been set before him. 'Duncan,' he asked suddenly, 'you remember that party of Anthea Gender's? Did you have any further talk with Christopher Cressy at it later on?'

'No, I didn't.' This abrupt change of subject took me by surprise. 'But I met him again at a dinner-party the other evening.'

'Did he have anything to say about that tedious business?'

'The letter-book? Yes, he did – and quite unprompted by me, I need hardly tell you. I had a feeling he was up to something. You must know him better than I do, Charles. *Would* he be up to something?'

'Christopher's enormously entertaining.'

'No doubt. In fact, I don't deny it. He talked amusingly enough to me. But that's not the point.' I said this rather sharply, having grown tired of these tributes to Cressy's social charm.

'It might be the point, in a way.' Atlas again glanced circumspectly round the table. 'He likes to have a good thing to tell. Would you be inclined to say he was disposed to whet your curiosity?'

'I think he wanted me to go round whetting other people's curiosity. He was producing the tip of a mystery.'

'That sounds just like Christopher. What sort of mystery?'

'I'm not going to tell you, Charles. Don't misunderstand me. It's simply that I decided not to play – not to run around, that is, reporting his enigmatical remarks. He doesn't get any curiosities whetted by me.'

'But Duncan!' Forgetting his low-toned caution, Atlas cried out in dismay. 'That precisely *is* to whet. You can't leave me all agog. Do say.'

'Then I'll tell you just one thing. Cressy declared it to be wise and charitable in him to hold on to that hunk of stolen property. And if you can make anything of that, Charles, you're a long way ahead of me.'

# XV

W E  W E R E  N O W  over the hump of the Sixth Week, coasting
downhill towards the Christmas vacation with a rising breeze
behind us. For the undergraduates there would be an abrupt dispersal:
singly or in consort or in small faithful flotillas, they would scatter over
England, the continent, the habitable globe. The state of feeling this
prospect engendered I could remember clearly. It was complex,
compounded of regrets for ploys and relationships suspended and
impatience to get cracking on some fresh scheme whether of pleasure
or improvement according to the temperament of the individual
concerned.

The dons too felt the gale, but not quite to the same effect of
tacking idly round before being blown afar. For them their corporate
life would continue, and although their present pupils would cease
hammering importunately on their doors as the clock struck the hour
they themselves would be hard at work on the entrance examination,
knowing that the boys on whom their choice fell would be privileged
so to hammer through three or four long years to come. When the
examining was over, learned leisure would be theirs for a time.

Later on, I was going to find that the vacations – periods of
academic recess culpably generous in the regard of an outer world –
afforded interesting evidence on the varying contours of my colleagues'
private lives. Alike among the married and the single, there were men
who simply disappeared abruptly from the scene. In others the centre
of gravity could be observed to shift substantially but not radically;
they were around, but around less often. Yet others appeared to admit

in their habits no necessity for change. And the fact of so many people being away made the continuing presence of these the more noticeable, so that they had the appearance of haunting the place, of hanging around the quads, of lunching and dining in an awkwardly pertinacious manner.

But it was the coming and going of the young men and women that controlled, finally, the rhythm of our year. For their own better ease the dons had evolved a system whereby their juniors never lingered for long on the academic stage, yet their lives – even the lives of those who would have declared themselves as at no time disturbedly aware of the phenomena of undergraduate existence – were much conditioned by these mass exits and entrances. It was as if the ebb and flow of strong animal spirits owned a subtle and not clearly acknowledged influence on the rest of us. I concluded that there was something schizogenous in the pulse of Oxford life.

In relation to all this I wasn't yet clear where I myself stood. Excepting various short-term commitments entered into from time to time, I had never been other than a self-employed person before: now I had a permanent job – but one constructed on these patchy term-and-vacation lines. I had deliberately disrupted a good deal in the way of habit and assumption to make the change, my sufficient postulate being that when one feels a certain futility gathering around one it is wise to accept a break if it comes along. But now – and symptomatically in quite small and insignificant ways – I just didn't know. Was I going to remain in Oxford over Christmas? My house in Ravello awaited me, but I had never wintered there and wasn't sure I wanted to try. Should I go back to London; turn on the gas, the refrigerator, the immersion heater; ring up the Army and Navy Stores; resume (in default of a ministrant Plot) polishing my own shoes?

I found myself considering these questions as if they were matters of weight. Unattached people as a class have to be wary of self-absorption, and I decided I wasn't doing too well in the way of subordinating my own concerns to those larger and more impersonal purposes that a university is about. I thought a good deal about Fiona

– and a good deal, too, to the effect that any such thinking was of an irresponsible sort. It wasn't merely a matter of my being old enough – so famously just old enough – to be her father. That was self-evident, and I'd come out with it at once when Timbermill had revealed his bizarrely motivated design on us. It was also that Fiona's handling of the growth of our relationship exhibited so much waywardness and mockery and distancing persiflage that I'd be very well advised to think twice before thinking at all. What Fiona seriously thought about me, I couldn't know. It would be only prudent to suppose I came seldom into her head. Her crisp and open address, commonly comradely and asexual in tone, supported such a view. But what about that problematical occasion when she had talked ironically about us as possible marriage partners? It hadn't been serious, and it hadn't quite been straightforward fun either. It was as if there were something hovering in her that I hadn't got round to elucidating, and that I might or might not find agreeable if I did.

I didn't in the least distrust myself in thinking about Janet. Our relationship at that time seemed to me so marked by non-complication as virtually to be marked by nothing else at all.

Janet's having amazingly turned up in Oxford married to Ranald McKechnie struck me as one of those rare artistries of chance that are wholly beautiful and wholly innocent. It wasn't in my mind that we should again tumble out our hearts and histories to each other as when we were boy and girl on the balcony of an Edinburgh tea-shop. That would be inappropriate to our situation and our years. But I had a vision of, as it were, the passage into eternity of that moment at Anthea Gender's party in the middle of term when, across a crowded room, I had smiled at Janet and Janet had smiled at me.

And now I was going to lunch with the McKechnies at the end of this, the Seventh Week. It was a salient fact of the calendar, standing between me and those small perplexities over what I was to do with myself in the Christmas vacation, and it drove such college matters as I had been caught up in out of my head. Ivo Mumford had obligingly begged me not to worry about him. As I drove out of Oxford on a crisp late November morning I was worrying about nothing at all –

except certain *lacunae* (as Albert Talbert would have called them) in the otherwise copious directions McKechnie had scribbled out for me.

Where a man chooses to live is commonly his own affair, provided he is prepared to clock in for work at some prescribed hour. Oxford knows nothing of such chronometrical demands, and therefore goes in for topographical ones instead. Colleges, I had gathered, could in theory house their fellows, like grooms and gardeners, in specified dwellings for which the laws applicable to tied cottages were in force. In practice, however, these people lived where they pleased: Cambridge, for example, if the fancy took them that way. The university, on the other hand, did in general insist that its professors and similar persons should live within a certain radius of the centre of the city. The distance may have been ten miles or twenty; living, as I did, in college, the point was irrelevant to me, and I had never inquired; what was now clear was that the McKechnies must dwell at, or even beyond, the extreme verge of this confine. I found myself driving across Berkshire with my distinguished schoolfellow's crumpled envelope on the seat beside me.

I wondered whether it was Janet who had chosen a retreat so rural as I appeared to be heading for. McKechnie himself I'd have thought of as an urban man: the son and grandson and great-grandson of a scholar, he would surely think of civilised living in terms of ready access to learned colleagues and great libraries. Janet as a child had been a townee like myself, but whereas I had formed no more than a reasonably positive response to the kind of country life intermittently presented to me at Glencorry, Janet had nourished a steady passion for a region so remote in my imagination that I had thought of it, quite inaccurately, as among the farthest Hebrides. It seemed possible that, in some obscure fashion, the retired situation of her second conjugal dwelling had been made to mirror that of her first.

I was indulging in these reflections when I ought to have been keeping a wary eye on McKechnie's itinerary at its crucial points, and as a result I made a false turn which presently looked like costing me a good deal of time. I didn't know whether Janet's was to be a party or, so to speak, a domestic Edinburgh occasion, but in either case I oughtn't to be late for it.

The surrounding terrain was flat and with patches of woodland that precluded much of a view: only now and then there was a glimpse ahead of the line of the downs bounding the Vale of White Horse to the south. At one point I thought I saw the nick or hiccup on this skyline that marks the vallum of Uffington Castle. This put me in mind of the White Horse itself, to which J. B. Timbermill had once invited my attention as connected in some interesting and learned fashion with the coinage of a non-Belgic tribe called the Dobunni. In the hamlet of Uffington – he had on another occasion assured me – there were to be found a good many people of the name of Bunn – not necessarily connected (as in Happy Families) with the baking trade, but undoubtedly descended from those more or less Iron Age persons. Twenty years later, I knew, Timbermill had provided Fiona with the same picturesque if speculative information. So I was thinking of Fiona again when I eventually found what was undoubtedly the McKechnies' drive.

It was a long and winding drive, with some tide to be called an avenue, and at present inches deep in fallen leaves which treacherously masked formidable potholes. Beyond it rose the outline of a large, or at least lofty, red-brick dwelling. I slowed up, and as I did so become aware simultaneously of a great deal of noise and of the appearance of a small tornado or maelstrom of whirling leaves advancing with unnerving speed. I came to a halt, and a moment later was confronted by a Juggernaut-like mechanical monster swaying and bucketing alarmingly down upon me. Perched high on this, and clinging hazardously to its steering-wheel, was McKechnie himself.

At least he managed to stop the thing, with the result that our respective conveyances confronted each other nose to nose. I scrambled from my car. For a moment McKechnie stared down at me blankly. Then he spoke.

'Oh, yes – of course,' McKechnie said. And for a moment he seemed quite at a loss. 'Duncan,' he then added, 'how nice to see you.'

'I hope I'm not late.'

'No, of course not.' McKechnie descended from his perch, and I supposed that my last words had given him a clue to the situation. 'You're in very good time.' He eyed my car. 'Only, I'm terribly afraid you'll have to back. To the foot of the drive, that is. You see, when I have this leaf-gathering thing on, I can't back myself. I can turn easily enough where there's room for it. Quite a tight U-turn, as a matter of fact. I'll show you later. But with this in tow reversing tends to break the shackle. It's the same when I'm using it with the flail-mower in the paddock. But not with the rotary mower that's built into it. I can whizz backwards with that.' As he offered these abundant particulars, McKechnie was making elucidatory gestures in the direction of various parts of the Juggernaut. 'The leaves,' he said happily, 'are quite a job, just at the moment.'

I'm sure they must be.' I inspected the leaf-gathering component. It was a gleaming metallic receptacle, and appeared to me to own the dimensions of a small cottage. There were no leaves in it. I had a dim impression that it had somehow or other been hitched on the wrong way round. The effect recalled one of those films of the Wonders of Nature which run to frank exposure of the bizarre copulatory postures favoured by certain denizens of the deep. Some such technical slip-up perhaps explained the dervish dance the leaves had been achieving. 'I'll back down,' I said. 'Just a matter of *reculer pour mieux sauter*.' With this rather feeble witticism I returned to my car, reversed cautiously down the drive, and with equal caution swung round on the lane beyond. McKechnie's vehicle had already sprung into action again – so abruptly as to recall those advertisements for sports-cars which deal in miles per hour to be achieved in so many seconds from a standing start. It charged down the drive and hurtled into the road. McKechnie waved to me with one hand and with the other swung the wheel. It was clear that I was to witness the U-turn there and then. It happened – beneath the bonnet of an advancing lorry and with wheels shaving the farther ditch. McKechnie shouted what I took to be an injunction to follow him, and went swaying back up the drive, with dead leaves gyrating madly behind him.

This rapid revelation of a Ranald McKechnie hitherto unknown to me was bewildering but satisfactory. I wondered whether his attachment to rural pursuits was extensive and catholic or confined to the triumphs of mechanisation in the manner just exhibited. But now we had turned a corner and the house was before us. Even if it hadn't been possible to glimpse the village church standing just beyond a belt of trees I'd have been certain that it could have had only one start in life. Here was one of those architecturally unfortunate but abundantly commodious vicarages which the genius of the Anglican Church scattered around the countryside in the later decades of the nineteenth century. There would be a new vicarage now – one reflecting, if not the diminished consequence of the clergy, at least their more controlled procreative propensities. This one – together, no doubt, with the land constituting its glebe – had been acquired by the McKechnies when it had perhaps been in some disrepair. Although far from tumbledown, it didn't look in very good order now. Neither McKechnie nor Janet, the children of academic fathers as they were, could have any money in the rentier's sense of the term. But at least they weren't poor. They had no bills, for example, coming in from public schools.

McKechnie turned into a stable yard, I followed him, and we dismounted together. He was wearing old flannel trousers and a black pull-over so clerical in suggestion that I wondered whether he had found it abandoned on the premises. To this extent he retained at home that clerkly or subfusc appearance which characterised him at Oxford.

'I ought to have got changed earlier,' he said – although I don't think he could have noticed my eye on him. 'But there really is such a lot to do. I'm badly behind with the winter pruning. The hedges take time, too. I must show you what I've just got for them.' He dived into a shed, and reappeared a moment later carrying a complicated pair of shears on a trailing electric cable. 'You compress both hand-grips,' he said, 'and it operates. Like this.' The shears began to pulse, whirl and click violently. 'But as soon as you remove either hand it stops at once. They call it a fail-safe arrangement. And it will cut through practically anything.'

Including the flex,' I said.

'Well, yes – I suppose you might damage it that way.'

'I suppose you might.' I glanced at McKechnie apprehensively, rather wondering whether he ought to be allowed even a toy train. As if to reinforce this rational fear, he had perched the shears negligently on a window-sill beside us. They failed to fail safe, and were, indeed, emitting sinister green sparks in an alarming manner. They were also perceptibly creeping in an undesirable direction. Immediately below the window was an open water butt. 'Ranald,' I said, 'are you sure you've read all the directions? They don't seem to be behaving quite as they should.'

'You're perfectly right.' McKechnie looked at the shears in mild reproach and surprise. 'I'll switch off at the plug.' He vanished again – this time, it seemed to me, much at leisure – into the shed. The shears gave a loud click and were still. My sense of relief occurred simultaneously with the loud clanging of a bell. My first thought was that, after all, something fatal had occurred. Then I realised that the sound came from the direction of the house. McKechnie emerged again – not at all at leisure this time.

'Oh, dear!' he said. 'That's Janet.'

'Janet? Why, Ranald, it's exactly like Miss Clarke!'

'So it is!'

For a moment McKechnie and I stared at each other in an odd delight. Miss Clarke had been the head-mistress of the most junior department of that long-life Scottish academy in which we had both passed a full decade of our lives. And at the end of every 'play-time' she had certainly wielded just such a bell.

'And do you remember, Duncan? She screamed at the same time. At the top of her voice. As if we couldn't hear that ghastly tintinnabulation.' For the first time in my acquaintance with him, Ranald McKechnie laughed boisterously. I remembered how, at the Gaudy dinner six months before, he had quoted Lord Chesterfield to me as deprecating anything so ill-bred as audible laughter. We were both being ill-bred now.

'And clapped her hands,' I said, 'with demoniac violence.'

'So she did! She used to be utterly terrified. Only she couldn't have—could she? Clapped and tintinnabulated, I mean, simultaneously.

It wouldn't be possible.'

'No more it would. But she did, all the same.'

'Yes, indeed. There isn't a doubt about it.' For a further moment McKechnie and I contemplated this mystery with deep satisfaction. Then he waved a hand towards the house. 'I've just remembered,' he said. 'There are several other people coming to lunch, Duncan. I think we'd better hurry.'

'Yes,' I said – and I believe I was as scared as my host. 'I think we better had.'

The 'several other people' included, for a start, Fiona and her fellow-householder Miss Mountain. This puzzled me; indeed, I found it almost as perturbing as McKechnie's injudicious enthusiasm for mechanical contrivances. At Anthea Gender's party Janet hadn't known Fiona from Eve. Her first glimpse of my cousin had been at the moment I was receiving that cousinly kiss. She hadn't known Margaret Mountain either; and although she had read *The Orrery* she had spoken of it without enthusiasm. All this made it remarkable that she had so briskly cultivated the acquaintance of the two young women.

A lesser surprise was the presence of Arnold Lempriere, whom I'd not have thought of as frequenting the drawing- rooms and luncheon tables of collegiate ladies. Then I realised that his presence could be very simply explained. McKechnie, although not commonly attentive to such matters, had heard that Lempriere and I were related, and when this information was relayed to Janet it had occurred to her that my Aunt Charlotte's granddaughter was distantly related to him too. If she had invited him to lunch for the purpose of meeting Fiona he would certainly have accepted. He hadn't been pleased, I remembered, that Fiona's residence in Oxford had been unknown to him hitherto. And I had myself failed so far in my promise to bring them together.

However all this might be, it was plain that Lempriere and I were thought of as balancing the young people from the Woodstock Road. The other guests were the Bedworths.

Janet probably knew that Cyril Bedworth was my oldest friend in the college; indeed, it was quite likely that I had endeavoured to amuse her with some account of him long ago.

During sherry I addressed myself to eliciting from Miss Mountain some token of an ability to converse. It looked like the hardest job to hand at the moment. Not that Miss Mountain was exactly sulking. Her line was once more that of brooding in what I took to be a professionally attentive manner. At least I possessed the advantage of having read *The Orrery* by now. I thought better of it than Janet had apparently done. Being a writer who felt the twitch of his tether as soon as he had made an unassuming naturalism mildly amusing, I had a proper respect for fiction interwoven with symbolic implications of an elusive but presumably pregnant sort. *The Orrery* seemed to be like that. Its hero's passion for his aunt had to be received (like much in Holy Scripture, the Provost would have said if pressed) in a mysterious sense. So, perhaps, had much else in the novel. *The Orrery* wasn't like *Le Rouge et Le Noir* or *Madame Bovary.* But why should it be?

'I'd like it suppressed.' This was Miss Mountain's response, drily uttered rather in Fiona's manner, to the civil remarks I'd offered about the book – a legitimate conversational resource, I'd felt, in the light of my standing as a *confrère* of sorts.

'You've come on the scene too late for that, I'm afraid. Fifty years ago it would have been suppressed, without a doubt.'

'I don't think you think I mean that.' Miss Mountain, although continuing to regard me broodingly, seemed unoffended and even amused. 'Withdrawn by the publisher – or called in, or whatever the proper phrase is. I'd like to write it again. I see it differently. But publishers don't like that sort of thing.'

'I suppose not. Couldn't you forget about it as it now lingers in the bookshops, and rewrite it for reissue some years ahead?'

'I'm not a don, Mr Pattullo. I have to make a living, and I'm in the middle of another book.' 'I see the difficulty.' It hadn't hitherto occurred to me that by becoming a don I had ceased to be under the kind of economic necessity Miss Mountain had invoked. 'You must just press ahead.'

'*The Orrery* – and where it goes wrong in the most ghastly and juvenile fashion – keeps on coming between me and this other thing.

Fiona says I ought to develop two independent working personalities – and keep one in England and one in France.'

'Have you a base in France?'

'My parents live in Paris – if that can be called having a base.'

I didn't see why it couldn't. Miss Mountain's schooldays were barely behind her – or so it was possible to feel – and there seemed nothing inappropriate in the idea of her periodic domestication in a parental home. She had spoken however, as of an evident absurdity. I wondered whether Fiona thought that Paris would be a good idea from time to time. The relationship of these two young women remained opaque to me. They might be devoted to each other or simply stuck with each other's society. I didn't know.

But I had at least succeeded in transforming Miss Mountain into quite a talkative person, and I wondered whether this new disposition would survive our being joined by anybody else. The question looked like receiving an immediate answer, for Lempriere now came up to us. I wondered whether he would introduce the subject of lady novelists in the succession to Mrs Humphry Ward. It proved, however, that there was another matter on his mind. Having already been introduced, he came out with it at once.

'Do you happen,' he demanded, 'to be descended from poor Armine Mountain, who died at Futtyghur?'

'I don't think so.' Miss Mountain was not discomposed. 'Was he a friend of yours, Mr Lempriere?'

'He died round about 1850. One of the Quebec Mountains. I've some connection with them.'

'Oh, the Quebec Mountains! Bishops and people. I've heard of them. Not relations of mine at all.'

'Well, it's something to be positive.' Lempriere gave his chuckle in a somewhat perfunctory or half-hearted manner. He was not in a good temper, so that I wondered whether he had failed to impress Fiona with the significance of their consanguinity. 'Duncan here wouldn't bother to inform himself about his own grandmother.' As he said this Lempriere glanced at me severely, and his eyebrows effected the curious horizontal glide intimating his wish that one should retire with him into a corner for some confidential purpose – a code- signal to which I had first tumbled at the Gaudy breakfast. Since we were isolated for the moment with Miss Mountain it was an impracticable proposal; he might have been imagining himself in a common room, where one man can break away from another in mid-sentence with no more than a ritual glance of apology. Now, realising that I was going to stay put, he resolved upon confidence on the spot, and actually raised his hand to his mouth by way of indicating the fact.

'Uncommonly awkward cat got out of the bag, Dunkie.' He contrived to speak in what must be called a gruff whisper. 'Concerns poor old Edward. Say nothing to anybody. Tell you later.' He nodded to the two of us indifferently, and walked away.

Miss Mountain offered no comment on this behaviour, although she must have been conscious of it as censurable in one who had plainly enjoyed the advantages of a well-conducted nursery. The subject to which she turned, however, suggested that Lempriere had brought the theme of *tristis senectus* to mind.

'Fiona,' she said, 'is very anxious about Dr Timbermill.'

'So am I.'

'She thinks something ought to be done, and I believe she's right. But I'm afraid I'm out of it. The old man doesn't like me.'

'So I noticed.' 'It sticks out a mile. He thinks I'm a bad influence on Fiona.'

'It's a very arbitrary point of view.'

'Do you mean that it's Fiona who is a bad influence on me?'

'No, I don't. Why ever should I! I haven't thought of either of you that way at all.' I realised that this comprehensive disclaimer wasn't quite honest, since I had at least wondered whether one of these young women notably ran the other.

'I've heard it's said that Fiona has deflected me in my writing – that it has taken a slant from her cast of mind.'

'People get all sorts of ideas about writers.' This was a feeble remark. But Miss Mountain's statement, although interesting, had been a little awkwardly on the self-absorbed side. She was very young, indeed, and the very young have the privilege of taking themselves seriously even on socially inapposite occasions. I felt back to our previous topic. 'But, Margaret, why should Timbermill disapprove of you?'

'Because I'm not a scholar, I suppose.' Miss Mountain had given me a swift look. 'He's convinced I'll lead Fiona into frivolous courses – intellectually speaking, that is. *He* sees it *that* way on. Of course he's conscious of something of the sort in himself.'

'I don't quite follow that.'

'The *Magic Quest* thing. It kept him from completing some enormous academic labour or other, and now he regrets having been lured away by it.'

'Then he's wrong.'

'I agree.' Miss Mountain's head – which just came up to my shoulder – gave a decided nod. 'It mayn't be a work of the most enduring quality, but it's miles ahead of any labour of conservative scholarship. So what the old man has is a false conscience.'

'You may be right.'

'Not that he isn't still capable of scraps of imaginative thinking. That's what enables him to say the most frightful things from time to time. Do you understand me?'

'Yes, I do. Frightful things should be said only in novels. But I suppose we must put up with old people's notions. Unless, of course, we believe in euthanasia, or something of that kind.'

'I don't.'

'Or that the old can be quietly tucked away.'

'I'm afraid I don't believe in that either, Mr Pattullo. Or not for somebody like J. B. Timbermill.'

'He must be let go down with his colours flying?'

'Something like that. Which is why there's a problem.'

This colloquy came to an end upon a summons to luncheon. We had assembled in a drawing-room which had been rescued only in part from somewhat oppressive ecclesiastical associations. The windows were high, pointed, embellished with tracery in their upward parts, and pervasively fringed or scalloped in stained glass; through them one looked across a leaf-strewn lawn to a rustic summer-house and the surviving framework of a child's swing. Within, a seemly clerical austerity was conveyed through the instrumentality of much highly varnished pitch-pine, and there was an enormous fireplace guarded on either hand by sword-bearing archangels hewn from the same material. The hall through which we made our way to the dining-room contrived a similar effect, particularly in being entirely floored with slippery encaustic tiles in a pattern of obscurely liturgical association. It struck me what a barn of a place the whole house was for a childless couple.

I had gone ahead with Janet, and it was hard upon this thought that I found myself alone with her for a moment – and viewing, over a less intimidating mantelpiece, something totally unexpected: a small landscape painting by my father.

'Isn't it fun?' Janet said. She was suddenly more animated than I had known her since we were restored to each other. 'It's probably worth as much as everything else in the house put together.'

'Getting on that way.' I was so delighted by this outrageous remark that – although it was nonsense – I concurred at once. 'I like it very much. Have you had it long?'

'Yes, of course, Dunkie. Your father gave it to me as his wedding-present. I love it. Calum loved it too.'

This unexpected information quite overwhelmed me. The act had been my father all over. He had liked Janet. He had liked her without – I had long since come to understand – remotely sharing my mother's persuasion that she would ever be his daughter-in-law.

'Janet,' I said, 'I used to imagine you and your family in your home. By your fireside, mostly. But I didn't know to put this above it.'

'You can do that now. Mr Duncan Pattullo, where are you going to sit?'

I came to my senses as this problem was being coped with. *Placement-wise,* four married couples are an impossibility, and even four males and four females require thought. Janet put Mabel Bedworth at one end of the table and herself at the other. I was on Mrs Bedworth's right and Fiona was on mine with Bedworth on her other side. Opposite me was McKechnie and opposite Bedworth was Lempriere with Miss Mountain between them. As this got Mrs Bedworth on the right of her host and Lempriere on the right of his hostess it must have been eminently correct. Watching these middle-aged *convenances* transacting themselves, however, I might have been asking myself, with the poet, about the whereabouts of the penny world I bought to eat with Pipit behind the screen. Janet and I had buried our eagles and our trumpets. Or so it was proper to believe.

'I want you to come to London with me,' Fiona announced.

'I'd love to. For a show?'

'A lecture at Burlington House.'

'Oh.' I didn't make this an exclamation of delight. 'I suppose we could have dinner somewhere afterwards. What's the lecture about?'

'It's about Types of Manorial Structure in the Northern Danelaw.'

'You must be joking.' I had tried to remember Nick Junkin's manner of making this rejoinder.

'It might interest you very much. It would have at one time, wouldn't it?'

'No, Fiona. You've got that impression from Timbermill, and he remembers it all wrong. I admired him enormously, as I think I've told you, and it made me work for him like a black. But it wasn't honestly my sort of thing. And I'm miles and miles away from it now. An infant as clever as you are must see that clearly enough.'

'Well, yes. But J. B. thinks we could rekindle your interest. He's very keen you should hear Steenstrup.'

'Is that the lecturer's name?'

'Yes. He's a great authority on Danish institutions in England.'

'Steenstrup? How very interesting!' It was Bedworth on Fiona's other side who broke in with this, no doubt feeling that interruption was in order on a learned topic. 'Is it at the British Academy, Miss Petrie? I can't have had a card about it. The period isn't exactly mine, of course. But I've read in it to some extent.'

I had no doubt that this was true. Bedworth, although scarcely advanced in middle age, was the old-fashioned kind of don who despised what he would have called narrow specialisation and went in for encyclopaedic studies. To what extent anything in his mind pulled them together, I didn't know. But he was now well launched with Fiona. They discussed the Great Commendation to King Edgar, which appeared to be something that had happened in the year 973.

I was left for a short space to my own thoughts. The unexpected sight of my father's painting' had bumped me back a quarter of a century, and I was asking myself why I hadn't sent my own wedding-present to Janet and her Calum. I had written a letter I couldn't recall, although I knew I needn't be ashamed of it. But I had left undone the thing I ought to have done – which was to pack up my *Young Picts watching the arrival of Saint Columba* and despatch it to her. The obviousness of this, starting up after half a lifetime, was daunting. I stared at it.

Suddenly I became aware that Mabel Bedworth, although continuing to lend her ear to McKechnie, had her eye on me. This would have been noteworthy at any time – her ocular habits being as they were – but now it arrested me. I was confirmed in the perception that, like Margaret Mountain sitting opposite her, she was a person of an observing habit. I'd hardly reflected on the fact before it struck me that Janet at the head of her table was doing a certain amount of observing too. We were like a bunch of candidates – I told myself – at some horrible newfangled Civil Service examination, manipulating knives and forks while keeping a wary regard on one another.

At this point my right shoulder, as if mysteriously sensitised, told me that Fiona was becoming restless, and I detached her with some ruthlessness from the affairs of King Edgar or whoever.

'Look,' I said, 'I'll come to that lecture, and we'll have a tremendous feast afterwards. But it must stop there.'

'The feasting, Duncan?'

'No, not at all. The lecture-going, or any other charade for J.B.'s benefit. It wouldn't *be* for his benefit. Margaret'—I felt that Miss Mountain must be thus referred to now—'has more sense than you have. A great man isn't to be cosseted.'

'Very well.' Fiona took this instantly. 'But it puts his ball in your court, cousin. Rescue's up to you.'

I was about to say that the conception of rescue was a dubious one when a small distraction occurred. McKechnie had got to his feet and was effecting a belated distribution of wine. He was far from being an inhospitable man but was undeniably an absent-minded one. And Bedworth – who ought to have been talking to Janet, since Lempriere had fallen into an abstraction – addressed him across the table, it having apparently come into his head that his host ought to be publicly congratulated on the spaciousness of his dwelling. Bedworth admired spaciousness. Had he not, in the very first half-hour of my acquaintance with him, commented favourably on the dimensions of his low-hutched attic study on Surrey Four?

'Yes, indeed,' McKechnie said. He was gauging with some exactness the point to which he should fill Miss Mountain's glass. 'It's rather too large for us, really. For instance, there's a whole nursery wing. But that will be quite useful as the books pile up.'

I have been conscious, from time to time, of men echoing with a total unawareness words celebrated on the lips of a dramatic personage, but as a prime example this would have taken some beating. McKechnie was perhaps quite like George Tesman, although his scholarship was certainly of a weightier sort. Janet, on the other hand, wasn't in the least like Hedda Gabler.

Because effected across the table, the exchange had been heard by everybody, and its infelicitous character remarked. Curiously enough, the situation was dealt with promptly by Lempriere. A moment before, he had appeared totally withdrawn after the fashion he often exhibited at high table. Now he was smiling at Janet with an air of alert attention, and offering an adequate emergency remark on the subtle character of the dish in front of him. It was a flicker of the social expertness which had no doubt been in full play during the period of his telling lies for his country abroad. Janet named with composure the ingredients of a sauce.

Miss Mountain was to be observed as paying more attention to Lempriere during the remainder of the meal, her interest having been caught by such prompt action on the part of one whom she probably regarded as virtually ready for entombment or incineration. I wondered whether, like numerous English novelists at that time, she was projecting a romance devoted to octogenarian and nonagenarian persons. I also wondered, but almost equally idly, what grave matter Lempriere had to communicate to me about the Provost. He had spoken of a cat being let out of a bag, an expression commonly used in a context of emergent scandal. But it was impossible to think of scandal in connection with Edward Pococke; one could as plausibly postulate some wild frivolity on the part of the Dalai Lama or the Pope of Rome. Nor was I impressed by Lempriere's deploying of his habitual injunction to reticence, since he commonly underestimated the existing currency of the intelligence he proposed to confide to one. So much did I see it this way, indeed, that had the opportunity occurred I'd have asked Bedworth whether Lempriere had made him a similar promise of piquant disclosure. But after lunch we all went into the garden, where there was bright sunshine but not much warmth in the air, and Bedworth was carried off by McKechnie, no doubt to have sundry resources in the way of mechanised horticulture exhibited to him. I found myself still with Fiona. We surveyed a derelict tennis court. It was a hard court, but cracked and undulating. Bindweed was at work on it in a big way.

'You'd think they might at least have a dog,' Fiona said.

'It wouldn't do. It would get chewed up by one of McKechnie's monsters. Or be electrocuted.'

'Canaries, then. Or budgies.'

'Fiona, don't be disagreeable.'

'How long have they been married?'

'I don't know.'

'How odd!'

'There's nothing odd about it.' I said this with the more emphasis because it wasn't true. There was indeed something surprising in my having avoided the acquisition of this simple information. 'But for several years, I'd suppose.'

'Why did she ask Margaret and me to lunch?'

'The slighter your acquaintance, the nicer of her it was.'

'One can look at it that way.'

'If you can't look at it more graciously, you'd better not look at it at all, Miss Petrie.'

'Wasn't she—'

'Stop calling your hostess "she". It's monstrously uncivil.'

'You're quite the Glencorry, Duncan. My grandfather would have said just that.'

'No, he wouldn't. Uncle Rory would have said nothing at all. Or just given an order to leave the room.'

'Your memory's good, too. I suppose it comes with age. Do you remember a lot about Mrs McKechnie?'

'Yes, a great deal. But not quite as much as I'd like to.'

'I love our chats, Duncan.' But Fiona, as she made this light remark, had stopped, and was looking at me gravely. 'What's Janet McKechnie after?' she asked.

'You mustn't impute designs to people. It's small-minded.'

'Please, that's enough of the governess-in-trousers turn, Duncan. Answer me seriously.'

'There's no serious answer. Janet's not after anything.'

'Would you say there's a standard resource when old adorers turn up?'

'There may be.'

'You *were* an adorer?'

'Yes. We were both extremely young. Much younger than you are now, Fiona.'

'Has it occurred to you she's match-making? That at this moment, as she shows your dotty old colleague her herbaceous border, she's hoping we're already clasped in one another's arms?'

'Shut up, Fiona!'

'I call *that* monstrously uncivil.'

'Then just be quiet.' I was myself silent for a moment. I believe I was very displeased. Once had been enough for Fiona's mockery at the notion of a lovers' relationship between us, and I'd had that at another party. But I was upset less by this than by the imagination of Janet's in any sense planning for me. It was a wholly disconcerting importation into our new relationship as I'd been thinking of it. 'We'd better go and find the others,' I said.

'Duncan's scared. Duncan's fetting.'

I hadn't heard this insulting Scots word since I left school, and I wondered where Fiona could have picked it up. Conceivably her brothers used it when prompted to impute abject terror to somebody. So potent are childish associations that it at once turned me childishly truculent.

'You're a very tiresome young person,' I said. 'You ought to be spanked.'

'Try it.'

At this the years rolled back in earnest. For the first time in my acquaintance with Fiona I was really aware of her as my cousin Anna Glencorry's daughter. Her challenge had been flung at me as an immediate physical possibility, sharply actual. Just so, in fact, had Anna and I occasionally initiated those tumblings and pantings in the heather which still sometimes returned to me in dreams. And suddenly I thought I saw where the power of Fiona's pull on me lay. She wasn't a bit like her mother: this I had been aware of on my first glimpse of her. She was like my own mother – which doubtless imported a Freudian factor into our situation. But the crucial fact was the depth at which, in Fiona, a sexuality quite as strong as Anna's moved beneath the androgynous or 'unisex' persona she had created for herself. Her rebarbative surfaces were like the barrier of thorn surrounding the desirable mistress in the mediaeval allegory.

If this poetic image really came to me it didn't help much to clarify my feelings at the moment. I was simply aware of Fiona as being more attractive to me than it was at all likely I could be to her.

'No sadism today,' I said. 'And not when we go to town for that lecture and dinner either.'

'Then come on.' Fiona tossed her head and laughed. She may have felt that she had gone a little far in inviting castigation in the garden of a Regius Professor. 'I'll ring you up about it. And shall I send you a preliminary reading list?'

'Fiona, dear,' I said, 'don't make me laugh.'

# XVI

L EMPRIERE HAD COME out to the McKechnies' house by taxi in the confident expectation of getting a lift back to Oxford from a fellow-guest – and this it was up to me to provide, since I could drive him straight into college. He made an irritable business of settling into the car, and snubbed me when I offered him a rug. Here was confirmation of the view that he had formed an unfavourable impression of his new-found kinswoman. Learned women must have come his way professionally from time to time, but he was of a generation that still hadn't schooled itself to take them for granted. He suffered from what somebody at that period was calling the flying pig syndrome, or a disposition to marvel that a woman could do this or that at all. With women content to be treated to courtliness and banter he would get on tolerably well, although he mightn't be easy with them. But a stringent young scholar like Fiona, existing with that prickly hedge all round her and emerging briefly with intent to shock, was beyond the scope of his sympathy. He would be restored to good humour, I judged, only if he made a satisfactory effect with whatever news he had to give me.

He wasn't in a hurry to begin. Or rather he was, but didn't care to admit it. Just as on the occasion when he had thought to inform me of the existence of Peter Lusby, he preserved silence for a time. It may have been his calculation that he was building up a high state of expectation in me. This wasn't so. For one thing, I had no belief in sensation of any sort as likely to be associated with Edward Pococke. For another, I was busy thinking about Janet.

We had not had much talk together at her luncheon party: almost notably little, indeed, considering that it had been a small-scale affair. The fact didn't worry or offend me, since it seemed to me that we had our remaining lifetimes to be fast friends in. And as I took even casual glances to be a kind of communion this was a satisfactory thought. Perhaps I was in a peculiar state of mind. If some of my feelings about Fiona were thrown in, it became very peculiar indeed. John Keats's Endymion, in a high old muddle between his elusive goddess and the Indian Maid, commanded cold clarity in comparison. Not that my brains were in a whirl, or anything of that kind. I was giving the situation (if there was a situation) what journalists had not yet begun to dub a low profile. I did pay further attention to the one thing that had disturbed me at the party, which was Fiona's attributing some match-making intention to our hostess. And here was something I felt lucid about. It wasn't true. In no circumstances could such an activity (although blameless in itself) be other than foreign to Janet's character. And that was that. If any further conclusion flowed from this, I didn't trouble to hunt for it.

We were skirting Frilford golf course. It had been the scene, long ago, of that famous misadventure which had befallen Tony Mumford, Cyril Bedworth and myself in our freshman phase. The memory of this might well have set my thoughts dwelling on the Provost, since it was he whom Bedworth's inexpert brassy-shot had winged. Instead, I was wondering whether I had ever told the story to Janet; whether the extent of my communication with her in that ill-starred year had still been such as to make it likely. My memories of those days were various and abundant, and they couldn't in the nature of things be other than vivid; some of them were painfully so. Yet it was extraordinary how they lay in my mind in a state of chronological confusion. Had this come before that? In which vacation had one or another sign appeared or definitive occasion occurred? I had kept a journal throughout the period, but it had aimed at being an intellectual chronicle of impressive scope. It still lay in a drawer. It would be more interesting now had it concerned itself with a more unassuming Duncan Pattullo, the confused youth whom I had judged unworthy of the dignity of chronicle.

'Remember that confounded letter-book, Dunkie?'

Lempriere came out with this question as I slowed to join the main Faringdon-Oxford road. I turned and glanced at him blankly.

'Letter-book, Arnold?' I repeated.

'Good God, man! Stop wool-gathering. That Blunderville thing.'

'Yes, of course. What about it?'

'It's in the news.' Lempriere's tone and accompanying chuckle conveyed a malicious effect which was new from him in my experience. The sardonic was his mode. 'You know about poor old Edward's having suddenly become mad keen to get hold of it?'

'I suppose it might be put that way. You and I have discussed this before. I don't think I'd always be quite confident about what the Provost's after.' (I had heard 'poor old Edward' from Lempriere several times that term; it seemed a perverse way in which to refer to a man a good deal younger than himself.) 'I'd say he's given to windlasses and assays of bias, you know.' It was sometimes tempting to tease Lempriere with nonsense of this sort. 'By indirections finding directions out.'

'A Polonius complex, Dunkie?' This time Lempriere's was an innocent chuckle. 'Perhaps so – although the man's no dotard. But the point is that this thing's all over Oxford.'

'This thing that you're going to tell me about so confidentially?'

'One wouldn't care to be identified as a principal agent of dissemination.' The chuckle had gained by several decibels, now seeming to involve Lempriere's nose as well as his gullet. I supposed him to have been recalling the jargon of his diplomatic days. 'I hear,' he went on, 'you've met that fellow Cressy?'

'Yes, I have.'

'Charles told me. Charles says you were a bit close about it.'

'Perhaps I was, Arnold. I have a feeling I was being invited to spread gossip – act as a disseminating agent, in fact.'

'Did Cressy say anything about this rubbishing collection of Blunderville letters and so forth?'

'Yes, he did.' I had an instinct that there was no longer any point in being cagey about the encounter at the dining club. 'He said the volume has a lot to do with Blunderville domestic affairs. There would be, for example, material for what he called an interesting little paper on the relations of masters and servants at that time.'

'Exactly! The letter-book reveals that poor old Edward's great-grandfather was the fourth marquis's butler.'

Lempriere's words had been offered as a bombshell. I believe he expected me to brake sharply, or swerve madly towards the kerb. Keeping without much effort on a steady course, I gave a moment to finding an appropriate reaction.

'So what?' I asked.

'Don't be silly, Dunkie.' Lempriere was seriously displeased with me. 'How would you feel yourself at such a thing bobbing up about your great-grandfather?'

'I take it I had four great-grandfathers, just like other people. The Pattullo one I've always supposed to have given most of his time to thinning out his turnips and carrots. So if I heard he'd really been butler to some grandee I'd think of it as a rise in the world.'

'I detest the affecting of robust egalitarian sentiments.'

This was Lempriere in one of his explosively arrogant moments, but I had in honesty to wonder whether he had a point. I owned that tenuous connection by marriage with his family – old-established gentry, I vaguely imagined, of Huguenot extraction. But wasn't I also the lineal descendant of King Gorse – a personage of an antiquity so extreme that it was highly probable he had never existed at all? What was Charlemagne to that – or even Pippin the Short? Perhaps there lurked in me a strain of feeling in these matters as dotty as that animating my Uncle Rory himself.

But this was irrelevant, and I turned back to the nub of the situation.

'Whatever you think of the Provost,' I said, 'and I have a wholesome regard for him myself, you can't claim *he's* silly.'

'He's a very sensitive man.'

'Arnold – just what's the idea? Did Christopher Cressy stumble on this piece of backstairs history, sit on the evidence out of regard for a former colleague, and then launch the ludicrous disclosure, for no reason at all, twenty years on?'

'Ludicrous – that's precisely it.' Lempriere waited for some response I didn't produce. 'A ludicrous time-bomb. I don't condone the thing. You mustn't think that. The Cressys came over with William. But, like any other family, they can produce a beggar on horseback from time to time.' Lempriere paused on this gleam of sanity. Then, for the first time in my memory of him, he laughed aloud. 'Poor old Edward,' he said, 'might set up a kind of trade union in the Lodging with that fellow Honey.'

This flash of glee baffled and dismayed me. It was a relief when the gates of the college were before us.

There was a note from the Provost on my mantelpiece. I opened it at once.

> Dear Duncan,
> I wonder whether you can possibly dine with me, *en garçon,* in the Lodging tomorrow? (Camilla has to be in town.) Marchpayne is coming up, not without some matters of moment to discuss. As, I believe, his oldest friend in college, and as one having some insight into our affairs, your presence would be invaluable to me. So I do hope I may prevail upon you – whose kindness is so invariable. Eight o'clock for a little later. Marchpayne has a Cabinet committee in the afternoon.
>
> Yours ever, EDWARD

Having briefly considered this summons, I rang up Tony, and was surprised to get through to him at once. I think I'd have done my best to have him hauled out of the Cabinet Room itself.

'Tony, this is Duncan. I've been asked to muck in at your dinner with the Provost tomorrow.'

'That's fine.'

'It's nothing of the sort. I don't think I like what it's in aid of.'

'What do you think it's in aid of?'

'More airing of your obsession with Ivo's academic career. And an attempt at horse-trading about it.'

'Oh, come! It's not quite like that, Duncan. I've got the chap to see sense.'

'Ivo?'

'Pococke, you idiot. All that's needed now is just a little dignified accommodation all round. So come and do your bit, like an old pal.'

'Listen, Tony. I've something to tell you. It's about that damned letter-book.'

'That what?'

'Those Blunderville papers that Christopher Cressy filched, and that I went with the Provost to Otby to see your father about, because of your father's having become some sort of trustee. You know perfectly well what I'm talking about.'

'Oh, yes – I do remember.' Tony said this perfectly composedly. 'I'm not quite sure you've got that occasion right. But never mind for the moment. What about the blessed letter-book?'

'The Provost's reason for going madly out of his way to get it back—'

'Yes, you have got it cock-eyed, all right. But go on.'

'It's because it chronicles the portentous information that the fourth marquis's butler was Edward Pococke's great-grandfather. Tony, you just *can't* trade on such an absurd and demeaning—'

'How absolutely splendid!' Tony had shouted with most indecent delight. 'What an awful pity it isn't true.'

'Isn't true?'

'My dear Duncan! Cressy still has this thing?'

'You know perfectly well he has.'

'It's because he has told somebody or other about Pococke the butler that somebody else has been able to tell you?'

'Yes – and half Oxford as well, it seems.'

'God, Duncan, you are an innocent.'

'What the hell do you mean by that?'

'My dear man, did you ever write a bedroom comedy?'

'A bedroom comedy?' I was so bewildered that for a moment the point of the question actually eluded me.

'Your precious friend Cressy clearly goes in for such impromptu inventions. And do you know where I think that letter-book is now? On the way back to your librarian, I'd say, with a polite note apologising for having retained it rather longer than he'd intended. And no depth of research will find a menial Pococke in it. Don't you know the Provost is descended from an eminent Orientalist of the same name, who flourished in the seventeenth century? Cressy has simply thought up a new joke that can't last a week. Look, it's nice of you to have rung up. But can we now talk sense?'

'Very well. Can you tell me why, on your view of the thing, the Provost was so keen of a sudden to recover this Blunderville lumber that he dragged me out to Otby, all set to explain to your quite impossible father—'

'You leave my old dad alone.'

'All right. But all set to explain how anxious the college was to be fair to Ivo, and how wonderful it is to be an Honorary Fellow, and heaven knows what?'

'Because of the Trust, of course.'

'The Trust?'

'The Blunderville Trust, or the Mountclandon Trust, or whatever it's called.'

'I don't know very much about it.'

'Nor did I, till the other day – except that they were making my father a key man on it, God help them. But it's clear your blessed Provost did. Only he's been keeping it under his hat.'

'Keeping just what under his hat? For the Lord's sake, Tony!'

'The glorious truth. Our trump card, my boy.' The telephone suddenly made strange noises which must have been occasioned by boisterous laughter. 'The whole concern has to be wound up next year, and there's provision for enormous charitable benefactions. They're to be entirely at the discretion of the trustees. I'd be inclined to estimate – having made an inquiry or two – that what the Provost has his sights on for the college may be half a million or thereabout. Well, *Paris vaut bien une messe.*' Again Tony laughed loudly, apparently much pleased with this historical parallel. 'Which is more than that absurd letter-book is. Your wily boss was using that simply as a stalking-horse. By way of sounding out my father's temper, if you like.'

'He certainly managed that.'

'Or approaching under cover. But let's take it that things are in the open now. So you'll come to that dinner?'

'I suppose I bloody well must.'

'Sunshine Dunkie had ever a gracious word.' Tony was obviously in the highest spirits. 'Until then, then.'

'Tony, just a minute. Do you mind if I ask you one question? It's about Ivo.'

'Go ahead.'

'It's about his expectations. Do they depend more on you, or on his grandfather?'

'What a rum curiosity! On me ultimately, I'd suppose – although I haven't a bean at present. It's even reasonable to say that my ministerial salary is quite a consideration with me.'

'Poor Marchpayne – the unmistakable stamp of poverty on everything.'

'Yes, yes – Henry James: I know. But I think Ivo's eye is chiefly on his grandfather, lolly-wise. He's not exactly a far- sighted boy. Have you heard anything about that magazine?'

'I rather think it must be printed by now.'

'I hope it isn't altogether too . . . but never mind. Duncan, I've a queue of people outside my door in this wretched morgue, all weighed down with affairs of state. See you tomorrow. Good-bye.'

I wasn't pleased with myself for having relayed the story of the fourth marquis's butler to Tony on what my inner ear now told me had been a note of ingenuous credulity. I wasn't pleased with Christopher Cressy, whose conversation with me about the letter-book had probably been the occasion of the fable first starting up in his fancy. And hadn't I, at the time, got the likelihood of its *being* a fable firmly by the tail – only to let it slip from me afterwards? This was thoroughly mortifying. And although I sympathised with the Provost (at whose supposed lowly and inconsiderable generation some appreciable part of Oxford was now conceivably laughing, although he was probably in total ignorance of the fact) I found myself, on consideration, pleased with him least of all.

The Provost had taken me on a ride to Otby in more senses than one, having evolved, it seemed to me, a totally unnecessary subtlety of approach to the monstrous Cedric Mumford which had necessitated some disingenuous remarks – to say the least of it – to myself. It was true that he now stood revealed as having been opening a campaign in the serious interests of the college, and this in a context in which the wretched Ivo constituted an uncomfortable complication. I supposed he had seen the alienated letter-book and the possibility of recovering it by way of the Blunderville trustees as a means of flattering Cedric Mumford's self-consequence and kindling his interest in his old college. It was a plan that had failed to pay off – which probably tends to be the fate of many plans conceived in an unnecessarily devious manner. I judged, however, that I'd have been amenable to trying it out had it been frankly disclosed to me. The Provost's councils-of- princes foible had got in the way of that, with the result that I was left in a state of resentment over the whole manoeuvre. It was not an attitude I must take along to the forthcoming dinner. My job was to use the new information that had come to me (although again not from the Provost) to further any reputable hunt for a great deal of money. And what *was* reputable could be left with some confidence to Edward Pococke. Every man has his price. But I doubted whether the Provost would judge Paris worth a mass if for 'mass' one was to read any improper indulgence to Cedric Mumford's grandson. About Ivo's future, nevertheless, it was apparent that he was keeping his options open. He had discovered excellent reasons for possible charity towards Nicolas Junkin, who was under the same threat of eternal banishment as his neighbour on Surrey Four. So the dinner-party promised interest.

I encountered Junkin later that day. He came tumbling down our staircase with his usual precipitation, but while unarming a young woman and kissing her as they ran. This complex behaviour almost resulted in a collision in my doorway.

'Oh, hullo!' Junkin said. 'This is Moggy. Isn't she splendid?'

'Yes, indeed. How do you do?' I shook hands with Moggy, whose photograph it was that now graced Junkin's room. She was a good-looking girl, with a healthy complexion and a straight glance. 'Are you both in a hurry,' I asked, 'or can you come in and have a drink?'

'Ten minutes,' Junkin said with decision. 'Because we're a bit late for a party. We've been asleep.'

I wondered whether Junkin would have given this candid information to Plot. Moggy seemed to find its being imparted to me quite without embarrassing connotation; she smiled and took Junkin's hand. So we entered my room in good order and I hastened to find a drink.

'Is that the Columba thing?' Moggy asked sharply. She had walked over to the fireplace, above which *Young Piets* had its prescriptive position.

'Yes, it is.' Junkin must have given Moggy an account of his neighbours on Surrey Four, and with some particularity in my own case. 'But you can hardly see him, I'm afraid. In the big picture he's clear enough through the spindrift, standing in the prow of the boat and holding up a Celtic cross.'

'Are the two boys historical? Are they going to be saints too after he converts them?'

'I don't think so. They're just representative Picts. They're also my elder brother and myself.'

'Which has the bare bottom?'

'That's me. The wind's supposed to have caught my kilt.'

'I think it's a lovely picture. Is it funny having a famous father? I've never met anybody who had before.'

'Yes, it is, rather.' I felt it was my turn to ask a question, and failed to think of very striking one. 'Are you in Oxford for long?'

'I'm staying until Nick's examination finishes, and then we'll go back to Cokeville together.'

'I got jittery,' Junkin said. 'It came of buying a paperback – the day after you had tea with me. It was about exams, and I thought there might be some useful gen in it. But it was mostly on about neurosis and anxiety states. A lot of crap, I expect, but somehow it got me down. I tell you, I saw myself writing those papers in the seclusion of the local bughouse. So I whistled up Moggy, and she's going to see me through. Isn't she a dream? I can't look at her and think of anything else.'

'It's a very good arrangement, Nick.' I hoped that this was true. 'Do you think your neighbour Ivo Mumford has been having jitters too?'

'I'd say he's more likely to be getting the DTs than the willies. He told me he was going to live for the rest of the term on oysters and champagne. But I don't know much about him. That essay-business petered out. And so our concordat wore a bit thin.' Junkin seemed pleased with his command of this expression, which had presumably come to him from his historical studies. 'His magazine's supposed to be coming out tomorrow. Have you seen the stickers for it?'

'No, I haven't.'

'They're up here and there in Oxford today. Just a pillar or pedestal or something with a question-mark perched on top of it and a kind of silvan scene behind. It's meant to stimulate curiosity, I suppose. I ask you.'

'But it has the title of the thing as well?'

'Oh, yes. *Priapus,* for Christ's sake. Mumford wouldn't know the difference between Priapus and Pithecanthropus if he met them both in the High.'

'I suppose Priapus is to be on the pedestal,' Moggy said. Moggy, it struck me, was cleverer than Junkin. Perhaps there was no harm in that.

'Do you know?' Junkin demanded suddenly. 'Do you know why I'm going to pass their silly exam? It's because I'm not going to be in the same bleeding gallery'—he broke off and turned to me—'*is* it gallery?'

'Galley, Nick.'

'—the same bleeding galley as that ignorant gnome. I'm buggered if I am.'

'That's a very good reason,' I said. 'Good luck to it.'

255

'On your feet, Moggy!' Junkin, having glanced at his watch, produced this commandingly – although Moggy had not, in fact, got off them. 'Thanks a lot,' he said, putting down his glass.

I opened the door for this devoted couple, and wished them an enjoyable party.

# XVII

O N THE FOLLOWING evening I was surprised to meet Bedworth on the doorstep of the Lodging. It hadn't occurred to me that the Provost's proposal was for other than a threesome. Then I remembered that, as Senior Tutor, Bedworth was Number Two in the college. However much I was supposed to be in the confidence of the Mumford family, I could hardly be brought in *solus* on a negotiation in the background of which there hovered a possible windfall of half a million pounds.

'Cyril,' I asked, 'have you rung the bell yet?'

'No. I was going to, and then I saw you coming across the quad.'

'Then let's walk round it. We're in good time. Tony can't have arrived yet, or his bloody great car would be on view.'

'So it would. So come on. It's dark enough to conspire in, Duncan.' This was quite a flight of fancy from Bedworth. 'I find it odd, somehow, Tony Mumford being in the Cabinet. I thought of him as a very frivolous young man.'

'You admired him as a very frivolous young man.'

'That's perfectly true.' Bedworth spoke as if he had never reflected on this before. 'And I admired you too, Duncan, in just the same way. It's funny what happens to people.'

'Funny when it isn't appalling. Do you think there's anybody else dining with the Provost tonight?'

'I know there isn't.'

'Then it's another oddity. Do you remember the golf course, Cyril? You, me, Tony, and the Provost.'

'Mrs Pococke was there too then.' Bedworth had the scholar's care for accuracy. 'But it is rum. Who'd have thought?'

'Who, indeed? The whirligig of time, as Feste says.'

'Yes. Do you know what a whirligig was?'

'A spinning top, I suppose.'

'It was a revolving cage for the ducking of petty criminals.' Bedworth's tutorial habit had momentarily asserted itself. 'You know about all this money?'

'Tony told me on the telephone yesterday.'

'I had a letter about it from Edward. He regards it as very confidential still. Wisely, I think. No point in having the place agog with it at this stage. There are some delicate issues.'

'So there are. Can you believe that Cedric Mumford will really have the principal say in who gets what? It seems incredible. It sticks out a mile that he's a malign old dotard.'

'Perhaps it's apparent only in certain contexts.'

'Like this uncommonly awkward one of ours.'

'Precisely. Duncan, I wish that wretched boy had never come up here.'

'Too late for wishing. You ought all to have taken a harder look at him at the start. Do you think the Provost will play?'

'No.'

'Not even in – well, some highly manipulative fashion?'

'I see no scope for it.'

We were now half-way round the quad. It was rather chilly,

'Just suppose,' I said. 'Could the college keep young Ivo in residence for a full three years without his ever troubling – or call it managing – to pass a damned thing? That's his grandfather's vision, and it doesn't surprise me. But it seems to be his father's too – which I find utterly amazing.'

'Duncan, wouldn't Tony, in a crunch, do as you tell him? We all know you ended by running him.'

'Running him!' This freak in the recovery of time past staggered me.

'Mrs Pococke says you had him right under your thumb. And she had much the clearest head in college in those days.'

'Would you say she has been advising the Provost?'

'It's possible. But as for your question – yes. The college is entirely its own master there. It could elect the little brute into the Provostship, if it wanted to. But there's another question – another question of influence. If Tony could be made to see sense, could he – again in a crunch – enforce it upon that old man? On the main issue, I mean. The utter propriety of the college's benefiting substantially when this Trust is wound up. The late Lord Mountclandon – and he was the last of his line – was our most distinguished member in a century. And himself most faithful to us. There already exist, as you probably know, three open scholarships he founded off his own bat. Including the one you came up on, as it happens.'

'The John Ruskin?' This information astonished me. It was the final instance of the fact that, in our college, nobody ever told one anything.

'Yes, of course. But here's the bloody great car.'

The dining part of our occasion didn't bear a working character. The Provost led a conversation on general topics. Tony was subdued. He looked tired. I wondered whether that government shuffle was something he was now hard up against. How this might affect his attitude to personal matters I just didn't know. It might make him reasonable. On the other hand it might just bring out the streak of Mumford family outrageousness in him. There was no telling. Bedworth was distinguishably impatient. He was a conscientious and hard-working man who liked to get on with things. But we were in the Provost's library, and with brandy in front of us, before the Provost spoke up. When he did so it was with no effect of crisis.

'And now, Marchpayne,' he said, 'I suppose we ought to have a word about your son's position. We touched on it when you so kindly found time to lunch with me in my club. It is very important – and here in the college we are all agreed upon that – to consider with great care the special circumstances which may be bearing upon one young man or another. Particularly in these days, when the tendency in the university as a whole is to be rather rule-of-thumb.'

'I'm all attention, Provost.' Tony said this in an admirably uncoloured way. He had paused politely in the act of lighting a cigar. I glanced at Bedworth. He was compressing his lips in a manner reminding me of Charles Atlas. I didn't think he'd liked what he'd just heard.

'An instance was in my mind only the other day. It related to a contemporary of Ivo's, one Nicolas Junkin, who is in much Ivo's difficulty over an examination. Junkin is not academically distinguished – or even, I fear, assiduous. But he is an excellent college lad, active in various ways. In his first year he was responsible for our winning what the young men call Drama Cuppers. Duncan, you will appreciate the satisfactoriness of that.'

'It's no doubt a point in his favour, Provost.'

'Precisely. One would hesitate before seeing him depart – or at least depart for good.' The Provost let this last clause fall without emphasis. 'And we have sometimes to weigh, too, the relevance of more private matters. I have lately had a letter from Arnold Lempriere. Marchpayne, you know Lempriere, no doubt.'

'Hardly at all.' I could see that Tony was now very alert. 'He hadn't returned to Oxford when Duncan and I were up.'

'He has interested himself in your son – or at least in your son's position. Not unnaturally. For he was, I believe, your father's tutor.'

'He was, indeed.'

'That was a long time ago. Lempriere is the most senior of my colleagues, and a man of great experience both here in Oxford and in other and wider fields of action.' The Provost paused on this impressively; he must have been referring to Lempriere's achievements in professional mendacity in America. 'It is not invidious, therefore, to say that there is nobody in college whose advice I rate more highly. Although he has not, it seems, so much made your son's acquaintance, it is no exaggeration to say that he has his interest very much at heart.'

'It's very kind of him,' Tony said – this time in a tone I liked less. He had developed an almost instinctive sense, no doubt, of when he was beginning to be led up a garden path.

'And now, my dear Marchpayne, you must forgive me if I have to touch upon a painful matter. Have you by any chance been made familiar with the name of Lusby?'

'I know all about that, Provost. No need to enlarge on it.'

'Quite so. It is sufficient to bear in mind that Ivo was in some degree implicated in the occasioning of that very sad event. Lempriere points out to me that Lusby's death must have been a very great shock to him. We must not exaggerate this consideration. It would scarcely be reasonable, for example, to regard the present term as one in which Ivo's sole duty has been to pass through a period of convalescence. Still, something it should be possible to allow when coming to any decision on this perplexed affair. I hope, Marchpayne, I am not being tedious.'

'I'll know presently.'

This was less promising still. At any moment – I felt extravagantly – the features of Lord Marchpayne might dissolve behind the cigar smoke, and those of Cedric Mumford appear there instead.

'So let us consider one possibility. Should Ivo – as unfortunately appears almost certain – again fail his examination, it might be reasonable to proceed to no more than rustication. You understand what the phrase implies. He would not be sent down once and for all, but would be required to withdraw from Oxford and study privately until the examination is held again. He would take it, "from rustication" as we say, but of course coming up to Oxford for the purpose. Were he successful, he would then be at liberty to return into residence. Cyril, you would agree that this is a regular procedure?'

'It happens from time to time, Provost.' Bedworth paused. 'In deserving cases,' he added firmly.

'But the boy doesn't want to hang around London or Otby for six months, or whatever it is!' I saw that Tony was suddenly and fatally angry. 'He wants to stay in Oxford.'

'Are we not taking that rather for granted?' I asked. For the first time since the discussion began, I felt I had better say something. 'Lempriere would take it for granted; it's axiomatic with him that all young men want to stay in Oxford for ever and ever. But perhaps Ivo doesn't. Perhaps he has more sense.'

'I don't find your suggestion helpful, Provost.' Tony had ignored my intervention. He put his cigar down on an ashtray, and was looking calmly at its glowing tip. 'If we can't make a little further progress in this matter, it will be useless to go on to any others.'

The naked ultimatum produced silence. I wondered whether the Provost would suggest any means of securing the progress Tony required. It was my guess that he would not.

But I was never to know. The door of the library had opened, and Honey stood revealed in it. He was bearing the unnecessarily large silver salver that he affected for the carrying of messages. What lay on it now was a foolscap envelope.

'Excuse me, sir'—Honey advanced into the room—'but one of the gentlemen has called with this.'

'An undergraduate, Honey?' The Provost asked this sharply, although, in the language of the college, Honey could mean nothing else.

'Yes, sir – and said it was most urgent. He gave his name, which is why I've ventured to disturb you.' Honey glanced swiftly at Tony. 'Mr Ivo Mumford, sir.'

'If – only for a moment – you will excuse me.' The Provost had never been more courtly than when, with these words, he carried off Ivo's envelope to a table at the far end of the room. It was as if he wanted to ensure that a letter-bomb didn't inconvenience his guests.

With varying degrees of clarity, I suppose, we recognised that it was indeed something of the kind. I had the advantage of more information than my companions. It wasn't a far leap from it to the conclusion that Ivo had been kind enough to deliver a copy of *Priapus* to the head of his college.

'I think perhaps if you would gather round.' The Provost's voice was not quite steady. 'I scarcely think that what I have received need detain us for long.'

We rose, all three, and trooped across the room. I hadn't been astray. *Priapus* lay on the table, cover-upwards. What Junkin had described as a silvan scene proved to be a misty but identifiable photograph of Parson's Pleasure, with naked youths disporting themselves in and out of the river. The pedestal was in the foreground, but not topped by a question- mark. What perched on it was the figure of Arnold Lempriere, also naked, and cut off just above the knees. It was, of course, the body of a very old man, and the evidences of decrepitude were painfully prominent.

'The theme recurs,' the Provost said, and turned over the pages. There were several other photographs of Lempriere, always unclad, and they had been fitted into crudely sketched lubricious occasions.

Bedworth was the first to speak, or to try to speak.

'I can't imagine how—'

'Ivo has a thing called a candid camera,' I said. It was given to him by a Japanese associate of his grandfather's. Incidentally, he wasn't aware of Arnold Lempriere's identity when he concocted all this.'

"But he was,' the Provost asked gently, 'before he put his horrible rag into circulation?'

'Yes, he was.'

'Marchpayne, I am so sorry.' The genuineness of Edward Pococke's distress was unmistakable. 'But before we destroy at least this copy, perhaps we ought to glance at the letterpress. I fear a couple of minutes will be enough.'

A couple of minutes were enough. *Priapus* was, of course, pervasively indecent. And it was this with a crudity and oafishness hard to believe. We watched the Provost drop it into his waste-paper basket. And then we returned to our seats. Tony hadn't said a word. It was again Bedworth who broke the silence.

It's dreadful!' he said. 'Tony, I'm deeply, deeply sorry. But we have to get it clear. It ends any uncertainty about your son's immediate future.'

'I don't think I understand you,' Tony said, and reached for his brandy with a trembling hand. For some moments, I believe, his mind simply didn't function.

'I don't know whether this thing can be said to be on sale all over Oxford now. I'd suppose it hard to get anyone to handle it. But that's the plain intention. So it's a university matter, and quite out of college hands. I must be frank with you. The Proctors will have sent Ivo down by noon tomorrow.'

'It would be censorship, that.' Tony produced a flicker of fight. 'They may think twice about it, in the present state of undergraduate feeling.'

'No. That thing is an obscene libel, and they'll be protecting Ivo from the law by getting in their own penalty at once. Go and ask Jimmy Gender, if you don't believe me.'

'We must do anything we can,' the Provost said, 'to help your boy to shape himself another career. We ought not to exaggerate, once more. The consequences here in Oxford will be indeed as Cyril says. But we may think in terms of an aberration of adolescence and not of Ivo's settled character. There is much good in him, I don't doubt.'

Whether these were – to Tony in his humiliated condition – assuaging words, I didn't know. I judged quite probably not. And an alternative line occurred to me. (Once more, I had the advantage of superior information.)

'At least,' I said, 'Ivo's got where he wants to be. And been pretty ruthless in getting there.'

'Dunkie, what the hell do you mean?' Tony had straightened up from a slumped position, and was staring at me, alerted by what came to him as wholly commendatory words.

'He's got himself out of this dump.' I caught a startled glance from the Provost, and made a decent retreat. 'From what he'd call, if he had the gift of eloquence, this damned self-congratulatory dump. Do you think he ever wanted to come near the place? If he did, he pretty soon wanted to get away again. It isn't him. He hasn't the brains for it, for one thing. He's a decent boy – which is what the Provost has been saying – but don't think his brains are just not academic brains. They're not all that good, any way on. So he's been miserable here, with both schoolfellows and what he thinks of as young proles making rings round him. He's only stuck it because of what they call father-eclipse – a great confident heavy-weight dad sitting on top of him. But at least he's got devil in him.'

'Devil?' Gropingly, Tony found this conception of his son attractive.

'Unfortunately – but perhaps just for the moment – Ivo has swopped father-eclipse for grandfather-eclipse. But it's been a shrewd move.'

'Shrewd?' Tony's note was again hopeful.

'Ivo believes it's with his grandfather that his fortune lies – as you and I agreed on the telephone. Well, he tumbled to something. His grandfather was dead keen that he stick it out here in defiance of all good sense as to what an Oxford college is about. For that matter, it has been your own damned silly idea too.'

'You have a point.' Tony's glance was still fixed on me. 'Go on.'

'What came to him was this: that if he *didn't* stick it out, what he *could* do was leave in a stink of sulphur. Manage that spectacularly enough, and he was his grandfather's golden boy.'

'Yes – you're right.'

'Then we needn't dot the *i*'s and cross the *t*'s. His means have been pretty drastic. At the start, it's true, Lempriere was just an unknown elderly frequenter of that bathing place. Ivo had never so much as noticed his presence round the college. When he discovered who his proposed victim was, he was certainly a little startled. It was I who told him, as it happens, that Lempriere had been his grandfather's tutor. What then dawned on him was that for his grandfather this would make the thing funnier still.'

'He probably wasn't wrong.' Tony said this with a decent grimness. Then he lifted his chin. 'It can't be said to add to the engagingness of the general picture.'

'Ivo hasn't had much luck here, one way and another. You'll have to plan for him. And perhaps we should say goodnight to the Provost, and go over to help the boy pack.'

My suggestion – the second part of which I hadn't intended quite literally – at least took us out of the Lodging and into open air. It was very dark. Beyond Bernini's fountain the light at the college gate shone dimly amid a halo of its own creating; this, and a damp breath on our faces, spoke of a nocturnal fog so dense that the Great Quadrangle might have been thought of as a vast tureen filled with cold soup. We had taken, only a few paces when Tony put a hand on my arm and drew me to a halt. Perhaps he was disoriented. He was certainly bewildered – as what he now said showed.

'Duncan,' he said, 'I can't believe it! How *could* Ivo do such a damned low thing? How could any gentleman imagine it?'

'Young gentlemen aren't always gentlemen, I suppose. They have to be given time – or some do. Give Ivo time, and he'll be all right. He wanted to commit an enormity, you know, and at least he managed it. Of course the Lempriere side of his prank has been abominable. But he might never have thought of it if it hadn't been for his beastly little camera. All manner of unfortunate things come Ivo Mumford's way.'

'How would you describe Lempriere, Duncan? I hardly know him.'

'In the particular context of the moment, I'd describe him as a harmless old *voyeur*. And why not? Even parsons allow themselves such pleasures.'

'No doubt.' Tony had rightly thought ill of this feeble joke. 'And he'd be a non-player?'

'Good God, yes. A total abstainer, I'd say, since the day he left school. Of course, old age has its hazards for his type – as he probably knows.'

"Would he go to law?'

'Sue Ivo, you mean? It would be inconceivable to him. And remember he's been Ivo's man. He'll remain so – *Priapus* and all. For he's an obstinate old creature. Take comfort from that.' I was becoming impatient of heartening Tony, perhaps as knowing that he had a notably rapid power of heartening himself. Ivo was a much more vulnerable Mumford. In eight weeks I had become enough of a don to be mortified that I'd made no sort of job of his case, and it was my instinct that some sign ought now to be made to him. 'Come on,' I said. 'We'll go over to Surrey and see how the land lies.'

We moved forward again, almost gropingly, and in silence for some moments. The sounds customary at that hour – chatter from a party, a man playing a piano, many feet pounding a staircase – came to us faintly as if through some insulating integument; the plop-plop of drops of moisture on the flagstones beneath our feet made a sharper effect; Oxford's bells when they chimed the hour would have dwindled to the tinkle of a musical-box played covertly beneath the blankets.

'But he'll feel it,' Tony muttered suddenly.

'He bloody well will,' I said – and with an involuntary savageness that dismayed me. Tony had been offering – on Arnold Lempriere still – what seemed a singularly unnecessary remark. 'Or perhaps not terribly,' I added hastily. 'The very old sometimes develop an unshakable self-confidence. Nothing can really touch them or embarrass them. It's a sort of protective induration.' These words sounded to me so stupid as I uttered them that my dismay deepened. 'Let's hope Lempriere will prove to be like that.'

On this fatuity we fell silent again. The tunnel leading to Surrey held a just-audible susurration: some faint current of air flowing through had stirred a few sodden leaves into sluggish motion. Then suddenly we were both brought to a halt. There was uproar in Surrey – and of a kind carrying to both of us a sharp reminiscence of an earlier time. For on a first impression what was going on might have been a simple re-enactment of the occasion on which we had first spoken to one another. We could even hear empty bottles going through windows, and it was hard not to believe that in a moment a full one would turn up miraculously at our feet, thus enabling us to cement our alliance in stolen champagne.

In a moment this impression corrected itself. The present occasion was not quite like that one. There loomed up in front of us—for we had walked straight across the grass towards Surrey Four—a massive shape, darker than the dark of night except when lit up by a flicker of electric torches playing around it. Directly above it there was a blaze of light through the two open windows of Ivo's room. The room appeared crowded with young men. Some were tossing unidentifiable objects into the waiting arms of companions in the quad below. Others were taking pot shots, slant-wise, at any windows within reach. The missiles were, I imagine, textbooks. At one time or another, somebody had probably bought Ivo quite a lot of them.

'It's a car,' Tony said incredulously. A car in Surrey was an unheard of thing, although there were massive iron gates through which the most gigantic char-a-banc or articulated lorry could have been admitted. 'And—by God!—it's mine.'

'So it is.'

'Martin has been driving that Ministry car for years.'

'He's engaged in furniture-removing now.'

'And there's my personal dick—Detective-Sergeant some- body-or-other. A really tough chap. The thing's incredible.'

'Not at all, Tony. Ivo has just been suitably imperious. He'll go far.'

'He knows he'll be sent down ?'

'Of course he knows, you idiot. Haven't we got all that clear? He's been playing for it. And this is what you might call his going-down party. It will be memorable.'

'You don't think he'll have called in the press ?' Of a sudden Tony's voice was sharp with anxiety.

"No, I don't. Not to watch what's happening to that Ministry car. Ivo, if you want to know, probably has quite a regard for his father in the Cabinet.'

'He seems to have friends.'

'And they appear to be active ones.' As I said this, I was aware that Tony's spirits were taking their inevitable bouncing course. He was already rather proud of Ivo again.

'Look!' Tony said.

We had moved to where we had a direct view of the staircase and its opening upon the quad. Down it were coming two young men, carrying some large flat object apparently thought unsuitable for tossing through air. They began to edge it with difficulty into the big car. A gleam of light fell on its surface and revealed that masterpiece of discreet Victorian volupte which three generations of Mumfords had trundled in and out of their prescriptive set in Surrey. I don't know that I have anywhere recorded the tide of this work of art. It was A Languid Afternoon—which suggested a persuasion that Roman bawdy-houses ran to morning sessions. I wondered whether it would ever again ornament the wall with which 1 associated it.

'I suppose,' Tony said, 'we'd better leave them to it for the moment.'

'Yes—and it's not much use my asking you in for a quiet drink.' Not for the first time, I reflected on the rashness of a grown man's domesticating himself cheek by jowl with a huddle of youths liable to turn either cheerfully or viciously disorderly any night of the week. 'We'll go over to common room. It will probably be deserted. The butler locks up the cigars but leaves the whisky. And I suppose your car will come round to the gate again.'

'Ivo and I can have a talk on the run back to town. If there's room for me, that is.' This sardonic reflection must have pleased Tony, for he was laughing softly as we turned away again into the dark. 'That pompous old donkey,' he said. 'He didn't do too badly.'

'The Provost ? He did very well. Of course, Tony, he has his hopes of you.'

'Hopes?'

'Well—rather stronger than that. All that money. It's up to you to get the college its whack. Have yourself made a trustee too, if that's the best way of going about it. But go about it you must. It will be the Mumfords' Reply—that sort of thing. And Edward Pococke knows it.'

'The wee Scotch laddie nannying round again. However, the Minister is grateful to his honourable friend, and will study his suggestion with care.'

This reply, although it had begun disobligingly, was satisfactory in its fashion. Tony said nothing more until, standing in the big shabby deserted common room, festooned with the portraits of dead dons whose names nobody remembered, he had his modicum of whisky in his hand.

'Well, yes,' he then said, 'I might have a shot at being made a trustee. After all, I'm not—' He broke off, I think when about to say something like 'wholly unknown in the world'. For a moment he surveyed the surrounding nonentities, sunk alike in faded photographic sepia and learned abstraction. 'An army of unalterable law,' he said. And he raised his glass to them: rank upon rank of academic shades.'

# Madonna of The Astrolabe

In the fourth of J.I.M. Stewart's acclaimed 'Staircase in Surrey' quintet the gravity of a surveyor's report given to the Governing Body is the initial focus. The document is alarming. The Governing Body, an assembly of which Pattullo was in awe, was equally awed by the dimensions of the crisis revealed. It would seem that the consideration was whether there would literally be a roof over their heads for much longer. The first rumblings from the college tower brings the thought well and truly home to Pattullo.

'Professor Sanctuary,' the Provost said evenly, 'favours the immediate launching of an appeal . . .' And so it begins . . . In J.I.M. Stewart's superbly melding of wit, mystery, observation and literary prowess a gripping novel develops that will enthral the reader from cover to cover. This can be read as part of the series, or as a standalone novel.

# Full Term

The final volume in the 'A Staircase in Surrey' quintet. Duncan Pattullo is coming to the end of his term as 'narrator' and is thinking of re-marrying, although his former wife continues to cause difficulties. His intended is also providing gossip for the college, but that is as nothing compared to the scandal caused by Watershute, an eminent nuclear physicist. His misdemeanours range from abandoning his family and conducting an affair in Venice, to being drunk at High Table. However, things get very serious when he appears to be involved in activities that might amount to treason. An interesting and convoluted plot, which is a fitting end to this acclaimed series, is carried forward with J.I.M. Stewart's hallmark skill and wit. Full Term can be read in order, or as a standalone novel.

# Andrew and Tobias

The Feltons are a family with a long lineage stretching back beyond the Norman Conquest. They now have a daughter, Ianthe, but prior to her birth Tobias, or Toby, was fostered and then adopted as their heir after he had miraculously survived the sinking of a refugee ship by a German U-Boat. Then, someone who is clearly Toby's twin turns up as an under-gardener. He had been fostered by a Scottish couple, now dead. There is now general and disturbed confusion on everyone's part – including the boys themselves. Stewart explores magnificently the nature of the complicated relationships, including those from outside of the family such as Toby's lover; the irony of the situation; and the many ramifications of class and culture in the absurd situation the characters find themselves.

# The Naylors

George Naylor, an Anglican priest, has doubts about his faith. He goes to stay with his brother's family, who unfortunately regard religion with some disdain and George as a bit of a joke. Enter Father Potter, sent by the establishment to regain their wayward cleric. There then occurs a series of adventures including the discovery of a secret research laboratory which is conducting testing on animals, and the prospect of George and Father Potter being involved in a protest rally which includes nuclear disarmers and anti-vivisectionists. All is brought to a hilarious conclusion in this fine example of Stewart's witty writing.

# Villa in France

Penelope, the daughter of a local priest, is lured to a villa in the south of France where she is the victim of a cruel hoax. As to how she came into the situation, we are first introduced to her as a child and the background is set out with Stewart's usual wit and highly descriptive writing. Fulke Ferneydale, now a rich novelist, knew Penelope then – indeed, in her later teenage years he suddenly proposed to her, but she turned him down. At the time, he had something of a chip on his shoulder as his father was 'in trade', which is something Penelope's father looked down upon in a snobbish manner, although it didn't affect her. Accordingly, Ferneydale went off and married Sophie, although he subsequently managed to enjoy a string of mistresses and young boys. Penelope married Caspar, but he is withdrawn, scholarly and boring, not to mention materially unsuccessful. So what is to become of her in France? There are many twists to this tale, not least the final surprise.

Made in the USA
Middletown, DE
26 October 2022